C
NIGHT

BLISSFUL
SEDUCTION

ONE NIGHT OF CONSEQUENCES COLLECTION

October 2017

November 2017

December 2017

January 2018

February 2018

March 2018

ONE NIGHT

BLISSFUL SEDUCTION

LYNNE
GRAHAM

HEIDI
BETTS

CATHY
WILLIAMS

Published in Great Britain 2017
By Mills & Boon, an imprint of HarperCollins*Publishers*
1 London Bridge Street, London, SE1 9GF

ONE NIGHT: BLISSFUL SEDUCTION © 2017 Harlequin Books S.A.

The Secret His Mistress Carried © 2015 Lynne Graham
Secrets, Lies & Lullabies © 2012 Heidi Betts
To Sin with the Tycoon © 2015 Cathy Williams

ISBN: 978-0-263-93172-3

09-1217

THE SECRET HIS MISTRESS CARRIED

LYNNE GRAHAM

Lynne Graham was born in Northern Ireland and has been a keen romance reader since her teens. She is very happily married, with an understanding husband who has learned to cook since she started to write! Her five children keep her on her toes. She has a very large dog, which knocks everything over, a very small terrier, which barks a lot, and two cats. When time allows, Lynne is a keen gardener.

CHAPTER ONE

THE GREEK OIL BILLIONAIRE, Giorgios Letsos was throwing the party of the year at his London town house. Yet, instead of socialising, he was answering his emails, escaping the predatory females who had dogged his every footstep since the news of his divorce became public.

'*I heard,*' a female voice murmured outside the library door, which stood ajar after a maid had served her employer with a drink and failed to close it, 'that he got rid of her because she did drugs.'

'*I heard,*' another voice piped up, 'that he dumped her back on her father's doorstep in the middle of the night with all her things.'

'*I heard,*' a third voice interposed,.'that the pre-nup was *so* tight she didn't get a cent.'

Gio was sardonically amused that speculation was keeping his neglected guests entertained. His cell phone pulsed and he answered it.

'Mr Letsos? It's Joe Henley from Henley Investigations…'

'Yes?' Gio asked absently, assuming it was the

usual quarterly callback to report a negative result, his attention still on his laptop as he mulled over the purchase of another company with the kind of concentration and enjoyment he would never find at any party.

'We've found her…er, at least I'm ninety per cent certain *this* time,' the older man carefully framed because neither of them would ever forget the mistake he had once made when Gio had gone racing across the city in his limo only to find himself looking at a complete stranger. 'I took a photo and emailed it to you. Perhaps you'd like to check it out before we go any further.'

We've found her… Suddenly, Gio was galvanised into action, springing out of his chair to his full imposing height of six feet four inches, squaring his wide shoulders while he flicked back to the emails. Fierce intensity had fired his dark golden eyes while he identified the right email before clicking on the attachment.

It wasn't a great photo but the small curvaceous figure in the floral raincoat was instantly recognisable to his hard, searching gaze. Excitement and satisfaction roared in an intoxicating wave through Gio's lean, powerful length.

'You will be generously paid for this piece of detection,' Gio breathed with rare warmth as he stared at the picture as though it might disappear at any moment. *As she had done.* She had contrived to lose herself so completely he had honestly begun to believe that even with all the resources he had at his disposal he would never track her down.

'*Where* is she?' he pressed.

'I have the address, Mr Letsos, but I haven't yet acquired sufficient info to make up a proper background report,' Joe Henley explained. 'If you give me a couple of days, I'll proceed the usual way—'

'All I need, all I *want*,' Gio stressed with rippling impatience at the thought of waiting even an hour, 'is her address.'

And suddenly, Gio was smiling for the first time in a very long time. He had finally found her. Of course that didn't automatically mean he intended to forgive her, he swiftly qualified, straightening his muscular shoulders. His wide, sensual mouth compressed in a manner that would have made his chief executives quail, for he was a tough man, an inflexible, stubborn man, very much feared in the business world. After all, Billie had walked out on him, was, in fact, the only woman *ever* to pull that stunt on Gio Letsos. But there she was on screen, *his* Billie, still wearing flowery clothes like a nature explosion, a shock of caramel-coloured blonde curls flowing round her heart-shaped elfin face, her wide green eyes unusually serious.

'You're not a very active host,' a voice remarked from the doorway. The speaker was as short as Gio was tall and as fair as Gio was dark but Gio and Leandros Conistis had been friends since their schooldays, both of them born into wealthy, privileged and pedigreed, if dysfunctional, Greek families and sent to England to board at exclusive fee-paying schools.

Gio closed down his laptop and studied his old friend. 'Did you expect anything different?'

'Even for you, that sounds arrogant,' Leandros countered.

'We both know that even if I threw a non-alcoholic party in a cave, it would be packed,' Gio said drily, well aware of the pulling power of his vast wealth.

'I didn't know you were going to throw a divorce party.'

'That would be tasteless. It's *not* a divorce party.'

'You can't fool me,' Leandros warned him.

Gio's lean, strong face was expressionless, his famed reserve kicking in hard and fast. 'Calisto and I had a very civilised divorce—'

'And now you're back on the market and the piranhas are circling,' Leandros commented.

'I will never marry again,' Gio declared grimly.

'Never is a long time…'

'I mean it,' Gio emphasised darkly.

His friend said nothing and then tried to lighten the atmosphere with an old joke, 'At least you could trust Calisto to know that Canaletto isn't the name of a race horse!'

Momentarily, Gio froze, his lean, dark, devastating features tightening, for that gag had worn thin years before he stopped hearing it. Sadly, not Billie's most shining moment.

'I mean…' Leandros was still grinning '…I don't blame you for ditching that one…what an airhead!'

Gio said nothing. Even with his oldest friend Gio was not given to making confidences or baring his soul. In actuality, Gio had not ditched Billie; he simply hadn't taken her out with him in public again.

In the garage, Billie was going through garments and costume jewellery that she had acquired during the week to sell in her vintage clothes shop. She was sorting items into piles for washing, repair or specialist cleaning while dumping anything past its prime. While she worked, she talked non-stop to her son. 'You're absolutely the most cute and adorable baby ever born,' she told Theo warmly as he kicked his legs in his high chair, smiled beatifically and happily got on with eating his mid-morning snacks.

With a sigh, she straightened her aching back, reflecting that all the bending and stretching had at least started knocking off a few pounds of the extra baby weight she had been carrying for months. The doctor had told her that that was normal but Billie had always had to watch her weight and she knew that while putting it on was easy, getting it back off again was not. And the problem with being only five feet two inches tall with an overly large bust and hips was that it only took a few surplus pounds and a thicker waistline to make her look like a little barrel.

She would take all the kids to the playground and walk round and round and round the little park with the pram, she decided ruefully.

'Coffee?' Dee called out of the back door.

'I'd love one,' Billie told her cousin and housemate, Dee, with a smile.

Thankfully, she hadn't been lonely since she had

rediscovered her friendship with Dee, yet they might so easily have missed out on meeting up again. Billie had been four months pregnant when she attended her aunt's funeral in Yorkshire and got talking to Dee, whom she had gone to primary school with although Dee was several years older. Her housemate was a single parent as well. At her mother's funeral her cousin had sported a fading black eye and more bruises than a boxer. Back then Dee had been living in a refuge for battered women with her twins. Jade and Davis were now five years old and had started school. For all of them life in the small town where Billie had bought a terraced house was a fresh start.

And life was *good*, Billie told herself firmly as she nursed a cup of coffee and listened to Dee complain about the amount of homework Jade was getting, which related more to Dee's inability to understand maths in any shape or form than the teacher overloading Dee's daughter with work. *This* life was ordinary and safe, she reasoned thoughtfully, soothed into relaxation by the hum of the washing machine and the silence of the children while they watched television in the sitting room next door. Admittedly there were no highs of exciting moments but there were no gigantic lows either.

Billie would never forget the agonies of her own worst low, a slough of despair that had lasted for endless weeks. That phase of her life had almost destroyed her and she could still barely repress a shudder when she recalled the depression that had engulfed her. She had been hurting so badly and there had seemed to be no way of either stopping or avoiding that pain. In fact, in the end it had taken an extraordinary and rather frightening development to show Billie a light at the end of the tunnel and a future she could actually face. She contemplated Theo with glowing satisfaction.

'It's not healthy to love a baby so much,' Dee warned her with a frown. 'Babies grow up and eventually leave you. Theo's a lovely baby but he's still just a child, Billie, and you can't continue building your whole life round him. You *need* a man—'

'I need a man like a fish needs a bicycle,' Billie interposed without hesitation, reckoning that the disaster zone of her one and only real relationship was quite sufficient to have put her off men for life. 'And who are you to talk?'

A tall, whip-thin blonde with grey eyes, Dee grimaced to concede the point. 'Been there, done that.'

'Exactly,' Billie agreed.

'But I don't have the options you have,' Dee argued. 'If I were you, I'd be out there dating up a storm!'

Theo clutched Billie's ankles and slowly levered himself upright, beaming with triumph at his achievement. Considering her son had had both legs in a special cast for months to cure his hip dysplasia, he was catching up on his mobility fast. For a split second he also reminded her powerfully of his father and she didn't like that, didn't go *there* in her mind because she didn't allow herself to dwell on the past. Looking back on the mistakes she had made was counterproductive. Those experiences had taught her hard lessons and she had forced herself to move on past them.

Dee studied her cousin in frank frustration. Billie Smith was the equivalent of a man magnet. With the figure of a pocket Venus, a foaming mane of dense toffee-coloured curls and an exceptionally pretty face, Billie exuded the kind of natural warm and approachable sex appeal that attracted the opposite sex in droves. Men tried to chat Billie up in the supermarket, in car parks or in the street and if they were behind a car wheel they honked their horns, whistled out of the window and stopped to offer her lifts. Had it not been for Billie's modest take on her own assets and her innate kindness, Dee was convinced she would have been consumed with envy. Of course she would have been the last to envy Billie's unfortunate long-term affair with the ruthless, selfish swine who had broken her tender heart, she thought guiltily. Like Dee, Billie had paid a high price for falling in love with the wrong man.

The knocker on the front door sounded loudly. 'I'll get it,' Billie declared because Dee was doing the ironing and Billie hated ironing with a passion.

Davis hurtled out of the sitting room, almost tripping over Theo, who was crawling earnestly in his mother's wake. 'There's a big car...a really big car on the street!' the little boy exclaimed.

It was probably a lorry with a delivery, Billie assumed, aware that any vehicle with wheels fascinated Dee's son. She unlocked the door and then took an immediate and very abrupt step back, astonishment and panic shooting up inside her like a sudden jarring surge of adrenalin.

'You're a hard woman to track down,' Gio murmured with supreme assurance.

Billie's facial muscles were locked tight by shock. She couldn't have shown him an expression to save her life but her wide green eyes were huge and anxious. 'What are you doing here? Why would you have wanted to track me down, for goodness' sake?'

Gio feasted his shrewd, dark gaze on her. Twenty four freckles adorned her nose and her upper cheekbones: having once counted them, he knew that for a fact. Her clear eyes, delicate features and lush mouth were utterly unchanged, he was relieved to note, his attention sliding inexorably down over her in a staged appraisal because he was strictly rationing himself. A faded blue cotton tee shirt stretched to capacity over her high, rounded breasts and his attention lingered there against his will, lust sending his libido leaping for the first time in a long time.

Relief rather than irritation consumed Gio because it had been far too long since he had experienced that reaction to a woman, so long indeed that he had feared that his marriage had stripped him of his essential masculinity in some peculiar fashion. But then, he would have been the first to acknowledge that he had never wanted any woman the way he had always wanted Billie. He had once flown her out to New York for a single night because he literally could not get through another week without her in his bed.

Billie was so worked up, so horrified that Gio Let-

sos had come looking and found her, that her feet
were glued to the hall carpet. She stared at Gio, unwilling to credit that he was really there in the flesh
in front of her, the man she had once loved, the man
she had believed she would never see again. Her heart
started to thump very, very hard and she sucked in a
sudden snatch of oxygen, flinching as Theo drew her
back to reality by hauling on her jeans-clad legs with
his little fat hands to pull himself upright.

'Billie…?' Dee asked from the kitchen doorway.
'Who is it? Is there something up?'

'Nothing.' Billie rescued her voice from her convulsed throat and stooped down in a jerky movement
to scoop up Theo, her dazed gaze roaming over her
cousin's children who were studying Gio as though
he had just dropped in from Mars. 'Dee…could you
take the kids?'

Her voice emerged all husky and shaken and she
had to force herself to direct her attention back to Gio
while Dee put out her arms for Theo and urged her
own children into the kitchen with her. The kitchen
door closed, sealing the hall into a sudden claustro-
phobic silence.

'I asked you why you were here and why you
would have looked for me in the first place,' Billie
reminded her unwelcome visitor doggedly.

'Are you really planning to stage this long-overdue
meeting on the doorstep?' Gio drawled, all velvety
smoothness and sophistication. He was taking control
the way he always did and it unnerved her.

'Why not?' Billie whispered helplessly, struggling

to drag her eyes from his devastatingly handsome features, remembering all the many times she had run her fingers through his thick black hair, loving him, loving each and every thing about him, even his flaws. 'I don't owe you the time of day!'

Gio was disconcerted by that comeback from a woman who had once respected his every word and done everything possible to please him, and his lean, strong face set taut and hard. 'You're being rude,' he told her icily.

Billie's hand clutched at the edge of the front door while she wondered if its support was all that was keeping her upright. He was so cool, so collected and such a bully, really couldn't help being one. Life had spoilt Gio Letsos although he had never seen it that way. People flattered him to an extraordinary degree and went out of their way to win his approval. And once she had been the same, she acknowledged wretchedly. She had never stood up to him, never told him how she really felt, had always been far too afraid of spoiling things and then losing him. Only a very naïve woman would have failed to foresee that naturally Gio would choose to walk away from her first.

Her abstracted gaze took in the fact that her neighbour was staring over the fence at them, possibly even close enough to catch snippets of the conversation. Embarrassment made her step back from the door. 'You'd better come in.'

Gio strode into the tiny sitting room, stepping with care round the toys strewn untidily about the room. He swallowed up all the available space, Billie thought numbly as she hastily switched off the television, which was playing a noisy children's cartoon. He was so tall, so broad and she had forgotten the way he dominated any room he occupied.

'You said I was rude,' she said flatly as she carefully shut the sitting room door, ensuring their privacy.

She kept her back turned to him as long as possible, shielding herself from the explosive effects of Gio's potent charisma as best she could. It wasn't fair that just being in the same room with him should send a shower of sparks tingling through her and give her that oh, so dangerous sense of excitement and anticipation that had once seduced her into behaving like a very stupid woman. He was so very, very good-looking that it hurt to look at him and the effect of seeing him on the doorstep had stimulated her memories. In her mind's eye, she was seeing the straight black brows, the utterly gorgeous dark golden eyes, the distinctly imperious blade of his nose, the high cheekbones, the bronzed Mediterranean skin, the beautiful, wide, sensual mouth that had made seduction an indescribable pleasure.

'You *were* rude,' Gio told her without hesitation.

'But I was entitled to be. Two years ago, you married another woman,' Billie reminded him over her shoulder, angry that it could *still* hurt her to have to force that statement out. Unhappily there was no escaping the demeaning truth that she had been good enough to sleep with but not good enough to be considered for anything more important or permanent in Gio's life. 'You're nothing to do with me any more!'

'I'm divorced,' Gio breathed in a raw-edged under-tone because nothing was going as he had expected. Billie had never attacked him before, never dared to question his behaviour. This new version of Billie was taking him by surprise.

'How is that my business?' Billie shot back at him, quick as a flash, while refusing to think that startling declaration of divorce through or react to it in any way. 'I still remember you telling me that your marriage was *none* of my business.'

'But then you made it your business by using it as an excuse to walk out on me.'

'I didn't *need* an excuse!' A familiar sense of won-derment was gripping Billie while she listened, once again, to Gio vocalise his supremely selfish and ar-rogant outlook. 'The minute you married, we were over and done. I never pretended it would be any other way—'

'You were my mistress!'

Colour lashed Billie's cheeks as though he had slapped her. 'In your mind, not mine. I was only with you because I fell in love with you, not for the jew-ellery and the clothes and the fancy apartment,' she spelled out thinly, her hands curling together in front of her in a defensive, nervous gesture.

'But there was no reason for you to leave. My bride had no objection to me keeping a mistress,' Gio stressed with growing impatience.

My bride. Even the label still hurt. The back of

her eyelids stung with tears and she hated herself but she hated him more. Gio was so insensitive, so self-centred. How on earth had she ever contrived to love him? And why the heck would he have tracked her down? For what possible reason?

'Sometimes I honestly think you talk like an alien from another planet, Gio,' Billie countered, tightly controlling her anger and her pain. 'In my world decent men do *not* marry one woman and continue sleeping with another. That is not acceptable to me and the idea that you found a woman to marry who didn't care *who* you slept with just depresses me.'

'But I am free now,' Gio reminded her, frowning while he wondered what the hell had happened to Billie to change her so much that she could start arguing with him the minute he reappeared.

'I don't want to be rude but I'd like you to leave,' Billie admitted unevenly.

'You haven't even heard what I have to say. What the hell is the matter with you?' Gio demanded, shaken into outright disbelief by her aggressive attitude.

'I don't *want* to hear what you have to say. Why would I? We broke up a long time ago!'

'We didn't break up—you walked out, *vanished*,' Gio contradicted with harsh censorious emphasis.

'Gio…you told me I needed to wise up when you informed me you were getting married and I did exactly like you said…the way I always did,' Billie muttered tartly. '*I wised up* and that means not listening to a word you have to say.'

'I don't know you like this.'

'Why would you? It's been two years since we were together and I'm not the same person any more,' Billie told him with pride.

'It might help if you could actually look me in the eye and tell me that,' Gio quipped, scrutinising her rigid back.

Reddening, Billie finally spun round and collided dangerously with stunning deep-set dark eyes, heavily fringed with lashes. The very first time she had seen those eyes he had been ill, running a high temperature and a dangerous fever, but those eyes had been no less mesmerising. She swallowed hard. 'I've changed—'

'Not convinced, *moli mou.*' Gio gazed steadily back at her, enjoying the burst of sexual static now thickening the atmosphere. That her tension mirrored his told him everything he needed to know. Nothing had changed, certainly not the most basic chemistry of all. 'I want you back.'

In shock, Billie stopped breathing, but within seconds his admission made a crazy kind of Gio-based sense to her. By any standards, his marriage had lasted a ludicrously short time and she knew Gio didn't like change in his private life. To his skewed way of thinking, reconciling with his former mistress might well now seem the most attractive and convenient option. 'No way,' she said breathlessly.

'I still want you and you still want me—'

'I've built a whole new life here. I can't just abandon it,' Billie muttered, wondering why on earth she was stooping to making such empty excuses. 'You and me…it didn't work—'

'It worked brilliantly,' he contradicted.

'And your marriage *didn't*?' Billie could not resist asking.

His hard facial bones locked in an expression she remembered from the past. It closed her out, warned she had crossed a boundary. 'Since I'm divorced, obviously not,' he fielded, smooth as glass.

'But you and I,' Gio husked, reaching out to grasp her hands before she could guess his intention, 'did work very successfully—'

'Depends on your definition of successful,' Billie parried, her hands trembling in his, perspiration dampening her entire skin surface. 'I wasn't happy—'

'You were always happy,' Gio had no hesitation in asserting, because her chirpy, sunny nature was what he remembered most about her.

Billie tried and failed to draw her hands free of his without making a production out of it. 'I *wasn't* happy,' she repeated again, shivering as the almost forgotten scent of him assailed her nostrils: clean, fresh male overlaid with tones of citrus and something that was uniquely Gio, so familiar even after all the time that had passed that for a charged and very dangerous split second she wanted to lean closer and sniff him up like an intoxicating drug. 'Please let go, Gio. Coming here was a waste of your time.'

His hot urgent mouth swooped down on hers and he feasted on her parted lips with fiery enthusiasm, plundering and ravishing with a hunger she had never

forgotten. Electrifying excitement shot through Billie like a lightning bolt to stimulate every skin cell
in her body. The erotic thrust of his tongue into her
mouth consumed her with burning heat and a crazy
urge to get even closer to that lean, virile body of his.
Wild hunger started a glow of warmth in her pelvis
and made her nipples tighten and strain. She wanted,
she *wanted*...and then sanity returned like a cold drop
of water on her overheated skin when Theo wailed
from the kitchen, jarring every maternal sense she
possessed back to wakefulness.

Wrenching her mouth free of his, Billie looked
up into the smouldering dark golden eyes that had
once broken her heart and said what she needed to
say, what she *owed* it to herself to say. 'Please leave,
Gio...'

Billie stood at the window watching Gio climb
into his long black limousine on the street outside, her
fingernails biting into her palms like sharp-pointed
knives. Without even trying he had torn her in two,
teaching her that her recovery was not as complete
as she had imagined. Letting Gio walk away from
her had almost killed her and there was still a weak,
wicked part of her that longed to snatch him back
with both hands. But she knew it was pointless, because Gio would be furious if he ever found out that
Theo was his child.

Right from the start, Billie had known and accepted that truth when, finding herself accidentally
pregnant, she had chosen to give birth to a baby fathered by a male who had only wanted her for her

body. There would be no support or understanding from Gio on the score of an illegitimate child, whom he would prefer not to have been born. She had only been with him a few weeks when he had told her that if she ever fell pregnant he would regard it as a disaster and that it would destroy their relationship, so she couldn't say she hadn't been warned. She had finally decided that what he didn't know about wouldn't hurt him and she had so much love to give their son that she had convinced herself that Theo would not suffer from the lack of a father.

Or so she had thought…until after Theo's birth when concerns began to steadily nibble gaping holes in her one-time conviction that she had made the right decision. Then she had guiltily asked herself if she was the most selfish woman alive to have chosen to have a child in secrecy who would never have a father and she had worried even more about how Theo might react when he was older to what little she would have to tell him.

Would her son despise her some day for the role she had played in Gio's bed? Would Theo resent the fact that although his father was rich he had grown up in comparative poverty? Would he blame her then for having brought him into the world on such terms?

CHAPTER TWO

BILLIE STUFFED HER face in the pillow and sobbed her heart out for the first time in two long years and once again Gio had provided the spur. When she had finally cried out all the pain and the many other unidentifiable emotions attacking her, Dee was by her side, seated on the edge of the bed and stroking her head in an effort to comfort her.

'Where's Theo?' Billie whispered instantly.

'I put him down for his nap.'

'Sorry about this,' Billie mumbled, sliding off the bed to go into the bathroom and splash her face with cold water because her eyes and her nose were red.

When she reappeared, Dee gave her an uncomfortable look. 'That was *him*, wasn't it? Theo's dad?'

Billie didn't trust herself to speak and she simply nodded.

'He's absolutely gorgeous,' Dee remarked guiltily. 'I'm not surprised you fell for him but what's with the limousine? You said he was well off, not that he was minted...'

'He's minted,' Billie confirmed gruffly. 'Seeing him again was upsetting.'

'What did he want?'

'Something he's not going to get.'

Rejection was the very last thing Gio had anticipated. After assigning two of his security team to watch Billie round the clock and ensure that she did not disappear again, it occurred to him that perhaps there was another man in her life. The idea sent him into such a violent maelstrom of reaction that he couldn't think straight for several rage-charged minutes. For the very first time ever he wondered how Billie had felt when he had told her about Calisto and he groaned out loud. He didn't do complicated with women but Billie was certainly making it that way.

How had he believed it would be when he turned up out of nowhere? he asked himself impatiently. Billie had asked him to leave: he still couldn't *believe* that. She was angry with him: that reality had sunk in. He had married another woman and she was holding that against him but how could she? Gio raked long brown fingers of frustration through the curly black hair he kept close cropped to his skull. She could not possibly have believed that he might marry *her*…could she?

He was the acknowledged head of his family owing to his grandfather's long-term ill health, and it had always been Gio's role and responsibility to rebuild the aristocratic, conservative and hugely wealthy Letsos clan. He had vowed as a boy that he would never repeat the mistakes his own father had made. His great-grandfather had had a mistress, his grandfather had had a mistress but Gio's father had been less conventional. Dmitri Letsos had divorced Gio's mother to marry his mistress in a seriously destructive act of disloyalty to his own blood. Family unity had never recovered from that blow and the older man had forfeited all respect. Gio's mother had died and he and his sisters' childhoods had been wrecked while Dmitri had almost bankrupted the family business in an effort to satisfy his spendthrift second wife's caviar tastes.

Well, if there was another man in Billie's bed, he would soon find out, Gio rationalised with clenched teeth and a jaw line set rock hard with tension. In twenty-four hours he would have the background report from Henley Investigations. Regrettably he was not a patient man and he had assumed she would throw herself back into his arms the instant he told her that he was divorced. Why hadn't she?

Her response when he'd kissed her had been...*hot*. In fact Gio got hard just thinking about it, his libido as much as his brain telling him exactly what and who he needed back in his life. He wondered if he should send her flowers. She was *crazy* about flowers, had always been buying them, arranging them, sniffing them, growing them. It had been selfish of him not to buy her a house with a garden, he conceded darkly, wondering what other oversights he must've made when the woman who had once worshipped the ground he walked on now felt able to show him the door. No woman had *ever* done that to Gio Letsos. He knew he could have virtually any woman he wanted but that wasn't a consolation when he only wanted Billie back where she belonged: in his bed.

After a disturbed night of sleep, Billie rose around dawn, fed all the kids and tidied up. It was only at weekends that she and Dee saw much of each other. On weekdays, she took the kids to school to allow Dee, who worked evenings as a bartender in a local pub, a little longer in bed. Theo went to work with Billie in the mornings and Dee collected him at lunchtime and minded the three kids for the afternoon. After the shop closed, they all ate an early evening meal together before Dee went off to do her shift. It was an arrangement that worked very well for both women and Billie was fond of Dee and her company because her two years in a city apartment where Gio was only an occasional visitor had been full of lonely days and nights.

Of course, in those days she had learned to make good use of her free time, she acknowledged wryly. In those two years with Gio she had acquired GCSEs and two A-levels, not to mention certificates in various courses ranging from cordon-bleu cookery and flower arranging to business start-up qualifications. Gio might not have noticed any of that or have shown the smallest interest in what she did when he wasn't around, but making up for the education she had missed out on while she was acting as her grandmother's carer throughout the teenage years had done much to raise Billie's low self-esteem. After all, when she had first met Gio she had been working as a cleaner because she had lacked the qualifications that would have helped her to aspire to a better-paid job.

As she placed the new pieces of costume jewellery on display in the battered antique armoire she had bought for that purpose, she was a thousand mental miles away on an instinctive walk down the memory lane of her past. Unlike Gio, Billie did not have a proper family tree or at least if she did it was unknown to her. Her mother, Sally, had been an only child, who had reputedly gone wild as a teenager. As Billie's only source of information about her mother had been her mean-spirited grandmother she was inclined to take that story with a pinch of salt. Billie had no memory of ever meeting Sally and absolutely no idea who had fathered her, although she strongly suspected that his name had been Billy.

Billie's grandma and her mother had lived separate lives for years before the day Sally turned up without warning on her parents' doorstep with Billie as a baby. Her grandfather had persuaded her grandmother to allow Sally to stay for one night, a decision she had had Billie's lifetime to loudly and repeatedly regret because when the older woman got up the next morning she had discovered that Sally had gone, leaving her child behind her.

Unfortunately, Billie's grandma had neither wanted nor loved her and, even though she received an allowance from social services for raising her grandchild, her resentment of the responsibility had never faded. Billie's grandpa had been more caring but he had also been a drunk and only occasionally in a fit state to take an interest in her. Indeed, Billie had often thought that her background was the main reason why she had been such a pushover for Gio. His desire for her, his apparent need to look after her, had been the closest thing to love that she had ever known. So, although she would never have admitted it to him, she had been madly, insanely happy with Gio because he had made her *feel* loved…right up until the dreadful day he'd told her that he had to get married and father a child for the sake of his all-important snobby Greek family and his precious business empire.

Chilled by the sobering and humiliating recollection that Gio had not even considered her a possible candidate for a ring, Billie brought out the new garments she had prepared at home and began to price the stock. Theo was napping peacefully in his travel cot in his little cubbyhole at the back of the shop. Customers browsed, purchased and departed as she served them while she worked. Only a month earlier, she had hired her first employee, a Polish woman called Iwona, who did part-time hours when Billie couldn't be at the shop. In fact, the business was doing well and was steadily fulfilling all Billie's hopes. But then she had always loved the character and superior workmanship of vintage clothes and she was careful only to stock quality items. Slowly but surely she had built up a list of regular customers.

Gio climbed out of his limo while his chauffeur argued with the traffic warden and his security team

were disgorged from the vehicle behind. He scanned
the shop front, adorned with the name, 'Billie's Vintage', and frowned, positively transfixed by the idea
that Billie could have opened up her own business.
Yet there was the proof in front of him. *Theos!* He
shook his arrogant dark head, thinking that women
were strange, unpredictable creatures and finally
wondering if he had ever really known Billie at all
because nothing that she had done or said so far had
appeared on his list of her potential reactions. His
frown grew even darker, lending a saturnine quality
to his hard, dark features. He had important projects
to manage and people to see and yet here he was still
stuck after twenty-four exceedingly boring hours in
a back-end-of-nowhere Yorkshire town chasing Billie! What kind of sense did that make?

Dee and Iwona arrived at the shop within minutes
of each other. Dee strapped Theo into his pram and
asked Billie what she fancied eating for supper while
Iwona wrapped a purchase for a customer. That was
when Gio strode in, utterly frying Billie's brain cells
because she stopped mid-conversation with Dee and
totally forgot what she had been about to say.

Garbed in a charcoal designer pinstripe suit that
sheathed his tall, muscular body like a tailor-made
glove, Gio simply took her breath away. His white
shirt accentuated his bronzed complexion and the
very masculine black stubble already beginning to
shadow his handsome jaw line. A startling sunburst of
honeyed heat blossomed between Billie's thighs and
she pressed them tight together, her colour steadily

climbing. She was even more painfully aware of the swelling heaviness of her breasts and the sudden tightening of her nipples. She was appalled that Gio could still have that immediate an effect on her, an effect that was markedly more intense than the day before when she had blamed her surrender to that kiss on the fact that he had caught her unprepared. What was her excuse this time?

'Billie…' Gio breathed in his dark, velvet drawl, poised several feet away and acting as if his appearance in her shop were the most natural thing in the world.

'G-Gio…' she stammered half under her breath, quickly closing the space between them, fearful of being overheard. 'Why are you here?'

'You're not stupid, don't act it,' Gio advised, glancing around. 'So, you left me to open a shop—'

'You. Left. Me,' Billie spelt out with a bitterness she could not restrain but it was the truth: he had left her to place a wedding ring on another woman's finger.

'We can't talk here. We'll catch up back at my hotel over lunch,' Gio decreed, closing a hand round her arm.

'If you don't let go, I'll slap you!' Billie hissed, determined not to be railroaded by his overpowering personality and drive.

His dark eyes glittered like pyrite as if the prospect of a good slap was an entertaining challenge. 'Lunch, *pouli mou*?'

'We've got nothing to say to each other,' Billie told

him, noting that his entire hand was still wrapped round her arm, forcing her to stay by his side.

His sensual mouth quirked as he studied her full pink mouth. 'Then you can *listen*—'

Butterflies danced in her tummy as she looked up at him. 'Don't want to talk, don't want to listen either—'

'Tough,' Gio pronounced and then he did something she would never ever have dreamt he would do in public. He just bent down and scooped her up off her feet and headed for the door.

'Put me down, Gio!' she gasped, making a wild grab at the flouncy skirt of her dress, which had flown up to expose her thighs. 'Have you gone crazy?'

Gio glanced at the two women standing together behind the counter. 'I'm taking Billie out for lunch. She'll be back in a couple of hours,' he explained with complete cool.

'*Gio!*' Billie launched in disbelief, catching a glimpse of Dee's laughing face before Gio shouldered open the door and hid her cousin from view.

The chauffeur swept open the passenger door as if they were royalty and Gio shoved her into the back seat with scant ceremony. 'You should've known that I wouldn't stand there arguing with an audience,' he pointed out smoothly. 'In any case, I'm out of patience and I'm hungry.'

In a series of angry motions, Billie smoothed down her dress, tugging it over her knees. 'Why didn't you go back to London yesterday?'

'You should know by now that saying no to me only makes me try harder.'

Billie rolled her bright green eyes in mockery and said angrily, 'Well, how would I know that when I never did say no to you?'

Disconcertingly Gio laughed, genuine amusement illuminating his darkly handsome face. 'I've missed you, Billie.'

Her annoyance fell away and she turned her head in a sharp movement, both shaken and hurt by that claim and by how very empty it was. 'You got married. How could you possibly have missed me?'

'I don't know but I did,' Gio ground out truthfully. 'You were so much a part of my life.'

'No, I was like one tiny little drawer in a big busy cabinet of drawers,' Billie countered. 'I was never part of the rest of your life.'

Gio was sincerely astonished by that statement. He had phoned her twice a day every day no matter where he was in the world and no matter how busy he was. Her soothing happy-go-lucky chatter had provided him with necessary downtime from a hectic schedule. In truth he had never had so close a relationship with any woman either before or after her. He had trusted her and he had been honest with her, which was a very rare thing between a single man and a single woman in Gio's world. *But* it was steadily sinking in on him that none of that mattered because he had married Calisto. Billie, who had never shown a jealous, distrustful streak in her life, had clearly been jealous and distressed by that development. He didn't like that idea, he didn't like it at all, and he kicked out that thought so fast it might never have existed.

Gio had constructed a protective shell while he was still a child to ensure that he could remain untouched by emotional reactions. Emotion didn't need to get involved. Emotion complicated and only exacerbated an already difficult situation. Calm, common sense and control had always worked far more efficiently for Gio in every field of his life, only *not* with Billie, he acknowledged grudgingly. But the past was the past and he couldn't change it, while life had taught him that with enough money, energy and purpose he could form the future into any shape he wanted.

Billie, however, was not practical; she was all about emotion and perhaps that essential difference between them had been one of the things that attracted him to her and which was now sending her in the wrong direction. His shrewd, dark eyes rested on her angry, flushed face and suddenly he wanted to flatten her to the seat of the limo and teach her that there were far more satisfying responses. Inky spiky lashes lowering, he scanned her from her bright eyes to her lush mouth right down over the glorious breasts he had loved to play with and the long shapely legs he had loved to slide between. Sex with Billie was *amazing*. Just thinking about her made heaviness stir at his groin. Being with her without being able to reach out and take what he wanted, what he had once taken for granted, not only felt weird, but also struck him as a form of refined torture.

'I want you back,' Gio declared with stubborn force. 'I've been looking for you ever since you disappeared.'

'Your wife must've liked that.'

'Leave Calisto out of this…'

Even the sound of her name on Gio's lips stung Billie like a whip across tender skin. She knew she was being too sensitive. He had married another woman two years ago and she needed to move on. Even if *he* hadn't moved on? That was too complex for her, shouted too loudly of wishful thinking. And, my goodness, she had done enough of that while she was still with him and what had those optimistic hopes got her? A broken heart and, right now, the pieces of that foolish heart were rattling like funeral bells. This was the guy she had loved as she had never dreamt she could ever love anyone and he had damaged her beyond forgiveness. Even walking away as she had known she must had almost destroyed her, but not even for him would she have sunk low enough to sleep with another woman's husband.

'I can't believe you're wasting your time with this,' Billie admitted abruptly, her soft full mouth compressed to a flat, tense line. 'I mean, what are you doing here? Why do you even want to see me again? It makes no sense for either of us!'

Gio searched her animated face and wondered what made her seem so beautiful to him. In some corner of his brain, he knew that from a purist's point of view she never had met and never would meet the standard tenets of beauty because her nose turned up at the end and her eyes and her mouth were too big for her face and in a sudden shower of rain her hair turned into an unbelievably frizzy mess. But dry it fell in a silky tangle of curls the colour of toffee half-way to her waist and that hair had cloaked his body many, many times on occasions so intimate it hurt to remember them and still be deprived of the right to repeat them.

'Stop looking at me like that,' Billie told him thinly, the colour of awareness mantling her cheeks, a warm glow unfurling low in her body to remind her of how much time had passed since she had last been touched. She had got pregnant, become a new mother, set up a new home and business and kept so busy-busy-busy for months on end that she fell into bed exhausted every night. It took Gio's reappearance to remind her that life could offer more self-indulgent pastimes.

'Like what?'

'Like we're still…you know,' she completed, eye-lashes lowering.

'Like I still want to be inside you?' Gio queried thickly. 'But I do and right at this very minute I'm aching for you…'

A tiny clenching sensation in a place she refused to think about forced Billie to shift uneasily on the seat. 'I really didn't need to know that, Gio. That was a *very* inappropriate comment to make—'

Gio skated a long forefinger down over the back of the hand she had tautly braced to the leather seat. 'At least it was honest and you're not being honest—'

'I'm not coming back to you!' Billie interrupted loudly. 'I've got another life now—'

'Another man?' Gio slotted in, deep accented voice raw with unspoken vibrations.

And Billie seized on that convenient excuse like a drowning swimmer thrown a lifebelt. 'Yes. There's someone else.'

Every lean, long line of Gio's big body tensed. 'Tell me about him.'

Billie was thinking about her son. 'He's extremely important to me and I would never do anything to hurt or upset him.'

'There's nothing I won't do to get you back,' Gio warned as the limousine drew up outside his country-house hotel and the chauffeur leapt out to open the door. He also grasped at that same moment that he was not as law-abiding as he had always assumed because he knew that he was willing to break rules in order to get Billie back.

Billie stole a reluctant glance at his lean, hard face, clashing with the golden glitter of his stunning eyes. She froze in consternation at that expression of menace she had never seen there before. 'Is there some reason you can't let me be happy without you?' she asked suddenly. 'I think I've paid my dues, Gio.'

Gio's nostrils flared at that declaration, exasperation roughening the edges of an anger he knew he had no right to express. If she had another man, she would naturally get rid of him because he refused to credit that any other man could set her on fire the way he did. But nothing could assuage his bone-deep ferocious reaction to being forced to imagine Billie in bed with someone else. Billie had always been his alone, indisputably *his*.

As they crossed the foyer of the opulent hotel a familiar voice hailed Billie and she stopped dead and flipped round with a smile as a tall blond man in expensive country casuals moved towards her eagerly to greet her.

'Simon, how are you?' she said warmly.

'I've got an address for you.' Simon dug into his wallet to produce a piece of paper. 'Got a pen?'

Billie realised her bag had been left behind at the shop and looked expectantly at Gio. 'Pen?' she pressed.

Totally unaccustomed to being ignored while others went about their business around him, Gio withdrew a gold pen from his pocket with pronounced reluctance, his beautiful obstinate mouth sardonic.

Simon borrowed the pen and wrote the address on the back of a business card. 'There's a heap of stuff there you'll like and it won't cost you much either. The seller just wants the house cleared.'

Impervious to the reality that Gio was standing by her side like a towering and forbidding pillar of black ice, Billie beamed at the taller man. 'Thanks, Simon. I really appreciate this.'

Simon studied her with the same appreciation Gio had often seen on male faces around Billie and his perfect white teeth gritted. 'Maybe you'll let me treat you to lunch here some day soon?'

Gio shot an arm like a statement round Billie's slender spine. 'Regrettably she's already taken.'

Ignoring that intercession, Billie reddened but kept on valiantly smiling. 'I'd like that, Simon. Call me,' she suggested while knowing that she was only encouraging the other man to make a point for Gio's benefit and feeling guilty about that because Gio was making her behave badly as well.

'What was that all about?' Gio demanded grittily as he urged her into the lift.

'Simon's an antique dealer. He tips me off about house clearances. I know a lot of dealers. That's how I built up my business,' Billie advanced with pride.

'You can open a shop in London. I'll pay for it,' Gio told her grimly.

Unimpressed, Billie glanced wryly at him. 'Well, in a roundabout way you paid for this one *and* my house, so I don't think it would be right for you to pay anything more.'

'What are you talking about?'

'I sold a piece of jewellery for cash. It was something you gave me.'

Gio frowned. 'You left everything I ever gave you behind.'

'No, I took one piece. Your very first gift,' Billie extended. 'I had no idea how much it was worth. That was a surprise, I can tell you.'

'Was it?' Gio couldn't even remember his first gift to her and he would have been prepared to swear, having checked the jewellery she left behind, that she had taken nothing with her when she walked out.

'Yes, you're so extravagant it's a wonder you're not broke. You hardly knew me and yet you spent an absolute fortune on that diamond pendant,' Billie told him critically. 'It paid for my house and setting up the shop. I couldn't believe how valuable it was!'

Gio thrust open the door of his suite. And just like that, the memory of the gift returned to him. He had bought the pendant after their first night together and he was furious that she had just sold it as if it meant nothing to her. 'I don't believe that there's another man in your life.'

'I'm not coming back to you,' Billie told him in the most ludicrously apologetic tone. 'Why would I want a shop in London? Why would I want to move? I'm happy here. And believe it or not there are men out there who would take me out with them into a public restaurant instead of hiding me inside their suite!'

Billie had served a direct hit. Gio paled beneath his Mediterranean tan. 'We're in my suite only because we need a private setting in which to talk.'

Billie gave him a wry smile. 'Maybe that's true this one time, Gio, but when it went on for almost two years, even I got the message. You might as well have been married from the moment I met you. I was like a guilty, dirty secret in your life.'

'That is not true.'

'No point arguing about the past now,' Billie parried with determination. 'It's not worth it.'

'Of course it is…I want you back.' A spasm of open exasperation crossed Gio's lean dark face when a knock sounded on the door, announcing the arrival of two waiters pushing a rattling trolley: lunch had arrived.

Billie folded her arms, thinking of her grandpa's favourite winning racehorse, Canaletto, and the reality that just four years ago she had never heard of the artist called Canaletto before. Recalling that blunder still made Billie cringe and die inside herself, for the moment she had entered the conversation she had known her mistake but it had been far too late to cover it up. Unhappily for her, the one and only time Gio had taken her out to mix with his friends she had made an outsize fool of herself…*and* him.

Although he had reacted with neither anger nor criticism, he had dismissed her attempts to talk about the incident and explain that she had grown up more at home in betting shops than museums. But she had known that she had seriously embarrassed him in public in a way that would not be forgotten and, even worse, in a manner that had literally signposted the reality that she and Gio came from worlds and educational backgrounds that were light years apart.

That was why she had never complained about being excluded from his social life and why she had happily settled for dinners out alone in discreet locations where he was unlikely to meet anyone he knew. She had guessed that he was worried she would let him down again and without his awareness she had swiftly set about a self-improvement course in the hope that eventually he would notice and give her another chance. Sadness filled Billie when she recalled that naivety born in the early months of their relationship before she had reached the daunting moment of discovery and slow, painful acceptance that she was *not* Gio's girlfriend but instead his mistress, there to dispense sexual entertainment and not much else and never ever to be taken seriously.

'You're so quiet. I'm not accustomed to you being quiet with me,' Gio confessed in growing frustration, closing his hands over her slender, taut shoulders, massaging the tense muscles there as the door flipped shut behind the waiters. 'Talk to me, Billie. Tell me what you want.'

Feeling the warm tingling of his touch snaking down her rigid spine and the pinching tautness of her nipples while resisting a powerfully seductive urge to lean back into the strong, sheltering heat of Gio, Billie pulled away and quickly sank down into one of the chairs by the beautifully set table. *Talk to me.* That was an insanely perplexing invitation to receive from a male like Gio, who didn't like serious conversations and who smoothly sidestepped or downright ignored emotional moments and phrases.

'We've got nothing to discuss,' she pointed out, tucking into the first course with sudden appetite because while she ate she did not have to speak and had less excuse to be looking at Gio. Gio, surely one of the most beautiful men ever born? She glanced at him from below her lashes, roaming with helpless appreciation across his sculpted features to relish the spectacular slash of his high cheekbones and the tough masculine angle of his jaw. He was out of her reach. He was rich and successful, handsome and sophisticated, educated and pedigreed, everything she was not. He had *always* been out of her reach. If only she had had the wit to accept that obvious fact, she would never have got involved and never have got hurt.

'Is there really another man?' Gio asked very quietly, the rich velvety depth of his accented drawl filling her with pleasure, no matter how hard she tried not to react that way. But that was the same voice she had once lived to hear on the phone when he was away from her, and she could not break her instinctive appreciation.

Billie worked out the question and flushed as she collided with stunning tigerish golden eyes surrounded by ebony lashes. She breathed in, intending to lie, breathed out, knew that for some reason she didn't want to lie. Perhaps it was because if she lied he would come down on her like a granite block to get further information about the supposed man in her life and would eventually cleverly trip her up and learn that she was lying, which would only make her look stupid. 'No, there isn't,' she admitted grudgingly. 'But that doesn't change anything between us.'

'Then we're both free,' Gio murmured lazily, topping up her glass with the bottle of wine.

'I have no intention of getting involved with you again,' Billie declared, taking a hasty gulp of the mellow red, wondering if he would laugh if she told him what the flavour reminded her of. After all, she had once attended a wine course as well as an art-appreciation course and had never had the opportunity to show off what she had learned there.

'But we work well together.'

Billie shook her head in vehement rejection of that statement and concentrated on her food again.

Sipping his wine, Gio watched her. He suspected she was wearing vintage clothes and the pale green linen dress she wore teamed with a light blouse-like jacket embroidered with flowers didn't bear any resemblance to what he deemed to be current fashion, but the colours and plain styling had an understated elegance. The minute she sat down, however, the fabric of the dress pulled taut across the swell of her ample bosom. Gio tensed, hunger stabbing through him while he wondered how he was supposed to tempt a woman so utterly lacking in greed. She didn't want his money, had never wanted his money, had once told him in no uncertain terms that he didn't need a yacht because he would never take the time off to use it. His yacht, sitting idle and costing a fortune to maintain, was currently moored at Southampton.

The waiters came back to serve the main course. She saw their sidewise glances and recognised their curiosity about her. By now the hotel staff would have established who Gio was—Giorgios Letsos, the oil billionaire was a legend the world over. The press loved him because he lived a rich man's life and looked great in print. Calisto had looked brilliant in print too with her sleek straight blonde hair, her perfect features and her terrifyingly tiny size-zero body. Beside her, Billie would have appeared plump, short and ungainly and, from seeing that first photo, Billie had accepted that no comparison could ever be made between them. After all, she and Calisto weren't even on the same page in the looks department.

Gio wound down the tension by talking about his recent travels round the world. She asked small, safe, impersonal questions about some of his staff, a couple of whom she had met and some she had only got to know by speaking to them often on the phone.

While eating her dessert, a glorious concoction of fresh berries and meringue, she enquired whether or not he still had the apartment.

'No…like you, it's long gone,' he stated.

Billie took that to mean that he had not installed a more malleable woman in her place and when a sense of relief filtered through her she gulped more of her wine and tried hard to direct her thoughts to safer topics. It was no longer her business to wonder who he slept with. Once he had married Calisto the question had become academic. Billie had been re-placed in every way. Calisto had been chosen to sit at the other end of the dining table in his probably very beautiful Greek home, which Billie had naturally never visited. Gio would have socialised *with* Calisto because they were a real couple and obviously he had planned to make Calisto the mother of his children…

CHAPTER THREE

AS THE PAIN of that never-to-be-forgotten reality pierced Billie, she suddenly reached the limits of her tolerance. Her attempt to be civilised for the sake of appearances was shattered and, forced cruelly out of her comfort zone, she thrust her hands down on the edge of the table and suddenly stood up. 'I can't *do* this!' she told Gio with ragged abruptness. 'I want to go home right now!'

Taken aback, Gio sprang upright, a frown line drawing his ebony brows together, his lustrous dark eyes locked to her flushed and unhappy face with wary, searching curiosity. 'What's wrong?'

'Only you would ask that in this set-up!' Billie exclaimed helplessly. 'I didn't want to see you ever again. I don't want to be reminded of the past!'

'Billie…' Gio murmured, closing strong hands over her shaking shoulders while his keen gaze collided with her translucent green eyes. 'Calm down…'

'I can't…I'm not like you…I never was. I'm no good at avoiding the obvious and pretending!' She gasped strickenly, tears clogging up her throat and

terrifying her because in the past she had always contrived to hide her emotional breakdowns from Gio
and she was proud of the restraint she had demonstrated in spite of the provocation and the pain he had
put her through. 'You really shouldn't be here...you
should've left me alone in my new life.'

Gio trailed a blunt forefinger along the lower line
of her lush bottom lip. 'I would if I could. I *had* to
see you again.'

'Why?' Billie demanded baldly.

'Because we weren't done when you walked away.'

A great scream of agonising hurt and frustration was rising up inside Billie. '*Of course* we were
done—you were getting married!' she reminded him
doggedly.

'I had to see you again to find out if I still wanted
you.' Long brown fingers rose to cup her cheekbones.
'And the answer to that is that I *do* still want you.'

In a sudden rage at his nerve in admitting that,
Billie jerked her head back out of reach to detach his
fingers. 'That means nothing.'

'It means a hell of a lot more to me than you seem
to appreciate!' Gio growled, patience splintering, because he was well aware that he was fighting blind in
the sort of emotional confrontation he had absolutely
no experience of dealing with.

'Not enough to make a difference!' Billie snapped
back, a kind of madness in the strong emotions powering her while she fought a humiliatingly defensive
urge to just race out of the door and run away like a
scared kid.

Gio imprisoned her in the strong circle of his arms in an unforewarned movement that jolted her. Brilliant dark eyes blazed pure gold fire down at her. 'There's more than enough for *both* of us,' he spelt out, marvelling that she was still fighting him when it was more normal for him to be fighting off the women who ceaselessly pursued him with flirtation and flattery.

'Let me go!' she told him shakily.

'No.' Gio studied her with smouldering determination. 'You'll only run away again. I can feel it in you and I won't let you do something that stupid again.'

'You can't make me do anything I don't want to—'

'But what about what you *want* to do?' Gio savoured the comeback, bending his handsome dark head to run his tongue along the seam of her closed lips.

Taken by surprise, Billie jerked, her blood running heavily and slowly through her veins as if time itself had slowed down to give her the chance to catch up. His breath fanned her cheek and his lips connected with hers in a heart-stopping collision that tripped her ability to breathe. His lips were smooth and unusually gentle and soft and somehow she couldn't prevent herself from turning up her chin to ask for more of the same.

Gio smiled against her lush mouth, hunger beating through him like a jackhammer. He wanted her more than he had ever wanted anything or anybody in his life and he was all fired up to fight hard for what he wanted because he knew she would restore the oasis of peace he needed in his private life. Long fingers smoothed over her back, his other hand curving to her waist. He nipped at her soft lower lip and then glided his sensual mouth over hers in a move that swallowed her tiny cry of surprise. His hand moved up to tangle in her mane of curls and the pressure of his mouth increased until her head tilted back, allowing him greater access.

Her breasts crushed against the solid wall of his broad chest, Billie was struggling to breathe and being bombarded by sensations she had forced herself to forget. She had forgotten how gentle he could be and how inventive and her heartbeat was racing like an express train because it had been too long since she had been touched, too long since she had allowed herself to be the passionate woman that she was.

His tongue darted between her teeth, searching out the moist welcome beyond and then tasting her deep and slow with a rough sensuality that lit a string of firecrackers low in her pelvis. She squirmed as the heat of his mouth on hers grew and the hunger she had tried to deny leapt up inside her in explosive response. The rhythmic plunge of his tongue was matched by the small rocking motions of his hips against hers and her body went nuclear on memories she had suppressed for two years. The barrier of their clothing could not conceal the fact that Gio was erect and ready for her.

Billie felt him lift her but she was so drunk on the taste and texture of his passionate kisses she ignored the fact. He was more intoxicating than wine and her head swam while powerful pulses of reaction were coiling up from the tight knot forming at the heart of her body. Her back connected with a soft yielding surface and he lifted his proud, dark head, black cropped hair ruffled by her seeking fingers, burnished dark golden eyes holding hers in an exchange so familiar it shook her to her very depths.

'My tie's choking me,' he confided huskily, yanking at the offending item, ripping loose the collar of his shirt and, in his impatience, sending the button flying.

That comment was typical of Gio: an emotional moment instinctively avoided. When she looked at him, though, everything else melted away for her. It was a desire so all-encompassing it thrummed through Billie like a sensual drugging pulse. He shrugged out of his jacket, used his feet to push off her shoes.

'I can't let you go again, *pouli mou.*'

'You have to...we can't do this,' Billie whispered unevenly, her awareness returning to encompass the giant bed and the elegant furnishings of what was obviously the bedroom of his suite. She was stunned, still dimly wondering how she had got there.

'Open your mouth for me,' Gio urged with stubborn single-minded zeal. '*Theos*, I love your mouth—'

Just one more kiss, she bargained with herself frantically, her body coming alive in the most fatally seductive fashion because with the life came the cravings she had successfully shut down. And he tasted like heaven, a banquet for the starving, a delicious drink for the terminally thirsty. Her hands kneaded his bulging biceps and, brushing aside his collar, she pushed her mouth against the corded strength of his neck, licking the salt from his skin. His big body shifted in a jerk against hers, sealing every line of his muscled mass to hers, and the awesomely familiar weight of him and the scent of his skin plunged her back into the past.

Gio rolled onto his side to drag off her jacket and locate the zip of the dress. He ran it down, stroked it down her arms and fell on the heavenly globes of her full breasts with a hunger he could no more have controlled than he could have stopped breathing.

Billie surfaced from her sensual spell as her bra fell away and Gio cupped her breasts, thumbing the straining strawberry-pink peaks into swollen buds and then using his mouth, the gliding caress of his teeth and the lash of his tongue to stimulate the sensitive nubs beyond bearing. She couldn't stay still. Somewhere in the back of her mind she knew she was going to have regrets but she couldn't listen to them, couldn't detach herself long enough from the scorching urgency of Gio's passion or the staggering strength of her own increasing need.

With a skilled hand he traced the taut triangle of lace stretched between her restive thighs and an inarticulate sound of helpless encouragement broke from her lips. He ravaged her mouth with a wild, devouring kiss and her hips rose, her hands clawing in frustration down the lithe, strong length of his shirt-clad back. Wetness surged to the tender flesh that throbbed. He teased her, stroked her in a sensual torment that drove her to the edge…

'Stop messing about, Gio!' she suddenly gasped in stricken reproach, her body on such a high it was aching and hurting.

Unholy amusement lit up neon signs inside Gio's head and he laughed against her mouth, recalling that she was the only woman who had ever made him laugh in bed. She was also most probably the only woman who could reduce him to the juvenile level of having sex with half his clothes still on. He blanked the thought, the barometer of his mood suddenly darkening, lean, strong face shadowing, but it was no use because he wasn't in control at that moment, didn't even want to be in control, simply craved the hot, wet oblivion of burying himself in her as deeply as possible.

Billie arched up and suddenly he was there, nudging against her indescribably sensitive entrance before driving his long, hard thickness into her tight channel. She cried out, flung her head back and her back arched as she convulsed around him, her cries of helpless pleasure filling the air as he angled back from her and plunged again with dominant force. The hot excitement of his every virile thrust consumed her, sending out eddying ripples of ever-growing pleasure from her womb. The pace became fast and frantic and the friction of his powerful rhythm stimulated her response to an unbearable height, and she bucked before he sent her flying into another powerful climax, ecstasy flooding every inch of her body.

Within seconds of satiation, Gio turned cold, pushing off the bed and grabbing what little clothing he had removed to head for the bathroom. He was outraged and downright unnerved by the sheer intensity of his own need. Without a doubt, Billie was special, terrific in bed but nothing more, nothing greater, for nobody knew better than Gio Letsos that any form of attachment endangered a man's power and control. He could keep his hands off her if he had to; *obviously* he could exist perfectly well without her. Billie was an indulgence, not a necessity.

As he ripped off what remained of his clothes he rested his hot, damp forehead against the cold tiled wall for several tense seconds, hands coiled into tight fists of angry restraint. For an instant images from the worst day of his life reclaimed him and he broke out into a cold sweat, his quick and clever brain reacting accordingly. Wanting or needing a woman too much was weak and foolish; enjoying good sex was normal: he had just enjoyed very, *very* good sex.

CHAPTER FOUR

LIKE AN ACCIDENT VICTIM, Billie sat up in the tangled and creased remnants of her clothes. She blinked and then the realisation of what had just happened kicked in and she hated herself with a virulence that literally hurt. In shock, she struggled to deal with a colossal self-betrayal. Gio would never believe she wanted to be left alone now, would he? Not when she glugged down a couple of glasses of wine over lunch with him as if they were old and dear friends and then got upset and *still* went to bed with him!

How could I have? Theo's trusting little face below his mop of black curls swam inside her head. What had happened to her self-respect? She had wanted Gio with a desperate hunger that in retrospect shook her inside out. Had she missed sex that much? She fought her way into her knickers with clumsy, trembling hands. The bathroom door opened and she froze before sliding off the bed, gathering up her discarded clothing, locked in a cocoon of almost-sick mortification.

'I didn't plan for this to happen…' Gio breathed curtly.

Engaged in getting her bra back on, it was as much as Billie could do to even spare a glance in his direction. She was surprised that he wasn't sporting a triumphant smile because he had won and Gio liked to win much more than most people. It was the high-voltage combination of that essential drive, innate aggression and competitiveness that made Gio Letsos a global success.

'Like I believe that,' Billie framed dully while she slid into her dress because she knew how intensely manipulative and devious he could be. He used those qualities in business. She was quite sure he had used them on her and was still doing so. Conscience didn't get much of a look-in with Gio when it came to anything he wanted.

'Let me...' He strode round the foot of the bed to run up her zip and she wanted to slap his hands away and scream, only that would have humiliated her even more by exposing just how much he had wounded her. 'I didn't plan it,' he repeated.

'Right, you didn't plan it,' Billie echoed like a well-taught parrot, pushing her feet into her shoes, wanting a shower badly but desperate to escape his presence and reach the sanctuary of her home and her son.

'Next week you have your twenty-fifth birthday,' Gio told her.

Billie grimaced. 'My twenty-third—'

Gio looked back at her in bewilderment. 'Twenty-fifth—'

'I lied when we first met,' Billie volunteered carelessly. 'You said you didn't date teenagers and I was nineteen, so I said I was two years older.'

Taken aback, Gio stared at her. 'You *lied*? You were only nineteen?'

Billie nodded and shrugged. 'What does it matter now?'

Biting back a sharp retort, Gio compressed his handsome mouth, his absolute trust in her taking a severe hit because right from the start of their acquaintance he had been disarmed by her apparent honesty. Aside of that he was less than pleased that he had taken a teenager to his bed without even realising it. It had been a much more unequal relationship than he had ever appreciated, he recognised grudgingly. He had been twenty-six years old and about a thousand years of sexual savoir faire and sophistication ahead of her.

'Call me a taxi,' she prompted in the strained silence. 'I want to go home.'

'We haven't agreed anything yet—'

'And we're not going to,' Billie interposed. 'What just happened was an accident, a mistake…a case of familiarity breeding contempt, whatever you choose to call it. But it didn't mean anything to either of us and it didn't change anything…'

Billie waited for Gio to protest but the silence stretched and she was suddenly wretchedly, unhappily aware of how much that silence of agreement hurt. He had travelled from hot-pursuit mode to apparent indifference: it seemed the sex had acted like a miracle cure. And why was she surprised? She had always been surprised that Gio stayed interested in her. She had been surprised throughout their relationship, had never contrived to work out what he saw in her that he could not find in a more beautiful and glossier woman.

'The limo will drop you back,' Gio breathed flatly, his spectacular eyes veiled. 'I have work to catch up on. My business team are joining me here within the hour. I'll call you tomorrow.'

Shot from the conviction that she was being rejected to the news that once again she had read him wrong, Billie slowly shook her head. 'There's no point. End it here, Gio. Leave me alone. You go your way, I go mine. It's the only sensible option after all this time.'

A sliver of dark fury shot through Gio that Billie should still feel detached enough to believe that she could easily walk away from him. This was the woman he had once believed *loved* him. This was the woman he had spent a fortune tracking down. Well, so much for love, he reflected without wonder at that change in her and her lack of appreciation for a persistent and flattering pursuit that many women would have killed to receive from him. Was his less-than-stellar performance between the sheets at fault? Shorn of his usual cool, he had been too fast and too eager. His perfect white teeth gritted.

'You're starting to offend me,' Gio admitted with the disconcerting honesty he could occasionally employ to unsettle the opposition. He tugged out his phone and voiced terse instructions in Greek. 'Perhaps it's better that you leave now and think over what you're doing.'

Billie flushed, hands linking tightly in front of her. 'I've already thought—'

'If I leave, I never come back,' Gio spelt out in pure challenge. 'Think carefully before I give you what you say you want.'

A pang of dismay shot through Billie. She wanted him to go away and leave her alone, of course she did. She didn't have a single doubt. She had to protect Theo because Gio would hit the roof if he found out about him. His Greek family was very traditional and old-fashioned and children born on the proverbial wrong side of the blanket were not welcomed. She knew his father had had an illegitimate child with a lover, a half-sister of Gio's, whom his family did not acknowledge or accept into their select circle.

Gio was finally coming round to her arguments, she decided, striving to feel pleased that her objections were finally getting through to him and being taken seriously. But just then, as Gio showed her back out to the lift and turned away again without a backward glance to vanish into his suite, it was impossible for Billie to feel good about anything that had happened. She was a mess inside and out and she hadn't even brushed her hair. The mirrored wall in the lift showed a woman with a reddened swollen mouth, a wild torrent of tousled curls and guilty troubled eyes gritty with the tears she was denying. Did she blame the wine? Being sex-starved? Old memories and familiarity? Or did she have a fatal weakness called Gio Letsos? And without any warning, time was sweeping her boldly back to their very first meeting.

Billie's grandfather had died when she was eleven. Seven years later, her grandma had passed away after a very long illness. The older woman had willed her house to a local charity and had essentially left Billie homeless. Billie had travelled down to London with another girl, moved into a hostel and found work as a cleaner in a luxury block of apartments. She had cleaned Gio's palatial apartment daily for several months before she met him.

Before she'd entered any apartment she had rung the bell to check whether anyone was at home and there had been no answer that day. Billie had been dusting shelves in the vast open-plan living area when a sudden unexpected noise had made her jump in fright. Whirling round, she had belatedly realised that there was a man lying slumped on one of the sofas. For an instant she had believed he was asleep, but his dark golden brown eyes had opened to stare at her and he had immediately begun trying to sit up, his movements clumsy and uncoordinated. She had watched in shock as, instead of standing, he had ended up rolling off the sofa and falling heavily to the polished wooden floor.

'For goodness' sake…are you all right?' she had exclaimed, wondering if he was in a drunken stupor.

But having grown up with a grandfather and school friends who liked to overindulge in alcohol at every opportunity, Billie had trusted her ability to recognise when someone was drunk. Gio had tried and failed to lift his head and he had groaned. She had noted that there was no sign of a bottle or a glass anywhere and no smell of drink before she had finally risked moving closer to see if he was simply ill.

'Flu...' he had mumbled, ridiculously long black lashes dropping back down over his stunning eyes as if even the effort of speech was too much for him.

Billie had rested cool fingers fleetingly on his forehead and registered that he was running one heck of a fever. 'I think you need an ambulance,' she had whispered.

'No...doctor...phone,' he had framed with difficulty, patting the pocket of his business suit jacket.

Billie had dug out the phone for him and slotted it into his hand. He had fumbled with buttons and cursed. 'No, you do it.'

But the contacts list had been written in some weird script that was definitely not the alphabet and most probably a foreign equivalent. She had had to shake his shoulder to bring that to his attention and with some difficulty at focusing he had stabbed out the name for her and she had had to make the call to the doctor for him. Mercifully the doctor had spoken English and, sounding very concerned about the male he'd referred to as 'Gio', he had promised to be with them in twenty minutes.

Feeling uncomfortable but knowing she had to wait to let the doctor into the apartment, Billie had got on with the cleaning while Gio had lain there on the floor. She had felt helpless and useless because he was simply too big and heavy in build for her to lift him in an effort to make him more comfortable. The doctor, young and fit, had been shocked to see

Gio lying on the floor and had immediately hauled him up and practically carried him into the first bedroom off the corridor.

Ten minutes later, the doctor had sought her out in the kitchen. 'He's a workaholic and he's exhausted, which is probably why he's ill. It's a bad dose of the flu and he won't go to hospital. I'll bring back his prescription and look into getting a private nurse…in the short term, can you stay for a while? He shouldn't be alone but I'm on emergency call—'

'I'm only here to clean and I'm already behind,' Billie had explained apologetically. 'I should be starting on the apartment next door—'

'Gio owns the building. He's probably the man who signs your pay cheque through the management company. I wouldn't worry about the place next door,' the doctor had told her drily. 'He asked for you to go in and see him—'

'But why?'

The doctor had shrugged on his way out. 'Maybe he wants to thank you for being a good Samaritan. You could've run and left him lying there.'

She had knocked on the bedroom door and when it wasn't answered had peeped in, seeing Gio sprawled naked but for a pair of black silk pyjama trousers on the biggest bed she had ever seen. Even ill, pale below his olive skin and fast asleep, he had been the most beautiful specimen of masculinity she had ever seen, from his ruffled black curly hair to his unshaven chin and his incredibly impressive bronzed and muscular torso and flat stomach.

She had cleaned the guest bathrooms, waited an hour and then gone back into the bedroom, finding him awake.

'Do you need anything?'

'Water would be welcome…what's your name?' he had asked limply, breathing heavily as he'd tried to sit up but had lurched sideways instead.

'Billie.'

'Short for?'

'Billie. Do you want me to fix your pillows?'

And she had fixed the pillows and straightened the sheet and fetched him a glass of water. He had seemed stunned by the discovery that she cleaned his apartment regularly sight unseen.

'There's never much to do here,' she had admitted. 'You don't seem to use the kitchen.'

'I travel a lot, eat out or order in when I'm here.'

The bell had buzzed. 'That'll be the nurse the doctor mentioned,' she remarked.

'I don't need a nurse.'

'You're too weak and sick to be left alone,' Billie had informed him bluntly.

'I was hoping you'd hang around…'

'I have other apartments to cleanI'll be working late tonight as it is,' she had said before she hurried to answer the door to a beautiful uniformed blonde with the face of a madonna.

The next morning when she had clocked in, her manager had emerged from his office to say, 'You've been seconded full-time to Mr Letsos' apartment until further notice.'

'But how…why on earth? *Full-time?*' she had queried in astonishment.

'The order came down from higher up. Maybe the
guy had a party last night and needs the place gutted,' he had muttered without interest. 'It's not our
business to question why.'

She had used the bell but nobody had answered
and she had let herself in with her pass key, moving
quietly round the silent apartment before knocking
on the bedroom door.

'Where's the nurse?' she had asked straight away.

Even more badly in need of a shave and still flat
on the pillows, Gio had given her a wry look. 'She
tried to get into bed with me… I told her to leave.'

Thoroughly disconcerted by that bald admission,
Billie had surveyed him wide-eyed, recognising the
level of his primal male attraction even in sickness.
He was gorgeous. Just looking at him had made butterflies take flight in her tummy.

'For that reason, I hope you don't mind that I arranged for you to take care of me because you haven't
demonstrated any desire to get into bed with me—'

Billie had reddened to the roots of her hair. 'Of
course not…how did you arrange it?'

'Do you mind?'

'What would taking care of you entail?' Billie had
prompted suspiciously. 'I'm no nurse—'

'I haven't eaten since breakfast yesterday,' Gio had
confided, stunning lustrous dark eyes locking onto
hers in clear search of sympathy. 'Food would be
very welcome.'

She had felt sorry for him, had even contrived to feel guilty that she hadn't offered him a meal the day before. And after all, taking care of the sick was pretty much all Billie had done from the age of eleven right up until her grandmother had passed away. For the following three days, Billie had done what came naturally without fuss or fanfare. She had looked after Gio, shopping for him, cooking meals, changing the bed, passing out his medication and arguing with him every time he prematurely announced that he was well enough to get out of bed because his state of exhaustion was still etched in his pallor and sunken eyes. Indeed she had established an amazingly easy camaraderie with Gio Letsos that took no note whatsoever of their divergent status in life and she had laughed out loud when he had announced that he would take her out to dinner as a thank you as soon as he was stronger.

'What age are you?' he had suddenly demanded, staring at her. 'I don't date teenagers.'

And the minute that Billie had appreciated that the dinner suggestion could actually be described as a date, she had lied without shame to fulfil the conditions of acceptance because *any* kind of a date with a male like Gio had struck her as a dream come true.

As the images of the past receded, Billie swallowed hard, shaken up by those recollections and her own innocence, for in those days she had very definitely viewed Gio as a knight on a white horse. He had seemed so perfect to her, so very considerate and courteous. Well, she conceded painfully, she knew how well that belief had turned out... Gio could say the most dreadful things in the politest way without even raising his voice. He could graciously open the door for you while saying something that flayed the skin from your bones and ripped your heart to shreds. His superb manners and self-control had only added another layer of pain to the end game because he was clever enough to voice intolerable expectations in an acceptable, seemingly civilised way.

That same day the head of Gio's security, Damon Kitzakis, came to see him after dinner. Wearing a rare air of discomfiture for a man who was generally very relaxed with his employer, Damon hovered and took his time about speaking up.

'Something worrying you?' Gio encouraged with a frown.

'As you instructed, Stavros has been keeping an eye on Miss Smith and in the course of doing that he got chatting to one of her neighbours,' Damon volunteered stiffly. 'Quite accidentally he picked up something you probably already know about...of course, *but*—'

Gio was steadily becoming very still behind the desk, his broad shoulders taut. 'What is this something?'

'Miss Smith has a child.'

Gio shot him a startled look. 'The woman she lives with has kids.'

Damon winced. 'Apparently when...Miss Smith

moved in when she was pregnant. The youngest kid…
the baby…is hers.'

Suddenly something was buzzing in Gio's head,
interfering with his ability to think clearly. He blinked
rapidly, fighting to clear his thoughts. Billie had a
baby, another man's child. There *had* been another
man. *Theos,* he should never have approached her in
advance of seeing the background report he had yet
to receive from Henley. This was his reward for his
ridiculous impatience, he reflected grimly. The least
she could have done was *tell* him, he thought then
with the dull, unfeeling anger of shock.

Pallor framed his mouth as he compressed his lips
hard and phoned Joe Henley. Yes, there was a child,
the older man confirmed without hesitation, but he
hadn't yet got hold of a copy of the birth certificate
and couldn't offer any further details until he did.

Why the hell hadn't Billie just told him that she
was a mother? After all, she had had the perfect
excuse for not resuming their relationship, so why
hadn't she used it? Surely she would have guessed
that he would no longer want her with a kid in tow?
Gio sprang upright. His anger, cold from sheer
shock, was heading towards sizzling temperatures
very fast indeed because Billie had achieved a feat
few people lived to boast about: she had made Gio
feel foolish. He would never have gone to bed with
her again had he known she had a child. Was Billie
playing some silly waiting game, planning to entrap
him with the lure of sex before admitting that she
now had a kid?

* * *

Billie sank into a deep bath and whisked her fingers through the bubbles coating the surface of the water. It was treat night, when she spoiled herself with her favourite things. The children were in bed fast asleep. The kitchen was clean. She would curl up on the sofa and watch a romantic movie and have some chocolate. Even if she no longer quite believed in true love or the staying power of romance she could still enjoy the fantasy, she acknowledged ruefully.

The doorbell went when she was drying herself. And she grimaced, hurriedly reaching for her robe and tying the sash tight round her waist as she sped barefoot down the stairs, keen to prevent her caller from pressing the bell again and disturbing the children. Jade was a light sleeper and once she was up she would be up and there would be no prospect of peace and tranquillity. No, then it would be cartoons and endless chatter until Jade got sleepy again.

Billie yanked open the door and stiffened in dismay. It was Gio, shorn of his usual business suit, wearing black jeans and a leather jacket. She dragged her attention from the rare sight of him in casual clothing up to his lean, hard-boned face. Dark eyes glittered like golden fireworks at her and colour surged up in a hot wave over her cheeks because all she could think about at that instant was the thrusting potency of him over and in her and the earth-shattering pleasure that had followed.

'Why didn't you tell me you had a child?' Gio demanded in a raw undertone.

Billie jerked and lost colour even faster than she had gained it at the recollection of how they had spent the afternoon. She pushed the door wider, immediately recognising that this was not a conversation she could keep outdoors. 'You'd better come in.'

'You're damned right I'm coming in,' Gio all but snarled at her, striding past her and thrusting open the sitting-room door with all the annoying assurance of a regular and more welcome visitor.

He knew. Oh, dear heaven, he knew, and that was why he was furious, Billie assumed in consternation.

Gio swung round from the window, all fluid grace and driving aggression, stunning eyes blistering over her as if she had deeply offended him in some way. 'I'd never have touched you if I'd known you'd had some other man's child!'

Some other man's child. The worst of the tension holding Billie uncannily still evaporated as she realised that by some mysterious good fortune her secret was still a secret. Evidently it had not even occurred to Gio that her child might be his, but she was disconcerted by the unexpected flash of sexual possessiveness he was revealing. 'Yes, I have a child,' she confirmed flatly. 'But I don't see that as your business—'

'*Theos*… Of course it was *my* business when I was asking you to come back to me!' he flung back at her, his spectacular bone structure rigid with condemnation.

So, he didn't want her with the encumbrance of a child. That was no surprise to Billie. He might have wanted a legitimate heir from Calisto but that want had been firmly rooted in his pride in his family line and his apparent desire to have a child to inherit his business empire. He had no particular fondness for children or interest in them that she had ever noticed. He had nephews and nieces because at least two of his sisters had married and produced but he had never mentioned those kids in a positive way, choosing instead to complain about the noise, inconvenience and indiscipline they displayed at adult gatherings.

'But I didn't *owe* you the information that I had a child when I had no plans to come back to you,' Billie countered evenly, slight shoulders setting straight now that she no longer felt threatened, green eyes bright with defiance.

'Then what was this afternoon all about?' Gio demanded with cutting derision.

'A mistake, as I said earlier,' she reminded him doggedly. 'A mistake we will obviously never repeat.'

Gio studied Billie, all pink and tousled and undoubtedly naked below the robe. As she moved her breasts swayed, pointed nubs making faint indents on the fabric, and within seconds he was hard as iron and furious that the hunger he had so recently assuaged could return without his volition. 'Who was the guy?'

'That's not relevant,' Billie fielded.

The fury still powering Gio wouldn't quit. He breathed in slow and deep, disturbed by the level of anger still burning through him, questioning its source. 'What age is the kid?' he asked, although he didn't know why he was asking because he could see no reason why he should want to know.

'A year old,' Billie answered, trimming a couple of months from Theo's tally for safety's sake, fearful of rousing Gio's curiosity and making him wonder if there was the smallest possibility that her child might also be *his* child.

Involved in fast mental calculations as he counted the months, Gio compressed his wide sensual mouth into a hard line of distaste. 'So, it was some kind of rebound thing after me,' he assumed.

'Not everything in my life is about you!' Billie snapped back defensively.

'But obviously the kid's father isn't still around—'

'Not all men are cut out to be fathers,' she parried.

'The least a man should do is stand by his own child,' Gio pronounced, startling her with that opinion. 'It's his most basic duty.'

'Well, mine didn't…' and she almost reminded him that his father hadn't either but that felt like too sensitive a point to raise in the mood he was in.

'Whatever.' Gio shifted a broad shoulder sheathed in butter-soft leather in a Mediterranean shrug as he moved past her to the door, clearly eager to be gone this time around. 'You should've told me about the child the minute I reappeared. It's a game changer, not something I could accept.'

Once, Billie would have assumed that she would experience a certain bitter satisfaction from Gio, in his ignorance, rejecting his own child, but instead guilt bit deep into her uneasy conscience. The passage of time had softened her outlook. Nothing was as black and white as she had believed when she had given birth to Theo without Gio's knowledge. Less emotional now than she had been then, she knew that Gio had wronged her but that Gio's wrong did not necessarily make her decisions right. A child wasn't a trophy or a payback for an adult's unkindness. A child was only a small human being, who might well not appreciate the choice she had made when he was old enough to have an opinion.

For Gio the next morning started with a bang when the fax spewed out a document and kept on printing. He scooped up the first page on the way to the shower and froze when he realised that he was looking at a facsimile of a birth certificate.

Theon Giorgios, a little boy aged fifteen months, had been born to Billie Smith. Theon was his grandfather's name and the child's age left no doubt of when conception had occurred.

Gio swept up the other pages of the report that had come through. His hands were trembling with rage. He was so angry, so incredulous that he wanted to smash something. He had trusted Billie and yet self-evidently she had *betrayed* his trust. He struggled to cool down for long enough to take a rational appraisal of the facts. No method of birth control was fool proof. He knew that intellectually, but he had always been careful, determined never to be caught in that net by something as basic as biology.

Billie had been on the contraceptive pill but side

effects had led to her trying several brands before finally choosing to have an implant put in her arm instead. In short he had allowed her to take contraceptive responsibility and it was very possible that she had simply fallen victim to the failure rate. He set down the report, strode into the shower and, below the pounding beat of the overhead power shower, he thought with an incredulous wonder that was entirely new to his experience, *I have a son.*

An illegitimate son. He didn't like that; he didn't like that aspect at all. Gio was rigid in his views in that line and was well aware that his half-sister had suffered from having neither a father nor the acceptance and support of her own family. Times had changed since then and the world in general was much less concerned about whether or not children were born within marriage. In the Letsos family, however, such formal acknowledgements of inheritance, status and honour still mattered a great deal.

That Billie had lied outright to him shocked Gio the most and by the time he had finished reading that report and had learned about his son's surgery, Billie's unacceptable childcare arrangements and the unsavoury character of the woman she was living with, he wasted no time in setting up a video-conference meeting with his legal team in London to get advice. That discussion concluded, Gio knew what his options were and they were very few and the fierce temper he usually kept under wraps was boiling up like lava below his calm surface. He was in a situation he would never have chosen and, worst of all, a situation he could not necessarily control. He would fight dirty if he had to, *very* dirty if need be. Billie might have taken him by surprise but Gio knew where his priorities lay.

That same morning, Billie felt washed out because she had tossed and turned through the night and she got up early and was sitting with a cup of tea when Dee came downstairs smothering a yawn and swearing she was going straight back to bed.

'I've done something awful,' she confided to her cousin, quickly filling in the details and wincing when Dee looked at her in surprise and dismay. 'I know, it was totally wrong of me to tell Gio that Theo was another man's child—'

'What came over you?'

Billie groaned. 'I felt cornered and threatened. I didn't get the chance to think anything through. I know Gio's going to be furious when he finds out the truth.' She pushed away the curls flopping on her brow and groaned. 'I'm going to text him and ask him to come over.'

'I think you'd better. I mean…the minute you re-alised that he knew you had a child, you should've come clean. After all, if you don't tell Gio, what happens if Theo decides that he wants to meet his father ten or fifteen years from now?' the blonde woman asked anxiously. 'I know Gio hurt you but that doesn't mean that he couldn't be a good father.'

Dee wasn't telling Billie anything she hadn't thought herself during the long lonely hours of the night. Gio walking back into her life had changed everything. It was no longer acceptable to conceal the truth of Theo's paternity and pretending that some other man was responsible for his conception had been downright unforgivable, she acknowledged with eyes that ached from the tears she was holding back. Ashamed of that moment of cowardice, she swallowed hard and lifted her phone, selecting the number she had never deleted, hoping it remained unchanged, texting…

I have to speak to you today. It's very important.

Gio texted back.

Eleven, your house.

Clearly, Billie was planning to tell him the truth. Gio's mouth curled; he wasn't impressed. The truth would still be coming fifteen months and more too late…

CHAPTER FIVE

RESTIVE AS A cat on hot bricks, Billie peered out of the window as Gio sprang out of the limo and she tensed up even more at the sight of his formal attire. He wore a faultlessly tailored black business suit teamed with a white shirt and purple tie. This was Gio in full tycoon mode, eyes veiled, lean, strong face taut with reserve, and unsmiling.

'I have something to tell you,' she said breathlessly in the hall.

Gio withdrew a folded sheet of paper from his jacket and simply extended it. 'I already know…'

Her heart beating very fast, Billie shook open the sheet, lashes fluttering in disconcertion when she saw the photocopy of the birth certificate. 'I don't know what to say—'

'There's nothing you can say,' Gio pronounced icily. 'You lied last night. You deliberately concealed the truth from me for well over a year. Evidently you had no intention of *ever* telling me that I was a father.'

'I never expected to see you again,' Billie muttered weakly.

'I want to see him,' Gio breathed in a driven undertone.

'He's having a nap—'

Poised at the foot of the stairs, Gio sent her a sardonic appraisal. 'I will still see him...'

Billie breathed in deep and started up the stairs, brushing damp palms down over her jeans. If she was reasonable, even a touch conciliating, they could deal with this situation in a perfectly civilised fashion, she told herself soothingly. Naturally, Gio's first reaction was curiosity and, since he was divorced, Theo's existence was probably less of an embarrassment than it might otherwise have been.

'We need to be quiet,' she whispered. 'Dee's very tired and she went back to bed. I don't want to wake her.'

Billie pressed open the door of the room that the three children shared. Theo's cot was in the corner. Gio strode up to the rails and gazed down with a powerful sense of disbelief at the baby peacefully sleeping in a tangle of covers. *His son.* Even at first glance, the family resemblance was staggering. Theo had a shock of black curls, a strong little nose and the set of his eyes was the same as Gio's. Gio breathed in deep and slow, his broad chest tightening on a surge of emotion unlike anything he had ever felt. This was *his* little boy and he had gone through serious surgery *without* Gio. Any sort of surgery on babies was risky. His child could have died without Gio ever having known of his existence. Rage shot through Gio like a rejuvenating drug, ripping through the carapace of uncertainty and shock. Not trusting himself to remain quiet, he swung away from the cot and walked back to the door.

Billie studied him uneasily. Colour scored along the high blades of his cheekbones. His eyes were a glossy brilliant black she couldn't read and his wide sensual mouth was clenched into a hard line.

'*Theos*...I will never ever forgive you for this,' Gio ground out at the top of the stairs, his dark velvety drawl as chilling as an icicle shot into her flesh.

Consternation winging through her at that inflexible assurance, Billie's tummy flipped and her legs felt hollow and clumsy as she descended the stairs.

In the sitting room she turned round to face him. 'Why won't you forgive me?' she prompted. 'Because I got pregnant?'

A tall, dark, brooding figure in the doorway, Gio stared across the room at her. 'I'm not that stupid. It takes two people to make a baby. I know you couldn't have schemed behind my back to have him because if that had been the case your goal would have been to claim child support. As you made no attempt to contact me to tell me that you had had my child, I can, at least, absolve you of a motive of greed.'

'Am I supposed to say thank you for that vote of confidence?' Billie asked with raised brows.

'No.' Gio closed the door behind him. 'You're supposed to explain why you chose not to tell me.'

'I'm surprised you can ask me that.'

'Are you really?' Gio prompted in a gritty undertone.

'Yes…you were getting married,' Billie pointed out flatly.

'That's not an excuse,' Gio declared harshly. 'Whether I was single, married or divorced that child upstairs was my business and will *always* be my business and that's why you should have told me the minute you realised that you were pregnant.'

'I didn't think you'd want to know,' Billie admitted uncomfortably, wondering exactly what he expected her to say. 'You once warned me that if I got pregnant it would be a disaster and the end of our relationship.'

'That's not an excuse either, particularly as, according to you, our relationship was already at an end,' Gio reminded her staunchly.

'Gio, you know you would've been furious and that you probably would've blamed me for it. I *knew* you wouldn't want me to have your child!' she exclaimed in frustration, resenting his refusal to acknowledge the limits of their relationship at the time.

'What you want and what you get in life are often two very different things,' Gio pointed out cynically. 'I'm adult enough to accept that reality.'

'Oh, thanks a bundle!' Billie snapped back at him, her face flaming. 'How dare you sneer at me because I have your child? I believed that if I'd told you back then, you would have asked me to have a termination—'

Gio shot her a chilling appraisal. 'On what grounds do you base that assumption?'

Aware of the rise of hostile vibrations in the atmosphere, Billie fumbled to find the right words. 'Well, obviously—'

An ebony brow lifted. 'Did I ever make any comment about expecting you to have a termination if the situation arose?'

Put so unerringly on the spot, Billie shifted her feet uneasily. 'Well, no, but once you had admitted what your attitude would be to an unplanned pregnancy it was a natural assumption for me to make.'

'I don't think so.'

'So, you're saying that you wouldn't have suggested a termination?' Billie prompted.

'That's exactly what I'm saying. And considering that we only once briefly discussed how I would feel about you getting pregnant, you made one hell of a lot of assumptions about how I would react to having a child!' Gio condemned.

'At the time you were getting married to *have* a child with another woman. My being pregnant was nothing but bad news on every level!' Billie proclaimed emotively. 'And maybe I didn't care to be the bearer of such bad news, maybe I didn't want to tell you what I knew you didn't want to hear, maybe, just maybe, I had a little pride of my own...'

'I would never have married Calisto had I known you were pregnant,' Gio declared grimly. 'I would always have put the needs of my child first.'

Billie was rocked by that blunt announcement and she frowned. 'I don't understand.'

Gio was beginning to grasp that reality for himself and his temper was on a hair trigger. 'No, you don't understand what you've done,' he told her flatly. 'Do you?'

'What have I done?' Billie fired back defensively. 'I brought Theo into the world and I've looked after him ever since to the best of my ability. He has everything that he needs—'

Gio's eyes flared golden as luminous torches, the force of his anger obvious in the harsh angular lines stamped on his darkly handsome features. 'No, he has not. He has no father—'

Her brow furrowed. 'If you want to play a part in Theo's life, I'll support that…if that's what you're worrying about—'

'You think it's acceptable to offer me a part?' Gio derided in a tone that cracked like a whiplash in the silence. 'You think it's acceptable to let my son go through surgery without even telling me? To raise him here in a dump? To drag him to a shop while you work? To keep him ignorant of my language, his heritage, his father's family, when you don't even have a family of your own to offer him? Let me tell you now that *nothing* you have done is acceptable to me!'

Shaken by that comprehensive denunciation of what she had to offer her child and the fury he couldn't hide, Billie backed off a step. 'My home is not a dump—'

'It *is* on my terms,' Gio fired back unapologetically.

'How did you know that Theo had to have surgery?' Billie asked, thrown by Gio's attitude, which was the exact opposite of what she had expected, and then finally making the leap to guess the most likely source of his information. 'Oh, you've had us investigated, haven't you?'

'Why was my son over six months old before he received surgery?' Gio demanded. 'Hip dysplasia is usually recognised early.'

'His wasn't and when it was other treatments were tried first. You seem to know something about it—'

'Of course I do—there's a genetic link to the condition in my family. My half-sister and one of my full sisters were born with it as well as one nephew and one niece. It's less common in boys. Theo having suffered it was almost as good as a DNA test,' Gio spelt out with sardonic bite. 'He is a Letsos in all but name—'

Billie lifted her chin. 'No, he's a Smith.'

Ramping down his anger, Gio looked at her, lustrous dark golden eyes semi-veiled by the thickness of his lashes. Even dressed in old jeans and a blue cotton top, her lush feminine curves sang a siren's song to him. He hardened, knowing that, no matter how angry he was with her, he still wanted her on the most visceral level. Once had not been enough; once had not sated him. 'I want my son,' he said simply.

Billie turned pale, eyes flickering uncertainly over his lean, tight face, skimming uneasily over the lithe, lethal power of his very well-built body. 'What's that supposed to mean?'

'It means exactly what I said—I *want* my son. I want to be there for him as my father was not there for me,' Gio extended curtly, wide sensual mouth compressing on the grudging admission, reminding her that his background and his family had always been a thorny topic on which he was only prepared to offer the barest details.

'And how do you propose to do that?'

'By fighting you for custody,' Gio countered, throwing his big shoulders back, standing tall. 'My son deserves no less from me.'

Her brow furrowed, consternation and disbelief running through her in a debilitating wave as she collided with his fiery gaze. That visual connection seemed to make the very blood in her veins move sluggishly even while her heartbeat quickened. In turmoil, she shivered. 'You can't be serious. You can't mean that you would try to take Theo away from me?'

'I will not allow him to stay here.'

Anger powered by a deep sense of fear smashed through the wall of Billie's astonishment. 'It doesn't matter what you allow. I'm Theo's mother and what you have to say has nothing to do with it!'

'You're wrong,' Gio told her succinctly. 'I have every right to object to the manner in which you care for my son and I will be happy to fully explain to the children's authorities why I believe my son's current living conditions are unacceptable.'

Gio was threatening her. Gio was actually telling her that he was prepared to report her to the social services for what he evidently saw as inadequate or neglectful childcare. The very thought made Billie shake with rage, a flush running across her cheekbones, her chin up, her green eyes defiant. 'Well, maybe you'd be happy to tell me because quite frankly I don't know what your problem is!'

'You are living with a prostitute and leaving my child in her care. I will not tolerate that,' he asserted with icy precision.

Off-balanced by that condemnation coming at her out of nowhere, Billie sank weakly down on the sofa, her legs suddenly giving way beneath her. It had not occurred to her that a routine investigation of her life would also dig up Dee's biggest secret. Pale, her clear eyes reflecting her strain and distress, she stared back at Gio. 'Dee's a bartender now. She's put her past behind her…'

'I don't put a time limit on a past like that, nor do I want such a woman in close contact with my son or taking care of him,' Gio delivered with inflexible cool.

'People make mistakes, people change, turn their lives around. Don't be so narrow-minded!' Billie urged, stricken, appalled that he had uncovered her cousin's troubled history and leapt straight to a disparaging conclusion.

Dee had got involved with an older man in her teens and had dropped out of school and ended up as a drug addict on the streets. Dee had been brutally honest with Billie about her past and Billie had tremendous respect for the amount of work and effort the other woman had put into making a fresh start for her and the twins.

'I'm glad for her sake that she's turned her life around but I still don't want her anywhere near my son,' Gio growled without apology. 'How do you know she's not still turning tricks at the bar where she works at night?'

'Because I know her and how much she values what she has now!' Billie slammed back furiously.

'I want my son out of this house right now,' Gio admitted. 'I want the two of you to move into my hotel with me until we get this situation sorted out.'

Wildly disconcerted by that demand, Billie stared back at him. 'No,' she said straight away.

'Say no and take the consequences,' Gio drawled softly, chillingly.

'What's that supposed to mean?'

'That I will use whatever I have against you to make the case for gaining custody of my son,' Gio advanced with measured force. 'I will go to social services with my concerns and they are bound by law to investigate.'

'I don't believe I'm hearing this!' Billie exclaimed jerkily, appalled by what he was telling her and cringing at the prospect of Dee being investigated once again by suspicious hypercritical officials, who would disinter the past that Dee had worked so hard to leave behind her. 'You're threatening me and my cousin!'

'If it is in my son's best interests, there's nothing I won't do for his benefit,' Gio intoned harshly. 'He is my primary concern here. I don't care what it takes or who else it hurts but I will always do my absolute best for him by whatever means possible.'

'How can you feel like that about a son you haven't even met yet?' Billie demanded shakily.

'Because he has my blood in his veins. He is mine, he is a Letsos and I must fight his battles for him because it is my duty to do that while he is still too young to have a voice.' Gio glanced down at the wafer-thin gold watch barely visible below his immaculate white shirt cuff. 'You have fifteen minutes to pack.'

'Leaving here is absolutely out of the question.'

'No, it is your one chance to escape the penalty for defying me. If I leave this house without my son today, I will fight to win custody and I will use whatever means are at my disposal,' Gio warned her with chilling bite.

Her eyes rounding, Billie's upper lip parted company from her lower. 'You're not being reasonable!'

'Why would I be? You've stolen the first fifteen months of my son's life from me,' Gio pronounced with lethal cool. 'How can you be surprised that I refuse to allow you to steal one day more?'

In receipt of that caveat, Billie could feel the blood draining slowly from below her skin, shock smacking through her in a dizzy wave. He was angry, he was bitter, but he couldn't possibly be thinking through what he was doing. 'Are you crazy? Theo needs *both* of us,' she told him tightly.

His lean, strong face clenched hard. 'Of course he does…in a perfect world. And this, I need hardly remind you, is not a perfect world.'

'Where are you planning to make time for a baby in your schedule?' Billie demanded with scorn. 'You won't. You don't really want him. You're behaving as if Theo is some kind of a trophy.'

'Pack,' Gio urged, one long brown forefinger tapping his watch face. 'You need only bring what you need for twenty-four hours. Naturally I will cover any necessities you need.'

Frozen to the spot, Billie stared at him, unwilling to believe that he could threaten everything she held dear in her life on the strength of what could only be a whim. 'Gio—'

'Not one word,' Gio cut in fiercely. 'I *want* my son. You've had all the time with him that you ever wanted. It's my turn now and I'm taking it.'

Billie reached a sudden decision. She would go to the hotel and allow Gio the time and space to get acquainted with Theo. Surely that major concession would cool his temper and calm him down? Sadly, she couldn't feel sure of the outcome. Gio's anger was shockingly new to her and she could still feel that anger sizzling from him in invisible sparks that could ignite into an explosion. Right now, opposition would probably only make him angrier and given a few hours' respite he would surely cool off and develop a more practical outlook, she reasoned frantically.

Billie withdrew a case from the hall cupboard and carried it up to her room. She packed the basics for herself and her son and then went downstairs to throw Theo's feeding essentials into a holdall. In the kitchen she scribbled a note to Dee, telling her where she had gone and that she would phone.

'Dee won't be able to work tonight if I'm not here to babysit for her,' Billie protested as she pulled on a light cotton jacket. Beneath the onslaught of Gio's appraisal she suddenly felt like a complete mess and she turned her head away, stiff with self-loathing. Her toffee-coloured corkscrew curls were never going to compare to Calisto's blade-straight blonde locks. Her hips were never going to be boyishly lean, nor would her boobs ever be dainty handfuls. Short of a body transplant, she was what she was. Wearing only a smattering of make-up, she looked very ordinary. It was ironic that she was so casually dressed because she hadn't wanted Gio to think that she had made a special effort for him. It was not a comfort that looking less than her best now felt like striking an own goal.

'I'll hire a babysitter for your cousin.'

'I can't let her down like this, Gio. It took so long for her to find a job with hours that suited.'

'I said I'll take care of it and I will,' Gio incised, grabbing her case from the hall and yanking open the front door, determined to let nothing come between him and his ultimate objective. 'Trust me.'

His chauffeur was waiting on the step to collect her case. After a moment's hesitation, Billie passed over her holdall as well, snatched a tiny jacket off the handles of the pram below the stairs and went up to lift Theo out of his cot. *Trust me!* Perhaps the strangest thing was that she *did* trust Gio because he had told her the truth even when she didn't want to hear it and he had never broken his word to her.

Her son was sleepy and warm as toast. She nuzzled her cheek against his smooth skin and breathed in his glorious baby scent before threading his short little arms into the jacket. Even in the very dark mood he was in, Gio had stated that their son needed both of his parents, she reminded herself staunchly. He wasn't trying to split them up; he was only making threats to make her listen and do what he wanted. Possibly all he really wanted was a couple of days with free access to Theo so that he could get to know him and he couldn't have that opportunity without including Billie in the arrangements.

A built-in safety seat for a child sat in the rear seat of the limousine. Billie settled Theo in and did up the buckle while her son craned his head to stare at Gio with big brown eyes. Silence fell while the two of them sized each other up. Gio had a cell phone in his hand and the light danced across the metallic finish. Theo stretched out a hand to grab the phone and Billie was incredulous when Gio handed it over.

'You can't give him that!' Billie exclaimed as the phone went straight into Theo's mouth to be chewed. 'He tries to eat everything.'

Billie filched the phone back. Theo looked at his empty hand and wailed while Billie passed the phone back to Gio out of her son's view. She dug a toy out of the holdall to give her son. He studied it with a jutting lower lip and threw it down.

'He wants the phone back,' Gio breathed in wonderment.

'Of course he does…it's got lots of buttons. The brightest, shiniest new toy always gets his interest.'

They drew up outside the hotel. Billie climbed out

and leant back into the car to unbuckle Theo but Gio was one step ahead of her and was already hoisting Theo into his arms. She followed them into the hotel. Theo loved new places just as much as new toys and his curly dark head was turning this way and that with keen interest. Billie stepped into the lift. Theo beamed at her from the vantage point of his father's arms, clearly very pleased with the exchange.

Billie was surprised to enter a different suite from the one that Gio had previously used. 'Have you changed to another floor?'

'Of course, we needed more space,' Gio pointed out while Theo frantically wriggled in his arms. With a sigh, Gio gave way and gently lowered Theo to the wooden floor. The little boy crawled off at high speed, grabbed at the leg of a fancy sofa and hauled himself upright, grinning with satisfaction.

'Theo's a clever boy,' Billie praised warmly.

Her son's sturdy little legs began to wobble and he toppled down onto his bottom in a sudden loss of balance and burst into floods of tears. Gio scooped him up again and held him high above his head. In his usual mercurial fashion, Theo forgot his moment of misery and burst out laughing instead at finding himself airborne. Gio made aeroplane noises like a little boy and whirled his son energetically round the room while Billie watched with a dropped jaw, not entirely sure that she could credit what she was seeing. Gio, shedding his dignity and distance, Gio smiling with unabashed enjoyment.

'It's time he had lunch,' Billie remarked.

The game between father and son concluded. A high chair was delivered along with the case and Billie started to feed Theo, who wanted to feed himself and complained vociferously between mouthfuls until she finally gave him the spoon. Theo stuck the spoon in the carton of yogurt with a victorious smile. Billie was still in a daze, her mind still engaged in replaying Gio acting as she had never before seen him act. Only an hour earlier, he had been threatening her with an adverse report to social services.

It had been an utterly ruthless threat that had chilled Billie to the marrow. A couple of years earlier, before Dee began getting her life straightened out, Dee's children had been put into care. Although she had got the twins back again and no longer even received visits to check on her progress, any allegation of negligent childcare made against the household where Dee lived would certainly result in a full investigation being made by the authorities. Billie could not bear the threat of that happening to her cousin again. It would flatten Dee's confidence, make her feel like an unfit mother again and if people realised that social services were checking up on her it would rouse local gossip. There was very little that Billie would not have done to protect Dee from such a development.

Yet the same male who had voiced that chilling threat had shown an entirely different side of himself to their son. With Theo, Gio had been playful, uninhibited, almost joyful, three traits she would never ever have associated with Gio's cool, calm and reserved nature. She recognised that Gio's interest in his son was considerably more powerful than she had ever dreamt it would be and she wondered uneasily where that left her in the triangle. He had said he wanted his son. What exactly did that mean?

Gio strode into one of the rooms leading off the spacious reception room and reappeared in jeans and a trendy striped cotton sweater. Billie couldn't drag her eyes from his lean, dark, devastating face as he watched entranced while Theo piled up his bricks and smashed them down again, giggling at the noise he was making. The tight jeans delineated every muscle in Gio's long, powerful thighs and narrow hips as he squatted down on the floor beside Theo. Billie's gaze ran over his washboard-flat stomach to the bulge below his belt and she averted her eyes, as hot and cold as someone with a fever. And mortifyingly, she knew precisely what was wrong with her. The kind of craving she had for Gio didn't go away, didn't take a back seat when you wanted it to, didn't fade when you knew it should; it just went on and on, the gift that kept on giving.

Sometimes wanting Gio had felt like a life sentence to Billie. Her pregnancy had only accelerated her exit from his life because she had been afraid that he might guess her secret. She had believed that that would be the ultimate humiliation because she had assumed that Gio would foist all the blame on her for her inconvenient pregnancy and make her feel dreadful as well as guilty and unworthy. Yet now he was telling her differently, insisting that he would never have suggested she have a termination.

Yet how much faith could she have in what Gio was currently saying? Gio, after all, was speaking with the benefit of hindsight, aware that his dynastic marriage was destined to fail. But two years ago that marriage had been very important to him and Billie's pregnancy would have been a severe embarrassment at the very least. What on earth had he meant when he had sworn he would never have married had he known about Billie's pregnancy?

It would never have occurred to Billie then that she could set the clock forward by two years and would see Gio, down on his jeans-clad knees, creating a precarious tower of bricks for Theo's benefit and actually laughing when Theo smacked it down with a chubby fist.

'You said you wanted Theo,' Billie murmured quietly, having finally worked up the courage to press for answers. 'What does that mean exactly?'

'That now that I've found him, I'm not walking away again,' Gio intoned, level dark golden eyes resting on her above Theo's head. Such beautiful eyes he had that even thinking was a challenge when she looked at them.

'No…er obviously,' she managed gruffly, 'you want to get to know him and stay in contact.'

Keeping very still, Gio lifted an ebony brow. 'I want much more than that.'

'How much more?' she pressed, struggling to breathe while level with those stunning eyes of his.

A sardonic smile curled Gio's wide sensual mouth. 'I don't like half measures…I want it *all*.'

'And what does "all" encompass?' Billie asked shakily.

Gio surveyed her with grim amusement. He had thought she would work it out for herself. He was ready to give her what she had always wanted from him and what he had never dreamt of offering before. Now he had very sound reasons for offering and anything else he gained as a by-product did not have to be measured or considered. The ever-ready pulse at his groin grew heavy while his attention roved to the deep valley between her full breasts, which was tantalisingly visible every time she angled her head down to speak to him. He wanted to rip her clothes off and slide between her thighs and stay there until he had worked off the powerful hunger riding him.

'Gio…?' she prompted, crystalline green eyes very serious.

'I want it all…as in marriage,' Gio filled in smoothly, long fingers smoothing back the curls on Theo's brow as his son slumped back against him for support. 'It's the only serviceable option we have.'

CHAPTER SIX

'LET ME GET this straight…' Billie framed between bloodless lips, barely able to credit what he was implying. 'You're suggesting that *we* get *married*?'

'If we marry, Theo's birth is automatically legitimised under British law.'

'But that scarcely matters when anyone who knows his age will guess that he was born while you were married to another woman,' Billie pointed out flatly.

'That's immaterial. The end result is what I want most—Theo legitimised, his place as my heir legally secured and recognised,' Gio spelt out very quietly, his dark, velvet drawl lowered to the level of an insidious husky murmur. 'That is his birthright and I want him to have it.'

'Even if it means you have to marry me to achieve that?' Billie prompted in disbelief.

'You will marry me for his sake and I will marry you for the same reason. We're responsible for his birth and we should put him first,' Gio told her squarely. 'We owe him that.'

Her skin clammy with disconcertion, Billie was

trembling where she sat. Long, long ago, she had dreamt of being Gio's wife, indeed she had dreamt the whole fairy tale before being forced to accept in the most painful way possible that it was just a fantasy. She could hardly bring herself to accept that he was actually talking about marrying her because it was like opening a locked door to let the silly fairy tale back in. She wrapped her arms protectively round herself. 'And you're quite sure that Theo's rights as your heir couldn't be secured any other way?'

'I could have legal agreements drawn up to officially acknowledge him as my son but nothing of that nature would be as watertight as marriage to his mother. In such agreements there is almost always a loophole or an irregularity and a clever enough lawyer can always find those weaknesses and build on them to make a claim.'

'And who on earth do you think is likely to make a claim?' Billie pressed in wonderment, sufficiently challenged to even picture her infant son as a child of future means.

'Have you any idea how wealthy I am?' Gio asked with lethal quietness of tone. 'Or of the lengths even wealthy people will go to in an effort to enrich themselves or their children even more?'

'Probably not,' she conceded ruefully, knowing when she was out of her depth.

'When I was fourteen, my stepmother tried to have me disinherited from the family trust in favour of her son, who was eight years old. The claim was only thrown out of court when my grandfather was able to prove that *her* son was not his grandson,' Gio completed.

Billie was sharply disconcerted, never having had any suspicion that Gio's place in his family had been challenged before he even reached adulthood. She frowned, shaken on Gio's behalf, wondering what on earth his childhood could have been like with such a spiteful and grasping stepmother and finally comprehending his fears on Theo's behalf.

'We can get married within a matter of days,' Gio told her smoothly, as if he had already worked out that he had won the battle. 'After the ceremony, we'll fly out to Greece and I'll introduce my wife and child to my family.'

Quite unable to credit such an event even taking place with her in a starring role, Billie sprang out of her seat and walked over to the window. 'That would be crazy, me trying to pretend I was your wife... We can't do this!'

'You will *be* my wife, you won't be pretending. What it comes down to is...how much do you love your son?' Gio enquired with almost casual cruelty.

Billie went rigid. 'That's not fair!'

'Isn't it? You *chose* to make yourself solely responsible for Theo and his future happiness. I'm only asking you to make good on your mistakes and ensure that he receives everything that should be his by right of birth,' he asserted glibly.

Billie inwardly squirmed at the accusation that she had made a serious mistake where Theo was concerned in not immediately informing Gio that he had a child, but the reference to Greece had sent her thoughts racing in another direction. 'If the marriage is only a legal formality why would you need me to accompany you to Greece?'

'Would you allow me to take Theo to Greece without you?' Gio asked in apparent surprise.

'No!' Billie proclaimed instantly.

'And while the marriage may appear to be little more than a legal formality to you,' Gio continued in the same reasonable tone, 'it is essential that it appears to be a normal marriage.'

Billie closed her arms round herself again, feeling threatened, cornered, bewildered, fighting that disorientation on every level as her chin tilted and her green eyes flared bold and bright as emeralds. 'But why should it have to appear normal?' she demanded.

'Do you want our son to feel guilty when he's older that you were forced to marry me for his benefit?' Gio enquired.

Billie frowned. 'Of course not—'

'Making it seem normal is a whitewash. There's nothing I can do about that,' Gio swore, manipulating the argument to the very best of his ability, flexing a level of cunning he had never utilised on Billie before. 'The more people who accept that the marriage is normal, the fewer the awkward questions that will be asked and the less comment it will create.'

'Nobody's going to accept that you freely *chose* to marry your mistress!' Billie slashed back at him angrily, hating to use that label on herself but willing to use it if it forced him to see sense.

'But we are the only people who know that you were my mistress. We didn't broadcast the fact and now we can be grateful that we kept a low profile. *Ne...*yes, you've had my child,' Gio conceded, sliding fluidly upright and moving towards her. 'All that proves is that we had a relationship.'

Billie clashed with spectacular dark eyes and her heart raced. 'All that proves is that we had, at least, a one-night stand.'

'*Diavelos...*you're not a one-night-stand woman and no man looking at you could believe that one night would be enough, *pouli mou,*' Gio purred soft and low, closing his hands firmly over hers to draw her close to his lean, powerful body. 'You will be my wife, the mother of my son. You will have nothing to be embarrassed about...'

It was a seductive image because Billie had always been embarrassed about the reality of her relationship with Gio. He had not been her knight on a white horse and she had not been his one true love. Her power had never stretched beyond the bedroom door and that was a demeaning truth that Billie had always felt shamed by, for what sort of woman settled for that kind of half-relationship? Her hands trembled in the grasp of his. A whitewash, he called it. But to the woman whose heart he had broken, and in spite of the fact that love wasn't involved, it still seemed more like a fairy tale to be offered what he had once tacitly refused to offer her.

'I can't leave Dee or the shop to go to Greece,' Billie told him abruptly. 'It's impossible. The shop is my livelihood and I can't just up and leave it...'

Gio closed his arms round her. Freed, one of her hands skimmed up over his muscular torso and came to rest uncertainly on a broad shoulder while the other lifted of its own volition to delve into his cropped black hair. 'I'll look after everything,' he told her.

'I have to have my independence,' Billie muttered unsteadily, her mouth drying and her breathing quickening as he ran the tip of his tongue along the closed seam of her lips. Her mouth tingled, stinging tightness pinching her nipples to send a current of liquefied heat into her pelvis. 'Listen to me, Gio,' she urged even as her fingers massaged his well-shaped skull, fluffing up the short strands of hair that were never allowed to amount to curls.

Gio rocked his hips lightly against hers and she tensed, suddenly insanely aware of his arousal and her own. 'Theo's my son. It's my duty to look after *both* of you.'

With a mighty effort of self-control, Billie yanked herself back from Gio and temptation. He could always make her want him but she could not afford to be stretched thin by that fierce wanting while she was trying to concentrate on the need to conserve her own life. With a slight shudder of loss, she straightened her slight shoulders and breathed in deep and slow to compose her scattered wits.

'Sell the shop or let me hire a manager for it. You decide which option will suit you best,' Gio urged, his lean dark features taut with impatience.

Billie looked at him with wide eyes of disbelief.

'Gio…I worked very hard to build up my business. You can't expect me to walk away from it.'

'Not even for Theo?' Gio prompted, glancing down at the little boy now clinging precariously to his jeans-clad leg and gazing up at both of them. 'Our son needs both of us and will do for some time. I want a normal family rapport with him. At the very least you will have to relocate your life to London, so that I can have regular access to him.'

Unexpectedly that statement jolted Billie because Gio spent most of his time in Greece. No, he was definitely not offering her a fairy-tale for-ever marriage because he was clearly already envisaging a future in which they were separated and sharing custody of their son. Billie paled, feeling as though he had slapped her in the face with reality, but ironically it was her own silly thoughts she needed to put a guard on, she conceded painfully. Of course, Gio wasn't suggesting a real marriage and a whitewash marriage would naturally have a sell-by date beyond which it was no longer required.

'I need to think about all this,' Billie admitted tightly. 'You're talking about turning my life upside down.'

'And my own,' Gio added softly. 'None of this was on my bucket list either.'

That obvious fact struck Billie like a second slap when she least required it. She did not need the reminder that Gio would never have chosen to marry her were it not for Theo. That reality was engraved on her soul because he had once rejected her in favour of Calisto. She bent down and scooped up Theo, loving the warm cuddliness of his solid little body and using it as a comfort to the chill spreading through her stomach. 'I need to change him,' she explained, walking away to scoop up the holdall and locate the nearest bathroom.

Why were women so complicated? Gio thought in seething frustration. He had offered her what he had assumed she had always wanted and she was behaving as if he had offered her a dirty deal. What did she have to think about? How many women had to run off to the bathroom and change a nappy before they could decide whether or not they wanted to marry a billionaire? Was it possible that she suspected that he had a motivation that he wasn't sharing?

His lean, strong face set like granite. Admittedly, he had not told her the whole truth, could not possibly tell her the whole truth because that would make her fear him. He was fighting for what he believed in, fighting for what Theo needed most. In every battle there were winners and losers and Gio had no plans to be a loser or to stand by powerless while Theo received less than his due. In the rarefied world of the super-rich Billie could only be a trusting babe in arms. She was so ignorant of the utter ruthlessness that could make Theo a target for the greedy that she had no concept of how best to protect their son. But Gio knew and there was nothing he would not do to achieve that objective.

Billie hovered by the vanity while Theo crawled across the tiled floor and pulled himself up on the

side of the bath. Her brain was in turmoil, inescapable
fear rammed down behind every thought. Gio wanted
her to marry him for Theo's sake and she wanted to
give her son the best possible start in life. But there
would be a steep price to pay for such a rise in her social status, she acknowledged unhappily. She would
inevitably be an embarrassment to Gio, and his precious family were certain to disapprove of her. But
then doubtless Gio planned to pension her off once
all the legalities and his son's place in life had been
affirmed. So, it wouldn't be a real for-ever marriage
and would probably be set aside once Theo was old
enough to go and visit his father without his mother
in tow. Everything, she assumed, would happen exactly the way Gio wanted it to happen because he
left nothing to chance. She foresaw that reality and
froze at the terrifying prospect of being left so powerless, shorn of her home and her business. Did she
have a choice? Could she trust Gio with their son's
future well-being?

Theo anchored on her hip, Billie walked back into
the gracious reception room. Gio had removed his
jacket, loosened his tie and pushed up the sleeves of
his white silk shirt. The super-fine expensive material accentuated the muscles that rippled with his
every movement and his impossibly taut, flat stomach. Her gaze lingered there, feverish memories of
torrid moments awakening, fingers and lips gliding
along his hard ribcage, smoothing over his abdomen
before stroking down the furrow of silky hair disappearing below his waistband. Her tummy flipped

and she gave herself a stern, frowning little shake as she emerged from her reverie. Black lashes flicking up on shrewd eyes, Gio completed the phone call he was making and set the phone down.

'OK. I'll marry you,' Billie spelled out tautly, her colour high. 'But that means I'm trusting you not to do anything that might harm Theo or me. If I find out that I can't trust you I'll leave you.'

Gio flashed her a deeply appreciative smile. She would never leave him again. Not unless she was prepared to leave her son behind with him, he reflected with immense satisfaction. She might not know it yet but her days of running were at an end.

'And you have to be totally, one hundred per cent faithful,' Billie decreed.

'I always was with you,' Gio responded airily.

'But there's that saying about how when a man marries his mistress he creates a vacancy,' Billie remarked flatly, her lush mouth compressing on a sense of humiliation.

'I think my life is complicated enough,' Gio fielded.

And of course he wouldn't be expecting to be married to her until he was old and grey and, since he would always have an end to their arrangement in sight, straying through boredom was less likely to be a problem, Billie affixed grimly, striving not to be hurt by that truth.

'Now that you've got what you wanted, can I go home?' Billie pressed.

'I want you here. Presumably you want to be in-

volved in making your own wedding arrangements.'
A straight ebony brow inclined. 'We'll have a small
wedding in the Greek Orthodox church I attend in
London. I've already applied for the required li-
cences.'

Billie's eyes flared in surprise. 'You took a lot for
granted.'

Gio's steady gaze held hers. 'I can afford to. Why
would you refuse to marry me when that was presumably what you wanted two years ago?'

Billie reddened as though she had been slapped.
So, he had finally worked that obvious fact out, had
he? Mortification drenched her like a tidal wave. 'I
don't buy into fairy tales any more.'

'But I want you to *have* the fairy tale, *pouli mou*,'
Gio breathed curtly, thoroughly disconcerting her
with that statement. 'I want you to wear a fancy dress
and all the trimmings.'

'Why? Because it will look good in the photos?'
Billie forced her strained eyes away from him, her
heart-shaped face stiff because she knew that he could
never give her the fairy tale. After all, the one essential facet of her fairy-tale denouement had been his
love. She was also wounded that he was so sure that
she would have married him like a shot two years
earlier, particularly when he had coolly turned away
from her to marry another, more suitable woman.
Her love had meant nothing to him in those days but
then she had offered her love too freely. Was it fair to
judge him harshly for not being able to love her back?

'A normal marriage,' he reminded her quietly. 'That is what I want and that is what we will have.'

His uncompromising arrogance set Billie's teeth on edge. Even though he was divorced he still had no fear of matrimonial failure. But then he wanted Theo and he wanted her, Billie conceded ruefully, and she knew that high-voltage libido of Gio's probably drove him harder than love ever could. He was, to say the least, an electrifyingly sexual personality. Had he ever loved Calisto? Or merely wanted the beautiful blonde? What had ultimately killed that wanting? And what did it matter to Billie? After all, she was only finally getting that wedding ring by default.

Gio's business team arrived to work with him that afternoon while Billie viewed images of wedding dresses online, sent at Gio's behest by a well-known designer. She squirmed over taking her measurements and sending them off and then buried the memory by picking her dream dress, her dream veil and her dream shoes while planning a timely trip to her favourite lingerie shop. But when she headed for the door with Theo in her arms, Gio asked coolly, 'Where are you going?'

'I have some shopping to do,' Billie told him, soft mouth settling into a firm line. 'And I want to do it with Dee.'

His stunning gaze iced over. 'No,' he said simply as he scrawled his signature on a document placed in front of him by an aide.

'Yes,' Billie said equally simply and walked on out of the door.

'Billie!' Gio roared down the corridor after her as she headed to the lift.

With reluctance she turned.

'I said no,' Gio reminded her icily.

Green eyes sparkling, Billie wandered back closer. 'And I wasn't going to argue with you in front of your staff but I have to see Dee.'

'You know I've arranged for a sitter for her for the next two weeks.'

'She's my cousin and my friend and she has always been there for me when I needed her,' Billie countered gently. 'I don't care what you say or how you feel about it but I will *not* turn my back on her.'

'Then leave Theo with me,' Gio urged, reaching out to take his son.

Billie retained a hold on Theo. 'You couldn't look after him on your own—'

'I won't be on my own. I hired a nanny. She's in the hotel right now awaiting my call.'

His interference, his conviction that he knew what was best for her child, made Billie bridle. 'Then you've wasted your time and your money because I will not leave Theo with a stranger.'

'I'll tell her to come up and you can meet her.'

Billie pursed her lips. 'Theo comes with me. Sorry, if you don't like that, but that's the way it's going to be.'

'Don't try to fight me,' Gio warned her softly. 'If

you fight, I will fight back and inevitably you'll get hurt.'

'Nothing you do could hurt me now,' Billie declared staunchly, refusing to be intimidated. 'And why don't you quit while you're ahead, Gio? I've agreed to turn my whole life upside down, to marry you and meet your family. How much more do you want or expect? When do *you* learn to compromise?'

'I don't,' Gio said succinctly, his strong jaw line squared. 'Not when it comes to my son and your involvement with an individual I don't want you mixing with.'

'That individual you don't want me mixing with was with me when I was in labour for two endless days!' Billie snapped back at him in a low intense voice that shook with emotion. 'She was there for me and Theo when you weren't and I was darned glad to have her!'

An almost imperceptible pallor spread beneath Gio's bronzed skin and his thick lashes screened his gaze to grim darkness. 'I would have been there for you if you'd told me you were pregnant—'

'I don't think so, Gio. You were a newly married man back then,' Billie reminded him without any expression at all.

'Go, then, if it means so much to you,' he urged with chilling bite.

'It *does* mean that much to me. I'm always loyal to my friends,' Billie declared with quiet dignity.

Gio glowered at her, lustrous dark eyes shimmering gold. 'Once, first and foremost, you were loyal to me.'

Billie dealt him a wry look. 'And where did that loyalty get me at the end of the day?' she quipped, stepping into the lift.

Gio wanted to snatch her back out of the lift and Theo with her but her reference to that word, 'compromise' had sunk in. He had ninety per cent of what he wanted and he would have the whole once they were married. In the short term, he could afford to be generous, he told himself sternly. But Billie had changed and he could no longer ignore the fact. She was ready to go toe-to-toe with him and fight. In some ineffable way she had grown up and the girl who had looked at him with starry eyes as if he were a knight in shining armour was no more. He didn't like that one little bit.

Even less did Gio appreciate the way he was feeling, shaken up and stirred, insanely abandoned by her departure, all reactions totally at war with the cool, adult, detached reserve with which he preferred to view the world. Above all, he didn't like people to get too close; he didn't want or miss the messy emotional responses that encouraged weakness, self-delusion and loss of control. He could only be content when calm and discipline ruled.

So, what was it about Billie that could make him feel so at odds with himself? She disturbed him, made him overreact, he decided grimly, hoping that that was a temporary affliction he would soon overcome. It seemed particularly ironic that she was also the only woman who had ever given him a sense of peace and contentment. But that was *not* the effect she was having on him at present. He had a great deal of work to accomplish before he could hope to take time off after the wedding. Mulling over the problem and the challenges, Gio was quick to decide that it would be more sensible to take a short break from Billie and the unwelcome and disturbing hothouse emotions she unleashed.

'You can't give me the house,' Dee told Billie squarely. 'I'm not going to live off you. I can afford to pay rent.'

Billie was reluctant to hurt her cousin's feelings by pointing out that once she was married to Gio she would have little use for the rental payment. Dee was fiercely independent and had learned young that she had to be that way. The few times she had depended on others, Dee had been let down.

'Are you hoping to sell the shop as a going concern?' Dee asked.

'It's as much my baby as Theo is,' Billie admitted. 'I really don't want to part with it at all.'

Dee looked at her anxiously and then, biting her lower lip, leant forward. 'Would you let me try to run it for a three-month trial period?' she asked hesitantly. 'I picked up quite a bit from you when I was helping you set it up and as long as I used a bookkeeper I think I could manage.'

Billie studied the blonde woman in surprise, never having suspected that her cousin had a yen to work in the shop. 'I had no idea you would be interested.'

'Well, I am interested, always have been to be honest…but I knew you couldn't afford a full-time

employee, so there wasn't much point mention-
ing it.'

The two women talked at length and an agreement
was reached. Billie was smiling by the end of their
discussion, happy to think of Dee taking over her
business, much preferring that to the option of selling.

'If you're willing to go to Greece, you must really
trust Gio,' Dee remarked.

'He's always been straight with me, even when I
didn't want to hear what he had to say,' Billie pointed
out wryly. 'If he's prepared to marry me for Theo's
benefit, I'm prepared to trust him.'

'You've got far too big a heart, Billie. Don't let him
hurt you again,' Dee warned her worriedly.

It was a piece of advice that Billie wished she
could take to heart after she returned to the hotel
and discovered that Gio had checked out to fly back
to London 'to work'. Not that she was fooled by the
piece of fiction in the brief note he left for her. She
had annoyed Gio and he had turned his back on her
and walked away. She was familiar with the with-
drawal of approval and presence that always followed
such demonstrations of independent action. Once
long ago she had insisted on attending a tutorial interview while he was staying at the apartment. He
had been irritated that she should want to go out and
leave him, even if it was only for a couple of hours.
By the time she had got back, he had returned to
Greece. Lesson learned, she had thought then, sick
with disappointment and resolving never to mention the need to go anywhere else again. This time

around, however, Billie was exasperated and furious that he had removed her from the comfort of home and familiarity and marooned her in a luxury hotel with a nanny and a four-strong set of bodyguards to watch over her and Theo.

CHAPTER SEVEN

LEANDROS CONISTIS VERY nearly dropped his drink. 'You're getting married again?' he repeated like a well-trained parrot to the male who had so recently told him he would never remarry.

Gio dealt his best friend a forbidding look that dared irreverent comment. '*Ne*...yes.'

'Do I know the lady?' Leandros enquired somewhat stiffly.

'You met her briefly on one occasion,' Gio divulged grudgingly. 'Her name's Billie…'

Leandros knocked what remained of his drink down in one suicidal gulp because he knew in that same moment that Canaletto's name would never ever cross his lips again. 'I didn't realise…Billie was still a feature in your life. Have your family met her?' he asked.

Gio compressed his wide sensual mouth. 'No.'

'And when is this wedding at which you wish me to act as your best man to take place?'

'Tomorrow.' Gio threw in the necessary details of place and time in a demonstration of spectacular cool.

Leandros studied the date on his watch face, astonished that it wasn't the first of April and an April fool's joke because Gio, who was as a rule extremely conservative and never imprudent, had literally stunned him speechless. 'It seems…er…very sudden,' he commented cautiously.

'*Ne*…yes,' Gio conceded.

'Very…er hasty.' Leandros was gradually becoming more daring.

'Not hasty enough,' Gio told him drily. 'My son is fifteen months old.'

'Oh, Billie, you look amazing.' Dee sighed as she stepped back from tying the laces at the back of Billie's wedding gown.

Billie stared at her reflection in the cheval mirror and blinked several times at the still-unfamiliar furnishings of the opulent bedroom. Gio had taken a plush city apartment for her and Theo to stay in. She still couldn't quite believe that she was marrying Gio, indeed she kept on expecting some movie cameraman to show up and shout, 'Cut!' before things went any further. After all, in an hour's time she was going to marry a man she wasn't even speaking to. How's that for stupidity? she asked herself ruefully.

Gio had left her and Theo in the hotel in Yorkshire for four days. Of course he had made regular phone calls and had talked during those calls as though there were nothing wrong with his desertion while smoothly excusing himself in advance.

'I knew you had too much on your plate to accompany me down to London,' Gio had told her, ignoring the fact that he had put one of his aides in charge of dealing with all the wedding and removal arrangements for her.

'I knew you would want to spend time saying goodbye to your friends and sorting out your shop,' Gio had said optimistically, ignorant of the reality that Dee was walking Billie down the aisle while her twins were acting as a bridesmaid and pageboy.

'I knew that you would think it was a bad idea to subject Theo to another change of surroundings and more strangers when it wasn't strictly necessary,' Gio had opined complacently.

Billie was furious with him and her anger hadn't faded; it had only grown while Gio had acted as if leaving his bride-to-be and newly discovered son behind him in Yorkshire had been the only possible thing to do. Striving to keep a lid on that tight little knot of rage locked deep inside her, Billie surveyed her dress with faraway eyes. It was a romantic dress fashioned of Chantilly lace and chiffon, light and floaty and styled to make the most of her natural curves and waist. The flirty short veil and crown of flowers had a natural elegant simplicity. Pearl-studded shoes peeped out below the hem of her gown.

Someone knocked on the bedroom door. Since the only other person in the apartment was Irene, the pleasant middle-aged nanny whom Gio had hired, Dee answered it.

'Oh…' Dee backed off uneasily, her surprise unhidden when she recognised Gio.

Billie froze. 'You're not supposed to see me in my wedding dress!' she exclaimed in consternation.

Taken aback by Dee's appearance, Gio muttered a stiff acknowledgment in English while hungrily taking in the vision Billie made in her white dress. He had died and gone to heaven, he decided without hesitation. As Dee ducked out behind him, tactfully closing the door in her wake, he strode forward, his attention locked to the tantalising pout of Billie's ripe pink mouth and the creamy swell of her luscious breasts above the boned bodice of her gown. 'You look fantastic,' he breathed in a roughened undertone.

It was a challenge for Billie not to echo that sentiment. It might be a small wedding on Gio's terms, which was to say that it was a large wedding on *her* terms, but Gio had still chosen to embrace the formality of a full morning suit teamed with a striped black and silver cravat at his brown throat. The black jacket was exquisitely tailored to his tall, well-built form, delineating his broad shoulders and muscular chest, while the striped trousers enhanced his narrow hips and long powerful legs. Billie collided headily with smouldering dark golden eyes heavily fringed with curling black lashes. Gio looked absolutely gorgeous.

'What are you doing here?' she whispered and then tensed. 'Have you changed your mind? If you have, it's all right. I'm not going to make a fuss. It doesn't feel real anyway—'

'*Theos*…of course I haven't changed my mind!' Gio ground out, extending the jewel case he carried in one lean brown hand. 'I wanted to give you this…'

For a split second he too wondered what he was doing there for in truth he had acted on the kind of impulse he usually suppressed. On the way to the church he had realised that he *had* to see her before the wedding and there was nothing wrong with that, he reasoned uneasily, when he was about to take the very major step of marrying her. Desire was always an acceptable motivation as long as it stayed within rational bounds. And sex with Billie was incredible. He felt nothing else, needed nothing beyond her physical presence.

In a daze, Billie blinked and accepted the case, flipping it open to display a breathtaking triple string of pearls and dangling pearl earrings. The set would match her shoes and be a great deal more impressive than the cheap diamanté set she had purchased. 'It's beautiful,' she murmured weakly as he moved forward to detach the pearls from the case and fasten them round her neck.

His fingertips brushed the nape of her neck. 'I wanted to give you something special.'

The glowing pearls were cool at her throat and she bent over the case to detach the earrings. Threading her veil and her curls out of the way, she put the earrings on. 'Thank you,' she said woodenly, thinking that he hadn't changed one little bit in all the years she had known him. Here he was still trying to bribe and guilt her into ignoring his bad behaviour.

'I can't stand you talking to me in that chilly voice,' Gio informed her grimly. 'Obviously you're annoyed I left you behind in Yorkshire.'

Billie's teeth rattled together with rage. 'You mean…you actually noticed I was being cool on the phone?'

'Considering that you would once chat about nothing in particular for hours on end without the slightest encouragement, one-word responses *were* rather obvious,' Gio countered with sardonic emphasis. 'What's wrong with you? You never used to play games like that with me.'

'Shut up before I lose my temper!' Billie urged between clenched teeth, her facial muscles locked tight. 'You left me in that hotel with Theo and a bunch of bodyguards and a strange nanny!' she accused. 'You did it deliberately because I had annoyed you. You just took off for London. What happened to your all-consuming interest in getting to know your son? You *can't* just saunter in here and throw a bunch of priceless pearls at me and expect that to take the place of an apology and an explanation!' Billie launched at him in fiery denunciation.

'I have nothing to apologise for. Now that I have got on top of work, I will have far more time to spend with Theo and you *after* the wedding,' Gio told her stubbornly, watching her curls bounce round her animated features, the passion flaring in her green eyes, while noting how luminous the pearls were set against her creamy skin and the firm, sweet swell of her breasts. Hunger stormed through his tautening length in an uncontrollable wave, leaving him painfully aroused. 'I refuse to go through a wedding with you behaving like this. This is why I needed to see you.'

Billie was silenced. Suddenly she was the one at fault for straining their relationship beyond tolerance. Wide-eyed she stared back at him, the atmosphere dense and sending a curious little quiver through her belly. 'So…we…er call it off now and go our separate ways?' she whispered shakily.

Gio stared at her in rampant disbelief, his dark eyes golden-bronze spearheads of intimidation at the mere thought of her pulling a disappearing act again. 'You're not going anywhere without me.'

Billie didn't understand because that sudden shock of fear had destroyed her ability to think straight. Her heart was jumping up and down inside her ribcage like a rubber ball being bounced and making it very hard for her to breathe.

'*Ever again,*' Gio growled in menacing completion as he scooped her up in his arms and brought her down on the bed.

'What are you doing?' Billie gasped. 'Gio…*my dress*!'

Gio came down on top of her, almost squashing her flat. 'Stop struggling…you're more likely to rip something.'

Billie looked up at him with huge disconcerted eyes. 'Gio…we *can't*…this isn't the answer to anything.'

Gio rubbed his mouth sexily across hers with a sensual groan. 'It's the *only* answer for me.'

'You're wrecking my make-up,' she framed unevenly, fingertips dancing shyly through his cropped black hair, slowly dropping to frame his amazing cheekbones.

'You don't need make-up,' Gio told her thickly.

'Every bride needs make-up,' Billie argued, trying to slide unobtrusively out from beneath his weight without shredding her dress.

He lowered his head and devoured her mouth with a hungry driving urgency that made her every sense shift into superdrive with piercingly sweet longing. The taste and scent of him infiltrated her like a dangerous drug, blowing her control out of the water. 'I won't wreck the dress,' he promised, lifting his hips to tip the bundled skirt of her gown up to her waist.

'*Gio*…' Billie whispered pleadingly even as her back arched and her pelvis rocked up to his without her volition.

'*Diavelos*, Billie…I *hurt*,' he ground out, his breath fanning her cheek while he shifted revealingly against her, grinding the thrust of his erection into the cradle of her thighs.

And low down in her pelvis, deep in her feminine core a surge of moisture dampened her most tender flesh and she started to melt. 'We can't…we haven't got the time.'

'We'll make time,' he husked, yanking out his phone as it buzzed, clamping it to her ear and talking in fast Greek to a male voice that sounded both loud and agitated. 'Our day, nobody else's,' he spelled out fiercely.

Long fingers glided up her inner thigh, leaving

tingles of humming energy in their wake. Her eyes closing, her head fell back on the pillows, her neck extending as her spine arched. Her heart was racing thump-thump-thump at the foot of her throat. He stroked the taut triangle of satin between her thighs and the only thing in the world for her at that moment was the stupendous high of excitement and anticipation holding her fast. With a yank, Gio dislodged her bodice sufficiently to expose a creamy breast topped by a pale pink nipple. He closed his mouth urgently to that swollen peak and a stifled gasp escaped her, eyes squeezing tight shut.

'I need to know you're mine,' Gio growled against her throat.

He eased a finger below her lace-edged knickers and stroked along the petal-soft folds. Her thighs opened wider in helpless invitation and when he rubbed the little bud where she was most sensitive she moaned and shifted her hips, urging him on, helpless in the grip of the savage need he could induce. He thrust a long finger into her tight, wet sheath and she jerked, on the edge of crying out until he clamped his mouth to hers to silence the sounds she was making. The rhythmic play of his fingers over her tender flesh sent ripples of throbbing excitement through her. As the tension in her pelvis rose to an all-consuming ache that was unbearable, her every muscle clenched tight and she soared to a breathless shattering peak of ecstasy while biting the shoulder of his jacket to mute the sob of release building up inside her.

'Oh…' she mumbled afterwards, her body as languorous as a floating beach ball.

Gio's phone was screeching in his pocket. Scanning her dreamy face, he switched it off with an unsteady hand. Strangely, although he was still taut with sexual arousal, the inner tension driving him had dissolved. He felt like himself again for the first time in four days and snapped straight into rescue mode, propelling Billie off the bed, repositioning her bodice, brushing down the skirt of her gown before urging her into the bathroom where he stared in all male helplessness at the crushed veil hanging askew, the curls positively rioting round it and the smudges of the lipstick he had dislodged.

'Good grief,' Billie groaned, catching her mangled reflection. 'Gio, you're a menace.'

Gio washed with enviable cool and ran a comb through his tousled hair. A sharp knock sounded on the bedroom door and it opened the merest crack. 'The cars have arrived, Mr Letsos. We cannot be late…' It was Damon Kitzakis' voice.

'I'll get your friend to help you,' Gio breathed in sudden decision.

Billie was in full bridal panic mode, scanning her swollen mouth and tumbled hair and veil with withering scorn. You should have said no, she told herself furiously. Why didn't you say no? Why had she, once again, failed to call a halt? Sex had always been a slippery slope with Gio. She couldn't keep her hands off him, she couldn't resist his passion but she was convinced that he would respect her more if she was less spontaneous and more restrained. Yet he had received no satisfaction whatsoever from what they had done, she acknowledged in surprise as she waged a frantic war on her rebellious curls and hurriedly repaired her make-up.

Gio reappeared in the bathroom doorway, lean, strong face taut. 'Damon thought it best that your cousin, her children and Irene and Theo leave immediately for the church. You're travelling with Leandros and me.'

Billie turned from the mirror. 'But you and your best man are supposed to arrive *first.*'

'You can wait in the church porch for ten minutes, *koukla mou,*' Gio pointed out, lustrous dark eyes gleaming with sudden amusement. 'Why do you take all these silly little rules so seriously?'

Billie went pink and lifted her chin. 'I assume all brides do the same.'

Gio closed a hand over hers and pulled her towards the lift, sweeping her off her feet before she could reach the pavement and depositing her in a vast tumbling heap of lace and chiffon into the stretch limousine waiting by the kerb.

Billie forced a smile when Leandros Conistis looked at them both in frank astonishment. The heat of almost unbearable embarrassment engulfed her in a burning tide because she had never forgotten her one and only meeting with Gio's best friend and the incredulous look on his face that evening when he had realised that she had never heard of Canaletto.

Leandros tossed a handkerchief at Gio. 'You have lipstick on your face.'

Billie's mortification did not abate at that aside; indeed it worsened. Now the other man would think that she was not only stupid but also a slut with no idea of how to behave like a dignified bride. Even though she knew she was being ridiculously oversensitive, she could not overcome her attack of self-consciousness. Dee helped her climb out of the limousine and ushered her into the porch where she admired the pearl set, teased her cousin about what she saw as Gio's wildly romantic gesture at showing up at the apartment before the wedding and then fussed with the skirts of Billie's gown before checking that her daughter, Jade, was still carrying her basket and flowers and Davis, his lucky horseshoe.

Walking down the aisle of the half-empty church some minutes later, her hand resting lightly on her cousin's arm, Billie was earnestly instructing herself that she was not living a fairy tale and striving not to react to the lean dark charisma of Gio's sheer beauty as he looked down the aisle, brilliant dark eyes glimmering gold.

'This is your dream,' Dee whispered unhelpfully at that exact same moment. 'Stop fretting…enjoy your moment in the sun.'

Billie recalled the vanishing act that Gio had pulled in Yorkshire, her own frustrated rage, and breathed in deep. So, he wasn't straightforward, he was complex, secretive and arrogant, but as she focused on his tall, dark, powerful figure at the altar her heart sang its own deeply revealing signature tune. That was when she recognised and accepted the truth—the truth that vanity had made her deny. Gio was the man she loved, very probably would always be the man she loved, regardless of what he did in the future, because she was very steady in her affections.

Acknowledging the strength of her feelings was like breaking free of a constricting band round her chest. She had never got over Gio and now he was back and they had a child and she was about to become his wife. Instead of expecting, indeed almost inviting the roof to fall in on her, wasn't it time she went for a little positive thinking? And it was at that instant of sunny, optimistic thought with her emotions on a high that her eyes zeroed in on the blue-eyed blonde keenly studying her two pews back from the front. Her heart and her body froze in concert and even her feet became reluctant to do her bidding. Dee had to use momentum to move Billie on down the aisle.

Calisto was a guest at their very small wedding. Billie was in shock. What did Calisto's presence today of all days mean? Her hand trembled as Gio slid the ring onto her wedding finger. Her skin was clammy with shock, her knees in a rigid hold. In her mind's eye she was seeing not the priest but Calisto, her tiny proportions sheathed in a killer-blue fitted dress and lace jacket, a jaunty little feather confection adorning her head, waterfall-straight platinum-pale hair falling to her shoulders, framing a face of such perfection that angels would weep to look at it. In print she had been a beauty; in the flesh she was downright dazzling, setting a standard that Billie could never hope to reach. A deep chill spread through Billie like an unexpected frost on a summer day.

'What's your ex-wife doing here?' Billie whispered shakily on the church steps as the society photographer and his assistant got them to pose with linked hands.

Gio massaged the tender skin of her wrist with his thumbs, sending a delicious little thrill of awareness trickling through her tense body. 'Haven't a clue, but it wouldn't have been polite to ask her to leave.'

'Perhaps not.' Billie was in two minds about what being polite entailed in such circumstances. 'But how did she know about the wedding?'

Gio sent her a frowning glance. 'Naturally I told her about it. It would've been bad manners to let her find out from anyone else. Cal probably thinks that showing up is the socially "hip" thing to do. She likes to be "hip",' he completed drily.

Billie was sharply disconcerted by the news that Gio was still on good enough terms with his former wife to have automatically informed her of his remarriage. The comfortable way he referred to Calisto with the fond diminutive 'Cal' bothered her even more although she was quick to question her own reaction. Not all ex-wives and husbands loathed each other and it was perfectly possible that Calisto had turned up simply out of curiosity. And who could blame her for that? Gio and Calisto had only been divorced for a couple of months at most. She glanced across to where Calisto stood in animated conversation with Leandros and two other Greek friends.

'She's very friendly with everyone,' Billie remarked gingerly, quite frankly envying the blonde's confident assumption of her welcome. Calisto evidently didn't feel the slightest bit uncomfortable attending her ex-husband's wedding and Billie struggled to be equally accepting of the blonde's presence.

'Cal is Leandros' first cousin,' Gio advanced. 'And one of my lawyers is her stepbrother. She probably knows virtually everybody here.'

Dismay at those previously unknown close connections assailed Billie and her unease only increased when she saw Calisto climb with a tinkling girlish giggle into a limo with the three men. A wedding breakfast was being served at an exclusive London hotel. She seriously hoped Calisto wasn't going to push her way in there as well. It was a hope destined to disappointment, however, because the first person Billie saw in the foyer was Calisto, beaming smile all over her perfect face as she surged forward to kiss Gio on both cheeks and beg sweetly for an introduction to Billie.

'I've already met your son…what a little darling!' Calisto gushed, all dimples and flapping fake lashes. 'And what a clever, clever girl you are to have brought such a little angel into the world.'

Gio laughed softly. 'Theo's cute, isn't he?'

'*Super* cute,' Calisto purred in agreement, flexing manicured scarlet fingertips on Billie's arm to prevent her from moving away.

'Excuse us for a moment,' Dee interrupted in an undertone. 'Billie, you need your veil fixed. It's hanging by a thread.'

Relieved to have an excuse to escape, Billie followed her cousin to the other side of the foyer. She angled her head back to assist Dee's efforts to anchor her veil and she was in the perfect position to catch Dee's hissed enquiry, 'Who on earth is the pushy blonde?'

As Billie spun to fill in the details Dee's eyes got rounder and rounder. 'She's got a heck of a nerve coming today!' she commented angrily. 'No bride wants her predecessor as a guest!'

Billie coloured. 'I don't want to make a fuss about it when everybody else is quite happy.'

'By everybody else, you mean Gio,' Dee interpreted. 'She's spoiling your day and, like most men, he's just taking the easy way out by doing nothing!'

'He hates bitchiness and catfights. I'm not going to say anything,' Billie intoned as if she were mouthing a soothing mantra she badly needed to absorb. 'If Calisto can handle me then I can handle her.'

'Whatever you think,' Dee trilled, clearly unimpressed. 'But I wouldn't stand her being here like the spectre at the feast for longer than ten seconds.'

Billie greeted the other guests as they arrived with quiet poise. Several of Gio's British business colleagues were attending as well as his lawyers and a large group of London-based Greeks. She was surprised that he had not invited any of his family to attend their wedding and worried that they might have refused to attend because they disapproved of Gio marrying a woman from so ordinary a background.

She had met Gio's lawyers in Yorkshire when they had called at the hotel to present her with the pre-nuptial agreement. They had advised her to take independent advice before she signed but Billie really hadn't had the time to consult anyone, being far too busy packing up the life she had lived for two years and discarding what she no longer required. In any case, Gio was anything but mean when it came to money and, regardless of what might happen between them in the future, she didn't feel she needed documentary proof that he would always be fair. He had once mentioned that his father had been shamefully stingy in his monetary dealings with his mother after they had divorced and she was convinced he would never be guilty of committing the same sin.

As they ran out of guests to greet in the reception area beside the dining room, Billie saw Gio and Leandros approach Calisto. She watched that perfect face freeze and her scarlet-painted mouth open to deliver an obviously animated response before Billie forced herself to turn away and head for the cloakroom to freshen up. There was no denying that Calisto had cast a cloud over the day. Unfortunately, Calisto was Gio's ex and still part of his social circle and Billie was stuck with that reality. Making heavy weather of the fact wasn't going to change anything.

Billie was engaged in renewing her lipstick when the door slammed behind a new arrival and high heels smacked noisily across the tiles. Calisto appeared in the mirror beside Billie like the evil fairy. 'Don't waste your time feeling smug that Gio's asked me to leave. He's had long enough to regret our divorce and naturally he's upset at having to marry you to get his son and even more upset to see you and I together...well, there *is* no comparison, is there?' Calisto pointed out, lifting her chin to examine her perfect reflection with open admiration.

Billie turned away from the mirror, lifting her own chin in fear that she might have a slight suggestion of a double chin when she held her head at some angles and that was a humiliation she could not have borne in Calisto's presence. 'Gio divorced you?'

'Only because I wouldn't give him a baby,' Calisto told her cheerfully. 'But now that he's got one... thank you *so* much for taking care of that problem for me. He can have me *and* his precious son and heir. You've given us a textbook solution to our dilemma.'

'What on earth are you trying to say?' Billie asked in genuine astonishment.

'That triangles never work and it won't be long before Gio takes his son off you and reclaims me as his wife,' Calisto trilled with satisfaction. 'You were his mistress and I'm afraid the background of his life is where a woman like you belongs.'

'A woman like me?' Billie prompted, her green eyes taking on a dangerous sparkle.

'A tart with a heart,' Calisto quipped, rolling her eyes. 'And let's not forget the pantomime big boobs and bum. But you were never destined to be a Letsos and your reign as one will be painfully short.'

Billie shook her head in silent wonderment as she walked to the door. How could Gio have married such a spiteful shrew? In comparison with Calisto, she was unquestionably rounder in certain areas but she was determined not to get drawn into a childish spat with the other woman. She was less sanguine, however, concerning Calisto's claims about Theo and why Gio had married her.

Was it possible that Gio had only married Billie to gain equal rights to his son? It was simply another angle to Gio's insistence that they marry to give Theo *his* birthright. Obviously Gio would benefit as well from the formal acknowledgement of his role as Theo's father. And was it true that Gio had divorced Calisto because she wouldn't give him a child? Stamping down on further conjecture about Calisto, Billie reminded herself comfortingly that Gio had asked his ex-wife to leave their wedding.

Feeling hot, flushed and distinctly out of sorts, Billie returned to the elegant function room and collected Theo from his nanny to give him a cuddle. While her son nestled close, she was relieved to see Gio and Leandros chatting away to Dee.

'She's pleasant,' Gio conceded later when they were all seated for the wedding breakfast. 'But that doesn't mean that I think she's a fit person for you to have as a friend.'

'Try to be less judgemental. If you hadn't seen that report, you wouldn't have known about her past,' Billie pointed out. 'And we've all made mistakes...you married Calypso.'

'Calisto,' Gio corrected. 'She's gone—'

'Good.' Lashes screening her gaze, Billie sipped her champagne.

'It wasn't appropriate for her to stay.'

'Why did you divorce her?' she heard herself ask.

'We were incompatible,' Gio fielded without hesitation.

'That's not telling me *any*—' Billie began heatedly as Gio lifted a hand and closed it into her curls to turn her back to him.

She clashed with smouldering dark golden eyes and a writhing inferno of heat rushed up inside her in response. Her heart stuttered, her breath shortened in her throat. The tip of his tongue traced the curve of her lower lip and the peaks of her full breasts stiffened and strained below her boned bodice.

'*Se thelo*...I want you,' Gio growled soft and low, ferocious tension etched in every taut athletic line of his lean, powerful body.

'*So much,*' she echoed in breathless agreement, her tummy performing a somersault as he ravaged her mouth in an electrifyingly passionate kiss.

As Leandros signalled to indicate his readiness to make a short speech and dealt him a highly amused smile, Gio set Billie back from him, shrewd eyes searching her bemused face. She was like a breath of fresh air in his life. Was that why she unsettled him? Tempted him into engaging in the kind of PDA he had never before indulged in? But then what other woman would have tolerated Calisto's appearance without throwing a big scene?

He watched Billie rise from her seat without hesitation to take Theo, who was stretching his arms out to her from a nearby table. Clearly tired and fed up, his son whimpered and clung to his mother like a little limpet before burying his head sleepily against her shoulder. Gio's rarely touched conscience was pierced by the sight when he thought of the iniquitous pre-nuptial agreement he had had drawn up to ensnare Billie. She was such an innocent. He had guessed that she wouldn't bother to read the terms, never mind the small print. Knowing she didn't give a damn about his money, he had taken ruthless advantage of her trusting nature....regardless of his awareness of how much she loved their son.

Of course, she need never know about the terms of the pre-nup, Gio reasoned, reckoning that he didn't want that coming back to haunt him at some inopportune time in the future. Billie would be shocked. Billie, who had always tried to see him as a nicer, kinder person than he could ever be, would for ever lose her rose-tinted view of him. He frowned, deciding that he would lose her copy of that document in a safe somewhere...

CHAPTER EIGHT

THE HELICOPTER LANDED in a clearing lit by torches on the island of Letsos.

'So, this is the island where you were born. Does it belong to you?' Billie remarked as Gio lifted her down to the ground and then went back to take Theo and assist the nanny in her descent.

'It still belongs to my grandfather, Theo's namesake. I imagine if it had ever passed to my father, it would've been sold long ago,' he opined drily. 'He sold everything that wasn't nailed down long before he died.'

'Did your family name the island after themselves?' she asked curiously.

'No, I believe my ancestors stole the name and began using it several generations back after a family dispute split them into two factions,' he explained, ushering her into the four-wheel-drive vehicle.

'I'm looking forward to meeting your family,' Billie lied because she felt she had to lie out of politeness.

While Billie was undeniably curious, she was also very apprehensive about the sort of reception she could expect to receive from Gio's wealthy relatives. In her own opinion she had so many strikes against her: the speed of their marriage, Theo's birth out of wedlock, never mind the reality that she was a complete stranger and a foreigner without either fancy lineage or cash. She was convinced that those facts would ensure that she was viewed with extreme suspicion and possibly even hostility.

'You'll meet them all tomorrow,' Gio told her calmly.

'But I assumed I'd be meeting them now…tonight,' she said tensely.

'It's been a very long day and we're not staying at the main house tonight. We'll introduce them to Theo in the morning.' Gio smoothed a hand down over Theo's back as his son squeezed out a cross little mutter as he secured him in a car seat. 'The sooner he's in bed, the better. Irene, you'll have the help of my old nursemaid tonight because I know you're tired. We're leaving Irene and Theo at Agata's house.'

'*Leaving*…Theo?' Billie parroted in dismay.

'Relax. It's not as though we're abandoning him on a park bench,' Gio censured with quiet amusement, dark eyes skimming her anxious face. 'We're spending our wedding night at the beach house. We'll pick up Theo in the morning before we go and meet the family. Agata will revel in being the first islander to get to know my son.'

When they drew up at Agata's house, Billie soon appreciated that Gio had not exaggerated because Theo's arrival was the source of much excitement and pleasure. Agata was middle-aged and rotund. She greeted Gio with overflowing affection and took hold of his son with a blissful smile while contriving simultaneously to offer Irene a warm welcome and the promise of a comfortable bed in her guest room.

Gio swept Billie back into the car. The road was soon travelling sharply downhill and the car finally stopped at the mouth of a sandy path. Their driver, a strapping youth, grabbed the heavy cases and trudged down the path, leaving them to follow.

'Watch your step. It's a steep track,' Gio warned, clamping a strong arm to her slender spine to steady her as her heels sank into the sandy surface.

'I'd never have worn these shoes if I'd realised we were going to a beach house!' Billie muttered ruefully. 'I'm dressed up in my fanciest togs because I thought I'd be meeting your family tonight.'

'I wanted to surprise you.'

'You've succeeded.' Billie laughed, staring down at the stretch of pristine beach coming into view as they descended. The sun had gone down but a brazier was burning, casting flickers of light across the sand and the dark waves washing into the cove.

The wooden beach house was tucked into a corner and lit up with fairy lights that looked like roses. 'Wow...that's *so* pretty!' Billie exclaimed, staring when she saw lights flickering beyond the floor-to-ceiling windows as well.

Gio carried her over the threshold and she lost one of her shoes and he said that was a good thing because she couldn't walk in them and she was smiling as he set her down on a polished wood floor. There were flowers everywhere she looked and lots of burning candles casting glimmers of moving light and shadow across the opulent interior. Their driver settled the cases in the adjoining bedroom and departed.

Billie wandered barefoot into the bedroom, appreciating the luxurious but plain furnishings and the wide, comfortable bed.

'Champagne?' Gio prompted.

'Maybe later. Right now, I want a shower more than anything,' she confided, keen to be free of the tailored dress and jacket she had worn to look smart. 'Could you unzip me?'

'If I unzip you,' Gio remarked as she shed her jacket and moved helpfully close, 'you'll never make it to the shower.'

The zip ran down. He spread the fabric back and pressed his mouth to the smooth slope of her shoulder. 'Your skin is so wondrously soft,' he told her huskily, skimming the short sleeves down her arms, giving the dress a helpful push downward as it threatened to settle at her waist, and lifting her out of the folds.

'I'm not going to get my shower,' Billie forecast as he turned her slowly round to face him.

'Well, possibly not until later and you might have to share it.' Gio grinned down at her, his eyes hot as the sun's rays on her exposed the lush curves of her figure in a green satin and lace bra and panties set. 'That's if I ever let you out of bed...'

Billie resisted a sudden urge to stupidly ask him if he thought her bottom was too large. She tried to stay a stable weight but she had never fussed about the curvy shape she had been born with, regarding that as a futile exercise destined to lead only to disappointment. Irritated by her sudden self-consciousness in his presence, she said instead, 'You're wearing way too many clothes.'

Gio hauled her up into his arms and kissed her with passionate force before bringing her down on the bed. 'A shower and food and civilised behaviour later...I promise,' he swore.

Billie's memory flew back to the many, many times in the past when Gio had barely stepped through the door of the apartment before grabbing her with the wild impatience and hunger she had always cherished in him, deeming that fervour proof that she was more important to him than he was ever likely to tell her. Of course, the fallout when he announced that he was marrying Calisto had been all the more painful to bear, she conceded ruefully. He had forced her to see the danger of wishful thinking, the foolishness of the assumptions that had made her feel secure. But as soon as she found herself thinking that way, Billie kicked out those negative thoughts and, reminding herself that this was their wedding night, she lay back on the bed where he had placed her.

Gio was her husband now and he was hers in so many ways that he had never been before, she conceded, trying to banish her worries. Together, she and Gio and Theo would be a family. They would also be part of a much bigger family, which she was praying would eventually accept her, even if it was only for Theo's sake.

'Who organised all this?' Billie asked, shifting a hand to indicate the flowers and the candles and the opulent comfort of the room's appointments. 'Is the beach house in regular use?'

'It hadn't been used in quite some time,' Gio admitted as he shed his shirt in a careless heap. 'Leandros' sister, Eva, is an interior designer and she agreed to do a rush job for me as a favour. She wasn't sure she would make the deadline until the last minute and only finished this afternoon. The household staff saw to the rest.'

'I love the candles and the flowers,' Billie admitted.

'I knew you would…you've always been such a romantic,' Gio teased.

'But you organised it so you must be a romantic too,' she pointed out, absolutely blown away by the gradually dawning realisation that Gio had had the beach house set up for their wedding night solely in an attempt to please her.

'I'll never be romantic,' he fielded wryly. 'But I am bright enough to work out what's required and deliver it, *glyka mou.*'

With the greatest difficulty, Billie dragged her attention from his washboard abs and the way his naturally golden skin sleekly delineated his ripcord musculature. He was gorgeous and yet he was with her and not with the equally gorgeous Calisto. For a split second she let that mystery unnerve her and then she squashed the thought flat, telling herself off for even thinking it. He was married to her now, *with* her, and Calisto was in the past. Gloriously unaware of her constant attacks of insecurity, Gio stepped out of his trousers and skimmed off his boxers in one fell swoop of impatience.

Her mouth ran dry, her heartbeat quickening. It had been so long since she had had the luxury of watching Gio strip. That day she had gone for lunch with him at his hotel and ended up in bed with him, he hadn't even got undressed. Her face burned at the recollection.

'What are you thinking about?' Gio breathed, stalking across the bedroom to join her on the bed.

And she told him and, surprisingly, he laughed. 'I wasn't exactly the cool seducer, was I? I was as hot for you as a teenage boy having sex for the first time but I did at least use a condom.'

'I got carried away too,' she soothed, running gentle fingers along his angular jaw line. 'But you'd best be careful. I'm not using any form of contraception.'

Gio tugged her down on the pillows beside him and leant over her. 'Do I need to be careful? I missed out on you being pregnant with Theo and I would be pretty excited if you were to conceive again,' he admitted, dark eyes shimmering gold in the candlelight.

That was the most confidence-boosting thing Gio could have said to her, Billie reflected dizzily. His interest in her having a second child took her by storm because it meant that he regarded their marriage as a long-term venture rather than an exercise to simply grant Theo his legal birthright.

'I put on a lot of weight when I'm pregnant,' she warned him.

'And in all the best places,' Gio husked, running an admiring finger across a bra cup overflowing with soft creamy flesh. '*Theos*, I *love* your body.'

'Honestly?' Billie prompted, loathing herself for pressing the point.

'I can't keep my hands off you, Billie,' Gio groaned, flipping open the catch on her bra and filling his hands with the bounty he had been admiring. 'I never could…'

Her wretched brain was still shooting in directions she didn't want it to. It was urging her to ask why he had then chosen to marry a woman like Calisto and suddenly she couldn't restrain that need to know any longer and she asked, 'Then why did you marry a woman half my size?'

There was a sudden deathly silence. His head bent while he toyed with the warm soft curves he had bared, Gio glanced up at her from below his ridiculously long lashes. 'For all the *wrong* reasons…and I paid the price,' he admitted in a roughened undertone.

Billie wanted to dig deeper into the topic but she also knew that she didn't want to spoil their wedding night with the shadow of past pain and loss. With an almighty effort she cleared her head of such morbid reflections and said nothing at all because regret had coloured every syllable he spoke. Regret was enough to satisfy her, wasn't it? How much of a pint of blood did she need to satisfy her damaged ego? Enough blood to cause ructions in their shiny new marriage when Gio had already mentioned a desire for another child? She thought not, decided it was better to leave the past where it belonged and look to a brighter future.

Gio captured a turgid nipple in his mouth and toyed with it until it was throbbing. Billie rested back, letting the heat flow through her, warming and moistening ever more sensitive parts. Her hips shifted, her fingers raked through his short hair, eyes sliding shut as she held him to her with a deep sense of happiness. Another baby? What a sign of optimism on his part! He was a child of a broken marriage and she was convinced he would not risk bringing a second child into the mix if he believed their relationship was likely to break down.

'Tomorrow's going to come too soon for me,' Gio complained huskily as he tugged up her knees and peeled down her knickers in one smooth operation. 'But if I make love to you all night, you'll be too tired to meet my family in the morning.'

'You've got every night with me that you want now,' Billie whispered as he shifted to trace the moist cleft between her legs with a roving forefinger and she quivered instantaneously, every tingling nerve ending instantly clamouring for more.

'And I'm going to make the most of every opportunity. I'm sex-starved,' Gio confided, working a trail of lusty nipping and sucking across the upper slope of her breasts to her throat. 'I never could get enough of you. Now I've finally got you round the clock, I'll be very demanding.'

'Promises…promises,' Billie quipped, warmed by that threat, for the more Gio expressed his desire for her, the more secure she felt.

As excitement began to claim Billie, conversation died because she couldn't think straight for long enough to vocalise. He touched her with the unerring skill of an expert and she writhed, hands digging into his cropped black hair as he used his mouth to bring her to a shattering climax.

Weak with satiation in the aftermath, she loosed a startled gasp as Gio flipped her over onto her stomach. 'What—?'

'I'm in a very dominant mood, *moro mou*,' Gio growled, gripping her hips and driving hard into her passion-moistened depths, stretching her to the limit with his length and girth and sending a renewed and arousing wash of hunger through her.

And Billie had always secretly liked it when Gio was forcefully passionate in bed. Then as now, his dominance somehow made her feel irresistible. A helpless shudder of response snaked through her quivering body, her breath rasping in her throat, her heart hammering as he plunged into her with pounding erotic urgency. It went on and on and on, igniting the bittersweet torment of need inside her again. A carnal finger stroked and encircled her clitoris and the tightening knot of tension in her womb started up a chain reaction. A string of tiny inner convulsions pulsed along her inner channel and finally merged into a rapturous explosion of soul-destroying pleasure.

'That's something you're very, very good at,' Billie mumbled unsteadily just as Gio began to pull away from her and she grabbed his arm, eyes flying wide in the candlelight. 'No, don't, *don't* move away. I hate it when you do that.'

'It's just the way I am,' Gio framed, frowning.

Billie brought up another hand to grip his shoulder. 'But it doesn't have to be like that. You can hug Theo.'

'That's different.'

Billie knew she was hitting barriers and that possibly she hadn't chosen the best time to complain, but his habit of shifting away from all contact in the immediate aftermath of intimacy had always hurt her feelings. 'You've never had a problem with hugging me if I'm upset about anything, have you?'

'Well, no, *but*—'

'So, pretend I'm upset,' Billie urged with all the enthusiasm of a woman who believed she had found the perfect solution to his lack in the affection department.

Gio settled dazed eyes on her. *'What?'* he breathed in disbelief.

'After sex,' Billie told him bluntly. 'Just think. She's upset, now I have to hug her.'

'I don't want to think of you being *upset* after we make love.'

'Have you got an argument against absolutely everything?' Billie asked him in a pained tone. 'I was trying to work out a strategy which would suit us both.'

'Forget the strategy,' Gio advised, anchoring both arms firmly round her and hauling her back against him with gritted teeth. 'I'll work on it…OK?'

'OK,' Billie agreed, satisfied, running an exploring hand down over his hair-roughened torso and then teasingly lower in an operation destined to prove to him there would be advantages to a change of behaviour that brought him physically closer.

'OK,' Gio said again but in a deep husky purr. '*Very* OK…'

An hour later they were outdoors, lying relaxed on the huge upholstered recliner on the deck and watching the flames from the brazier shooting up against the night sky. Discarded dishes from the packed fridge were scattered around, evidence of the substantial meal they had contrived to eat. Billie laced her fingers round the stem of her champagne flute and heaved a contented sigh. 'It's incredibly peaceful here with just the sound of the sea in the background.'

'I always loved that sound when I was a kid. My parents used to bring us down here and…' Gio's voice trailed away into silence.

Billie glanced up at him, aware of the tension now stiffening his long, lean length against her. 'And… *what*?' she pressed. 'It's great that you've got some good memories of your childhood.'

'My sisters and I were very young then. It was long before my parents broke up…before my father met *the love of his life.*' Gio voiced that emphasis with biting derision.

'Oh…and she was?' Billie jumped straight into the opening he had given her because he had always avoided the subject of his parents' divorce.

'An English fashion model called Marianne. She was his mistress and when she became *accidentally* pregnant—with the boy who later turned out not to be my father's—he decided that he couldn't live without her.'

'Oh,' Billie said in quite another tone, discomfited by the similarities she saw to their own previous relationship, wondering if she was at last learning the reason why Gio had always maintained an emotional distance in their relationship.

'My sisters and I returned from boarding school for our summer break and learned that our whole lives had changed. My father had divorced my mother and stuck her in an Athens apartment. Suddenly we weren't welcome on Letsos or in our childhood home any more because my father—and it is a challenge to compliment him with that label—had married Marianne and she refused to have the children of his first marriage hanging around.'

The depth of Gio's bitterness shocked Billie but she could imagine how horrible it must have been for him and his sisters to see their mother rejected and all of them excluded from everything they had become accustomed to believing was theirs. 'Didn't your grandfather intervene? You said he owned this island.'

'He couldn't disown his son though, and naturally

he didn't want to make an enemy of his new daughter-in-law. He does regret, however, that he didn't do more to help my mother, but at the time he was really struggling to repair the damage Dmitri's extravagance and marriage breakdown had already done to the family and the business.'

'Did you have much contact with your father after the divorce?' Billie asked.

'No, after that one meeting, I only saw him one more time. Marianne very much resented the fact that he had had other children. Love,' Gio breathed witheringly, 'can be a very destructive emotion. My father destroyed his family in the name of love and my mother never recovered from the treatment she suffered at his hands.'

Billie was thoughtful because she was finally seeing when Gio had reached the conclusion that the softer human emotions could be toxic. As a child, Gio had seen the consequences of what he believed to be love in all its selfish, dangerous glory when his father had sacrificed his family so that he could be with the woman he wanted.

'You can't say that a parent's love for their child is destructive,' she commented mildly. 'Most people see it as supportive.'

'A man of principle can do what he should do for his family without prating about love,' Gio asserted with a slight shudder as he tightened his arms round her. 'I don't need to love you to look after you.'

Billie's eyes stung painfully. He, most certainly, hadn't been looking after her when he had chosen to marry Calisto two years earlier but that was not a memory she wished to rouse. Instead she set down her glass and pillowed her head against his shoulder.

'I suppose,' Gio said, after a great deal of unusually introspective thought, 'I do love Theo but it's because he's little and helpless. He's got all the appeal of a puppy or a kitten. I took dozens of photos of him on my phone before I left Yorkshire and I couldn't wait to see him again.'

Billie thought it was sad that at that moment she envied her son for having that amount of pull with Gio after such a short acquaintance.

'I couldn't wait to see you either…as you know when I turned up today before you could even make it to the church,' Gio confided, nuzzling his unshaven jaw line softly along the line of her creamy throat, feeling extraordinarily at peace for the first time in a very long time and wondering what it was about her that had that effect on him. 'I don't know why I did that. It was absolutely crazy.'

'I didn't mind,' Billie interposed, squirming round in the circle of his arms to look down at him instead of up at the stars.

His lean, strong face was still a touch bemused by his own behaviour that morning and it was obvious that he was still mulling that over. 'You know, somewhere in the back of my mind, I honestly think I was afraid you mightn't turn up at the church… Isn't that insane?'

If he had known how much she loved him, he would have known he was quite safe on that score, she reflected ruefully. No, no matter how mad she had been with him she would never have jilted him at the altar.

'My goodness, it's a huge house,' Billie breathed as the four-wheel drive parked outside a very large sprawling villa set high on the hillside and surrounded by glorious tropical gardens.

'It has to be big for family get-togethers and it's been extended by almost every generation since it was built.' His tension pronounced enough to attract Billie's notice, Gio sprang out and turned back to unstrap Theo from the car seat while Irene and Agata headed up the wide, shallow steps that led to a front door that already stood wide.

The housekeeper hovering at the door fussed around them but Gio would not even linger long enough to perform an introduction and strode on past, knowing exactly where he was going and clearly determined not to be held back.

'Gio!' Billie exclaimed, hurrying out of breath in his wake. 'If we're going into a crowd, give me Theo. He can be awkward with strangers…'

His stubborn jaw line clenching, Gio passed their son to Billie, who settled the toddler comfortably on her hip. 'And smile, for goodness' sake,' she urged, troubled by the forbidding cast of his lean, darkly handsome features. 'It doesn't matter if your family aren't too sure about me…you have to give them time…'

The elegant reception room was in proportion with

the house and very big and Billie was disconcerted to peer in the glass doors and see an absolute throng of people, both standing and seated, on the marble floor. Gio had a much bigger family than she had appreciated. As they entered the room every head turned towards them and Billie sucked in her tummy by breathing in deep and slow, striving to steady her nerves.

'I asked you all here today to introduce you to my wife,' Gio declared in the rushing silence, his dark deep drawl measured and carrying to every corner of the room. 'This is Billie. We got married yesterday and—'

A noise erupted from the far corner as an older man stood up and banged his walking cane loudly on the floor. His lined face rigid, he shot a stream of furious Greek at Gio. Gio grated something back and then closed an arm to Billie's spine to thrust her back in the direction of the door. 'We are leaving,' he said curtly.

'Oh, please, don't go, Gio!' A tall, shapely brunette was chasing after them. 'I'm Sofia, Gio's youngest sister. Gio, why on earth didn't you tell us that you were getting married?'

Billie stopped dead and swopped Theo to her other hip because he was getting heavy. 'He *didn't* tell any of you?' She gasped in disbelief.

'No, he said he had a surprise to share with us and that's why we're all here.'

'We're leaving, Billie,' Gio reminded her doggedly.

But Billie spun round before he could open the

door and marched back into the room. 'Gio should have told you that we were getting married. I had no idea—'

'Billie,' Gio cut in, clamping an imprisoning hand to her shoulder.

'Well, I'm sorry to criticise you in front of your family but you really should have warned them. Obviously everybody's in shock and people say things they don't necessarily mean when you shock them,' Billie pointed out, studying the fuming older man, who she suspected was Gio's grandfather, Theon Letsos. 'There's no sense in storming out in a huff over it.'

'I am not in a huff,' Gio ground out between clenched teeth, outraged that she was defying his lead and his wishes with his own family.

'Perhaps we could talk about this,' the old man said gruffly, scanning Billie with astute dark eyes that reminded her strongly of Gio's. 'Your wife is correct. I spoke in haste and without thought.'

'He insulted you,' Gio bit out harshly.

'That's all right. I can only be offended if you abuse me in English,' Billie declared forgivingly. 'I don't speak a word of Greek!'

'Gio and his sisters attended English schools,' the older man told her with a sudden smile. 'Now come and sit down and tell me about yourself. I find it hard to stand for long.'

In a state of disbelief, Gio found himself in the rare position of being assigned second string within his family as Billie, chattering away to his grandfather as though she had known him for years rather than seconds, walked slowly over to the closest seats available.

'Forgive me for being so remiss in the courtesies,' Theon murmured. 'I am Gio's grandfather, Theon Letsos.'

'I'm Billie. It's not short for anything.'

'And your son?'

'*Our* son,' Gio corrected with pride. 'Theon Giorgios, your great-grandson, known as Theo.'

Taken aback by the revelation, the older man studied Theo as he crawled across the floor with all the energy of a toddler kept in restraint for too long. 'Theo…' he mused in the crashing silence that had once again engulfed the entire room. 'And you only married *yesterday*?'

'Gio only found out that Theo existed very recently,' Billie cut in hastily. 'We hadn't been in contact for a couple of years—'

Gio gritted his teeth. 'There is absolutely no need for you to talk about that.'

'Of course there is. I don't want anyone thinking that I had an on-going affair with a married man,' Billie declared without hesitation, marvelling at how slow on the uptake Gio could sometimes be because *he* was totally indifferent to what other people thought of him. But she didn't want that stigma within the family circle. She might not have liked Calisto, nonetheless she would not have engaged in a relationship with Gio with or without his wife's knowledge.

'A great-grandson named for me…' Theon was keen to concentrate on the positive and politely ignore Gio's brooding protective stance beside Billie's chair. 'A fine boy...not shy either!' he remarked with an appreciative laugh as Theo made his way over to another toddler with a small heap of toys in front of him and snatched at the first colourful item he could reach.

'So, tell me about yourself,' the older man invited.

'Billie's not here for an interview,' Gio incised coolly.

'My goodness, I'm *so* thirsty. I would really love a drink,' Billie informed Gio, shooting him an expectant look.

Of course, Gio simply snapped his fingers like some desert potentate and a uniformed maid materialised.

Billie met Theon's amused eyes and her own mouth twitched because her strategy had been lame but she really could have done without Gio standing over her in warrior mode as if she were defenceless in enemy territory. He had never acted that way around her before and the discovery that his reserve was as great within his own family as it had once been with her was a major shock to her expectations. Yet that insight saddened her as well. Gio was such a lone wolf. How had he contrived to become the guarded, unemotional male he was with such a large and, she sensed, loving family?

Theo crawled back and hauled himself up against Billie's knees and then clutched at his father's legs until Gio abandoned his rigid stance, smiled with a sudden brilliance that lit up his lean, strong face and swept his son up in his arms to carry him back to the toys.

'It's been a long time since I saw Gio smile,' Theon remarked.

'I don't have a fancy background or any money. I owned and ran a shop. I'm just an ordinary working woman,' Billie volunteered before Gio could return to censor the conversation. 'You might as well know that upfront.'

'In recent years, *very* recent years, I have learned the unimportance of such distinctions.' Theon gave an emphatic shrug and relaxed back into his armchair. 'And I'm afraid I must disagree with you on one point. No ordinary woman could handle Gio and the Letsos family with so much tolerance and common sense.'

That was Billie's last private moment with Theon. One by one she received introductions to Gio's uncles, aunts and sisters, including, to her surprise, his half-sister, Melissa, who had passed half a lifetime being royally ignored by her father's family because she was the result of Dmitri Letsos' illicit teenaged romance.

'They're not a bad bunch when you get to know them,' Melissa, a collected blonde teacher in her forties, pronounced with a wry smile. 'Oh, there's the usual sibling rivalry, but they are, one and all—I assure you—devoted to Gio. He brought me into this family and he's the first port of call for all of us when there's a crisis. I hope you can handle that. Calisto couldn't.'

From stray comments made and generally quickly leading to a subject change rather than risk causing offence, Billie began to suspect that Gio's first wife had not been well liked. She cursed her own curiosity about her predecessor: it was pointless and the gratification of that curiosity was more likely to lead to hurt. Gio had married another woman. *Get over it*, she urged herself impatiently, determined not to be haunted by the shadows of the past.

'If your wife is the woman she appears to be, she's solid gold,' Gio's grandfather told him disconcertingly.

Tight-mouthed, Gio breathed, 'When it comes to Billie, I have no need of anyone's approval.'

'But an invitation to the wedding would have been very much appreciated,' Theon countered drily.

Once Irene had taken Theo up for his bath and guests had begun to disperse to their own corners of the rambling villa, Billie slipped away to explore the wonderful gardens, finally sitting down in the shade of an ancient chestnut tree to appreciate the glorious bird's-eye view of the island and the ocean. Although she was exhausted she was quietly pleased that her meeting with Gio's family had ultimately gone well when it had so very nearly gone badly wrong.

When had Gio become so hot-tempered? He had been like a stick of dynamite with a smouldering string attached, aggressively ready to attack anyone who attacked her, over-sensitive to every comment and question that came in her direction. Billie sighed over that mystery and slowly relaxed, letting the tension drain out of her.

'I've been looking everywhere for you,' Gio delivered in a minatory tone, striding down the gravelled path towards her. 'Downstairs, upstairs...'

'Maybe you should microchip me and then you would know where I am at all times,' Billie told him deadpan.

Struggling to master his exasperation, Gio released his breath in a rush. There she was, curls foaming round her lovely face, eyes contemplative, clearly happy and content. He could not explain to her his personal fear that she had put on a fantastic sociable act all day for the benefit of his family while secretly masking her hurt at her less than welcoming reception. 'Are you all right?'

'Tired,' she admitted, sleepy green eyes locked to him while a wicked little current of remembered pleasure travelled through her. 'But then we didn't get much sleep last night...'

The faintest colour stung his stunning cheekbones, brilliant dark eyes flaring gold, lean bronzed features breathtaking in their perfect symmetry as his wide mouth took on a sensual curve. She loved him; she loved him so much, she acknowledged helplessly.

'What are you out here worrying about?'

'I'm not worrying,' Billie declared. 'This is a gorgeous garden and I'm enjoying it.'

Recalling the window boxes and pot plants she used to keep at the apartment, Gio felt his conscience ping. Just as quickly he recalled the hollow sensation he had suffered when, following her disappearance, he had seen those plants dead and withered and as always he buried the memory deep of that period in his life. 'I should've bought you a house with a garden a long time ago.'

'My only experience of gardening was visiting my granddad's allotment as a child,' Billie confided quietly. 'He used to plant vegetable seeds for me. That was in the days before the betting shop and the drink pushed him into a less active lifestyle.'

Gio frowned, astonished by the sudden realisation that he could know so little about his wife's background. Momentarily he marvelled that he had never asked her anything beyond the most basic questions, but, after learning that she had virtually no living relatives that she knew of, he had seen no reason to probe deeper. 'He was a drunk?'

'No, that's too harsh. He drank to escape my grandma's nagging. She was kind of sour in nature. If he was a drunk,' Billie extended, 'he was a nice drunk because he was never mean, but his liver failed and he was ill for a long time. That's when I first began missing school because my grandma wouldn't look after him the way he needed to be looked after and I felt so guilty leaving him to her care every day.'

'Surely there was some care offered by the state?'

'No, there's actually very little help available. Grandma was told he wasn't sick enough to get a bed in a nursing home even though he was terminally ill. Once he had passed, it was just her and me... and she never liked me, said I reminded her of my mother.' Billie grimaced. 'You can't really blame her. My mother dumped me on her and never came back. She was a bitter woman, who just never saw the good in anyone. I got to go back to school for a couple of years and then Grandma's health failed too and that was the end of that.'

Gio was stunned by what he was belatedly learning. 'How is it that I'm only finding out all this about you now?' he could not help asking, as if he thought the oversight might somehow be her fault.

Tactfully concealing her wonder at that question, Billie shot him a wry glance. 'Gio, back then, in your eyes, when I wasn't physically in front of you, I didn't exist.'

Gio tensed. 'That's untrue.'

'Do you recall that cabinet with drawers I once mentioned where I was tucked in my own tiny drawer, only to be taken out and appreciated by you on special occasions? Seriously, I wasn't joking—that *was* what it was like.'

His lean dark features were grim. 'What you're really saying is that I'm a colossally selfish individual.'

'You were self-absorbed and very driven. Let's face it, when we were together your main focus was always business. I also think you were too posh to be comfortable with the difference in our backgrounds. Ignoring it was easier. I think as long as I was willing to be quiet about it, you preferred not to be reminded that I was once a humble cleaner,' Billie told him gently.

'I can't believe we're even having this conversation!' Gio ground out angrily, his temper, kept on a short leash all day, whipping up in a sudden surge hotter than lava. 'Or that you could ever have had such a low opinion of me!'

In mute frustration, Billie closed her eyes and counted to ten. 'It's done and dusted, Gio—it's the past. I'm not attacking you. I'm only being honest. I wasn't perfect either. I should have stood up to you, demanded more, but I was too young and in my very first relationship.'

'You lied about your age.' Gio was quick to pounce on that reminder.

Billie nodded peaceably, refusing to rise to the bait because there was no way she was about to engage in a massive row with Gio about their past. After all, everything had changed now and they were making a new start at a very different level of intimacy.

'I've got some work to do,' Gio said in a tone of finality.

Billie smiled, knowing his first refuge when emotion threatened was work. 'I'll walk back indoors with you.'

Gio settled with his laptop in the library, which was set up like a high-tech office for his use. *Theos*, he still found himself thinking furiously, he was not and he never had been a selfish person. On one issue, Billie was correct: he had no need whatsoever to revisit the past. That conviction in place, Gio struggled to concentrate on the lines of figures on his laptop screen and he was fine until the moment that the matter of the pre-nuptial settlement contract squeezed into his mind and practically obliterated everything else in the process. He rang the housekeeper to dis-

cover where Billie's possessions had been stored since
being shipped out the previous week.

It occurred to him then without warning that even
the devil could not have devised a more colossally
selfish or fiendish document. He refused to act like a
male engaged in a covert operation, but on some level
of his brain he was astounded by what he was about
to do when he finally stood in the room confronted
with a heap of boxes. After all, when was Billie ever
likely to lift that contract out and reread it? Why the
hell was he so damned rattled by a very minor risk?
Perspiration dampened his lean, bronzed features. He
was engaging in a cover-up and the knowledge didn't
sit well with him. But prior to that contract he had
never once been dishonest with Billie. He hovered,
studying the boxes. That document could *hurt* her, he
reflected broodingly, and he latched onto that excuse
for what he was about to do with alacrity.

Gio had never unpacked a box in his life but he
wasn't surprised by the discovery that every box was
labelled and incredibly neatly filled because Billie
was very, very organised and always had been. In the
third box, he hit the pay dirt of finding files full of
papers and in the second file he espied the contract
and ripped it out, but not before he frowned down at
a certificate for wine tasting and found beneath it one
for art appreciation. He went through the whole file,
checking the dates, learning what he knew he should
have learned years sooner.

There was a burning behind his eyes that made
them feel scratchy and he felt oddly hollow, as though

someone had gutted him without warning. Feeling rather as though he had been beaten up, Gio replaced everything where he had found it with the exception of the contract and strode off to pour himself a very stiff drink. The contract went through the shredder but the relief he had expected to feel was utterly absent. He had gone digging where he had no business digging, he conceded sardonically, and he rather thought that in the process he had got what he deserved.

'Theon wants you to join him for afternoon tea,' Sofia told Billie cheerfully around three that afternoon. 'It's a big honour.'

Billie grinned. 'I liked him.'

'I think the feeling's reciprocated,' Gio's sister responded with a laugh as she guided Billie across the villa to the wing of the house Theon occupied.

A manservant showed her out onto a big shaded balcony where Theon awaited her. 'I believe this is an honour,' Billie remarked with a grin.

'How on earth have you escaped Gio?' his grandfather enquired mockingly.

'Something I said annoyed him... He's taken refuge in work,' Billie confided, marvelling at how very comfortable she felt in the older man's company.

'I overheard that conversation,' Theon admitted, disconcerting her. 'This balcony is directly overhead.'

Billie reddened but sat down. 'Oh, well, it's all within the family,' she said without great concern because it wasn't as if she and Gio had been hurling insults at each other or discussing anything she considered particularly private, although she knew that put in the same position Gio would have been furious.

'I thought I should bring you up to date on some family history, as I doubt very much that Gio has done the job for me,' Theon commented.

'I know about his parents' divorce,' Billie contributed. 'And I know his father really didn't have much to do with him after it.'

'Dmitri was a weak man. There, I have said it,' the older man said wryly. 'For years I wouldn't admit that to myself because he was my son...'

'It's challenging to accept faults in those we care about most,' Billie murmured soothingly.

'You love Gio a great deal—it shines from you,' his grandfather told her. 'He's a very lucky man.'

Billie flushed and decided not to embarrass herself with a denial while she poured the tea. 'I hope he always thinks so. He's much more complicated than I am...'

'And that's why I invited you for tea,' Theon told her. 'I'm very much afraid that his complexity can be laid at my door. I raised Gio from the age of eleven after his mother died.'

'I had no idea she died while he was still so young,' Billie said in surprise as she buttered a scone and deliberated with some gastronomic anticipation on whether to have raspberry or strawberry jam with her cream.

'Ianthe couldn't cope alone after Dmitri divorced her for Marianne. I had no idea how bad things had become for Gio's mother,' Theon told her heavily.

'Perhaps if my wife had still been alive she would have had the wisdom to foresee the problems and she would have encouraged me to offer help in time to prevent a tragedy.'

Billie set down her scone after one delicious bite. 'A tragedy?' she pressed.

'Ianthe hanged herself…and Gio found her,' the older man recounted with a shudder. 'I will carry the burden of my guilt to the end of my days.'

Eyes widening, Billie had lost colour. 'I had no idea…'

'I didn't think you would, which is why I told you,' Gio's grandfather confessed. 'The effect on Gio was catastrophic. He had lost his father, his home and then his mother, only a few months later.'

Billie shook her head slowly, cringing at the thought of such a huge loss being inflicted on Gio and his sisters while they were still so young. 'That must have been dreadful for him,' she muttered unsteadily, her heart swelling. 'He would've felt responsible—'

'I worried that Gio would inherit the same excessively emotional personality that both Dmitri and Ianthe demonstrated in the way they led their lives. That kind of emotional intensity leads to instability.'

'Not always,' Billie inserted gently.

Theon shook his white head. 'I wanted to be sure that Gio did not repeat his father's mistakes. It was too much responsibility to place on a child's shoulders. In many ways I taught him the wrong values,' he explained with unashamed guilt etched in his lined features. 'I expected, *wanted* him to marry well…

and we all know how successful that proved to be. I put far too much emphasis on wealth, status and family duty—'

'But,' Billie cut in with an apologetic look, 'at the end of the day, Gio is a highly intelligent adult and totally independent and he made his own decisions.'

'*Ne*...yes, and he married you without telling any of us because he refused even to risk the fact that I might have tried to interfere.'

'Probably,' Billie agreed thoughtfully. 'But he's not enough in touch with his own feelings to even know that.'

'You know him so well,' Theon pronounced with appreciation. 'Now we've got the difficult bit over, shall we enjoy our scones?'

Gio was on the phone to Leandros and Leandros was asking awkward questions, destined not to be answered. 'I just don't understand.' His best friend sighed. 'You only got married yesterday. You only arrived with your family today. Why would you want to fly back to Athens for one night simply to have some fancy dinner?'

'Tomorrow's Billie's birthday.'

'So, make it tomorrow, then.'

'I want to do it tonight. Are you joining us?' Gio prompted. 'And, Leandros, if you mention Canaletto, I'll cut your throat.'

'Of course I'll join you.'

Billie was engaged in drying Theo and slotting

him into his pyjamas when Gio appeared in the bathroom doorway of the nursery suite.

Gio swept up his son and hugged him and did
the flying thing again, which sent Theo into gales
of laughter. 'He's tired,' Gio acknowledged as Theo
then rested his curly head down on his father's shoulder and slumped.

'He's had a lot of excitement today and he's always
exhausted when he's been with other kids.' Billie carried her son through to the bedroom and settled him
down in the very fancy cot, from which she quickly
detached the flouncy hangings and everything else
within reach for such dangling temptations were not
a good idea with an active toddler.

'This place needs to be refurnished,' Gio commented tautly, watching her every move, it seemed,
unsettling her.

Billie laughed. 'It's perfectly fine. It might have
been done up for a little girl but Theo doesn't know
the difference yet.'

'It was decorated for Sofia's youngest daughter.
She had a difficult birth and her husband was travelling and Theon suggested she move back here while
he was away,' Gio volunteered.

'Sofia's lovely,' Billie said warmly.

'We're going out tonight,' Gio announced abruptly.

'Where to?'

'Athens.'

Billie blinked. '*Athens*? But we've only just got
here!'

'We'll be back tomorrow,' Gio sliced in. 'We're eating out with Leandros and his current girlfriend.'

'Are they getting engaged or something?'

'Not that I know of. Is going out with me such a big deal?' Gio demanded in frustration.

Billie almost said that, naturally, it was a big deal when he had never taken her anywhere public in years, aside of the wedding, but she thought better of that piece of one-upmanship. She was reluctant to hark back to the past when their marriage was, self-evidently, a very new and much altered situation. She supposed that, for Gio, taking a flight for one night out was almost normal, certainly nothing he appeared to have to think about, and she resolved to say no more while privately worrying about what she had to wear.

She blessed the foresight that had sent her out shopping for more sophisticated and expensive clothes before the wedding and pulled an elegant pewter-coloured dress from a closet in the luxurious dressing room where all her clothes had been carefully unpacked for her. While she showered and attended to renewing her make-up, she pondered Gio's strange mood.

'What do you think?' she asked, twirling a little apprehensively in front of him when she found him waiting in the bedroom for her.

Stunning dark golden eyes flared over her. 'You look incredible,' he intoned with convincing appreciation. 'Are you ready to leave?'

A warm sense of acceptance blossomed inside Billie even though she could still not understand how he could have been married to a beauty like Calisto and still deem his infinitely less-beautiful second wife equal to the label 'incredible'.

'Are we returning to Letsos tonight?' she prompted as she let Gio lift her into the helicopter.

'Yes, although the family own a city apartment if you would prefer to stay there,' he volunteered.

'No, I'd miss Theo at breakfast time when he's all warm and cuddly and glad to see me,' Billie confided sunnily.

As the helicopter rose in the air Gio leant closer, meshing long fingers into the tumble of her curls. He turned her face up and crushed her mouth under his in a breathtakingly hot kiss and that not only startled her, but also sent hunger crashing greedily through her body.

Billie rested disconcerted eyes on him in the aftermath. His lean, darkly beautiful face was slashed by a brilliant smile and he closed one hand firmly over hers. Wonderment filtered through Billie. There was something wrong but she didn't know what it was…

CHAPTER NINE

BILLIE WALKED INTO the upmarket art gallery with one hand resting on Gio's arm. The owner swam up to them wreathed in smiles. Wine was served while they were treated to a personalised tour of the exhibits. Billie was bored but worked hard not to show it, politely absorbing the pretentious descriptions of canvases that looked as though a toddler had thrown paint at them.

'Do you see anything you like?' Gio enquired, apparently surprised by his wife's unresponsive silence.

'I'm not an art buff. I sort of prefer more traditional paintings,' she whispered back guiltily, and then she stiffened, staring across the gallery at the unmistakeable figure of Calisto, sheathed in a scarlet minidress and virtually impossible to miss.

'What the hell…?' Gio breathed irritably above her head.

'I'll deal with this,' Billie announced, startling him, walking across the marble tiles with her wine glass clasped in one determined hand.

'How did you know we were going to be here?' Billie asked Gio's ex-wife without hesitation.

Calisto's ice-blue eyes glinted. 'I have my sources, but aren't you a little out of your depth in this milieu?'

'I believe you're the one out of your depth. Gio isn't coming back to you,' Billie responded stiffly. 'This is a waste of your time.'

'Oh, I don't think so. Once I heard the terms of your pre-nup, I knew you would be on your way out almost as soon as you arrived,' Calisto trilled with a scornful smirk. 'You signed it without reading it, didn't you? Silly, silly woman. Remember that when Gio dumps you back in the UK *without* your precious son!'

Billie refused to react in any way, determined not to give Calisto that much satisfaction. The woman hated her: she could see that. It was there in the dripping malevolence of her gaze and the sneering tone of her voice and Billie was challenged to understand what exactly she had done to incite such intense loathing. Simply marrying Gio? Her custody of Gio's son? Or was Calisto still in love with Gio and feeling scorned by his rapid remarriage?

Gio strolled up and without a word to even acknowledge his ex-wife walked Billie out of the gallery. 'Only two people knew we were coming here and one of them is Damon, whom I trust with my life,' he told her grimly. 'I've already called him. He will deal with the leak and the person concerned will be sacked.'

'I think that would be best,' Billie said rather woodenly. 'And perhaps the lawyer, whom you mentioned is her stepbrother? He seems to have talked out of turn about confidential matters as well.'

Gio frowned, making it obvious that he had not overheard Calisto's final salvo. 'What confidential matters?'

Billie shrugged as though she meant something trivial, reluctant to think the worst of Gio, averse to trusting anything that witch, Calisto, had claimed at his expense. She would dig out the pre-nup and check it out for herself or arrange to have it looked over by an independent lawyer. It couldn't be true; it couldn't possibly be true, she thought in an agony of fear. After all, if that claim of Calisto's was true, it would mean that their marriage was an empty charade, never intended to do anything but gain Gio legal custody of Theo and she could not, *would* not believe that of him!

'Your ex is a bit of a pyscho,' Billie remarked tentatively as they settled into the waiting limousine.

'And probably what I deserved,' Gio breathed in a raw undertone of stress.

'What's the matter with you?' Billie prompted before they entered the fashionable restaurant.

'Nothing's the matter,' Gio insisted.

If you can believe that, you can believe anything, Billie reflected, unimpressed, off-balanced by the odd way he was behaving. He was still holding her hand, still acting as if he were physically welded to her or, ridiculously, as though he were afraid that she might run away somewhere.

No way, Billie thought combatively. He had signed

up for a life sentence as far as she was concerned and he was going to serve it, she thought crazily, studying his lean, bronzed, totally gorgeous profile while he talked to Leandros and Billie listened to Leandros' girlfriend, Claire, who was a British model, talk about the joys of fake tan and the cosmetics range she was planning. It wasn't riveting stuff but Billie tried her best to be friendly while reaching the conclusion that Leandros was as shallow as a puddle when it came to the female sex.

Gio skated a teasing forefinger along Billie's thigh below the table and she tensed, thinking, not about what he probably hoped she was thinking about, but instead about what Calisto had said. I'm going to have to ask him, she accepted unhappily.

Was he capable of such a deception through the means of a legal document? Oh, yes, Billie had no doubts when it came to how ruthless Gio could be. After all, in spite of what she had deemed to be a very happy relationship and her warning that she would not be there when he returned, Gio had still gone off and married another woman because that was what he'd felt he *had* to do. Like a granite rock rolling down a hill on a set path, Gio was not given to second thoughts or doubts or insecurities like frailer personalities and he didn't think much about the damage he could be inflicting.

How could she love someone like that? Billie asked herself wretchedly as the limousine carried them back to the airport.

'What did you think of Claire?' Gio enquired in

the silence, desperate to know what Calisto had said to her. Calisto could be so vicious and, when she aimed it at Billie, even Gio was willing to admit that she had some excuse for her resentment.

'Very chatty and glam. She seems pleasant enough,' Billie commented.

'For a fake-tan expert. She must be great in bed,' Gio said sardonically.

'Why?' Billie heard herself say. 'Is that how you first thought about me? Let's face it, I didn't have much in the way of intellectual conversation to offer either.'

'We're not talking about you.' Gio gave her hand a little shake as though in rebuke. 'You were never that vain or frivolous.'

'Claire's looks are the basis of her whole career so I don't think it's fair to call her vain or frivolous.' And in the back of her mind, Billie was wondering why she was arguing with him about something that didn't matter in the slightest to her. Dimly it dawned on her that fear was working on her nerves, cutting through the sense of trust and security that she had begun to develop and throwing up friction in her every response to him.

What on earth was she planning to do if the man she loved turned out to be her worst enemy rather than her husband? How was she going to cope with Gio trying to take Theo away from her? Murder him in his bed? Hire a hit man? Her mind threw up crazier and crazier ideas and her tension rose steadily as she boarded the helicopter to sit stiff and silent by his side until the flight back to Letsos was complete.

'I wish you'd tell me what's wrong,' Gio breathed as she pulled away from his supporting arm and picked an uneven passage along the path from the helipad to the villa.

'We'll talk about it inside where nobody can hear us,' Billie framed in a flat tone he had never heard from her before.

Tension screaming from every line of his tall, powerful figure, Gio mounted the stairs a step in her harried wake. It was no comfort for him to flip through his list of sins and omissions with Billie because there were so many of them he didn't know where to start. He watched her stop dead in the living area of their suite and kick off her high heels, ensuring that she shrank greatly in stature.

Billie settled blazingly angry green eyes on Gio. 'Calisto told me that the pre-nup I signed contained something about you keeping Theo here in Greece if we broke up.'

Furious that something so highly confidential could have been leaked from what should have been the most trustworthy source, Gio turned pale, and for an instant he couldn't think of anything to say in his own defence.

Billie read his taut defensive expression and her shoulders slumped. 'So, it's true…this marriage has all been some cruel kind of game of deception.'

'The pre-nup no longer exists. I shredded your copy and mine and had my legal rep destroy all evidence of it,' Gio grated. 'It's gone, it's in the past. I should never have thought of such a thing.'

'How did you shred *my* copy?' Billie demanded in sudden wonderment.

'I went into your storage boxes,' Gio admitted, a tinge of heat accentuating his cheekbones at the look of disbelief growing in her gaze. 'I realised it was wrong and I wanted to destroy it. I didn't want you to realise what I'd tried to do at some later stage of our lives.'

'Well, you don't have that to worry about that now. It's come back to haunt you much sooner than you expected,' Billie pointed out, wondering how much she should be mollified by the apparent destruction of the document and his evident change of heart. At least he knew when he'd done something wrong, she thought limply, struggling to find a bright side to her predicament.

Gio studied her, his full attention locked to her flickering changes of expression. 'I didn't want to lose you.'

'You didn't want to lose Theo,' Billie corrected. 'I wish you'd just been honest from the beginning. I'm not unreasonable, Gio, and from the moment you reappeared I was willing to *share* Theo with you, honestly and fairly.'

'It was a very dirty trick to plant that clause in the pre-nup,' Gio acknowledged with a humility that astounded her.

'But very typical of you,' Billie responded. 'Clever, devious, cold-blooded.'

'I'm never cold-blooded when it comes to you. I had the pre-nup drawn up that way because…' Gio hesitated, lean, strong face rigid '…not because I was trying to take Theo off you, but because…'

'Because what?' Billie snapped in sudden frustration.

'*Because* I knew you'd never leave him and if I had the right to keep him, you wouldn't leave me either!' Gio yelled back at her full force, making her jump in fright.

Billie gaped at him. 'But I had no intention of leaving you.'

'You left me before!' Gio bit out rawly.

Billie stared at him, fighting to hide her fascination and astonishment. 'But don't you think there was some excuse for me leaving you then, when you were marrying another woman?' she reasoned very gently.

His lean, darkly handsome features froze as if she had slapped him. He released his breath in a long pent-up hiss. 'Marrying Calisto was the worst mistake I ever made…but I thought, I truly believed at the time that I was doing the right thing.'

Billie thought about what Theon had told her about the way he had raised Gio and the values he had emphasised and suppressed a sigh. 'But it wasn't the right thing for you.'

'I am so sorry for hurting you,' Gio framed in a roughened undertone, lustrous dark eyes unshielded and filled with overwhelming regret. 'If I could go back and change it, I would…but I can't. If it's any consolation, I hurt myself as well. For two years my life was miserable because you weren't part of it any longer, so I definitely paid for making the wrong choice. My happiest day since the day I lost you was the day when I finally found out where you were living.'

In her entire experience of Gio, Billie had never thought to hear such admissions from him. Initially the shock of what he was telling her almost struck her dumb and then the natural warmth of her nature sent her hurtling across the room to wrap both arms round him in comfort. 'Oh, Gio, you are an idiot sometimes,' she whispered helplessly.

'I honestly didn't believe you would leave me. When I found the apartment empty...well, it was a very bad moment for me and I did everything I could to fight feeling the way I did, but everything in my life felt wrong after that,' he confessed raggedly. 'Calisto got a bad deal from me as well. I didn't want her, I wanted you, and when you disappeared you were all I could think about.'

Belatedly Billie understood his ex-wife's hatred for her. 'Did she love you? She must've been jealous and hurt...'

'No, love wasn't part of our arrangement, nor was jealousy. If it had been she would never have agreed to me still keeping you in my life.'

'You *told* her about me? She actually agreed to you continuing to see me?' Billie prompted, shaken even though she recalled him saying something in that line before.

'I preferred to be honest with her from the start. Cal wanted social position. Her family are wealthy but have little status. She wanted to be Gio Letsos' wife for what it meant to the rest of the world. Unfortunately, I couldn't live with her,' Gio admitted with a grimace of recollection. 'She was nasty to my family and she lies at the drop of a hat about the most trivial things. After promising to have a family with me, she then confessed that she didn't *ever* want to have a child. In short, we were both dissatisfied with our marriage and she agreed to the divorce.'

'But then why is she carrying on this way trying to upset me and wreck our marriage?'

'I can only think I hurt her ego by not wanting her more than I wanted you. Obviously marrying you straight after the divorce offended her as well but we won't be having any more trouble from that quarter,' Gio asserted with conviction. 'That lawyer will be removed from my team and Leandros doesn't get on with Cal any better than I do, so there won't be any leaked info from him with regard to our lives.'

Ready to toss the issue of Calisto and his brief marriage on a back burner, Billie was instead thinking about what Gio had said about the pre-nup agreement he had had her sign. 'Why were you afraid of me leaving you again?' she murmured.

'My father left me, my mother left me and somehow you became even more important to me than they were,' Gio framed with dogged determination but obvious difficulty in explaining that to her. 'After I found my mother dead, I taught myself to close out emotions because it was the only way I could cope with the way my sisters' lives and mine had imploded. I preferred to stay in control. I felt threatened whenever emotion tried to take over. I found the way I seemed to *need* you totally unnerving...'

Billie was so stunned by that speech that the best she could manage was, 'Oh, dear...'

'I couldn't believe that you could try and send me away once I found you again.'

'Only because of Theo and I thought you'd be furious about him. And because you hurt me before and I didn't want to put myself out there for that again,' Billie told him truthfully.

'I did everything wrong, but then I would have done anything to get you back,' Gio confided. 'I shouldn't have used Dee's past as a weapon against you.'

'No, you shouldn't have.' Billie didn't pull her punches on that score. 'You blackmailed me into moving to your hotel!'

'I wanted you with me.'

'And then abandoned me at the hotel,' Billie reminded him stubbornly.

'My feelings around you were getting on top of me,' Gio breathed curtly. 'I couldn't handle them and I was getting angry and frustrated and I was afraid I might scare you off.'

'I didn't know you felt like that because until now you haven't shared anything with me,' she murmured ruefully.

Gio reached into his pocket and withdrew a ring

box, from which he removed a gleaming diamond solitaire. 'It's five minutes after midnight and your twenty-third birthday, *pethi mou*. Happy birthday.' He lifted her hand and threaded the beautiful ring onto her wedding finger. 'It belonged to my grandmother and now it belongs to you. They enjoyed a very long and happy marriage; consequently it comes with a worthy history for us to follow.'

Billie gazed down at her beautiful ring with tears of joy glittering in her eyes because that family gift meant so much more to her than a ring that he might have bought.

'I should have placed that ring on your finger two years ago but I didn't know my own heart then,' Gio confessed heavily. 'I had never stopped to evaluate what you actually meant to me and by the time that I did, it was too late and you were gone. Even after I found you again and married you, I genuinely *still* didn't appreciate that what I feel for you has to be love.'

'*Love?*' Billie exclaimed, jolted by surprise from her blissful perusal of her engagement ring.

'I do love you,' Gio declared with an endearing amount of self-consciousness about making such a statement. 'I probably always loved you but it was a very selfish love, so I didn't recognise it for what it was and neither could you have done.'

Billie was bemused. 'Gio…you just called your-self selfish…'

Gio frowned. 'I couldn't avoid that deduction after I found your exam certificates and all the courses which you had done while we were together two years back… I didn't know about even *one* of them,' he decried. 'I wish you'd told me.'

Billie was flushed. 'I was too embarrassed. You have a degree and there I was studying for the most basic qualifications,' she pointed out. 'My goodness, is that why you took me to that stupid art gallery tonight?'

'I thought you'd enjoy it,' Gio admitted.

'I only took the course because of that Canaletto thing,' she muttered ruefully. 'But to be frank, it's all a bit highbrow for me.'

'I'm not into art either. I wouldn't change a single thing about you. I'm proud of you and happy to show you off anywhere. I'm *really* proud that you're my wife,' Gio imparted with a brilliant beautiful smile as he scooped her up in his arms and carried her through to their bed.

'Honestly?' Billie pressed.

'Honestly,' Gio stressed. 'I only wish I'd understood the strength of what I felt for you a lot sooner because it would have saved us both a great deal of unhappiness. I would never willingly have let you go.'

'I still love you,' Billie told him with a forgiving grin that illuminated her whole face.

'I have to wonder why,' he said seriously.

'Maybe because I see a side of you that other people don't. I don't know. I just always loved you,' Billie mused, relaxed about her own feelings for the first time in years because he loved her back. A singing, dizzy sense of happiness was spreading through her, all her fears finally laid to rest.

'Bet I love you even more than you love me,' Gio husked, dark eyes smouldering gold as he kissed her with sweet, ravishing hunger. 'I'm hopelessly competitive.'

'You can win that competition any time you like,' Billie joked, feeling gloriously free to express her own feelings as she gripped his shirt collar and dragged him down to her again.

Billie watched Theo race into the waves with Jade and Davis while Gio kept a watch on the children.

'You know,' Dee remarked from her lounger by Billie's side on the deck of the beach house, 'Gio's totally different from the sort of man I thought he was. He's great with kids, for a start.'

'Oh, he's surprised me too in that line,' Billie confided lazily, her attention on the six-month-old daughter sleeping in her portable crib in the shadows. 'He adores Ianthe.'

'When does your family tree get a look-in with the names?' Dee asked.

'Are you joking?' Billie laughed. 'With Grandpa being a Wilfred and Grandma Ethel, I think Gio's family names have more promise. What were we talking about? Right, yes, Gio and children. He's surprised too by how much he enjoys having a family.'

'Billie, if you wanted a giraffe in the family, he'd try to give it to you,' her cousin said with a roll of her eyes. 'The man is besotted. I can see it every time he looks at you.'

'Maybe it'll be your turn soon,' Billie remarked quietly, because Dee had started seeing someone back home. It was early days yet, of course, but she was hoping Dee would be brave enough to try another relationship because her cousin spent too much time alone.

It had been two years since Billie had married Gio and Dee was currently in the process of buying Billie's vintage clothes shop, which she was still successfully managing. A lot had changed for Billie in that same period but Gio had changed too, opening up to his emotions and pulling free of an outlook that had once been set in stone. He would never be Dee's best friend but he could relax now with the other woman and accept her place in Billie's life without comment or tension. Billie suspected that their children had helped Gio become more relaxed and flexible.

Theo was tall for a three-year-old, like all the men in the Letsos family, and he had Gio's black hair messily combined with his mother's corkscrew curls, something he would no doubt complain bitterly about when he reached his teenaged years, Billie reflected fondly. Ianthe was a combination of their genes as well, for her eyes had turned as green as her mother's and she was fairer in colouring than her brother with dead straight hair with not even a hint of a curl.

Billie went into the beach house for a cold drink

and glanced around with a rather wicked smile because she knew that she and Gio would be spending the night there. Dee and the children were heading home in the afternoon and Irene, their trusty nanny, would collect Theo and Ianthe to take them back to the villa.

In the two years since she had married Gio, Billie had learned to make the most of their private time together. Gio travelled less than he once had and their lives were based on the island. Billie got on great with Gio's family and was particularly close to his sisters and never short of company. Sometimes she wanted to pinch herself because she had never dreamt that she could be so happy.

A pair of arms closed round her from behind and she jumped. *'Gio?'*

'Who else?' he breathed teasingly above her head.

'You gave me a fright,' she whispered, swivelling round in his arms to look up at him. 'Who's with the children?'

'Dee's taking a turn.'

Billie collided with smouldering dark golden eyes set in a stunning lean dark face and wrapped her arms round his neck, her heart hammering. 'You still rock my world, Mr Letsos,' she confided breathlessly.

Gio dealt her a thrillingly erotic smile of anticipation. 'Not until tonight, *agapi mou.*'

He called her 'my love' now, Billie reflected blissfully, for she now spoke a fair amount of Greek. Her curvaceous body sealed slowly to his with intense appreciation of the strength and protectiveness in his tall, well-built length. 'I love you, Gio...'

'And I am totally devoted to you,' Gio intoned huskily, bending his head to steal a kiss that went on until they had to break apart to breathe.

* * * * *

SECRETS, LIES & LULLABIES
HEIDI BETTS

To Rob and Michelle (Timko) Massung, for all of their amazing computer help recently.

You saved my butt more than you will ever know, and I just can't thank you enough.

An avid romance reader since junior high, *USA TODAY* bestselling author **Heidi Betts** knew early on that she wanted to write these wonderful stories of love and adventure. It wasn't until her first year of college, however, when she spent the entire night before finals reading a romance novel instead of studying, that she decided to take the road less travelled and follow her dream.

Soon after Heidi joined Romance Writers of America, her writing began to garner attention, including placing in the esteemed Golden Heart competition three years in a row. The recipient of numerous awards and stellar reviews, Heidi's books combine believable characters with compelling plotlines, and are consistently described as 'delightful,' 'sizzling' and 'wonderfully witty.'

For news, fun and information about new books, be sure to visit Heidi online at www.HeidiBetts.com.

One

Alexander Bajoran swiped his key card and pushed open the heavy oak door to his suite. He'd been halfway down the winding mile-long drive leading away from the luxurious yet rustic resort—aptly named Mountain View Lodge—when he realized he'd forgotten a stack of much-needed paperwork. Now he was late for his meeting, and it was going to be nearly impossible to make it into downtown Portland on time.

He let the door swing closed behind him as he marched toward the large cherrywood desk on the far side of the sitting area. Six steps in, he stopped short at the sound of someone else moving around in the suite. Turning toward the bedroom, he paused in the doorway, taking note of the woman stripping his bed and shaking her rear end to a song only she could hear.

She was wearing a maid's uniform, but sadly not one of the sexy French variety. Just a simple gray dress that did nothing to compliment her figure or coloring.

Her blond hair was pulled up and twisted at the back of her head, held in place by a large plastic clip, but he could still see bits of color peeking out here or there. A thin streak of black, then auburn, then blue running down one side and blending into the rest.

Yes, blue. The woman had blue hair. At least a few bits of it.

She was humming beneath her breath, the occasional odd lyric tripping off her tongue as she whipped back the top sheet, then a corner of the fitted one. The quilted coverlet was already in a heap on the floor.

As she danced around, oblivious to his presence, he noticed the glitter of earrings lining the entire length of one ear. Studs, hoops, dangles; there must have been seven or eight in her right ear alone. The left had only four that he could see—three near the lobe and one higher up near her temple.

Despite all the silver and gold and jeweled settings, he knew they had to be fake. No way could a chambermaid afford the real thing. Which was a shame, because she'd look good in diamonds. And he should know—diamonds were his business.

Soiled sheets balled up in her arms, she turned suddenly, jumping back and giving a high-pitched shriek when she saw him standing there.

He held his hands up in the universal I-mean-you-no-harm gesture. "I didn't mean to startle you," he offered by way of apology.

Reaching up, she yanked the buds from her ears and tucked them into the pocket of the white apron that must have held her MP3 player. He could hear the heavy beat of her music as she fumbled to turn down the volume.

Now that he could look at her straight on, he noticed she wasn't wearing makeup…or not much, at any rate. Strange, considering her hair and jewelry choices. She even had a small gold hoop with a tiny fleck of cubic zirconia hanging from the outer edge of her right eyebrow.

Eyes still wide from the scare he'd given her, she licked her lips. "I'm sorry, I didn't know anybody would be here. I didn't see the sign on the knob."

He shook his head. "There wasn't one. I expected to be gone for the day, but forgot something I need for a meeting."

He didn't know why he was telling her this. He didn't normally spend a lot of time explaining himself to anyone. But the longer he stood here talking, the longer he got to look at her. And he did enjoy looking at her.

That, too, was unusual for him. The women he dated tended to be socialites from wealthy families. Polished and sophisticated, the type who spent their days at the garden club doing nothing more strenuous than planning their next thousand-dollar-a-plate fundraiser for the charity du jour.

Never before had he found himself even remotely attracted to someone with multicolored hair and excessive piercings. But the young woman standing in front of him was fascinating in an exotic-animal, priceless-piece-of-artwork way.

She seemed to be slightly disconcerted by his presence, as well, staring at him as if she expected him to bite.

"Is there anything you need, as long as I'm here?" she asked, nervously licking her lips over and over again. "Extra towels or glasses, that sort of thing?"

He shook his head. "I'm fine, thank you."

Then, because he couldn't think of anything else to say or any other reason to stand there, staring at the help as though she was on display, he moved away, heading back across the sitting room and grabbing up the file he'd forgotten. It was her turn to stand in the bedroom doorway while he slapped the manila folder against his free hand a couple of times.

"Well," he murmured, for no particular reason, "I'll leave you to it, then."

She inclined her head in acknowledgment, still watching him warily.

Walking to the suite's main door, he pulled it open and set one foot across the threshold into the hall. But before walking off, he couldn't resist turning back and taking one last glance at the intriguing young woman who had already returned to her job of changing his sheets.

"It was Alexander Bajoran," Jessica said in a harsh whisper, leaning so far across the small round deli table that her nose very nearly touched her cousin's.

"You're kidding," Erin returned in an equally hushed voice, her eyes going wide in amazement.

Jessica shook her head, crossed her arms over her chest and flopped back in her chair, causing her cousin to move forward in hers. Their sandwiches sat untouched in front of them, their ice-filled fountain drinks slowly producing rivulets of condensation down the sides of the paper cups.

"Did he recognize you?" Erin asked.

"I don't know. He didn't say anything, but he *was* looking at me a little funny."

"Funny, how?"

Jessica flashed her a tiny grin. "The usual."

"Well, you do tend to stand out."

Jessica stuck her tongue out at her cousin's teasing. "We can't all be prim and proper Jackie O wannabes."

"Nobody's asking you to be Jackie O. The family just wishes you weren't quite so intent on being the next Courtney Love."

Following through on the natural instincts that had probably earned her that reputation in the first place, Jessica flipped her cousin a good-natured hand gesture. Not the least offended by the response, Erin merely rolled her eyes.

"Actually, your unique personal style may work in our

favor. You don't look at all the way you did five years ago. Chances are, Bajoran won't have a clue who you are."

"I hope not. I'll try to switch floors with Hilda, though. That should keep me from accidentally bumping into him again."

"No, don't do that!" Erin said quickly. "The fact that he doesn't recognize you is a good thing. You can move around his suite freely without arousing suspicion."

"Arousing suspicion?" Jessica repeated. "Who am I— James Bond?"

"If I could do it, I would, believe me," Erin told her with no small amount of bitterness leeching into her voice. "But you're the one he already thinks is a chambermaid."

Jessica narrowed her eyes. "Why does that matter?"

"Because it means you can move around the lodge without being noticed. You know what men like Bajoran are like. Rich and self-absorbed...to him, you'll be all but invisible."

Jessica understood her cousin's anger, really she did. Fifty years ago, Alexander Bajoran's grandfather and great-uncle had launched Bajoran Designs. Soon after, they'd begun a partnership with Jessica's and Erin's grandfathers, who owned Taylor Fine Jewels. Both companies had been based in Seattle, Washington, and together they'd been responsible for creating some of the most beautiful and valuable jewelry in the world. Million-dollar necklaces, bracelets and earrings worn by celebrities and royalty across the globe.

The Taylor-Bajoran partnership had lasted for decades, making both families extremely wealthy. And then one day about five years ago, Alexander had taken over Bajoran Designs from his father, and his first order of business had been to steal *her* family's company right out from under them.

Without warning he'd bought up a majority of shares of Taylor Fine Jewels and forced Jessica's and Erin's fathers off the Board of Directors so he could absorb the company into his own and essentially corner the market on priceless jewels and their settings.

Thanks to Alexander's treacherous move, the Taylor family had gone bankrupt and been driven out of Seattle almost overnight. They were far from destitute, but all the same, the Taylors were *not* used to living frugally. Jessica didn't think her mother was used to her new, more middle-class lifestyle even now, and Erin's mother had taken the reversal of fortune hardest of all.

Jessica was doing okay, though. Did she *enjoy* being a maid at a resort where she used to be a guest? Where she used to stay in a three-thousand-dollar-a-night suite and that her family could easily have purchased with a flick of the wrist?

Not always. But being a maid, working at a normal job like a normal person, gave her a freedom she'd never felt as a rich, well-known socialite. No way could she have gotten away with streaks in her hair and pierced everything when she'd been one of *those* Taylors. When she'd been attending luncheons at the country club with her mother and been the subject of regular snapshots by local and national paparazzi.

Money was good, but she thought anonymity might be a little bit better. For her, at least. For Erin, she knew the opposite was true.

"Why do I need to be invisible?" she asked finally. "It's lucky enough he didn't recognize me the first time. I should switch floors and maybe even shifts with one of the other girls before he does."

"No!" Erin exploded again. "Don't you see? This is our chance! Our chance to get back at that bastard for what he did to us."

"What are you talking about?" Thoroughly confused, Jessica shook her head. "How could we possibly get back at him for that? He's a millionaire. Billionaire. The CEO of a zillion-dollar company. We're nobodies. No money, no power, no leverage."

"That's right, we're nobodies. And he's the CEO of a zillion-dollar company that *used* to be ours. Maybe it could be again."

Before Jessica had the chance to respond, Erin rushed on. "He's here on business, right? That means he has to have business information with him. Paperwork, contracts, documents we could use to possibly get Taylor Fine Jewels back."

"Taylor Fine Jewels doesn't exist anymore. It's been absorbed into Bajoran Designs."

"So?" Erin replied with a shrug of one delicate shoulder. "It can always be un-absorbed."

Jessica didn't know how that would work. She wasn't sure it was even possible. But whether it was or it wasn't, what Erin was suggesting was insanity.

"I can't go poking around in his things. It's wrong. And dangerous. And corporate espionage. And *definitely* against Mountain View policy. I could lose my job!"

Her cousin made a sound low in her throat. "It's only corporate espionage if you're employed by a rival company. Which you're not, because Alexander Bajoran *stole* our company and put us all out on the street. And who cares if you lose that stupid job? Surely you can scrub toilets for the wealthy elite at some other high-priced hotel."

Jessica leaned back, stunned by the venom in her cousin's voice, as well as her obvious disdain for Jessica's occupation. Yes, she scrubbed toilets and stripped beds and vacuumed carpets instead of folding scarves and dressing mannequins at an upscale boutique like Erin, but she kind of liked it. She got to spend most of her time alone, got along well with the rest of the housekeeping staff and didn't have to claim her sometimes quite generous tips on her taxes.

And it kept her busy enough that she didn't have time to

dwell on the past or nurse a redwood-size grudge against an old enemy the way her cousin obviously did.

"Come on, Jess. Please," Erin begged. "You have to do this. For the family. We may never get another opportunity to find out what Bajoran is up to, or if there's some way—*any way*—to rebuild the business and our lives."

She wanted to refuse. *Should* refuse. But the pain in Erin's voice and in her eyes gave Jessica pause.

She could maybe poke around a little.

"What would I have to do?" she asked carefully. "What would I be looking for?"

"Just…see if you can find some paperwork. On the desk, in his briefcase if he leaves it. Interoffice memos, maybe, or documents outlining his next top secret, underhanded take-over."

Against her better judgment, Jessica gave a reluctant nod. "All right, I'll do it. But I'm not going to get caught. I'll *glance around*. Keep my eyes open. But I'm not going to rummage through his belongings like a common thief."

Erin's nod was much more exuberant. "Fine, I understand. Just look around. Maybe linger over fluffing the pillows if he's on the phone…listen in on his conversation."

She wasn't certain she could do that, either, but simply acting like she would seemed to make her cousin happy enough.

"Don't get your hopes up, Erin. This has 'Lucy and Ethel' written all over it, and you know how their crazy schemes always turned out. I'm not going to jail for you, either. A Taylor with a criminal record would get even more press than one having to work a menial, nine-to-five job cleaning other people's bathrooms."

Two

This was insane.

She was a former socialite turned chambermaid, not some stealthy spy trained to ferret out classified information. She didn't even know what she was looking for, let alone how to find it.

Her cart was in the hall, but she'd dragged nearly everything she needed to clean and restock the room in with her. Sheets, towels, toilet paper, the vacuum cleaner... If there were enough supplies spread out, she figured she would look busier and have more of an excuse for moving all over the suite in case anyone—specifically Alexander Bajoran—came in and caught her poking around.

The problem was, his suite was pretty much immaculate. She'd been cleaning it herself on a daily basis, even before he'd checked in, and the Mountain View's housekeeping standards were quite high. Add to that the fact that Alexander

Bajoran was apparently quite tidy himself, and there was almost *nothing* personal left out for her to snoop through.

Regardless of what she'd let her cousin believe, she was not going to ransack this room. She would glance through the desk, under the bed, in the nightstands, maybe inside the closet, but she was not going to root through his underwear drawer. Not when she didn't even know what she was supposed to be looking for.

Business-related what? Compromising…what?

Jessica couldn't blame her cousin for wanting to find *something* incriminating. Anything that might turn the tables on the man who had destroyed the Taylors' livelihood and a few members of the family personally.

But how realistic was that, really? It had been five years since Bajoran's hostile takeover. He had moved on and was certainly juggling a dozen other deals and business ventures by now. And even if *those* weren't entirely on the level, she doubted he was walking around with a paper trail detailing his treachery.

The sheets were already pulled off the bed and in a heap on the floor, so it looked as though she was busy working. And since she was close, she quickly, quietly slid open one of the nightstand drawers.

Her hands were shaking, her fingertips ice-cold with nerves, and she was shivering in her plain white tennis shoes. Sure, she was alone, but the hallway door was propped open—as was lodge policy—and at any moment someone could walk in to catch her snooping.

She didn't know which would be worse—being caught by Alexander Bajoran or by her supervisor. One could kick up enough of a stink to get her fired…the other could fire her on the spot.

But she didn't need to worry too much right that second, because the drawer was empty. It didn't hold so much as a

Bible or telephone directory. Mountain View wasn't *that* kind of resort. If you needed a Bible or phone book or anything else—even items of a personal nature—you simply called the front desk and they delivered it immediately and with the utmost discretion.

Closing the drawer on a whisper, she kicked the soiled sheets out of her way and shook out the clean fitted sheet over the bare mattress as she rounded the foot of the bed. She covered one corner and then another before releasing the sheet to open the drawer of the opposite nightstand.

This one wasn't empty, and her heart stuttered in her chest at the knowledge that she was actually going to have to follow through on this. She was going to have to search through her family's archenemy's belongings.

The bottom drawer of the bedside bureau held a decanter of amber liquid—scotch, she presumed, though she'd never really been in charge of restocking the rooms' bars—and a set of highball glasses. The top drawer held a thick, leather-bound folder and dark blue Montblanc pen.

She swallowed hard. Once she moved that pen and opened the folder, that was it…she was invading Alexander's privacy and violating the employee agreement she'd signed when she'd first started working at the lodge.

Taking a deep breath, she closed her eyes for just a split second, then reached for the pen. As quickly as she could she flipped open the folder and tried to get her racing mind to make sense of the papers inside.

Her eyes skimmed the print of the first two pages, but nothing jumped out at her as being important or damaging. And the rest was just pictures of jewelry. Snapshots of finished pieces and sketches of what she assumed were proposed designs.

Beautiful, beautiful jewelry. The kind her family used to create. The kind she used to dream of being responsible for.

She'd grown up pampered and protected, and was pretty sure her parents had never expected her to do anything more than marry well and become the perfect trophy wife. But what she'd truly aspired to all those years she'd spent primping and attending finishing school was to actually work for Taylor Fine Jewels. Or possibly more specifically their partner company, Bajoran Designs.

Like any young woman, she loved jewelry. But where most of her peers had only wanted to wear the sparkly stuff, she'd wanted to *make* it. She loved sifting through cut and uncut gems to find the perfect stone for a setting she'd drawn herself.

All through high school her notebooks and the margins of her papers had been filled with intricate doodles that were in reality her ideas for jewelry designs. Her father had even used a few for pieces that had gone on to sell for six and seven figures. And for her sixteenth birthday, he'd surprised her with a pearl-and-diamond ring in a setting that had always been one of her very favorites.

It was still one of her favorites, though she didn't get many opportunities to wear it these days. Instead, it was tucked safely at the bottom of her jewelry box, hidden amongst the much less valuable baubles that suited her current level of income.

But, heavens above, these designs were beautiful. Not perfect. She could see where the size of one outshone the sapphire at its center. Or how the filigree of another was too dainty for the diamonds it surrounded.

She could fix the sketches with a sharp pencil and a few flicks of her wrist, and her palms itched to do just that.

When she caught herself running her fingers longingly across the glossy surface of one of the photographs, she sucked in a startled breath. How long had she been standing there with a target on her back? All she needed was for Alexander or another maid to walk in and catch her staring at his portfolio as if she was planning a heist.

Slamming the folder shut, she returned it to the bedside drawer and placed the pen back on top in exactly the same position it had been to begin with. She hoped.

With the nightstand put to rights, she finished stretching the fitted sheet over the other two corners of the mattress, then added the top sheet. She needed to get the room cleaned, and the best way to snoop was to search the areas nearest where she was working, anyway.

So she got the bedroom fixed up and cleaned but didn't resupply the bathroom before moving back into the main sitting room. She ran the vacuum over every inch of the rug, just like she was supposed to, but took her time and even poked the nose of the sweeper into the closet near the hallway door. The only thing she found there, however, was the hotel safe, which she knew she didn't stand a chance of getting into.

The only place left that might hold something of interest to her cousin was the large desk along the far wall. She'd avoided it until now because she suspected she didn't really want to find anything. She didn't want to be put in that spot between a rock and a hard place; didn't want to hand something over to Erin that might put her cousin in an even more precarious situation; didn't want to stir up trouble and poke at a sore spot within her family that *she'd* thought was beginning to heal over. She'd thought they were all moving on.

Apparently, she'd been wrong.

Leaving the vacuum nearby, she did a quick sweep of the top of the desk. There were a few sheets of hotel stationery with random notes written on them, but the rest seemed to be the typical items supplied by the lodge. Hotel directory, room-service menu, et cetera.

Inside the desk, though, she found a heck of a lot more.

Namely a small stack of manila folders and a laptop computer.

Jessica licked her lips, breathing in shallow bursts that matched the too-fast beat of her heart against her rib cage.

She was not opening that laptop, she just wasn't. For one thing, that would be *too much* breaking and entering, and sticking her nose where it didn't belong, for her peace of mind. For another, it would take too long. By the time it booted up and she figured out how to explore the different files and documents, her supervisor would surely be kicking in the door demanding to know why she was still in this suite when she should have been done with the entire floor.

She was sticking to her guns on this one. Erin might not like that decision, but she would just have to deal with it.

So she stuck with the folders lying beside the laptop, opening them one at a time and scanning them as quickly as possible.

Nothing jumped out at her as being out of the ordinary—not that she really had a clue what she was looking at or for. It was all just business jargon, and she certainly hadn't gone to business school.

But there was no mention of Taylor Fine Jewels in any of the papers…not that she'd expected there to be. And there was no indication of anything else that put her instincts on red alert.

She was just letting out a huff of air that was part frustration, part relief when she heard a creak and knew someone was entering the suite behind her. Her eyes flashed wide and she all but slammed the desk drawer shut—but slowly and quietly to keep from looking as guilty as she felt.

Putting her hand on the rag that she'd left on top of the desk, she started to wipe it down, just as she was supposed to. *Act natural. Act natural. Try not to hyperventilate. Act natural.*

Even though she knew darn well someone was behind her…likely standing there staring at her butt in the unappealing, lifeless gray smock that was her work uniform…she didn't react. She was alone, simply doing her job, as usual. The trick would be to feign surprise when she turned around and "discovered" that she *wasn't* alone.

Schooling her breathing…*act natural, act natural*…she hoped her cheeks weren't pink with the guilt of a kid caught with her hand in the cookie jar. Luck was on her side, though, because as she finished wiping down the desktop and twisted toward where she'd left the upright vacuum cleaner, whoever was standing behind her, silently monitoring her every move, cleared his throat.

And it was a he. She could tell by the timbre of that low rumble as it reached her ears and skated straight down her spine.

The air caught in her lungs for a moment, and she chastised herself for having such a gut-level, feminine response to something so simple. This man was a complete stranger. Her family's sworn enemy. And since he was a guest of Mountain View, and she worked for the lodge, he might as well be her employer.

Those were only the first of many reasons why her breathing should not be shallow, her blood should not be heating, and the clearing of his throat should not cause her to shiver inside her skin.

Doing her best to snap herself out of it, she straightened and twisted around, her hand still on the handle of the vacuum cleaner.

"Oh!" she exclaimed, letting her eyes go wide in mock startlement, praying the man standing in front of her wouldn't see right through it. "Hello again."

"Hello there," Alexander Bajoran returned, his mouth curving up in a small smile.

Jessica's pulse kicked up a notch.

It was nerves, she told herself. Just nerves.

But the truth was, the man was devilishly handsome. Enemy or no enemy, a blind woman would be able to see that.

His ink-black hair was perfectly styled, yet long enough in places to look relaxed and carefree. Eyes the color of blue ice glittered against skin that was surprisingly tan for a resident of the Pacific Northwest. But she knew for a fact it wasn't the result of time spent in tanning beds or spray-on booths; the entire Bajoran family leaned toward dark skin, dark hair… and ruthless personalities.

She had to remember that. The ruthless part, anyway.

Never mind how amazing he looked in his black dress slacks and dark blue blazer. Like he belonged on the cover of *GQ*. Or *Forbes,* thanks to his ill-gotten millions.

Never mind that if she saw him on the street, she would probably give herself whiplash spinning around to get a second look.

"We seem to have conflicting schedules this week," he said in a light, amused tone. His voice immediately touched deep, dark places inside of her that she *really* didn't want to think about.

He gave her a look, one she'd seen thousands of times in her adult life and had no trouble recognizing. Then his voice dropped a fraction, becoming sensual and suggestive.

"Or maybe they're matching up just right."

The heat of his voice was like sunshine on budding little seedlings, making *something* low in her belly shiver, quiver and begin to unfurl.

Oh, no. No, no, no. No more charming-but-dangerous men for her—and Alexander Bajoran was the most dangerous of all.

She'd been hit on and leered at by any number of male guests in her time at Mountain View. Traveling businessmen, vacationing husbands with a wandering eye, rich but useless playboys with a sense of entitlement…. But whether they'd pinched her on the rear, slipped her hundred-dollar tips or attempted simple flattery, she had never once been attracted to a single one of them.

Yet here she was, face-to-face with the man who had stolen her family's company and whom she was supposed to be spying on, and caterpillars were crawling around under every inch of her skin.

He took a step toward her, and her hands fisted, one around the handle of the vacuum, the other near her right hip. But all he did was set his briefcase—which was really more of a soft leather messenger bag—on the nearby coffee table before sinking into the overstuffed cushions of the sofa behind it.

Releasing a pent-up breath and sending some of those annoying creepy-crawlies away with it, Jessica reached down to unplug the sweeper and started to coil up the cord. The sooner she got out of there now that he was back, the better.

"I can leave you alone, if you need to work," she said, because the growing silence in the room was killing her.

But even though he had the brown leather satchel open on the glass-topped table and had pulled out several stacks of paperwork, he shook his head.

"Go ahead and finish what you were doing," he told her. "I've just got a couple of things to look over, but you won't distract me. In fact, the background noise might do me some good."

Well, shoot. How was she supposed to make a smooth but timely exit now?

She guessed she wasn't.

Dragging the vacuum across the sitting room, she set it in the hallway just outside the door of the suite. Then she gathered up an armful of fresh towels and washcloths for the bathroom.

It wasn't hard to go about her business this far away from Alexander. It was almost as though the air was normal in this tiled, insulated room instead of thick with nerves and guilt and unspoken sexual awareness. From her standpoint, at any rate. From his the air probably seemed absolutely normal. After all, he wasn't the one snooping, breaking the law, fighting a completely unwanted sexual attraction to someone he was supposed to hate.

She spent an inordinate amount of time making sure the towels hung just right on the towel rods and were perfectly even in their little cubbies under the vanity. Even longer putting out new bottles of shampoo, conditioner, mouthwash and shaving cream.

There were decorative mints and chocolates to go on the pillows in the bedroom, but she didn't want to go back in there. From the bathroom she could wave a hasty goodbye and get the heck out of Dodge. But if she returned to the bedroom, she would have to pass by Alexander. See him, smile at him, risk having him speak to her again.

That was one corner she was willing to cut today. Even if he complained to her superiors and she got in trouble later, missing mints were easier to apologize for than snooping or blushing herself into heat stroke in front of a valued guest.

Stepping out of the marble-and-gilt bathroom, she rounded the corner and was just congratulating herself on a narrow escape when she lifted her head and almost ran smack into Alexander, who was leaning against the outside wall waiting for her.

She made a tiny *eep* sound, slapping a hand over her heart as she bounced back on her heels.

"Sorry," he apologized, reaching out to steady her. "Didn't

mean to scare you, I just wanted to catch you before you took off."

If ever there was a word she didn't want to hear pass this man's lips, it was *catch*. Was she caught? Had he noticed something out of place? Figured out that she'd rifled through his things?

She held her breath, waiting for the accusations he had every right to fling at her.

Instead, as soon as he was sure she wasn't going to topple over, he let go of her elbow and went back to leaning negligently against the wall. It was a casual pose, but all Jessica could think was that he was standing between her and the door, blocking her only exit from the suite.

"I know this is probably out of line," he murmured, "but I was hoping you'd have dinner with me tonight."

His words caused her heart to stutter and then stall out completely for several long seconds.

"I'm here on business, so after I finish with meetings and such during the day, my evening hours are a bit…empty."

He shrugged a shoulder, and because he'd taken off the blazer, she could see the play of muscle caused by the movement beneath his crisp white dress shirt. Something so minor shouldn't make her hormones sit up and take notice, but they did. Boy, howdy, did they ever.

Licking her lips, she cleared her throat and hoped her voice didn't squeak when she tried to speak. It was bad enough that her face was aflame with nerves; she could feel the heat all but setting her eyelashes on fire. She already looked like a clown, in many people's estimation—she didn't need to open her mouth and sound like one, too.

"Thank you, but fraternizing with guests is against resort policy."

Ooh, that sounded good. Very confident and professional—and squeak-free.

Alexander lifted a brow. "Somehow I find it hard to believe a woman with blue hair is afraid of breaking a few rules."

She reached up to toy with the strip of chemically altered hair he was referring to. "It's not *all* blue," she muttered.

That bought her a too-handsome grin and flash of very white, perfectly straight teeth. "Just enough to let the world know you're a rebel, right?"

Wow, he had her pegged, didn't he? And he wasn't taking no, thank you, for an answer.

Dropping the hank of hair, Jessica pushed her shoulders back. She was a rebel, as well as a confident, self-reliant woman. But she wasn't stupid.

"I could lose my job," she said simply.

He cocked his head. She wasn't the only self-assured person in the room.

"But you won't," he told her matter-of-factly. Then, after a brief pause, he added, "Would it make you feel better if I said I won't let that happen?"

With anybody else she would have scoffed. But knowing who Alexander Bajoran was and the power he held—even here in Portland—she had no doubt he meant what he said and had enough influence to make it stick.

"You'll be on your own time, not the resort's," he pointed out. "And I'll let you decide whether we order from room service or go out somewhere else."

She should say no. Any sensible person would. The entire situation screamed danger with a capital *D*.

But she had to admit, she was curious. She'd had male guests proposition her before, give her that salacious, skin-crawling look reserved for when they were on out-of-town business trips without their wives and thought they could get away with something.

Alexander was the first, though, to ask her to dinner without the creepy looks or attempts at groping. Which made her wonder why he was interested.

Did he suspect her of snooping around where she didn't belong, or was he just hitting on a pretty, no-strings-attached maid? Did he recognize her as a Taylor and think she was up to something, or just hope to get lucky?

Of course she *was* up to something, but now she wanted to know if *he* was up to something, too.

So even though she knew she should be running a hundred miles an hour in the opposite direction, she opened her mouth and made the biggest mistake of her life.

"All right."

Three

Jessica didn't get many opportunities to dress up these days. But she was having dinner this evening with a very wealthy, very handsome man, and even though she knew it was a terrible idea, she wanted to make the most of it. Not so much the man and the dinner but simply the act of going out and feeling special for a little while. Putting on something pretty rather than functional. Taking extra time with her makeup and hair. Wearing heels instead of ratty old tennies.

She even went so far as to dab on a couple drops of what was left of her favorite three-hundred-dollar-an-ounce designer perfume, Fanta C. Alexander Bajoran might not be worth a spritz or two, but she certainly was.

She was wearing a plain black skirt and flowy white blouse with a long, multi-strand necklace and large gold hoop earrings in her primary holes. The others held her usual array of studs and smaller hoops.

As she strode down the carpeted hallway, she fiddled with

every part of her outfit. Was her skirt too short? Did her blouse show too much cleavage? Would the necklace draw Alexander's eye to her breasts? Or worse yet, would the earrings pull too much of his attention to her face?

Flirting—even flirting with danger this way—was one thing. Truly risking being recognized by her family's greatest enemy, though... No, she didn't want that.

Which was why she'd chosen to meet him here, in his room at the resort, rather than going out to a public restaurant where they might be seen by someone they—especially she—knew.

Getting caught in a guest's room after work hours would be bad, but being spotted out on a date with Alexander by one of her relatives or somebody who might tell one of her relatives would be exponentially worse. She would rather be fired than deal with the familial fallout.

Reaching the door of his suite, Jessica stopped and took a deep breath. She straightened her clothes and jewelry for the thousandth time and checked her small clutch purse to be sure she had her cell phone, a lipstick, a few bucks just in case. She didn't know if she would end up needing any of those things, but wanted to have them, all the same.

When there was nothing left to double-check, no other reason to put off the inevitable, she took another deep, stabilizing breath, held it and let it out slowly as she tapped on the door.

The nerves she'd tamped down started to wiggle back toward the surface as she waited for him to answer. Then suddenly the door swung open, and there he was.

Six foot something of dark, imposing good-looks. Slacks still smooth and pressed, despite being worn all day. Pale, pale lavender dress shirt unbuttoned at his throat and sleeves rolled up to his elbows, but no less distinguished than when he'd been wearing a tie and suit jacket.

He smiled in welcome and a lump formed in her throat, making it hard to swallow. Suddenly she was almost pathologically afraid to be alone with him. It was two mature adults sharing a simple meal, but almost as though she was watching a horror movie, she could see around all the corners to where scary things and maniacal killers waited.

A thousand frightening scenarios and terrible outcomes flitted through her brain in the nanosecond it took him to say hello—or rather, a deep, masculine, "Hi, there"—and step back to let her into the suite.

She could have run. She could have begged off, hurriedly telling him she'd changed her mind, or that something important had come up and she couldn't stay.

She probably should have.

Instead, a tiny voice in her head whispered, *What's the worst that can happen?* and showed her images of a lovely, delicious meal at an establishment where she worked but never got the chance to indulge, with an attractive man the likes of which she probably wouldn't meet again for a very long time. Not given her current circumstances.

So she didn't run. She told herself she was here, he was a gentleman, and everything would be fine.

"Thank you," she murmured, surprised when her voice not only didn't crack, but came out in a low, almost smoky tone that sounded a lot sexier than she'd intended.

She stepped into the suite, and he closed the door behind her with a soft click. More familiar with these rooms than she cared to admit, she moved down the short hallway and into the sitting room where there was already a table set up with white linens and covered silver serving trays.

"I hope you don't mind, but I took the liberty of ordering," Alexander said, coming up behind her. "I thought it would save some time."

True enough. Mountain View employed one of the best

chefs in the country and served some of the best food on the West Coast, but room service was room service. It sometimes took longer than guests might have liked for their meals to arrive, especially if the kitchen was busy trying to get food out to the dining room.

Cupping her elbow, he steered her around the table and pulled out her chair. She tried not to let the heat of his hand do funny things to her pulse. Of course, her pulse had a mind of its own.

He helped her get seated, then began uncovering plates of food. The smells hit her first, and they were divine. Even before she could identify them all, she saw that he'd ordered a sampling of some of the very best culinary creations the resort had to offer.

From the appetizer section of the menu he'd asked for watermelon gazpacho with tomato; cucumber and borage; seafood tomato bisque; eggplant ravioli; and oysters in red wine mignonette.

As entrées, he'd gone with pheasant with green cabbage, port wine-infused pear and black truffle shavings, and something she could rarely resist—crab cakes. Mountain View's particular recipe consisted of large chunks of Dungeness crab, tiny bits of lobster, corn and faro lightly seared to a golden brown.

He had no way of knowing they were one of her all-time favorites, though. Most likely he'd ordered them because they were nearly world renowned and one of the most popular items on the resort's menu.

But her stomach rumbled and her mouth began to water at the very sight. She might work here, might have skated past the kitchen or dining room a time or two, but since she couldn't exactly afford fifty-dollar-a-plate dinners any longer, she'd never been lucky enough to actually taste them.

"I hope there's something here you'll like."

Like? She wanted to take her clothes off and roll around on the table of food, then lick her body clean.

Because she wasn't certain she could speak past the drool pooling on her tongue, she merely nodded and made an approving *mmm-hmm* sound.

"I ordered dessert, as well, but let's wait until we finish this before we dig into that."

Oh. She'd heard wonderful things about Mountain View's desserts, too.

"So…" he murmured, "where would you like to start? Or should I just hand over the crab cakes before someone gets hurt?"

The mention of crab cakes and the slight amusement in his tone brought her head up, and she realized she'd been concentrating rather intensely on that particular platter.

"Sorry, they just…smell really good."

He grinned at her candid response. Reaching to the side and lifting the plate, he set it back down directly in front of her.

"They're all yours," he told her. "As long as you don't mind if I keep the pheasant to myself."

Well, she would have liked at least a *tiny* bite—she'd never had the pleasure of trying that particular dish, either—but if the crab cakes were as delicious as they looked, smelled and she'd heard they were, she supposed it was a sacrifice worth making.

Her silence seemed to be answer enough. He moved the pheasant to his place setting, then reached for the bottle of wine in the center of the table and pulled the cork. While she shook out her napkin and laid it across her lap, he poured two glasses of the rich, dark liquid and handed one to her.

She took it with a murmured thank-you and brought it to her nose for a sniff. Mmm. It had been a while since she'd enjoyed a glass of really good, expensive wine. This one was full-bodied, with the scents of fruit, spice and just a hint of chocolate.

She was tempted to take a sip right away, but didn't want to ruin her first taste of the crab cakes and had also promised herself she would be careful tonight. A little bit of wine with dinner wouldn't hurt, but she didn't want to risk drinking too much and forgetting who she was…who he was… and exactly how much was on the line if she accidentally let any part of the truth slip past her lips.

So she set the glass aside and picked up her fork instead.

"At the risk of scaring you off now that you're already here," Alexander said, shaking out his own napkin and placing it across his lap, "it occurred to me that I invited you to dinner tonight without even knowing your name. Or introducing myself, for that matter."

Jessica paused with her first bite of crab cake halfway to her mouth. Uh-oh. She hadn't been concerned with introducing herself to Alexander because she already knew who he was. And keeping her own identity under wraps was critical, so she hadn't exactly been eager to share that information, either.

Now, however, she was cornered, and she'd better come up with a response soon or he would start to get suspicious.

To buy herself a little bit of time, she continued the trajectory of her fork and went ahead with that first bite of food she'd so been looking forward to. Her anticipation was dampened slightly by the tension thrumming through her body and causing her mind to race, but that didn't keep her taste buds from leaping with joy at the exquisite spices and textures filling her mouth.

Oh, this was so worth the stress and subterfuge of pretending to be someone she wasn't. With luck she would only have to lie to him for one night, and not only would he be none the wiser, but she'd have the experience of a lovely meal with a handsome, wealthy playboy-type tucked away in her memory banks.

The part about deceiving him and searching his suite like a wannabe spy would maybe have to be deleted, if she hoped to live with herself for the next fifty years, though.

Making a satisfied sound deep in her throat, she swallowed and finally turned her attention to Alexander—since she couldn't justify ignoring him any longer.

"My name is Jessica. Madison," she told him, using her middle name instead of her last. If he questioned anyone at the resort, they would either deny knowing her or correct her little fib without realizing they were revealing anything significant. He obviously hadn't asked around about her or he would already know her name, and she doubted he would bother after this, as long as she didn't give him cause to become curious.

He offered her a small grin and held his hand out across the table. She had to put her fork down to take it.

"Hello, Jessica. I'm Alexander Bajoran. You can call me Alex."

A shiver of heat went through her at both the familiarity of his invitation and the touch of his smooth, warm hand.

Darn it! Why did she have to like him so much? And she really did. He was charming and good-looking and self-assured. Knowing he had a nice, hefty bank account certainly didn't hurt, but it was his easy friendliness that made her regret her bargain with Erin and the fact that she was a Taylor.

If she didn't have that baggage, she suspected she would be extremely flattered by his apparent interest in her and excited about tonight's "date." But she would be self-conscious about the fact that she was a lowly chambermaid, while he was clearly blessed financially, even though there was a time when her fiscal worth possibly rivaled his own.

She would have been fidgeting in her seat, careful to say

and do all the right things in hopes of having him ask her out again.

And she probably also would have been imagining going to bed with him. Maybe not tonight, on their first date, or even on their second or third. But eventually—and sooner rather than later considering her deep and sudden hormonal reaction to him.

Shifting in her chair, she returned her attention to her plate, playing with her food in an attempt to get her rioting emotions under control. Not for the first time, she realized how truly foolish it was for her to have agreed to spend any more time alone with him than absolutely necessary.

Alexander—Alex—didn't seem to be suffering from any such second guesses, however.

"So…" he muttered casually, digging into his own perfectly roasted pheasant. "Tell me something about yourself. Were you born here in Portland? Did you grow up here? What about your family?"

All loaded questions, littered with pitfalls that could land her in very hot water. Without getting too detailed or giving away anything personal, she told him what she could, stretching the truth in some places and avoiding it altogether in others.

Before long, their plates were clean, their glasses of wine had been emptied and refilled at least once and they were chatting comfortably. More comfortably than Jessica ever would have expected. Almost like new friends. Or new ones, hoping to become even more….

Four

Reaching across the table, Alex topped off Jessica's glass before emptying the rest of the bottle into his own. He leaned back in his chair, watching her, letting the bouquet of the expensive wine fill his nostrils while his eyes took in every detail of the woman sitting before him.

He couldn't remember a time when he'd enjoyed a dinner more. So many of his meals were spent with business acquaintances, hammering out a new deal, discussing the aspects of a new publicity campaign or simply blowing smoke up someone's proverbial skirt in an effort to preserve continued goodwill. Even dinner with his family tended toward business talk over anything personal.

Jessica, however, was a breath of much-needed fresh air. Without a doubt she was a beautiful woman. It was hard to miss her streak of blue hair or the multiple piercings running along her ear lobes and right eyebrow, but rather than detracting from her attractiveness, they added a unique flare to her classic good looks.

She was also much smarter and more well-spoken than he would have expected from a hotel maid. Truth be told, he hadn't known what to expect from the evening after his completely impromptu invitation. But Jessica was turning out to be quite entertaining. Not only were her anecdotes amusing, but her warm, whiskey-soft voice was one he wouldn't mind hearing more of. For how long, he wasn't sure. The rest of the night might be nice. Possibly even in the morning over breakfast.

Jessica chuckled at whatever she'd just said—something he'd missed because he was preoccupied by the glossy pink of her bow-shaped mouth, the smooth half-moons of her neat but unmanicured nails and the soft bounce of her honey-blond curls. She tucked one of the shoulder-length strands behind her ear and licked those delectable lips, and Alex nearly shot straight up out of his chair. And while he managed—barely— to remain seated, other portions of his anatomy were beginning to inch their way north.

Knowing his behavior probably came across as bordering on strange, he shot to his feet, nearly tipping the heavy armchair over in the process. In the next instant he'd grabbed her hand and yanked her up, as well.

She made a small sound of surprised protest, but didn't resist. She did, however, dig in her heels and catch herself on the edge of the table just before she would have smacked straight into his chest.

Too bad; he would have liked to feel her pressed against him for a moment or two. Her warmth, her curves, the swell of her breasts.

When he'd walked into his suite to find her making his bed that first time, he'd caught a whiff of lemon and thought it came from whatever cleaning solutions she'd been using.

Now he realized the tangy scent had nothing to do with dusting or scrubbing. Instead, it came directly from her. From her shampoo or perfume, or maybe both. It was a peculiar blend of citrus and flowers that he'd never smelled before, but that seemed to suit her perfectly.

He took a deep breath to bring even more of the intoxicating fragrance into his lungs, then reached around her to pick up both glasses of wine.

"Come on," he invited, tipping his head toward the French doors and the balcony beyond.

He left her to follow—or not—but was pleased when she did. Even more pleased that it seemed to take her no time at all to decide. No sooner had he turned and started walking than she was on his heels.

Though Jessica had arrived while it was still light out, the sun had long ago slipped beyond the horizon, leaving the sky dark and star dappled. A slight breeze chilled the evening air, but nothing that required jackets or would hinder them from enjoying being outside for a while.

Moving to the stone balustrade, he set down the two glasses, then turned, leaning back on his rear and crossing his arms over his chest. As large as the Mountain View resort was, and as many guests as he was sure were in residence, the wide balcony that ran the entire length of his suite was completely private.

Tall, waffle-patterned trellises protected either side from the balconies beyond. He didn't know what the lodge did about them in the dead of winter, but at this time of year, they were covered with climbing flowering vines, creating a natural barrier to sound and sight.

When Jessica came close enough that he could have reached out and touched her, he uncrossed his arms and reached behind him instead. "Your wine," he offered in a low voice.

She took it, raising it to her mouth to sip. For long minutes neither of them said anything. Then she moved to the low chaise longue a few feet away and carefully lowered herself to its cushioned seat.

Her skirt rode up, flashing an extra couple of inches of smooth thigh. More than he'd been able to see while she'd cleaned his rooms in that frumpy gray uniform. A shame, too, since she had *amazing* legs. Long and sleek and deliciously toned.

He had the sudden urge to sit down next to her and run his hand along that silken length. Even through her stockings he wanted to feel the curve of her knee, the sensitive dip beneath, the line of her outer thigh and the perilous trail inside.

Alex sucked in a breath, his mouth gone suddenly dry.

When was the last time he'd been this attracted to a woman? Any woman?

He'd had affairs, certainly. A few relationships, even. At one time, he'd dated a woman long enough to consider marrying her. He hadn't loved her, not really, but it had seemed as if it might be the right thing to do. The most sensible next step, at any rate.

He was no stranger to lust, either. He'd been with women who'd caused it to flare hot and fast. But to the best of his recollection, he'd never been with a woman who stimulated his libido *and* his brain both at the same time.

Oh, it wasn't as though he and Jessica were waxing poetic about astrophysics or the effect of global warming on penguins in Antarctica. But that was just the point: he'd *had* those discussions—or similar ones, at least—with certain women without a single erotic nerve ending tingling to life. Just as he'd found himself burning with passion and rolling around on the sheets with others without a single intelligent thought passing between them.

And then there was Jessica Madison. Nearly anonymous

housekeeper at a resort he'd only decided to patronize a week and a half ago. If he'd booked a suite at the downtown Hilton instead, as had been his first inclination, he never would have bumped into her.

Damned if he wasn't glad they'd been booked up and someone had recommended Mountain View as a second choice. This dinner alone was worth every penny of the added expense and every extra mile it took to get into downtown Portland for his scheduled meetings.

Jessica wasn't just lovely to look at, but entertaining, too. Not only conversationally but in her silent self-assurance.

The hair and jewelry choices were the physical aspects of that, he supposed; a way to tell the world without words that she knew who she was and didn't care what anyone thought of her or how she lived her life. But whether she realized it or not, her body language conveyed the same message.

Once she'd spotted those crab cakes and decided she wanted them, it had been difficult to draw her attention away from the plate. And when he'd told her she could have them all to herself, she'd set about eating them as passionately as an artist struck by sudden creative inspiration.

No worries about how she'd looked or what he might think. Which wasn't to say she'd been a ravenous wolf about it. Her table manners had been flawless. But she'd enjoyed her meal the way he enjoyed a quick bout of neat, no-strings lovemaking.

And there it was. Sex. No matter where his mind started to wander when he got to thinking about this woman, it always seemed to circle right back around to *S-E-X*.

It didn't help that she was stretching now, lifting her legs onto the long seat of the chaise and leaning back until she was nearly sprawled out like a virgin sacrifice.

Blood pooled in his groin, heating, thrumming, creating a beat in his veins that matched the one in his brain. *Pa-dump*.

Pa-dump. Pa-dump. His heart, his pulse and his head kept the same rhythm, one that he could have sworn was saying, *Do it, do it, do it.*

He was very afraid "it" could be defined as something ill-advised. Like kissing her. Touching her. Taking her to bed.

Indulging in another sip of wine, Jessica let out a breathy sigh and crossed her legs—those damn tempting legs—at the ankle. She rested her arms on the armrests and her head back against the chaise.

"I'm sorry," she said. "I've been doing all the talking and not letting you get a word in edgewise."

Something he'd noticed, but certainly hadn't minded. He'd much rather listen to her speak than himself. On his best day he was a man of few words, and his only response now was to arch his brow and lift his own wine to his mouth for a drink.

"So…" she prompted. "Tell me about yourself. What do you do? Why are you in town? How long will you be staying at our fine establishment?"

"How long will you be making my bed and restocking my wet bar, you mean?" he retorted with a grin.

She chuckled, the sound filling the night air and doing nothing to quiet the pounding in his blood, his head, his gut.

"I don't stock the bars," she told him, returning his grin. "They don't trust us near the pricey liquor—because they're afraid we'll either steal it…or drink on the job."

He laughed at that. "I might be tempted to drink, too, if I had to clean up after strangers all day. Especially the kind who stay here. I imagine a lot of us come across as quite demanding and entitled."

She shrugged a shoulder. "It's not so bad. For one thing, I don't usually have to interact with you demanding, entitled types. Most of the time the rooms are empty when I clean, and I get to work alone. The pay could be better—and for rich people, you guys sure can cheap out when it comes to tipping—but I like my coworkers, and the view is stunning when I get the chance to stop and actually enjoy it."

He inclined his head. "Duly noted. In the future, I'll be sure to leave a generous tip anytime I stay out of town."

"Every morning before you leave your room," she clarified, "not just the day you check out. Shifts change, and the same maids don't always clean the same rooms every day."

As hard as he tried, he couldn't completely hold back the hint of a smile. She was a pretty good advocate for her fellow service workers.

"I'll remember that. Have my tips so far been acceptable?" he asked, half teasing, half genuinely curious of her opinion.

She slanted her head, thinking about it for a minute. Then she shrugged a shoulder. "You've been doing well enough. And tonight's dinner definitely makes up for any corners you may have cut."

"Glad to hear it," he drawled.

"You never answered my question," she said after a moment of silence passed. The only sounds in the growing darkness were the muted voices of guests far off in the distance, perhaps strolling along one of the lodge's moonlit paths, and the occasional chirp of crickets.

"Which one?"

"Any of them. All of them." She uncrossed her ankles only to cross them again the other way. "Just tell me something interesting so I won't feel like I monopolized the conversation tonight."

"All right," he replied. Pushing away from the stone barrier, he strode toward her, dragging the second chaise closer to hers one-handed and sitting down on the very end to face her.

"My family is in jewelry. Gems and design. Maybe you've heard of us—Bajoran Designs?"

Her eyes widened. "*You're* Bajoran Designs?"

"I'm one of the Bajorans of Bajoran Designs," he clarified. "As much as I might feel or wish otherwise at times, it
isn't a one-man operation."

"Wow. Your jewelry is amazing."

"You're familiar with it?"

"Isn't everybody?" she retorted. "Your ads are in all the
magazines, and on TV and billboards everywhere. Didn't you
design a bracelet for the Queen of England or something?"

"Again, *I* didn't, but our company did."

"Wow," she repeated. And then her head tilted to one side
and she raised a brow. Her lips curved. "I don't suppose you
have any free samples you'd like to share."

The sparkle in her eyes told him she was teasing, but he
wished suddenly that he had more than just a few proposed
design sketches with him. He wished he had a briefcase full
of priceless jewels surrounded by exquisite settings to re-
gale her with.

He would love to see her draped in emeralds and platinum
or diamonds and gold. Earrings, necklace, bracelet, perhaps
even a small tiara to tuck into those mostly blond curls.

He could think of any number of his companies' designs
that would look stunning with what she was wearing. But
he imagined that they'd look even better on her while she
was utterly naked.

Naked in his bed, her skin alabaster against dark sheets,
her hair falling loosely about her shoulders. And at her lobes,
her throat, her waist...maybe her ankle, too...*his* jewels, *his*
designs, in essence his *marks* lying cool on her warm, flushed
flesh.

The picture that filled his head was vibrant and erotic and
so real, he nearly reached out to touch her, fully expecting
to encounter nothing but the blessed nudity of a gorgeous
and waiting female.

Arousal smacked into him with the force of a freight train

late to its final destination. His fist closed on the wine in his hand, so tight he was surprised the glass didn't shatter. Every muscle in his body turned to iron, and that most important one—the one that desired her most of all—came to attention in a way that made its wishes clearly known.

Sweat broke out across Alex's brow and his lungs hitched with the effort to breathe. Jessica was still staring at him, the amusement at her teasing about the jewelry slowly seeping from her eyes as she realized he wasn't laughing.

She probably thought she'd insulted him. Or come across as a gold digger. The difference in their stations—her minimum wage chambermaid to his multimillionaire business tycoon—was patently obvious, and something he supposed she hadn't forgotten for a minute. Add to that the fact that he felt ready to explode, and he probably looked like Dr. Jekyll well on his way to becoming Mr. Hyde.

Forcing himself to loosen his grip on the wineglass, he concentrated on his breathing. *Relax,* he told himself. *Breathe in, breathe out. Don't scare her off before you have a chance to seduce her.*

And he was going to seduce her. He'd been attracted to her from the moment they'd first met, which, of course, meant he'd thought about sleeping with her about a thousand times since. But thinking about it and making a conscious decision to go through with it were two different things.

He hadn't realized until just this minute that he *was* going to make a move on her. He *was* going to kiss her and do his best to convince her to go to bed with him.

Pushing to his feet, he leaned across to set his wine on the wrought-iron table that had been between the two chaises. He locked his jaw and cursed himself when she jerked at his sudden movements. His only hope was that he hadn't frightened her so much that he couldn't smooth things over. Seducing a woman on the first date could be hard enough without adding "acted like a jackass" to the mix.

"Sorry," he said in a low voice, hoping the single word would be suitable as a blanket apology. And then in answer to her earlier question, "I don't have any samples. I'd need a 24/7 armed guard to carry that kind of merchandise around with me."

At his friendly tone, she seemed to relax. And when she did, he did.

"If you like, though, I can arrange a tour of our company. You can see how the pieces are put together, watch some gems being cut, maybe even catch a peek at a few designs that haven't been released yet. You'd have to come to Seattle, though. Think you can get the time off?"

If he'd expected her to be impressed, he was sorely disappointed. Her expression barely changed as her tongue darted out to lick her lips.

"That's all right," she said, instead of "Oh, wow, that would be awesome!" "I was just joking. I could never afford anything of yours, anyway. Better not to tempt myself."

It was on the tip of his tongue to tell her he'd gift her with a piece while she was there. He'd never done anything of the sort before, never even been tempted. Yet suddenly he didn't want to just imagine her covered in his family's fine jewelry, he wanted to literally cover her with it. Throw it at her feet like a humble servant making an offering to the gods. Diamonds, emeralds, opals, sapphires... Whatever she wanted. As much as she wanted.

He wasn't sure exactly when he'd become such a weak-kneed sycophant. He'd certainly never given women jewelry before; at least not easily or as willy-nilly as he was envisioning doing with Jessica.

To be honest, he wasn't sure he liked these feelings and the lack of control she seemed to evoke. It was the number one reason he thought he should probably call it a night and get as far away as possible from this woman.

That would be the smart thing to do, for certain.

So why didn't he?

Desire? Lust? Sheer stupidity?

But rather than thank her for coming and seeing her to the door, he held out his hand, indicating that she should give him her wineglass. When she did, he set it aside, then held out his hand again, this time inviting her to take it. He was equal parts surprised and relieved when she did so without a hint of reservation that he could detect.

Her fingers were cool and delicate. For a moment he savored the simple touch, not letting himself ruin it by imagining more just yet.

Then he gave her a tug, urging her to the edge of the chaise. A second tug pulled her to her feet.

She came into his arms as though she was tied to him and he was drawing on the string that bound them. Another step and she was pressed to his chest the way he'd wished she could be earlier.

Her blouse was silky against his palms and the front of his own dress shirt, her breasts rubbing just enough to give him ideas and get the blood pumping hot and thick to his groin once again. He held her there, enjoying the feel of her, stroking his hands up and down the line of her spine.

To his great delight she didn't pull away, but sank into him even more, her breath blowing out on a soft sigh.

With one hand at the small of her back, he brought the other up the length of her arm and the side of her throat until he cupped her jaw, his thumb brushing along the baby-soft curve of her cheek.

"I want to kiss you," he told her in a low, graveled voice, "but I'm afraid you'll think I'm moving too fast."

Afraid he was moving too fast and that he would scare her

off. Afraid that this overwhelming need he felt for her wasn't normal, wasn't the typical interest he felt when he was in the mood for a one-night stand.

"Did you notice my hair?" Jessica asked in little more than a murmur, reaching up to finger a few strands of blue.

His brows knit. What did her hair have to do with anything?

Still, he answered, "Yes."

"And my ears? My brow?" She flicked her wrist at both.

"Yes," he said again, more confused than ever.

"These are not the piercings and hairstyle choices of a girl who scares easily."

For a second, he didn't move, didn't dare breathe while her words sank in. Then a slow smile spread across his face.

"No," he murmured, even as his head lowered toward hers. "I guess they aren't."

Five

The minute Alex's lips touched hers, she was lost.

She knew this was a mistake. Everything was, from the moment she'd stepped into his suite tonight, to letting her guard down over wine and a moonlit stroll onto the secluded balcony. Maybe even before that, when she'd recognized him and not gone running, or when she'd agreed to her cousin's ridiculous scheme.

It hadn't been easy to sit still and pretend she didn't know who he was, but it *had* been somewhat enlightening to listen to him talk about himself and his business. Knowing what she did about him—namely that he'd stolen a portion of the company out from under her family—she would have expected him to be proud, arrogant, boastful.

Instead, he'd been humble, speaking highly of Bajoran Designs, but not taking any of the credit for the company's success for himself.

She thought that might have been when her head had

started to go fuzzy and stars had formed in her eyes. Her skin had been flushed with heat, too, but that was nothing new; that was just part of the attraction that had flared to life as soon as she'd walked into his arms.

She shouldn't be kissing him…or rather, allowing him to kiss her. It was a worse idea than agreeing to dinner with him, but she just couldn't seem to help herself.

The entire time they'd been talking, all she'd wanted was to cross the balcony and lay a hand on his chest. To see if it felt as hot and hard as it looked. And then to touch his mouth with her own to see if he tasted as delectable as she imagined.

The good news was, his chest *did* feel as hot and hard as she'd thought it would. Better, even, pressed up against her breasts and her belly.

And his lips were as delicious as she'd expected. Warm and soft but with a firmness that spoke of power and total self-confidence. He also tasted of the lush wine and food they'd shared earlier.

The *bad* news was that his chest felt exactly as she'd imagined, his mouth tasted even better, and instead of allaying her curiosity, it only made her want more.

With a groan she leaned farther into him, letting his heat and strong arms surround her, letting the passion sweep her away.

It was just a kiss, just one night, and he had no idea who she really was. What could it hurt to surrender to whatever this was igniting between them and just let go?

She didn't let her mind wander past that, didn't let her brain actually consider all the things that really could go wrong. She didn't want to think about it, didn't want to slow down—or worse, stop. For once she wanted to let go, be wild, be free and not worry about the consequences.

Besides, it wasn't as though anyone would ever find out. Erin would think she'd searched Alex's suite and come up with nothing, and Alex would think he'd gotten lucky with a near-anonymous hotel maid. No strings, no ties, no awkward morning after.

His mouth possessed her, but she certainly didn't mind. If anything, her moan, the melt of her body, her meeting his tongue swipe for swipe and thrust for thrust told him exactly how much she liked it.

Liked it? Loved it and was eager for more.

Not bothering to breathe—who needed oxygen?—Jessica wrapped her arms around Alex's neck, running her fingers through the hair at his nape and hanging on for dear life.

It was Alex's turn to groan. He hugged her tight and she felt his arousal standing proud, leaving no doubt that he was just as turned on as she was, just as carried away on this wave of uncontrollable lust.

Thank goodness. She would hate to be coiled in a haze of desire, only to discover he'd been after nothing more than a quick kiss.

But she needn't have worried. He was all but sucking her tonsils down his throat. And then his hands went to her waist, her hips, her thighs a second before he scooped her into his arms.

They broke apart, only because the change of position forced it, and it turned out people really did need oxygen eventually. They both gasped for breath as he carried her across the balcony and through the French doors, his long strides eating up the thickly carpeted floor all the way to the bedroom.

Once there, he set her on the end of the wide, king-size bed with more gentleness than she would have managed if their roles had been reversed. Standing over her, he stared into her eyes, his own crystal-blue ones blazing like hot ice.

With both hands, he cupped her face, tipping her head

back a fraction of an inch. Then he leaned in and kissed her softly, almost reverently.

Jessica's eyes slid closed, letting the sensation of his lips on hers wash over her, carrying her away.

A moment later, his mouth left her, but she felt his hands at her throat, his fingers trailing down the sides, over her collarbones and the slope of her chest. Goose bumps broke out on her skin as he grazed the insides of her breasts and started to unbutton her blouse.

She held her breath while he worked. This wasn't the first time a man had undressed her, but it was certainly the first time one had done it so slowly and had seemed to take such pleasure in the act. Either that or he was torturing her, but even the torture brought exquisite pleasure.

When he reached the last of the buttons, she straightened enough for him to tug the blouse from the waistband of her skirt. He flicked it over her shoulders and arms, then tossed it away completely.

Sitting there in her skirt and bra, Jessica suddenly realized she didn't have to be so passive. As much as she was enjoying his seductive treatment, she wanted to be in on the action. And, yes—if she was soon going to be naked in front of him, then she wanted to see him out of his clothes, too.

While he went for the zipper at the back of her skirt, she went for his belt buckle. He sucked air through his teeth, and she was delighted to see his nostrils flare, his jaw tic.

After undoing his belt, she got to work on his fly. She slid the tab down so slowly, each individual snick of the zipper's teeth echoed through the room. He was just as deliberate unzipping her skirt.

He pulled her to her feet by the elbows, tugging her against his chest again while he slipped the skirt past her hips. At the same time, he kicked off his shoes, letting her push his pants down so that both items of clothing fell to the floor together.

He set her back on the bed, then stepped out of the pants and kicked their clothes out of the way, unbuttoning his shirt and shrugging out of it all with urgent efficiency. Standing before her totally naked, Alex stared down at her with fire in his eyes and a set to his tall frame that told her without words that there was no turning back now. No escape.

As though she'd even want to. If she hadn't been sitting already, Jessica was pretty sure she would have melted into a steaming puddle on the floor. Her knees were jelly, her stomach doing somersaults worthy of an Olympic gold medal.

Her mouth felt as if it was filled with sand, and she licked her lips, swallowing in an attempt to bring some moisture back before the dehydration went to her head and sent her into a dead faint.

His gaze zeroed in on that tiny gesture, and she could have sworn she saw smoke spiraling out of his ears. He took a single, purposeful step toward her, bringing himself flush with the foot of the bed. Leaning in, he towered over her, fists flat on the mattress on either side of her hips.

"Scoot up," he told her in a low voice.

Even though her bones felt like rubber, she put her hands under her and did as he'd ordered, slowing moving back across the mattress toward the head of the bed. He followed her every inch of the way. Hovering over her, crawling with her, plucking the heels off her feet and pitching them over his shoulder as they went. She stopped when she reached the pillows, letting her head sink into one of the feather-stuffed cushions, still covered by the spread she'd tucked around them that morning.

"You're overdressed," Alex murmured a moment before he tucked his thumbs into the waistband of her barely there satin-and-lace panties and drew them down her legs. She helped him by kicking them off, then lifted up so he could unclasp and remove her bra.

For several long seconds he drank her in, his gaze so intense, she could hardly breathe. Just when she was about to hide her breasts self-consciously with her arms, Alex reached around her, loosening the bed's comforter and dragging it down, uncovering the pillows and sliding the slick fabric under her body until they were resting only on cool, freshly laundered sheets.

Once he was happy with the state of the bed, he lowered himself down on top of her. From chest to ankle he covered her like a blanket, the heat of his skin warming her and the hairs on his legs and chest tickling in all the right places.

He offered her a small, confident smile, and she couldn't resist rubbing against him, loving every single seductive sensation. Then she looped her arms around his shoulders and met him for a long, deep, soul-rattling kiss.

Alex ate at her mouth like he was enjoying their succulent dinner all over again. And she licked back as though she had moved on to the most decadent of desserts.

Alex's hands skimmed her body, up and down, all around, learning her shape and form and sweet spots. Her breasts swelled at his touch, and he rewarded them with added attention, squeezing, caressing, teasing until her nipples tightened into pebble-hard buds.

Tracing his mouth over her brows, her closed eyelids, the line of her jaw, he made his way down to suckle those pert tips, making her moan and wriggle beneath him.

She let her knees fall open, pulling him farther into the cradle of her thighs. He came more than willingly, settling against her, rubbing in all the right places.

Soon they were panting, writhing, clawing each other like wild animals. With a strangled groan, Alex grasped her waist, sitting back as he tugged her up to straddle his hips. Her arms tightened around him, her nails raking his skin.

The flats of his hands swept up either side of her spine,

sliding under her hair to cup the back of her skull. His fingers massaged, then dug in as he captured her mouth.

Long minutes ticked by while the only sounds in the room were their mingled breaths, their bodies moving together and the staccato interruption of deep growls and desperate moans.

Even though she was perched inches higher than Alex, he was definitely driving their passion. Which was fine, since he was really, *really* good at it. But she didn't want to be just a passenger on this bus, passively riding along wherever he decided to take them.

She wanted to *drive,* baby, and show him that a resort cleaning lady could blow his socks off just as easily as some silver-spoon socialite strumpet. Better, even, since she didn't give a flip about messing up her hair.

Bracing her legs on either side of him, she gripped his shoulders and pushed, toppling him backward and coming to rest over him with a satisfied smirk on her face. He returned her smile with a grin of his own, letting her know he was just as game for this position as any other.

"A take charge kind of woman," he said, running his hands along her torso until they cupped her breasts. His thumbs teased the undersides, coming just close enough to her nipples to make her bite her bottom lip in longing. "I like it."

Well, then, he should *love* her. She'd been taking charge of her life for as long as she could remember—to her parents' continued consternation. Even before it had become a necessity, Jessica had been more headstrong than was probably wise. Lord knew, it had gotten her into trouble on more than one occasion. She only hoped tonight wouldn't prove to be the biggest mistake of them all.

"So you're in charge," Alex told her, breaking into her fractured thoughts. His thumbs were growing bolder, finally brushing the very tips of her oversensitized breasts, causing them to grow almost painfully tight. "What's next?"

That pesky act-before-you-think gene had backfired on her again. Because her liberal, uninhibited streak seemed to have abandoned her, along with all the strength in her limbs. She no longer wanted to tower over him, but thought she would be better off sinking into the bedclothes in a pile of boneless flesh and nerve endings. That's what Alex's touch did to her—turned her to mindless, quivering mush.

But she needn't have worried. Alex might *say* he liked a strong-willed, take-charge woman—at least in bed—but he had no problem taking the reins when necessary. Abandoning her breasts, he splayed his palms at her waist and down her hips. Raising her slightly, he centered her over his burgeoning erection, brushing lightly between her folds with just the tip.

Jessica sucked in a breath, and Alex bared his teeth, nostrils flaring. Taking her hands, he wrapped them firmly around his hardened length. He was hot to the touch, soft velvet over tempered steel and throbbing beneath her fingers.

"Take me," he told her through gritted teeth. "Show me what you want, how you want it."

How could she resist? He was like a holiday buffet and she was a very hungry reveler.

Angling her hips just so, she brought him flush with her center. Then slowly…slowly, slowly, slowly…she sank down. Inch by inch he filled her, and the feeling was exquisite. To him, too, she guessed, judging by his long, low moan of satisfaction. His eyes fluttered closed, his hands clutched at her hips and beneath her rear, his thighs were as tense as iron beams.

She, however, was loose, almost liquid. Warmth spread through her veins, filled her belly, and surrounded him with moisture where they were connected. His body jerked, driving him higher inside of her, causing her internal muscles to spasm in response.

Though he was still breathing heavily, still holding himself gallantly in check, he smiled up at her, blue eyes flashing with devilish intent.

Oh, my. How had she resisted him for so long? Granted, their "relationship" had pretty much moved at the speed of light as it was. But gazing down at him now, knowing that he was not only movie-star handsome, but oozed sophistication and charm from every pore, she wondered how she hadn't fallen at his feet the very first day—first moment— they'd met. How every woman he came in contact with didn't simply drop to the nearest surface flat on her back like an upturned beetle.

That was the power he possessed—at least over her. He had the power not only to seduce her with barely a whisper, but wipe every ounce of sense straight out of her head.

What they were doing here tonight, in this room, in this bed, had nothing to do with good judgment and everything to do with pure, raw, primal instinct and desire.

Tossing her head from side to side, she shook her hair back over her shoulders and wriggled atop him to find just the right position. Alex growled, fingers digging into her flesh, and tensed even more between her thighs.

"Don't do that unless you're ready to relinquish control," he warned in something akin to a hiss, "because I'm about two seconds from rolling you over and finishing this, whether you like it or not."

A shiver rolled down her spine at his deep-throated threat. Oh, she suspected she would like that very much, indeed. She was tempted to say *yes, please* and let him do just that.

But staying in charge—at least for a while longer—was the only way she knew she'd be able to look herself in the mirror tomorrow. She wanted no doubts, no cracks in the story she might tell herself that would allow her to alter facts. She didn't want to wake up with enough doubts to convince herself that he'd taken advantage of her.

No, she wanted to be sure that if guilt was going to set in, it would rest squarely on her own shoulders. And that if anyone—especially anyone in her family, such as Erin—ever found out, she wouldn't give them further reason to paint Alexander Bajoran as a bad guy.

Running her tongue across her lip—slowly...from one side to the other...first the top...then the bottom—she watched his pupils dilate and his chest hitch with his ragged breathing.

"Poor baby," she murmured in her best sex kitten voice. "Am I being too rough on you?"

On the word *rough,* she flexed the inner walls of her feminine channel, squeezing him like a vise.

He moaned.

"Making this too...*hard?*"

She flexed again, this time coming up on her knees so that the friction, the rasping of their flesh drew sparks, sending currents of electricity outward to shock them both.

He groaned, snarled, muttered a colorful oath. And Jessica grinned at the knowledge that if their social circumstances were reversed—if they'd been doing this five years ago while her family still had control of their company—she could probably have gotten *him* to sign his company over to *her.*

That feeling of superiority, though, was short-lived. While he lifted off the bed and she continued to cant her hips back and forth in a slow, methodical motion, Alex reached for her breast again with one hand. To rub and squeeze and caress. He tweaked her nipples, making her shudder. Then, when it was her turn to let her eyes slide closed, he dropped his other hand between her legs and found the secret, swollen bud sure to send her spiraling out of control.

She moaned, biting her tongue until she thought she might draw blood, as ecstasy built to an almost unbearable pressure inside of her.

Alex stared at Jessica, fighting his own need to moan, possibly even whimper. Had he ever seen a woman so beautiful? Ever met anyone quite like Jessica Madison? He'd never gone to bed with one, of that he was certain.

He couldn't explain his overwhelming attraction to her, but he was sure as hell grateful for it—as well as her mutual enthusiasm. If she'd turned him down out there on the balcony, walked away after only a single too-brief kiss, he suspected he'd have spent the rest of the night taking out his frustrations by trying to punch a hole in one of the suite's walls with his forehead.

But she hadn't turned him down. She'd turned him *on,* then stuck around to do something about it.

Her skin was alabaster silk, running like water under his fingertips. Her mouth was equally soft: warm and inviting and sweeter than anything he'd ever tasted.

And the rest of her… He didn't think words had yet been invented to describe the rest of her. How she moved with him and around him. How she welcomed him and made him want to cherish her and ravish her both at the same time. How her hazel eyes turned dark and liquid when she looked at him. They were so wide and inviting, he thought he could drown in them without a single regret.

Those weren't exactly the thoughts he wanted to be thinking about a one-night stand, but they were there all the same.

And then he couldn't think at all because she was moving on him like sin itself. Long, sure strokes that drove him deeper. Made his jaw lock and his eyes roll back in his head.

He clutched her hips tight enough to leave bruises and had to make a concerted effort to loosen his hold before he did. Not that Jessica seemed to notice. Her straight white teeth were locked on her lower lip…her lashes trembled like butterfly wings as she struggled to keep her eyes open while passion coaxed them closed…and her pace never faltered as she undulated above him.

His own hips rose and fell with her movements, meeting her stroke for stroke, thrusting as deeply as possible and trying for more. Her hands flexed and curled on his chest until her nails dug into the muscles like claws and then released as she reached up to cup her breasts.

The sight of those slender fingers with their neatly trimmed but unmanicured nails curving over her soft, cushiony flesh, touching herself, bringing herself added pleasure, nearly sent him over the edge. Then she tweaked her nipples, arched her spine, and threw her head back on a rich-as-hundred-year-old-scotch moan, and he knew he was a goner.

In one sharp, fast motion, he flipped her to her back, drawing a yelp of surprise from those pink, swollen, delectable lips. Rising over her, he shifted her legs to his waist, encouraged when she linked them together at the base of his spine, heels digging in.

"Hold on, sweetheart." The endearment slipped past his lips before he could stop it, but he couldn't say he regretted it, not when her grip tightened around him, both inside and out.

"Yes," she gasped when he began to pound into her. Long, sure strokes, as deep as he could go to bring them both to the keenest, highest peak of satisfaction.

He moved faster, thrusting in time with her rapid-fire murmurs of *yesyesyesyesyes* until the world tilted, an invisible surf crashed in his ears and everything washed away to nothing except the woman beneath him and the startling, intense, overwhelming pleasure rocketing through him like a meteor crashing to earth.

When he came down, Jessica was breathing rapidly against him, her body splayed on the mattress in proverbial rag-doll fashion.

Well, wasn't he a heel. He'd enjoyed himself to the nth degree, but hadn't bothered to make sure she'd reached her completion first. So much for being a gentleman.

Then she lifted her gaze to his, arms going around his neck while her fingers combed through his hair near the nape. And she smiled.

"Better than dessert," she said just above a whisper.

Blowing out a relieved breath, he returned her grin before leaning in for a soft, lingering kiss. "Who says we can't have both?"

Six

Jessica had been right about the resort's desserts—they were delicious.

So how scary was it that she hadn't enjoyed that indulgence nearly as much as getting naked and rolling around with Alex?

Three times.

After that first amazing encounter, they'd only made it to the bathroom for a quick potty break before somehow ending up back in bed, getting sweaty all over again.

An hour after that, Alex had regained enough strength to reach for the phone and call for room service. She'd told him it wasn't necessary, that she wasn't even particularly hungry anymore. At least not for food.

But he'd insisted. The dishes had been preordered, so the kitchen was simply waiting for his call to send them up. Besides, he'd said, no dinner date was complete without dessert.

She thought heart-stopping, pulse-pounding, coma-inducing sex probably qualified as a decent substitute.

The fruits and pastries, crèmes and sauces that he'd spooned and then hand-fed her had been pretty yummy, too, though. She'd especially enjoyed the bits he'd eaten off her bare skin, and then let her lick off his.

Which had led to that third and final incredible experience that had started on the sitting room sofa…and somehow ended on the very desk she'd snooped through earlier.

Afterward he'd picked her up and carried her back to bed. Good thing, since she'd been doing her best impression of a jellyfish by that point.

She'd drifted off, tucked snuggly against Alex's solid warmth, his strong arm holding her close. And for a while she'd let herself pretend.

That it meant something.

That what they'd shared had a longer shelf life than expired milk.

That she wasn't deceiving him and he hadn't ruined her family.

But all too soon she came awake, reality slapping her hard across the face. Careful not to disturb him, she'd slipped from the bed, from his arms, and gathered her clothes, dressing as quickly and quietly as possible.

Tiptoeing from the bedroom, she moved through the sitting room, praying she could find her purse and get out before Alex noticed she was missing. Then she saw his briefcase, lying open on the coffee table. Frozen midstride, she stood staring at it, battling with herself over what to do next.

Should she turn around and leave, as she'd planned, ignoring the blatant invitation to snoop just a little more? Or should she peek, check to see if there was anything even remotely incriminating inside?

She felt like a dieter standing over a plate of fresh-baked chocolate chip cookies. Tempted. So very tempted.

With a quick glance toward the open bedroom door, she decided to risk it. Rushing forward, she put her clutch down beside the case and started riffling through the papers and manila folders.

It was too dark to see much, her eyes adjusting as best they could to the bit of moonlight shining through the French doors leading to the balcony.

As far as she could tell, it was more of what she'd found in the nightstand. Interoffice memos, contract notations, design sketches. Nothing worthy of fueling Erin's proposed plan of corporate espionage.

Then, at the very bottom of the case, she spotted one final packet. Not a plain manila folder, but a darker manila envelope stamped with giant red block letters she couldn't have missed, even if the room had been pitch-black: CONFIDENTIAL

Jessica's heart stopped. It was sealed. Well, tied closed with a thin red string, at least. But it was obviously private, not meant to be viewed by anyone but Alex and other authorized Bajoran Designs personnel.

Sparing another glimpse toward the bedroom, she took a deep breath and hurried to untie the stringed closure.

She didn't know what she'd been expecting...a treasure map or stack of secret security codes, maybe. Or maybe that was just her vivid imagination, replaying various scenes from her favorite action-adventure movies in her head while she pretended to be a poor man's Indiana Jones.

But what she found was no more surprising than anything else she'd stumbled upon so far. A stack of papers labeled Proposed Princess Line, with sketches of a dozen or so fresh designs included. They were for earrings, necklaces and rings, all in matching sets with similar design elements.

Obviously these were suggested pieces for a new line Bajoran Designs intended to launch in the near future. Likely a multimillion-dollar business venture.

Jessica couldn't have said what possessed her, but before she even realized what she was doing, she set the envelope under her clutch and replaced the other papers and folders inside the briefcase, making sure to leave it open exactly as she'd found it.

She was tired and maybe not thinking straight. But she would take the proposed designs with her to study more carefully in the safety of her apartment, and decide then whether or not to show them to her cousin.

With luck she could sneak them back into Alex's briefcase in the morning when she cleaned his room, long before he even noticed they were gone.

Pushing to her feet, she grabbed her purse and the envelope and rushed to the door, careful not to make a sound as she slipped out of Alex's suite, leaving him sleeping peacefully and hopefully none the wiser.

Seven

One Year Later

Alexander made his way down the hall toward his office with his nose buried in the company's latest financials. Not bad for a year when the country's economy was pretty much in the toilet, but he suspected they would have done better if someone else hadn't gotten the scoop on their Princess Line.

A deep scowl marred his brow. It had taken him a while to figure out, but now he knew exactly who was responsible for that little betrayal, too.

He was digging into his anger, mentally working up a good head of steam, when a peculiar sound caught his attention. Pausing midstride, he tilted his head to listen. Heard it again.

The unfamiliar noise seemed to be coming from the conference room he'd just passed. Backing up a few steps, he glanced through the open doorway.

His arms, along with the papers he was holding, fell to his sides. He blinked. Shook his head and blinked again.

He knew what he was seeing, and yet there was a part of his brain that refused to function, that told him it couldn't be what he thought it was. Obviously he was imagining things… but did illusions usually come with full surround sound?

The noise he'd heard earlier came again. This time he identified it easily, mainly because the source of that sound was sitting right in front of him.

In the center of the long conference table that was normally filled with high-ranking Bajoran Designs' employees sat a white plastic crescent-shaped carrier. And in the carrier, lined with bright material covered in Noah's ark cartoon animals, sat a baby.

A baby.

In his boardroom.

While the child continued to kick his legs and coo, Alex double-checked to be sure the room was empty. It was. No mother or father or grandparent or nanny in sight.

Stepping out of the room, he looked in both directions up and down the hall. It was completely deserted.

Since this was the floor where his office was located, it tended to be quiet and not heavily trafficked. Just the way he liked it. The majority of Bajoran Designs' employees were stationed on other floors of the building.

But that didn't mean someone wasn't visiting, child in tow. He couldn't say he thought much of their parenting skills, considering they'd left what looked to be their months-old infant completely unattended on a tabletop.

"Rose!" he shouted down the hall toward his personal assistant's workstation. He couldn't see her from where he was standing, but knew she would be there. She always was. "Rose!"

"Where's the fire?" she asked in an exasperated voice, coming into sight as she headed his way.

He ignored her tone. Having worked together for years, they knew each other better than some husbands and wives. He might be demanding and short-tempered at times, but Rose was twenty years his senior and only let him get away with so much before putting her foot down.

Rather than responding to her question, he pointed a finger and asked one of his own. "What is *that?*"

Rose paused beside him in the doorway, blinked once and said, "It's a baby."

"I *know* it's a baby," he snapped. "What is it *doing* here?"

"Well, how should I know?" Rose replied, equally short. "*I* didn't put it there."

A beat passed while Alex ground his teeth and struggled to get his growing outrage under control.

This was getting him nowhere. His secretary might be a woman, but she apparently wasn't teeming with maternal instincts.

Fine. He would handle the situation himself.

Stalking forward, he turned the baby carrier slightly to face the child head-on. Cute kid. Alex couldn't say he—or she—was any more or less cute than any other baby he'd ever seen, but then, he didn't pay much attention to children one way or another. They were—in his opinion—smelly, drippy, noisy things, and he didn't know why anybody would want or purposely set out to have one of their own.

Which still didn't explain why somebody had left *this one* in his conference room.

The baby smiled and blew a tiny spit bubble as it kicked its feet, sending the carrier rocking slightly. That's when Alex noticed the piece of paper tucked beneath the safety strap holding the infant in place.

Careful not to touch the baby any more than necessary, he removed the paper, unfolded it and read.

Alex—
I know this will come as a shock, but Henry is your son. I'm sorry I didn't tell you about him before now, but please don't hold that against him.

As much as I love him, I can't keep him with me any longer. He deserves so much more than I can offer right now.

Please take care of him. And no matter how you feel about me, please tell him that I love him very much and never would have left him if I'd had a choice.

It was signed simply "Jessica."

Jessica. Madison? Mountain View Jessica Madison?

The timing was right, he would admit that much. And he hadn't forgotten a single thing about their encounter, despite the year that had passed since she'd sneaked out of his hotel room—his bed—in the middle of the night.

A muscle ticked in his jaw as he clamped his teeth together more tightly than nine out of ten dentists would probably recommend.

She'd left without a word, which was bad enough. But it wasn't until later, much later, that he'd discovered the proposed designs for his company's Princess Line were also missing.

It hadn't taken more than three seconds for him to realize she'd taken them. That she'd apparently been some kind of spy, either sent by a competing corporation or come on her own to ferret out Bajoran Designs secrets.

And she'd found herself a doozy, hadn't she? He might be CEO of the family business, but it had been none too comfortable standing in front of the Board of Directors and explaining that he'd lost the Princess Line prospectus. Not just lost them, but had them stolen out from under him by what he could only assume was the competition.

Not that he'd told them the whole truth. He hadn't wanted to admit that he'd let himself be seduced and then robbed. He'd also hoped to get to the bottom of the theft on his own before coming totally clean. Which is why he'd talked them out of taking legal action or filing an insurance claim.

But he'd seethed for months. And though no one had said anything to his face—no one would dare, unless they had a death wish as well as a desire to be on the unemployment line—he knew he'd lost a certain amount of respect from his colleagues.

He wasn't sure which bothered him more—that, the loss of revenue for the company or his apparent gullibility at the hands of a beautiful woman.

Now, just when he'd finally begun to get his impromptu affair with Jessica the Chambermaid-slash-Evil Seductress out of his system and memory banks enough to focus more fully on the theft itself, here she was again. Popping into his life and claiming he'd fathered her child.

Not a single fiber of his being told him he could believe the note in his hand. If it was even from Jessica…or the woman he'd known as Jessica. After all, he had no proof that was her real name. Or that she'd actually written this letter…or that this was really her child…or that this was really *his* child.

Even so, he found himself studying the infant's features. Was there any hint of himself there? Any hint of Jessica?

"Call security," he told Rose without bothering to look in her direction. "Tell them to search the building for anyone who doesn't belong—especially a lone woman."

A lone woman with a streak of wild blue in her blond hair and eyes the color of smoky quartz. He thought the words, but didn't speak them.

"I also want to see the video footage from this floor."

Wrapping his fingers firmly around the handle of the carrier, he lifted the child off the table and marched away, certain his orders would be followed to the letter.

"I'll be in my office."

What the *hell* was he supposed to do with a baby?

At the moment, he was pacing a hole in the carpet of his home office, bouncing the squealing, squalling infant against his chest and shoulder. He still wasn't convinced this was his son, but the evidence certainly did point in that direction.

Security had searched Bajoran Designs' entire building—including the floors and offices that had no affiliation with the company. Nothing.

Then they'd reviewed the security tapes from Alex's floor, as well as the building's main entrance. Sure enough, there had been a woman who rang all kinds of bells and whistles for him.

She'd been wearing sunglasses and a knit cap pulled down over her ears, the collar of her denim jacket flipped up to cover as much of her features as possible. But her attempts at anonymity couldn't conceal the blond curls peeking out from beneath the cap, the high cheekbones holding up the shades or those lips that reminded him of sinful, delightful things better shared in the dark of night.

So while he couldn't say with one hundred percent certainty that the woman on the security tapes—toting a baby carrier on the way in but not on the way out—was the Jessica he knew from Mountain View Lodge, it was sure as hell looking that way. Which meant this *could* be his child.

According to Rose's best nonmaternal guess, she pegged the infant to be three or four months old. And given that he'd spent the night with the child's alleged mother a year ago… Yeah, the timing was more right than he cared to contemplate.

The question was: What did he do now?

Rose had been no help whatsoever. She'd told him to get himself some diapers and formula, and then take the baby out of the office because his coos—which were headed much more toward fussing by that point—were getting on her nerves.

Not having a better game plan, he'd done just that. Called his driver and ordered him to stop at the nearest grocery store on the way home.

Normally, he'd have sent his housekeeper out for baby supplies—and he probably still would. But at that very moment, he'd somehow known that he shouldn't wait much longer to have food for this kid's belly and clean Pampers on his bottom. Babies, he was quickly learning, were both demanding and smelled none too fresh after a while.

Thank God a clerk had come to his aid and pointed out a dozen items she insisted he couldn't do without. He'd been in no position to argue, so he'd bought them all.

No matter how rich he was, however, he learned the hard way that he couldn't snap his fingers and get a nanny to appear on his doorstep within the hour. He'd tried—asked Mrs. Sheppard to call every nanny placement agency in the city and offer whatever it took to have someone at his estate that night. She'd run into nothing but one stone wall after another.

No one was available on such short notice, and even if they had been, the agencies insisted he had to go through the official hiring process, which included filling out applications and running credit and background checks. He'd gotten on the phone himself and tried to throw his weight around in a way he rarely did, but suspected that had simply bumped him to the bottom of their waiting lists.

In a growing series of things that were just not going in

his favor today, it turned out Mrs. Sheppard was no more maternal than Rose. The minute she'd spotted him walking through the door carrying a whimpering child, she'd scowled like a storm cloud and firmly informed him with more than a hint of her usual Irish lilt that she "didna do babies," hadn't signed on to care for children and wasn't paid well enough to start now.

He *paid* her well enough to care for every child who passed through the gates of Disneyland on a daily basis, but understood her point. Until today he "didn't do babies," either.

Maybe that's why all of the people in his employ were less willing to volunteer for child-care duty than he was. Having an aversion to infants himself, he'd apparently hired staff who felt the same.

Which had worked perfectly well up to now. Suddenly, though, he wished he'd surrounded himself with more of the ticking-biological-clock types. A few women who couldn't wait to take a crying baby off his hands and work whatever natural magic they possessed to restore peace and quiet to his universe.

Before running out for a few more things he thought he might need before morning, Mrs. Sheppard had at least helped him stumble his way through his first diaper change and bottle preparation. He'd gotten the baby—Henry...the child's name was Henry, so he'd better start remembering it—fed and thought he was in the clear.

Still in the little rocking seat with the handle that made for easier toting around, the baby had started to drift off, eyes growing heavy as his tiny mouth tugged at the bottle's nipple like...well, like something he had no business thinking in the presence of an infant. Especially if that infant turned out to be his son and the image in his head was of the child's mother.

And then, just a few minutes after he'd emptied the bottle of formula, Baby Henry had jerked awake and started screaming at the top of his lungs. Alex had rocked the baby seat…shushed him in a voice he'd never used before in his life…and tried every trick he could think of—which weren't many, he was frustrated to realize.

Finally, having run out of options, he'd lifted the child from the padded seat and tucked him against his chest.

Surprised by his own actions, he'd begun patting the baby's back and bouncing slightly as he crossed the room. Back and forth, back and forth, back and forth in an effort to soothe the bawling child.

He didn't know where any of this came from, but it seemed the natural thing to do. Not that it was working. The baby was sobbing so hard, his little chest was heaving and his breaths were coming in hiccuping gasps.

If this lasted much longer, Alex was going to dial 9-1-1. It was the only option he could think of, given that he had no nanny and no personal knowledge of child rearing. Especially if it meant the difference between being thought a fool for overreacting or letting the poor kid suffocate on his own tears.

He was headed for the phone, intent on doing just that, when the doorbell rang. Halting in his tracks, he took a second to wonder who it could be at this hour—he wasn't expecting anyone except Mrs. Sheppard, and she had her own key—before Henry gave another hitching sob, driving him to action. Whoever it was, he hoped to hell they knew something, *anything* about babies.

Please, God, let this be Mary Poppins, he thought as he stalked out of his office and across the gleaming parquet foyer.

Yanking the door open, he jerked to a stop, shock reverberating through his system.

The person standing on the other side of the threshold was better than Mary Poppins…it was the baby's mother.

Jessica.

Eight

Jessica's heart was pounding like the bass of a hard rock ballad in her chest, tears pouring down her face. Coming here hadn't been part of the plan. And the last thing she'd intended was to knock on the front door.

But she couldn't stand it anymore. Henry's sobs were tearing her apart, causing a deep, throbbing physical pain that couldn't be ignored one second longer.

She'd been crying since she'd sneaked into Alex's office and left her sweet little baby on his boardroom table. No choice, nowhere else to turn.

She'd done everything she could on her own, and finally realized that turning Henry over to his father was the only option left unless she wanted to raise her child in a homeless shelter.

But doing the right thing, the *only* thing, didn't mean she could just walk away. She'd left Henry with a note for Alex to discover, praying he would believe her words and accept the baby as his son. That he would love and care for him the way their son deserved.

Then she'd sneaked back out of the building, but had stood across the street, waiting and watching. And crying. Crying so hard, she'd been afraid of attracting unwanted attention.

When she'd spotted Alex coming out of the building to meet his car at the curb, baby carrier balanced at his hip, her pulse had spiked. She'd taken it as a good sign, though, that he'd had the baby with him. And that he hadn't called the police to turn her in as an unfit mother, as well as for child abandonment.

She hadn't known where he was going, though, and suddenly she'd *needed* to know. Not that she could afford to hail a cab, and she'd sold her own car months ago.

With no other options, she'd taken a chance, using public transportation, then walking the rest of the way to Alex's estate. A gorgeous, sprawling sandstone mansion on fifteen private, perfectly landscaped acres in an area she was well familiar with from her own time living in Seattle.

It was also gated, but she'd lucked out—huffing and puffing from the uphill climb, she'd reached the entrance to Alex's property just as someone else had been leaving. The car had pulled out, turning onto the main road, and Jessica had slipped through the iron gate as it was slowly swinging closed.

Then she'd rounded the house, looking in every window she could reach until she'd spotted Alex and Henry. Heart in her throat, she'd used a less-than-sturdy hedge as a stepping stool, standing on tiptoe to watch. Just…watch.

She'd wanted so badly to go inside and hold her baby. To take him back and tell Alex it had all been a horrible mistake. But even if she had…even if it *was*…her circumstances would be exactly the same.

No choice. She had no choice.

It was when Henry had started crying—sobbing, really—and had refused to be calmed, that she couldn't stand it any longer. She wanted her baby, and he obviously needed her.

So here she stood, face-to-face with the one man she'd had no intention of ever being face-to-face with again.

She didn't know what to say to him, so she didn't mince words. "Give him to me," she said, plucking the baby out of his grasp.

She wasn't the least bit familiar with the layout of the house, but she didn't particularly care. Moving across the foyer, she headed in the direction she thought would take her to Alex's spacious office den. The one she'd been hiding outside of for the past half hour, spying on her child and ex-lover.

Pulling off her knit cap and shrugging out of her jacket—one arm at a time while balancing Henry in the other—she tossed them aside, bringing the baby even closer to her chest, tucking him in and crooning. From the moment he heard her voice, he began to relax.

It took what seemed like forever for his cries to die down, but she continued to sway, hum, pat him on the back. She whispered in his ear, telling him in a low, singsong voice how much she loved him, how sorry she was for leaving, and that everything would be okay. She wasn't sure she believed it, but she promised all the same.

A long time later, his tiny body stopped shuddering and she knew he was sleeping, his face turned in to her neck, his warm breath fanning her skin.

It was the most amazing sensation, one she hadn't thought she'd get to experience again anytime soon…if ever. Her own chest grew tight, moisture gathering behind her closed eyelids.

As much as she was trying to absorb every precious moment, she knew she was also stalling. Because Alex was standing behind her. Watching and waiting and likely fuming with fury.

She couldn't hide behind the baby forever, though. Time to pay the piper.

On a sigh, followed by a deep, fortifying breath, Jessica turned.

She'd been right. Alex was standing only a few feet away, arms crossed, blue eyes as cold as a glacier glaring at her. That look cut through her, chilling her to the bone.

Swallowing hard, she kept her voice low to avoid waking the baby, hoping Alex would take the hint and do the same.

"I'm sorry," she told him. "I shouldn't have abandoned him like that."

Abandoned. God, that made her sound like such a bad mother. But it was the truth, wasn't it?

She expected him to jump on that, throw all kinds of nasty accusations at her—though in a subdued tone, she hoped.

Instead, he pinned her in place with a sharp, angry stare. "Is he mine?"

"Yes," she answered simply. Honestly. "His middle name is Alexander, for you. Henry was my grandfather's name."

Without responding to that bit of information, he asked, "Are you willing to take a blood test to prove it?"

It hurt to have him ask, but she wasn't surprised. She'd lied to him—so many times, about so much…things he didn't even know about yet, let alone the things he did.

"Yes," she murmured again.

That seemed to give him pause. Had he expected her to refuse?

She wasn't exactly perched soundly on the higher ground, here. She had no room to complain and no right to be offended. If there were hoops he wanted her to jump through, and punishments he wanted to dole out, she had no choice but to acquiesce.

"I'll make an appointment first thing in the morning."

She nodded, though she knew he neither needed nor was waiting for her to agree.

"You'll stay here tonight," he continued, his tone brooking no argument. "In fact, you'll stay here until I know what's going on and have decided what to do about it."

As uncomfortable a prospect as that was, she was oddly okay with it. It wasn't as if she had anywhere else to go. Even after leaving Henry at Alex's office, her only plan had been to look for work here in Seattle or catch a bus back to Portland and try to find something there, but she suspected she probably would have ended up sleeping in the bus terminal instead. Provided Alex didn't intend to lock her in a dungeon somewhere in this giant house of his, it might be nice to sleep in a real bed for a change.

When she offered no resistance to his demands, he tipped his head and moved toward the door. "Follow me." He didn't look back, assuming—or rather, *knowing*—she would do exactly as he said.

Still holding a sleeping Henry, she trailed him out of the office, across the cavernous foyer and up a wide, carpeted stairwell to the second floor. He led her down a long hallway lined with what she could only assume was priceless artwork and credenzas topped with fresh-cut flowers in crystal and Ming-style vases.

Stopping suddenly, he pushed open one of the doors and stood aside for her to pass. It was a beautiful, professionally decorated guest room, complete with queen-size four-poster canopy bed and private bath. Done in varying shades of sage-green, it was unisex; not too masculine or too feminine.

"If you try to leave," Alex said from behind her, "I'll stop you. If you try to take my child from me—if he really is my child—I'll have both the police and my attorneys on you faster than you can blink."

She had no doubt he was rich enough, powerful enough and bitter enough to carry through with the threat. While she was broke, powerless and too exhausted to walk much farther, let alone attempt to run away.

Turning to face him, she continued to rub the baby's back. "I'm not going anywhere, Alex. I handled this badly, and for that, I apologize. This isn't how you should have found out you're a father. So whatever you need me to do...within reason," she added with a raised brow, "well, I figure I owe you one."

His raised brow told her he thought she owed him more than just one. And maybe he was right. But her response seemed to reassure him. Some of the tension went out of his shoulders and the lines bracketing his mouth lessened a fraction.

"Tell me what you need for him."

His eyes darted to Henry and she *thought* she saw a hint of softness there. Although she might have imagined it.

She had next to nothing. By the time she'd decided leaving Henry with Alex was her last resort, she'd been out of formula and down to her last diaper. If she hadn't, she probably wouldn't have been able to go through with it.

She could have gone to her parents, but that was still a can of worms she was trying to avoid opening. And the guilt of not alerting Alex to the fact that he was a father had started to eat at her, so she'd decided that he was a better "last resort."

"Everything," she said dejectedly.

"Make a list," he told her. "My housekeeper is picking up a few things right now. I'll try to catch her and have her get whatever else you need while she's out."

Jessica nodded, expecting him to go...unless he intended to pull up a chair and stand guard at the door all night. Instead, he remained rooted to the spot, his features drawn in contemplation.

"Will this be all right for him?" he finally asked. His arms swept out to encompass the room. "I don't have a crib or anything else...nursery-ish."

She offered a small smile. As angry as he was, he was still concerned about his son's safety and comfort. She found that endearing. And it gave her hope that his resentment would one day give way to understanding.

"We'll be fine," she assured him. "Henry can sleep in the bed with me, and I'll use pillows around the edges to keep him from rolling off."

He considered that for a moment, then said, "I'll make arrangements for someone to come by tomorrow and baby proof the place. Make a list for that, too—whatever you and Henry will need for an extended stay, and whatever needs to be done to keep him safe."

She wasn't sure what he meant by that. How *extended* a stay did he have in mind?

But now wasn't the time to question him. She was on thin enough ice as it was.

"We still have to talk," he informed her. "But you look tired, and I know he is. It can wait until tomorrow."

With that, he turned on his heel and walked out, closing the door behind him.

Jessica let out a breath, wishing it was one of relief. Instead, it was only...a short reprieve. As she set about readying the room, herself and the baby for bed, she felt as though a noose was hanging over her head.

Because as bad as today had been...tomorrow promised to be even worse.

Jessica didn't know what time it was when she finally came awake the next morning. Henry had had her up a few times during the night, needing to be changed or fed or simply lulled back to sleep. But she suspected yesterday's stress level had impacted him, as well, because he'd slept like a stone the rest of the time.

Stretching, she glanced beside her to find him awake and smiling around the pacifier in his mouth. His legs were kicking, and when he saw her looking down at him, he waved his arms, too.

"Good morning, sweetheart," she greeted him, unable to resist leaning over and kissing his soft cheek. He made a happy sound from deep in his belly, and she took a minute to blow raspberries on his tummy through his thin cotton T-shirt until he giggled.

Laughing in return, she scooped him up and finally looked at the clock. Ten-thirty. Later than she normally woke, but not quite as late as she'd expected, given the bright sunlight peeking through the drawn floor-to-ceiling curtains. As she started moving around, using the restroom and changing the baby, she heard noises from outside the bedroom door.

Last night, before she'd gone to bed, Alex's housekeeper had arrived with several large fabric totes bulging with baby items. Formula, bottles, pacifiers, toys, onesies, baby lotion, baby shampoo, baby powder…everything. More than Jessica would need to get through just the next few days. And now it sounded as though Alex had a construction crew in the house, building a nursery—or possibly an entire day care center—to his exact specifications.

With Henry at her hip, she opened the door only to find the hallway filled with oversize boxes and shopping bags. She stood rooted to the spot for a minute, stunned and confused.

Noises were coming from next door, and before she could decide which direction to turn—left toward the sounds of the pounding or right toward the stairs—Alex appeared. He strolled down the hall with two men on his heels who were carrying a large, flat cardboard box between them.

"In there," Alex instructed, pointing to the room where all

the building noises were coming from. He waited for them to pass, then waved her ahead of him.

They paused in the doorway of the room beside hers, where several men were busy putting furniture together and attaching shelving to the walls.

"What's all this?" she asked, though she could certainly guess. The half-assembled crib and changing table in the corner were dead giveaways.

"I'm putting a nursery in between our two rooms. That way we'll both be close to the baby in case he needs us during the night."

Jessica swallowed, not quite sure how to respond. Should she be more concerned that Alex's room was apparently only two doors down from where she'd spent last night…or that he seemed to believe she and Henry would be here long enough for a separate nursery to be necessary?

She owed him answers, and, of course, knew that he would want to spend time with his son now that he was aware of Henry's existence, but that didn't mean she—or the baby— were going to stick around forever.

Before she could decide how to respond, he continued.

"I've called Practically Perfect Au Pairs, the premiere nanny agency in the city. They'll be sending potential nannies out over the next few days to be interviewed. You can be there, if you like."

This time she wasn't at a loss for words. Her spine went straight and tight as outrage coursed through her system.

"Henry doesn't *need* a nanny. I'm his mother. I can care for him just fine by myself."

"As evidenced by the fact that you left him in the boardroom of my office building, with a note begging me to take him in," he replied, deadpan.

Jessica's chest squeezed. He was right, and they both knew it. But she'd changed her mind. She was here now, and damned if she'd let him foist her child off on some complete stranger.

"That was yesterday," she told him. "Today, I'm perfectly capable of watching out for my own child. I don't *need* a nanny," she stressed again.

She expected an argument. Worse, she expected him to toss more "unfit mother" accusations at her. Instead, he shrugged one shoulder encased in the fine silk-wool blend of a tailored dark blue suit.

"Humor me," he said in a tone that could only be described as wholly polite. "This is all rather new to me, and I'd feel better having a trained professional on hand for those times when you or I can't be with Henry."

Again the thought crossed her mind that she probably wouldn't be staying with him for long. Certainly not long enough to hire extra staff.

But what she asked him was, "Why wouldn't I be with him?" Her back was still stiff as a rod, her voice carrying more than a hint of wariness.

"We have a lot of ground to cover. You may need a nap after the grilling I plan to give you."

Her eyes widened at that, and suspicion gave way to fear.

"You missed breakfast," he added, jumping so easily from one topic to another that her head started to spin. "But I'm sure Mrs. Sheppard can see that you're fed."

"Oh, that's all right. I don't want to be a both—"

Alex took her elbow, forcibly turning her toward the other end of the house and leading her in that direction.

"Feed the baby," he told her. "Then get yourself something to eat. After that, we'll talk."

He said "we'll talk," but what Jessica heard was, "Let the inquisition begin."

Nine

Alex thought he deserved a damn Academy Award for his performance so far. Every second that he'd been with Jessica, he'd wanted to shake her. Every word that he'd spoken in calm, even tones, he'd wanted to shout at the top of his lungs. It had taken every ounce of control he possessed to hold a normal, mundane conversation with her rather than demand answers. Right there, right now, regardless of how many witnesses might hear.

But he'd bitten his tongue, fisted his hands so tightly he'd nearly drawn blood. Reminded himself that in most situations, one got further by keeping a cool, level head than losing one's temper and raging like a maniac.

As hard as it was to resist turning the full force of his fury on her, he told himself that would only frighten her and possibly cause her to run off again. This time taking *his son* with her.

Oh, there were going to be DNA tests to prove—or disprove—that claim. In addition to the nannies who would be dropping by on and off over the next several days, he had a doctor scheduled to stop in and conduct a paternity test as quickly as possible.

But until he knew for sure, he was going on the assumption that he *was* the child's father. Better safe than sorry, and if he was, he wanted to get a jump on being a dad.

He'd already missed… He didn't know how long. He did know, though, that he'd missed the entire pregnancy, the birth and any number of firsts. First feeding, first diaper change, first time being awakened in the middle of the night and rocking Henry back to sleep.

Alex clenched his teeth until they ached. One more thing to hold against Jessica. The list was getting pretty long.

Biding his time, he led her downstairs to the kitchen and asked Mrs. Sheppard to see to it that Jessica and the baby were both taken care of. Then he'd returned to the foyer to oversee the rest of the baby preparations.

He'd waited thirty minutes. Thirty-two to be exact, before returning to the kitchen, ready to get some answers to the questions burning a hole in his gut.

Walking into the room, he stopped short, taken aback by the sight before him.

Jessica sat at the table of the eat-in nook near the windows, a half-eaten plate of scrambled eggs and toast in front of her. She alternated between taking a bite of her own meal and slipping a spoonful of goopy gray cereal into the baby's mouth. He was perched on her thigh, nestled and in the crook of her arm.

"Why isn't he in the high chair?" Alex asked, his voice reverberating through the room more loudly than he'd intended, startling both Jessica and Henry. He'd ordered the expensive piece of infant furniture, though, so his son should darn well be using it.

Dipping the tiny spoon back into the baby goop, she said, "He's only three months old. He's not quite ready to sit up on his own yet."

Well, there was one question answered. Henry was three months old. The math worked.

He also made a mental note to buy some baby books. He didn't want to learn from Jessica or anyone else what his child could or couldn't do, or what he needed.

Feeling suddenly uncomfortable and slightly self-conscious, he cleared his throat. "When you're finished, come to my office. It's time to get down to business."

As she crossed the front of the house toward Alex's den, Jessica felt for all the world as if she'd been called to the principal's office. Her feet were lead weights and her heart was even heavier. Henry at her hip, in comparison, was light as a feather.

He was also happy today. She shouldn't have been quite so delighted about it, but from the moment she'd arrived last night and plucked him from Alex's arms, Henry had been relaxed and content. Something to be said for her mothering skills, she hoped, as well as their strong mommy/baby bond.

On the heels of that thought, though, came a wave of guilt. She'd had nine months of pregnancy and the three months since Henry was born to bond with him, while Alex had had only yesterday. And that hardly counted, since she'd sprung the baby on him with no warning and hadn't even stuck around to explain.

Which was why she was letting him get away with the strong-arm tactics. He was angry—with good reason. And she was guilty—for bad reasons.

The door was open when she arrived. Alex was seated behind his desk, another man—older and balding—sat in one of the guest armchairs with his back to her.

Alex spotted her almost the moment she stepped inside and stood to greet her.

"Come in," he said, rounding the desk as the other man also got to his feet.

"This is Dr. Crandall," he introduced them, closing the door behind her with a soft click. "Dr. Crandall, this is the young woman I was telling you about."

To Jessica, he added, "Dr. Crandall is here for the paternity test."

Having her integrity called into question stung, but in Alex's shoes she would have insisted on the very same thing. So she extended her arm and shook the doctor's hand.

"Nice to meet you, Doctor."

"You, too, my dear," he said, smiling gently. "And I don't want you to worry about a thing. This is a relatively painless procedure. Just a quick cheek swab, and I should have the results back from the lab by the middle of next week."

"I appreciate that, thank you."

The idea of having Henry's blood drawn hadn't appealed. He'd survived worse, of course, but that still didn't make it a fun prospect.

"Dr. Crandall assures me that the cheek swab tests are just as accurate as blood tests," Alex put in. "The only reason we'd have to have blood drawn later is if the initial tests come back as inconclusive or problematic."

Jessica nodded. "Whatever you need."

Ten minutes later, Alex was walking the doctor to the door, DNA samples labeled and tucked safely into his medical bag. She stood in the doorway of Alex's office, watching as he shook the physician's hand, then ducking back inside before Alex returned.

When he arrived, she was sitting in one of the leather guest chairs, bouncing a giggling Henry on one knee.

Alex stood for a moment, simply watching them. The

woman who'd seared some of the most passionate memories of his life into his brain, and the child they'd most likely made together.

His chest contracted. Without a doubt, he was furious. She'd used him, stolen from him, betrayed him and lied to him. Yet part of him wanted to cross the room, drop to one knee and wrap his arms around them, holding them close and cherishing them the way a family should be cherished.

He wondered what would have happened if his relationship with Jessica had played out differently. If she hadn't spent the night with him simply to steal company secrets. If she'd stuck around instead of running off before the sun rose the next morning so they could share breakfast, get to know each other better, perhaps agree to keep seeing one another.

Alex wasn't a man of fickle emotions, so when he'd awakened that morning after making love with her, looking forward to making love to her again…and possibly again…he'd known he'd found something special. Or thought so, at least. Reality had proven to be quite different.

But deep down, he knew the possibility of a good, old-fashioned romance had existed. They might have dated, shared a short engagement and walked down the aisle before deciding to start a family. Baby Henry would still have been part of the big picture, just a little further down the road.

Fate had a way of turning things upside down, though, then sitting back for a good chuckle at the expense of the humans who had been played with like marionettes.

Which meant he was now faced with fatherhood first and…he didn't know what else second.

Clearing his throat, he strode across the room, returning to his seat behind the desk. It was awkward to put such cold, professional distance between himself and the mother of his child, but he felt comfortable there, and if it intimidated Jessica at all, kept her on the level, then it was the right position to take.

"I think I'm going to need a quick rundown of events," he told her, careful to keep his tone level and unaccusatory. "Why did you take off in the middle of the night? And if Henry is my son, why didn't you contact me when you found out you were pregnant?"

He watched her eyes, saw the pulse in her throat jump as she swallowed.

"It was a one-night stand. I didn't think you'd want me to still be there in the morning," she murmured. "And then when I went back the next day to clean your room, you were gone."

"My business in Portland wrapped up a few days early, and I was needed back here in Seattle. I wanted to ask about you," he admitted—albeit against his better judgment, "or at least leave a note, but was afraid it might get you in trouble."

He very intentionally didn't mention the missing Princess Line prospectus. It was a subject that definitely needed to be discussed, but not now. Not until he knew for certain whether or not Henry was his son.

For the time being, the child and his possible unexpected fatherhood trumped everything else.

She nodded somewhat ruefully. "It probably would have gotten me fired."

Just as he'd suspected. "I called a while later, but whoever I talked to claimed there was no one by the name of Jessica Madison working at Mountain View. And that the only Jessica they'd had on staff had quit the week before."

He'd considered digging deeper, perhaps hiring a private investigator to track her down. But then he'd realized how that would look: desperate. Especially since he hadn't yet hired a P.I. to look into the theft. If their one night together hadn't meant enough to her to make her stick around, then he'd look pretty pathetic chasing after her like a lovelorn pup.

So he'd put her and what he still considered a spectacular intimate experience behind him. Or tried, at any rate. And he'd succeeded at putting her out of his everyday thoughts, if not his late-night, private ones.

"You must have called soon after I discovered I was pregnant," she said.

His mouth turned down in a frown. "You quit because of that?"

A strange look passed over her features, and it took a second for her to reply.

"I had to. It wouldn't have been long until I was unable to keep up with the workload, and the chemicals we used to clean wouldn't have been good for the baby. Besides, the owners of the resort weren't too fond of unwed mothers being on the payroll. They thought it tarnished the resort's pristine reputation and would have come up with a reason to let me go before long."

Alex made a mental note never to stay at Mountain View Lodge again. If anything, single and expectant mothers needed their jobs more than other employees. And considering some of the behavior that often took place at those types of high-scale resorts—adultery topping the list—he didn't think the owners had a lot of room to point fingers.

Getting back to the subject at hand, he said, "Why didn't you tell me when you found out? You knew who I was and where to find me."

It wasn't always easy to get in touch with him—Rose was an excellent guard dog—but if Jessica had left her name and at least a hint of what she needed to talk to him about, he would have returned her call. Hell, he would have relished the chance to see her again—for more reasons than one.

He didn't know how he would have handled the news of her unexpected pregnancy. Probably much the same as he was handling the news of Henry's existence now—with a fair dose of skepticism and trepidation. He liked to think he would have done the right thing, though, once he'd established the veracity of her claim. Much as he was trying to do now.

He was playing it smart, getting medical proof before accepting parental responsibility, but if Henry turned out to be his, he would do more than put a crib in one of the extra guest rooms and make sure his name was on the child's birth certificate. He would be laying full claim, taking whatever steps were necessary to be sure his son stayed with him. Whether Jessica liked it or not.

Why didn't you tell me when you found out you were pregnant?

It was the question Jessica had been dreading ever since she'd made the decision *not* to tell him.

It had been the wrong decision. Or at the very least, the wrong thing to do. There had been so many factors to consider, though, and she'd been so very frightened and alone.

To Alex, however, she said simply, "I didn't think you'd want to know. Most men wouldn't."

A muscle ticked in his jaw, and she got the distinct impression he was grinding his molars together to keep from doing—or saying—something violent.

"I'm not most men," he said slowly and very deliberately, almost as though each word was a statement unto itself. "I would have stepped up to the plate. And I most certainly would have wanted to know I'd fathered a child."

"I'm sorry."

Jessica didn't know what else to say, not without saying far too much. He was angry enough with her already; she didn't think telling him she was a Taylor and that she'd been poking around his hotel room looking for company secrets would do much to improve his mood.

So she kept her mouth shut, knowing he would find out eventually but hoping he would hate her a little less by then.

Ignoring her apology, both physically and verbally, he went on. "If you didn't want me to know about Henry, why did you dump him at my office yesterday?"

She flinched at his less-than-flattering description of her actions, even though that's exactly what she'd done—in his eyes and in her own.

"I didn't feel I had a choice," she told him quietly. "It's been rough being out of work and trying to care for a baby all by myself. I can't find a job until I put Henry in day care, and I can't afford day care until I get a job."

"Don't you have family to turn to? Parents? Relatives who could help you out?"

The short answer was no. The long answer would mean admitting she was a Taylor, and that rather than telling her family she was pregnant by Alexander Bajoran, she'd chosen to run away. Disappear and live one step up from on the streets.

She'd thought so many times about going home and telling her parents everything. But she hadn't wanted to see the disappointment on their faces when they found out who the father of her baby was. Even if she refused to tell them, she was afraid her mother would eventually wear her down and drag the truth out of her.

And if she'd managed to hold out against her mother's badgering, she'd been very much afraid her cousin would come along later and figure it out.

Because Erin knew what she'd been up to in Alex's room at the resort. And she knew that Jessica hadn't been dating anyone around that time. She'd have done the math in her head, become suspicious and started badgering Jessica until she confessed everything. Then Erin would tell Jessica's folks for sure, damn her meddling hide. Her cousin was the impetus behind all of this, yet Jessica was the one to suffer the consequences.

To Alex she said carefully, "No one who could help me out, no."

He considered that for a moment, the tension in his jaw easing slightly. "You should have come to me sooner. *Come* to me," he emphasized. "In person rather than sneaking around like a cat burglar."

"At least I left something instead of stealing something," she quipped in an attempt at levity.

"I'm not sure the authorities would see it that way," he replied with a withering glance that immediately wiped the lopsided smile from her face.

Before the adrenaline from his veiled threat made it into her bloodstream, however, he added, "You were actually pretty good at getting in and out of the building without being seen. How did you manage that?"

"Just lucky, I guess."

If *luck* included practically growing up there while her family was still part of the business, and knowing not only where all the security cameras and blind spots were, but also how the building's security functioned. Or how it *had* functioned, anyway. She'd taken a chance and hoped not much had changed in the past few years.

Alex's eyes narrowed, and she could see the questions swirling there, knew the interrogation wasn't even close to being over. And while he'd certainly earned the right to some answers, she didn't know how much longer she would be able to get away with partial ones and half-truths.

Then as though heaven actually heard her silent pleas, she was saved by the bell. Literally.

From the front of the house the doorbell rang. They heard footsteps, followed by muted voices, and then more footsteps. A minute later there was a soft knock at the office door.

"Come in," Alex called.

Mrs. Sheppard poked her head in. "One of the applicants from Practically Perfect Au Pairs is here," she said.

"Give us two minutes, then show her in," Alex instructed. "Bring us a tray of coffee and hot tea, as well. Thank you."

The housekeeper nodded, pulling the door closed behind her.

"This is only the first interview of many," Alex told Jessica. "Would you like to take Henry off to do something else, or would you like to stay?"

Another woman interviewing for the privilege of taking care of her son when she wasn't readily available? Oh, there was no way she'd leave that decision to anyone else. Not even her baby's father.

Ten

By the end of the day, they'd interviewed half a dozen nannies. They ranged in age from eighteen to probably forty-five or so; college-age girls needing a job and a place to stay while they attended school, to lifelong caregivers. Each of them came with a resumé and the stamp of approval from either Practically Perfect Au Pairs or one of the other professional nanny placement services Alex had contacted.

As nice as most of the people were, though, Jessica found herself balking at the idea of Alex hiring any of them. Credentials, references and background checks aside, none of them seemed quite good enough to be left alone with her child.

She stood in the foyer, waiting while Alex saw the last of the potential nannies out. Shutting the door behind him, he turned to face her.

"So…any possibilities?" he asked, his footfalls echoing on the parquet floor as he crossed to her.

She shrugged a shoulder, not saying anything.

One corner of his mouth quirked up in a half grin. A sexy half grin, she was troubled to note.

Damn him for being so attractive, even when he hated her. And damn herself for still *finding* him attractive when she had so very much to lose at his hands.

"Come on," he cajoled, raising a hand to rub one of Henry's cheeks with the side of his thumb before letting it drop… and stroking her arm with his cupped palm all the way down. The touch made her shiver as goose bumps broke out along her flesh.

"There has to be someone you liked at least a little. You can't be with Henry 24/7, and every child needs a babysitter at some point. So if you had to pick, who would it be?"

Taking a deep breath, she thought back to each of the interviews, the details playing through her memory. One jumped out over all the others.

"Wendy."

His gaze narrowed. "Why?"

"She was friendly and smart," Jessica told him. "And she engaged Henry almost as soon as she walked in. Spoke to him, smiled at him, played with him, split her attention evenly between the three of us. The others seemed more concerned with remaining professional and impressing you."

A beat passed while he digested that. Then he offered a curt nod. "I thought exactly the same thing."

"Really?" Jessica asked, more than a little surprised.

Taking her elbow, he turned her toward the stairs, leading her to the second floor.

"Absolutely. I may not know much about babies, but I do know that a nanny will be spending ninety percent of her time with Henry. Which means that whoever we hire should be more concerned with impressing him, not me."

He smiled at Henry while he spoke, earning himself a giggle and kick, which only made Alex smile wider.

Tweaking the baby's bare toes as they strolled down the hall, he said, "Besides, I noticed the same things you did. She was really quite good with him. I especially liked that she cleaned his toy giraffe with an antibacterial wipe from her purse before handing it back to him after it fell on the floor. All without a hitch in her conversation with us."

"Me, too," Jessica admitted. Actually, she'd loved that part of the interview. Even Jessica's first instinct would have been to simply take her chances that the floor wasn't that dirty, or maybe run the toy under some water if she was near a faucet. The fact that Wendy had come so well prepared before she'd even been hired definitely earned her bonus points.

"So we'll put her at the top of the list," Alex said. "There are still a few more potentials to meet with tomorrow, and then we can decide. But I think we should strike that Donna woman from the pool entirely. She was downright frightening."

Jessica chuckled, even as a shudder stole down her spine. "Definitely. She should be running a Russian prison, not caring for small children and infants."

Alex gave a short bark of laughter. "Maybe I'll mention that to the agency when they ask how the interviews went."

Jessica's eyes widened. "Don't you dare!" she exclaimed, slapping him playfully on the chest with the back of her hand.

She stopped in her tracks, both shocked and horrified at what she'd done. Dear God, what was she thinking? She was joking with him as if they were old friends. Never mind that he held her future in his hands and could decide to punish her in a million alarming ways at the drop of a hat.

She swallowed past the lump in her throat and forced her gaze up to his, an apology on the tip of her tongue. But his expression kept it from going any further.

Rather than looking annoyed or upset, his features were taut, his eyes blazing with something she hadn't seen since their time at the resort. It made her heart skip a beat and sent heat rushing through her system.

Or maybe she was imagining things. Maybe that blaze in his eyes really was annoyance, and she'd amused herself right into a boatload of trouble.

Chest tight, she licked her dry lips and wondered if she could distract him with a change of subject.

"What are we doing up here, by the way?"

For a moment, he continued to stare with that same barely controlled intensity. Then he pulled back just a fraction and gestured behind her.

"The nursery is ready," he said, leading her in that direction. "I thought you might like to see it."

The general decor of the room was the same as it had been before. Pale yellow walls, lacy white curtains at the windows and gleaming hardwood floors. But any original pieces of furniture had been replaced with top-of-the-line baby items.

A spacious oak half-circle crib rested against one wall, a large changing table and storage unit along another, and in the corner sat a beautiful rocking chair she'd be willing to bet was hand carved.

"What do you think?" Alex asked from just over her shoulder.

"It's lovely," she told him. Like something out of *House Beautiful* or *Babies Born with Silver Spoons in Their Mouths*. She was almost afraid to touch anything for fear she'd leave a smudge on the pristine interior. "I can't believe you had all of this done in only one day."

"Getting things done is easy when you have money and know the right people."

A fact she knew quite well from the good old days before Alex had destroyed her family.

"If there's anything else you or the baby need, anything you'd like to change, just say so," he continued. "I want everything to be perfect, and I'm afraid you're my only source of information at the moment where Henry is concerned."

He said it without a hint of censure. At least none that she could detect. But the guilt and underlying threat were there all the same.

"Why are you doing this?" she asked softly. Shifting Henry from one arm to the other, she turned to face Alex more fully. "You don't even know for sure that Henry is yours."

She did, of course, but she'd assumed that was the point of the paternity test they'd taken that afternoon.

Alex shrugged. "Better safe than sorry."

A very simple, off-the-cuff answer, but she suspected there was more to it than that.

"You're going to make us stay, aren't you?" she asked barely above a whisper.

"For the time being," he said without hesitation.

Then, surprising her yet again, he reached out and slid his hands beneath Henry's arms, lifting him out of her grasp and into his own.

For a split second, Jessica held her breath and nearly tried to tug the baby back. She had to remind herself that Alex *was* Henry's father. He *did* have a right to hold him, if he wanted to.

As distant as he'd been up to now, he didn't seem the least bit nervous about it. There was no hesitation, no pause while he considered the best way to position Henry against his thousand-dollar suit.

He was a natural. Either that, or he'd learned on the job during last night's screaming fit. Still, she couldn't resist stretching out a hand to smooth the baby's shirt down his back, making certain everything was just right and he was okay.

It was odd not holding her own baby, not having him almost surgically attached to her side when she was the only person who'd held him for any length of time since he was born. She didn't know what to do with her arms.

Letting them drop to her sides, she dug her hands into the front pockets of her jeans and told herself to leave them there, even though the urge was to fidget like crazy.

As hard as it was to admit, she made herself mumble, "You're really good at that."

"I've been watching you," he said, his gaze meeting and locking with hers. "I figured I should probably get the hang of it if I'm going to be responsible for this little guy from now on."

There it was again, the hint of a threat—or maybe just a reminder—that if Henry was his, Alex intended to exercise his full parental rights.

On the one hand, Jessica was impressed and sort of proud of him for that. A lot of men wouldn't have been the least bit pleased to discover they might have a child they hadn't known anything about.

On the other, she was scared almost spitless at what it might mean for her and Henry. What if Alex tried to take her son away from her? What if he wanted to keep Henry here with him, under his roof, but informed Jessica she was no longer welcome?

Jessica would fight—of course she would. But she already knew her chances were slim to none of winning any kind of battle against a man like Alex, let alone a custody one. Not given his money and influence and her total lack of either, not to mention her past actions and behavior where he was concerned.

Not for the first time she wanted to kick herself for bringing Alex into their lives. She hadn't had a choice; rationally, she knew that. And even more rationally, she knew he had the right to know about and *know* his own child.

But being here, disclosing Henry's existence to Alex, changed everything. It turned their world upside down and shook it like a snow globe.

To make matters worse, Jessica was afraid Henry was already showing signs of being a Daddy's Boy. He was leaning into Alex, completely trusting, completely content. One of his tiny hands was wrapped around Alex's silk tie, likely wrinkling it beyond repair, while his cheek rested on Alex's shoulder, his bow of a mouth working around his pacifier, his fine, light brown lashes fluttering toward sleep.

"He's getting tired," she told Alex, even as her heart cramped slightly at the sight. Until now she'd been the only one to see him get sleepy and doze off. She'd been the only one those miniature fingers had clung to.

"He missed his afternoon nap because of the interviews. We should probably give him a bottle and put him down for a while. If we don't, he's likely to get extremely cranky and keep us both up half the night."

"Only half?"

There was a twinkle of amusement in Alex's blue eyes. One Jessica couldn't help but respond to with a small smile of her own.

"If we're lucky."

Alex nodded. "Why don't you go downstairs for a bottle. I'll stay here with him. While you're down there, tell Mrs. Sheppard we'll be ready for dinner in thirty minutes. You'll join me, I hope."

That caught her off guard. "You're giving me a choice?"

"Of course."

"Would that choice happen to be eat a four-course meal

downstairs with you or enjoy a lovely serving of bread and water alone in my room?"

He chuckled. "My home isn't a prison, and you're not a prisoner."

"Are you sure?" It was a pointed question, one that had her holding her breath while she waited for the answer.

"After the way you've been living, I'd think staying here would almost be a vacation. Why don't you just enjoy it."

As responses went, it wasn't exactly a *You're free to leave anytime you like.* Although he did have a point; staying in this beautiful mansion was a far cry from worrying about where she was going to sleep that night or where her next meal might come from.

And yet she felt just as trapped as she would if he put her in her room and turned the key in the lock on the way out.

"You can't honestly refuse me this," he said when the silence between them had stretched on for several long seconds. "If Henry is my son, as you claim, I've missed the past three months of his life. The *only* three months of his life. I just want to spend some time with him, make up for a bit of that."

When all else fails, throw out a guilt bomb, she thought. And it hit its mark dead center. How could she possibly deny him time with his newly discovered son? Besides, it wasn't as though staying in a million-dollar house on a multimillion-dollar estate was going to be a hardship. Not physically, anyway.

Mentally, there was no telling yet what the toll would be. But she owed him at least this much.

Tipping her head, she kept her thoughts to herself, but let him know he'd won her over by saying, "I guess I'll go down for his bottle, then, and tell Mrs. Sheppard we're almost ready for dinner."

She patted Henry's tiny back, then stepped around them

and headed for the door. Just as she reached it, his voice stopped her.

"You can request bread and water, if your heart is set on it."

Her lips pursed as she fought a grin, but *his* chuckle of amusement followed her halfway down the hall.

Despite the beautiful new nursery just next door, Jessica couldn't bring herself to put Henry down in there for the entire night. He napped in the expensive new crib after his bottle and while Jessica and Alex ate dinner. But even though she left him there as she showered, changed into pajamas and got ready for bed, she hadn't been under the covers for ten whole minutes before leaping back up and marching next door to get him.

She hoped Alex hadn't gone into the nursery during the night to discover what she'd done. Or if he had, that he wouldn't say anything. She didn't feel like explaining her mild case of separation anxiety or the nagging worry that if she didn't have the baby in her sights at all times, Alex might take Henry away from her, hide him from her and never give him back.

Despite those very real concerns, however, Jessica had to admit that Alex had been perfectly pleasant at dinner. She'd been afraid to go down to the dining room with him, afraid to sit across the table from him—just the two of them alone in an almost cavernous room.

She'd expected more of the third degree. Inquisition, Part Two—only this time without the interruption of nanny interviews.

To her surprise and immense relief, he hadn't brought up even one uncomfortable topic of conversation. He'd asked about the baby. A few not-too-personal questions about her pregnancy. Even about where she'd been and what she'd done to support herself before Henry was born. And he'd spoken a bit about how he'd spent that time himself—mostly changes or new developments at Bajoran Designs.

It had actually been almost enjoyable, and she'd flashed back more than once to the only other meal they'd ever shared—that night at the resort. The night she'd let herself be led by her heart and her raging hormones instead of her head. The night Henry was conceived, though neither of them had had a clue about that at the time.

By the time dessert had been served—a simple but delicious fruit tart—he could have asked for her social security number and internet passwords…well, when she'd had use for internet passwords…and she probably would have turned them over as easily as she'd give someone the time of day. She was that comfortable, that lulled into a false sense of security.

But he hadn't. He'd remained a perfect gentleman, seeing her out of the dining room, then asking if she would be all right going back to the nursery and her room on her own while he went to his office to catch up on a bit of work.

It was the ideal opportunity to escape and put some distance between them. That should have made her happy, right? Just being this close to him, under the same roof, was dangerous with a capital *D*.

But she couldn't help feeling just a little disappointed. That what had turned out to be a lovely dinner had come to an end… That her memories of the last time they'd eaten together had been stirred up, warming her, yet leaving her somewhat frustrated by the fact that *this* meal wouldn't be ending the same way…. And possibly even that he wouldn't be accompanying her upstairs to check on Henry and say good-night.

Why she would want Alexander Bajoran to wish her a good-night, she had no idea. It was craziness to even imagine it. If anything she needed him to spend *less* time with her, watch her *less* closely.

In that, her prayers were answered, because he hadn't knocked on her door in the middle of the night to demand she return Henry to the nursery. He wasn't even waiting outside in the hall when she awoke the next morning and stepped out to begin the day.

Jessica did go to the nursery then, changing Henry's diaper and putting him into one of the matching baby-boy outfits Alex had had delivered the day before. He hadn't only ordered items for the baby, either, but had bought a good deal of stuff for her, as well. New clothes and toiletries; even a stack of puzzle books for her bedside table. Ostensibly in case she grew bored—something that rarely happened while caring for a three-month-old infant. Most nights she was asleep before her head hit the pillow.

But Alex's kindness hadn't gone unnoticed.

Henry was his son, a son he had every intention of laying claim to if those paternity tests came back with his name on them. So purchasing things for the boy was to be expected. Maybe not to the extent Alex had gone—"starting small" obviously wasn't a term that existed in his vocabulary—but buying diapers and formula and a few new pieces of clothing was completely within the realm of understanding.

He had absolutely *no* reason to feel the least bit generous toward her, however. He could have stripped the guest room of every creature comfort and left her to wear the same clothes she'd arrived in for the entire stay, and she would have considered it fair punishment for her deceptions.

But he was a bigger man—a kinder, more considerate man—than she could have anticipated. She only wondered how long it would last once he had the confirmation that Henry really was his son. Would he shower her with roses or take back everything and send her packing?

Hitching Henry higher in her arms, she strolled down the carpeted hallway and wide set of stairs, taking a right on her way to the kitchen. It was early yet, with the sun just beginning to cast purplish light through the windows as she passed.

But Henry was an early riser, especially when he was hungry. So she'd get him some cereal and juice, and make sure he was happy before looking for Alex and finding out what was on the agenda for the day. Likely more nanny interviews and questions from his long list of continued demands.

Half an hour later, she was sitting in the breakfast nook with Henry in his baby seat, his face and bib covered in splots of sticky and drying cereal. Mrs. Sheppard bustled around the center island, readying items for the meal she was about to prepare while Henry kicked his feet and sent the plastic seat rocking on the tabletop with every bite.

Jessica couldn't help grinning at her child's antics. He was so darn cute when he was happy and his belly was full. He was also extra adorable in the little choo-choo train overalls Alex had provided. He probably hadn't picked them out specifically, but whoever he'd put in charge of buying baby clothes had done an excellent job.

Raising a tightly closed fist into the air, Henry suddenly let out a squeal and jerked so hard, his seat scooted a good inch across the table. Jessica jumped, dropping the tiny Elmo spoon full of cereal and grabbing the seat before it could move any closer to the edge. Then she turned her head slightly to see what had gotten Henry so excited.

Alex stood only inches away, dressed in a charcoal suit and electric-blue tie that made his eyes pop like sapphires. He looked as though he'd just stepped off the pages of a men's fashion magazine. Or was maybe on the way to a photo shoot for one.

"Jeez, you scared me," she told him. Then she turned

back to Henry, picking up the fallen spoon and wiping up the spilled cereal with a damp cloth she had nearby.

When he didn't respond, and the awkward silence stretched from seconds into minutes, she craned her neck in his direction again. That's when she noticed the hard glint in his narrowed eyes and the still line of his mouth.

She swallowed and took a breath. "What's wrong?"

She'd never seen an expression like that on the face of anyone who wasn't there either to chew her out or tell her somebody had died. And with Alex she was betting on getting chewed out. What was it this time? she wondered.

"We need to talk," he told her simply, his voice sharp as a razor blade.

Uh-oh.

She looked back at Henry, her hand still on his carrier. His food-smeared smile was wide, his feet continuing to dance.

"Mrs. Sheppard," Alex intoned. "Can you please watch the baby while I have a word with Jessica?"

The housekeeper didn't seem thrilled with the prospect of babysitting duty, but dried her hands on a dish towel and crossed to the table, plucking the small plastic spoon from Jessica's fingers. Taking that as a sign that she didn't have much choice in the matter, Jessica relinquished the spoon and her seat, reluctantly following Alex from the kitchen.

Wordlessly, they walked to his office, where he waited for her to enter ahead of him, then shut the door behind them with a solid click of finality.

Much like the day before, she expected him to move behind his desk, and for both of them to sit down before he said whatever it was he had to say. Instead, he remained near the closed door, legs apart and arms crossing his chest in what could only be described as an aggressive stance.

"You're a Taylor," he blurted without preamble.

Her heart stuttered in her chest. "Excuse me?"

His eyes went to slits, a muscle ticking on one side of his jaw.

"Don't play dumb with me," he bit out. "Your name isn't Jessica Madison. It's Jessica Madison *Taylor*."

Eleven

The blood drained from Jessica's face. She felt it flush down her neck and through her body all the way to her toes, leaving her dizzy and light-headed.

Afraid she might actually faint, she took a step back, relieved when she bumped into one of the armchairs standing in front of his wide desk. She leaned her weight against it, reaching behind to dig her nails into the supple leather to help hold her upright and in place.

Licking her lips, she swallowed past the overwhelming drumbeat of her heart. Barely above a whisper, her voice grated out the only thought spiraling through her mind. "How did you find out?"

A flash of anger filled his expression. "DNA isn't the only thing I had tested. A friend on the police force ran your fingerprints for me, and they came back as Jessica Madison Taylor. No criminal record, I'm pleased to say, but it turns out you aren't at all who you claim to be. Your prints showed up as a former employee of both Mountain View and Bajoran Designs."

Well, not Bajoran Designs so much as Taylor Fine Jewels, when it existed. Still, she didn't know what to say. Shock that he'd found her out reverberated through every bone and nerve ending.

She certainly hadn't expected to be called out quite so soon. She'd actually been hoping she could find a time and place and way to tell him on her own. Eventually, when she couldn't keep it under wraps any longer.

"So what was your plan, exactly?" Alex asked, bitterness seeping into every syllable. "Seduce me for company secrets so you could sell them to the highest bidder? Or was the goal all along to get pregnant so you could blackmail me later with an heir?"

What little blood had worked its way back to her brain seeped out just as quickly. Her breath came in tiny, shallow gasps as her chest tightened and she swayed on her feet.

"What are you talking about?" she said, her jaw clenched. Partly because she was angry and partly because she was literally shaking. Her arms, her legs, her teeth. Every inch of her was quaking with the effort to hold back the maelstrom of emotions raging through her like a tidal wave. "I didn't get pregnant *on purpose*. And I didn't sell anything to anyone."

Alex didn't look as though he believed her.

"But I didn't get lucky with just a single, uninhibited chambermaid, did I? You're the daughter of Donald Taylor, granddaughter of *Henry* Taylor, both of whom used to be in partnership with Bajoran Designs. Aren't you?"

A beat passed before she answered. "Yes."

"And you just happened to be at the resort, cleaning *my* room."

She raised a brow, her grip on the chair at her back loosening as she began to regain some of her equilibrium.

"Actually, yes."

Doubt filled his stony features and was evident in his snort of derision.

"Call Mountain View. Give them my real name, and they'll tell you I was employed there long before you checked in. And the suite where you stayed was part of my regular rounds."

"Lucky for you that I landed there, then, wasn't it?"

"I wouldn't use the word *lucky,* no."

The day Alex had checked in to the resort was the beginning of her life's downward spiral. Except for Henry. He may have been unexpected, tossing her headfirst in a direction she wasn't ready to travel, but he was also the single greatest gift she'd ever been given.

"It was the perfect opportunity for you to take part in a bit of corporate espionage, though, hmm?"

Her pulse skipped in her veins. Wasn't that the exact term she'd used when Erin had first concocted her appalling plan? Of that, at least, she *was* guilty.

"I suppose you could say that, yes," she admitted. She wasn't proud of it, but the jig was obviously up, and she didn't intend to lie or deny any of it any longer.

"I recognized you the minute I saw you," she told him. "My family was devastated when you cut them off from Bajoran Designs and drove them out of business. I was okay with it, believe it or not. I might have ended up as merely a hotel maid, but I was happy and making enough of an income to live on. Unfortunately, the rest of my family didn't handle things quite as well."

Taking a deep breath, she released the rest of her hold on the armchair and moved on stiff legs to perch at the very edge of its overstuffed cushion. She was no longer facing Alex, cowering beneath his withering glare, but she didn't need to. His angry judgment filled the room like poison gas.

"When I mentioned to my cousin that you were staying at the resort, she convinced me to poke around your room. No excuses," she put in quickly, putting up a hand to hold off whatever his next verbal assault might be. "It was a stupid idea and I was wrong to ever agree to it, but I did. She wanted me to look for something that would hurt you—or rather, hurt Bajoran Designs. Something that could be used against you or put Taylor Fine Jewels back in operation."

"The design specs for the Princess Line," he said, his voice sharp as tacks.

Her head snapped up. So he knew she'd taken them. She'd kind of hoped she wouldn't have to confess that. But…

"Yes. I'm sorry about that."

"You seduced me to get them, and then sold the proposed designs to our competition."

The accusation struck her like a two-by-four. Her brows knit and she shook her head.

"No. No," she insisted. "I took them, but I didn't sell them. I never did anything with them."

"But you don't deny seducing me to get your hands on them," he tossed back with heavy sarcasm.

Spine straight, she lifted her chin and held his icy gaze. "Of course I do. I'm not a prostitute. I don't use my body to obtain information or anything else."

In for a penny, in for a pound, she thought before forging ahead. "I slept with you because I wanted to, and for no other reason. I'm also pretty sure *you* seduced me, not the other way around."

"I wouldn't be so certain of that," he muttered.

Stalking across the room, he rounded his desk and took a seat in front of the laptop set up there for his regular use. He tapped a few keys, waited a moment then turned the computer a hundred and eighty degrees so she could see the screen.

"Seduction aside, how do you explain this?" he asked.

She studied the images in front of her, growing colder by the second.

"I don't understand," she murmured.

Sliding forward, she looked even closer, narrowing her eyes, trying to figure out what was going on, how this had happened.

It had been months since she'd seen the original designs for the Princess Line, but she remembered them in acute detail. She'd even redesigned portions of them mentally and sketched changes in the margins of numerous pieces of paper that had passed through her hands since she'd taken them from his briefcase.

Nearly the *exact* designs from that folder were on the screen in front of her now, though, in rich, eye-popping color.

"What is this?" Swinging her gaze to Alex, she frowned. "Did Ignacio Jewelers buy the line concept from you? They needed work, but you shouldn't have given them up. They were perfect for Bajoran Designs."

His eyes turned to chips of blue glass, his fingers curling until the knuckles went white. "What kind of game are you playing, Jessica? I already know who you really are. I know what you were doing in my suite that night. You can stop with the lies."

"I'm not lying about anything," she said, growing more confused by the moment. "What are you talking about?"

"What are *you* talking about?" he demanded. "You know damn well you stole those designs from my briefcase that night after we slept together and sold them to Ignacio. I assume as part of your plot for revenge. Though why the hell you would have it in for me or my family's company, I'll never know."

Closing her eyes, Jessica shook her head and rubbed a spot near her temple where a headache was forming at record speed.

"No. This is…this is insane."

Opening her eyes again, she met his gaze head-on. "I told you I made a mistake in taking those designs. But I never did anything with them. I tried to return them the very next day, but you were already gone. Do you really think that if I'd sold them, I would be here now? That line of jewelry was worth millions. Even with a baby to care for, I couldn't have gone through that kind of money in under a year."

"I don't think you did," Alex told her. "I think you decided that showing up with a baby and telling me he's mine is all part of your plan to get even more money out of the Bajorans."

Tears prickled behind Jessica's lashes. "I'm sorry that I lied to you and betrayed your trust by taking those sketches," she said, struggling to keep her voice even and unwavering. "But no matter what you think of me, Henry *is* your son. I'm here because of him, *not* because I want anything from you. And I don't know what happened with that line," she rushed to add. "I don't know how Ignacio Jewelers got hold of it, but…I'll find out. Or at least I'll try."

Alex watched the myriad emotions playing over Jessica's delicate features. She looked truly distraught. Guilty and confused and hurt by his rapid-fire accusations.

It was no less than she deserved, of course, he thought to himself, clenching his jaw and refusing to be swayed by the moisture gathering in her eyes.

He wasn't sure what angered him most—the fact that she'd stolen the plans for one of his company's million-dollar ventures, or that she'd slept with him to get them.

That night might have been a one-night stand, but it sure as hell hadn't been meaningless. Not to him. Now he felt like a first class fool for ever thinking there was more between them than simply sex.

Crossing his arms in an attempt to rein in his temper, he arched a brow. "How, exactly, do you intend to do that?"

He could see the wheels in her head turning, desperately searching for a solution, a way out of the fix she was in.

Finally, she took a deep breath, her expression filling with resolve. "I left the proposal with the rest of my things when I stored them at my parents' house before leaving town. It should still be there."

"And who's to say you didn't simply make a copy before selling it out from under me?"

"I—" She screeched to a halt, blinking in confusion. "Why would I do that? I'd have no reason to keep a copy once I sold it for millions and millions of dollars to keep me in the wonderful lifestyle to which I've become so accustomed."

For having started out on a stammer, she ended with more than a fair note of snark. He had to bite the inside of his lip to keep from laughing aloud at her spunk.

Not for the first time, he was impressed by her resilience. She was in trouble, here. With his power and money, he could squash her like a bug if he so desired. Yet she was standing in front of him with her chin out and her "dare me" attitude wrapped around her like a shawl.

It also got him thinking. She was challenging him, and no one in their right mind would do that—not in this manner, about something so vital—unless they could back it up. Would they?

"So your assertion is that if the file is still there, hidden amongst your other belongings, then you couldn't have betrayed me and my family's company by selling it, is that it?"

"Yes."

"How do you intend to prove that?"

She took a deep breath, causing her breasts to rise beneath the lightweight material of her daffodil-yellow top. He wondered if it was one he'd had delivered for her, or if she'd brought it stuffed in that ridiculously small knapsack she'd been carrying when she'd arrived.

"I guess I'll have to go home and dig it out." A beat passed as she narrowed her gaze on him and pursed her lips. "Would you believe me if I did?"

Another challenge. Damned if he didn't like that about her. Not enough to give her a free pass, but the benefit of a doubt was a possibility.

"I'd consider it," he said carefully, not ready to promise anything he wouldn't later be willing to deliver.

"Well, that's encouraging," she mumbled half under her breath. Shaking her head, she straightened and looked him in the eye. "Tell me what you want me to do. Should I go to Portland and look for the file, or would you prefer to continue hating me for wrongs you *think* I committed?"

"Oh, you've committed plenty of wrongs, with or without the sale of that design line to our competitors," he reminded her even as he battled a grin.

She was guilty of so much, but she didn't let that hold her back one bit when it came to sticking up for herself. Arguing business with his contemporaries was definitely never this exhilarating.

Then again, no one at Bajoran Designs was as attractive or compelling as Jessica, and he'd never had quite as much to lose —or gain—if he suffered a defeat at their hands.

"We'll go together," he told her. "We can take the corporate jet. Be down there and back in a matter of hours."

Sucking her bottom lip between her teeth, she worried it for a moment, her face reflecting sudden alarm.

"What?" he asked. "Change your mind already? Decide to confess and put an end to the charade before we waste any more time or a load of jet fuel on a wild-goose chase?"

"You're an arrogant ass, do you know that?"

His brows rose. So much for the effectiveness of his harsh features and intimidating demeanor.

"If you must know," she continued sharply, "my parents don't know about Henry."

The shock must have shown in his expression because she flushed crimson and shifted guiltily in her chair.

"I know. I know how terrible that sounds," she admitted, tucking her hair behind one ear and running her fingertips through to the ends. "I'm a horrible daughter. It will crush them when they find out I've been lying and keeping a grandchild from them all this time."

"Then why did you?"

She cast him a glance meant to singe him on the spot. "Can you just hear that conversation? 'Hey, Mom and Dad, I know this will disappoint you, but I'm pregnant from a one-night stand. Oh, but that's not the best part. The *best* part is that the baby's father is our family's arch nemesis, Alexander Bajoran, the man who single-handedly ruined Taylor Fine Jewels and destroyed our lives. Surprise!'"

"Archenemy is a bit strong, don't you think?" he asked with an arched brow.

She gave a snort of derision. "Not amongst the Taylor clan. Your name might as well be Lucifer Bajoran, as far as they're concerned."

Which seemed to be an awfully harsh sentiment to have for a former business associate who hadn't had much at all to do with the split between their families. All of that had taken place quite literally before his time. Alex had been working at Bajoran Designs, of course, but hadn't taken over as CEO until well after the Taylors' departure.

He frowned to himself. Perhaps there was more to the story than he knew, more that he *should* know. He made a mental note to look into it when he got back to the Bajoran Designs offices. Out of curiosity, if nothing else.

"Then what do you propose?" he asked, focusing instead on the matter of visiting Portland so they could retrieve the Princess Line proposal. If it was even still where she claimed it was.

"If we go on Sunday, my parents will be at my aunt's house for brunch. They're usually gone three or four hours, so we should be able to get in and out before they get home."

He thought about that for a minute. "You're really going to sneak into town without letting your parents know you were there? After not seeing them in almost a year?"

Her chest shuddered as she took in a deep, unsteady breath. "If I have to, yes. I told you I was a terrible daughter," she added when he tipped his head quizzically. "I need to tell them, I know that. And I will. Soon. I just…I need time to work up to it, and frankly, I can only deal with one major crisis at a time. At the moment, *you* are the main crisis I'm dealing with."

"Then the sooner we get to the bottom of some very important facts, the better."

"Agreed."

"In that case, let me know exactly what time we need to be at your parents' house, and I'll make all of the arrangements for the trip, including someone to stay here with Henry."

He expected an argument over that, but all she did was nod. Apparently she, too, saw the wisdom in not dragging an infant along on a mission one step up from breaking and entering.

Twelve

"I don't understand. They were right here."

Jessica hoped her voice didn't reflect the panic beating in her chest and at her pulse points.

They were at her parents' home in Portland. A lovely two-story brick house at the end of cul-de-sac in a modest development.

The flight down had been uneventful, and only uncomfortable because Jessica didn't like being alone in such close quarters with Alex. If "alone" included a pilot in the cockpit and one very discreet flight attendant who made herself scarce between serving drinks and asking Mr. Bajoran if there was anything else he required. And if the private plane could be described as "close quarters." It wasn't as large as his mansion, but it wasn't exactly a broom closet, either.

She'd blamed her antsiness on a mild fear of flying and being away from Henry. Only one of those factors actually bothered her, but Alex didn't need to know that. And the sooner they found the folder and got back to Seattle, the better.

Back to her baby, who was probably even now being rocked to sleep by Wendy the nanny. She liked Wendy well enough; she was actually the nanny Jessica would have hired if it had been her choice alone. But that didn't mean she was keen on another woman caring for her child when she should be there with him instead.

The garage attached to her parents' home was large enough for two midsize cars—one of which was currently absent—and all of her belongings from when she'd had to clear out her apartment. Thankfully she didn't own much by way of material possessions.

Even so, she'd gone through everything. *Everything* because the folder with the Princess Line designs inside wasn't where she was almost positive she'd left it. She specifically remembered tucking it away with some of her other important papers and legal documents. Not only for safekeeping, but because she knew it would blend in and wasn't likely to be noticed if anyone snooped through her things.

She couldn't imagine her parents going through her stuff.

Her mother would be like a dog with a bone about the paternity of her first grandchild, but they weren't the nosy sort otherwise. For heaven's sake, she'd quit her job, given up her apartment and taken off for parts unknown, all on a whim, and they hadn't asked a single question. As far as they were concerned, she was traveling, sowing the female equivalent of wild oats and would call if she needed them. Otherwise they assumed no news was good news.

"Maybe they were never there to begin with, and this is just part of your elaborate ruse to convince me they were," Alex said from two or three feet behind her. He'd been standing there, hovering less than patiently while she searched.

"You'd like that, wouldn't you?" she retorted without turning around. She was still on her knees, digging through the same banker's box for the third time in thirty minutes. "One more nail to drive into my coffin. One more reason you'll give the courts to convince them I'm an unfit mother—a *criminal,* even—and that you deserve full custody of Henry."

Frustrated, angry and increasingly frightened he would do just that, she climbed to her feet, brushing off the knees of her jeans.

Facing him, she said, "Well, that isn't going to happen. I'm not lying, and this isn't a ruse. They were *there,* dammit, and I'm going to find out why they aren't anymore."

Big talk when she had no idea how to go about it. But she couldn't let Alex see her uncertainty, not when there was so much at stake.

Think. Think. Think.

Her erratic pulse suddenly slowed, and she realized she *wasn't* the only person who had known about the Princess Line proposal. She'd told her cousin. Shown her the designs, even.

Not to use them against Alex, but to prove she *had* poked around his room the way she'd promised, and also because she'd simply loved the designs. The artist in her had been impressed and unable to resist sharing them with someone she'd thought would appreciate their beauty and intricacy as much as she did. With a few notations on how she would improve upon them, if she could.

That's what they had discussed the morning she'd shown Erin the design sketches. *Not* how they could best go about selling them out from under Bajoran Designs. She would never have done that, regardless of what Alex might think.

As much as she wasn't looking forward to what she had to do, it needed to be done. She owed it to Alex, and at this point, to Henry and herself, too.

"Can I borrow your cell phone?" she asked.

Alex's eyes widened a fraction, the blue of the irises stormy and nearly gray. Whether due to mistrust or the dull light in the interior of the garage, she wasn't sure.

Without a word, he reached into the inside pocket of his suit jacket and removed his phone, handing it over.

Dialing by memory, she waited through three rings for her cousin to answer.

"Erin, it's Jessica." It was strange having this conversation in front of Alex, especially considering what she was about to say, but it wasn't as though she had much choice.

"Erin, this is important," she bit out, cutting into her cousin's fluffy, drawn-out greeting. Once Erin quieted, she said, "What did you do with the design folder I stole from Alexander Bajoran?"

Lord, it hurt to use that word—*stole*. But she'd taken it without permission, so she had to call it what it was.

"What do you mean?" her cousin asked. Too innocently. Even through the phone line, she could tell Erin was feigning naïveté.

"Don't play dumb with me, Erin. I mean it. This is important. I need you to tell me *right now* what you did with the Princess Line designs. I put them with my things in Mom and Dad's garage, but they're missing, and *you* are the only other person who even knew they existed."

Silence filled the space between them for several long seconds. Jessica didn't look at Alex. She couldn't. Instead, she pressed her fingers to the bridge of her nose and prayed she wouldn't break down in front of him, no matter how close to tears she felt.

Finally, in a tone of complete entitlement, her cousin said, "I sold them."

Jessica's heart sank. "Oh, Erin," she groaned, "tell me you didn't. *Please* tell me you didn't really do that."

"Of course I did," Erin replied without a hint of apology.

"That was the plan from the very beginning, after all. To stick it to those Bajoran bastards."

Despite her best efforts, tears leaked from Jessica's lashes. "No, it wasn't," she told her cousin, voice cracking. "That was never the plan. I *never* agreed to anything even close to that."

"Why else were you poking around the man's room, then?" Erin asked haughtily. As though she had any right to be offended.

"Because I was an idiot," Jessica snapped. "And because you convinced me I needed to do something to avenge the family against the evil Bajorans. Which is the most ridiculous idea in history and the stupidest thing I've ever done."

Taking a deep, shuddering breath, she dropped her hand from her face and turned away from Alex. She couldn't bear to look at him or have him look at her, at least directly, while she was making such a soul-shattering confession.

"You had no right to go through my things, Erin. No more right to take that proposal from me than I had to take it from Alex." Her voice was ragged, and she was skating close to the very edge of hysteria. "You have no idea what you've done, Erin."

"Oh, what did I do?" her cousin retorted, snottier than Jessica had ever heard her. "Get a little revenge against a corporate tycoon who used his money and influence to put our family out of business? Make some well-deserved money of my own while screwing the Bajorans out of another couple million they *didn't* deserve? So what."

"No," Jessica murmured, forcing herself to speak past the lump in her throat. "What you've done is betray my trust. Worse, you've done irreparable damage to my life. My reputation. My *son's* life. I can't forgive you for this, Erin. Not ever."

She clicked the button to end the call just as her voice

broke and her lungs started to fight against her efforts to draw in fresh oxygen.

How could Erin have done this to her? She'd convinced Jessica to do the wrong thing, true. And Jessica took full responsibility for having actually done the snooping and taking of the papers.

But she hadn't truly planned to do anything with them. Had fully intended to put them back, and suffered months of guilt when she hadn't been able to. She'd almost traveled all the way to Seattle to return them in person, but had been too afraid Alex would call the police and have her arrested.

That, in fact, had been one of her greatest fears about returning to Seattle with Henry. She'd been beyond lucky that he'd put their son first and not called the authorities on her the moment she stepped into his house.

"Are you all right?"

He spoke softly, his tone kinder than she would have expected given the circumstances. In fact, he hadn't sounded quite so nice since that night at the resort when he'd been intent on getting her into bed. Or according to him, open to allowing her to seduce him.

His hand touched her shoulder. Lightly, almost comfortingly.

Fresh moisture glazed her vision. How could he be so understanding *now* when the evidence was clearly stacked against her? He should be furious. Sharp and accusing, just like before.

"Jessica?" he prompted again.

She shook her head. "I am definitely not all right," she told him with a watery laugh.

Turning back to the stacks and boxes of her things, she started replacing lids and putting everything back in order. It was busywork, something to keep her hands occupied so she wouldn't sit down right in the middle of the hard concrete garage floor and sob uncontrollably.

"I guess that's it," she threw over her shoulder in Alex's general direction. "You win. Erin took the proposal and sold the designs to Ignacio, just like you thought I had. So there's no way to prove my innocence. No way to convince you I'm not the lying, thieving bitch you accused me of being."

"I don't remember using the term *bitch*."

Sliding the last cardboard box onto a short pile of other boxes, she turned to face him. Calmer now, more composed. Resigned.

"I'm pretty sure it was implied," she said, emotionless now.

"No, but perhaps it was inferred," he replied.

Moving toward her, he stopped mere inches away. She still couldn't bring herself to meet his eyes, so she stared at a spot on his blue-and-black-striped tie instead.

"I should probably apologize for that," he continued, surprising her enough that she lifted her head. "I might have been a bit more critical of your actions than was warranted."

Jessica's mouth didn't actually fall open in a big wide O, but she was certainly shocked enough that it should have.

He was apologizing? To her? But she didn't deserve it. She may not have been guilty of *exactly* what he'd accused her of, but she'd undoubtedly put it all in motion.

She hadn't set out to seduce him or to get pregnant, but both had happened because she'd been poking her nose where it didn't belong.

And she hadn't sold the designs for the Princess Line to a competing company, but she had taken them and shown them to her cousin, who'd done just that.

Cocking her head, she studied him through narrowed eyes. "Did I accidentally drop one of those boxes on your head?"

she asked him. And then, "Who are you and what have you done with Alexander Bajoran?"

She was too upset and emotionally wrung dry to mean it as a joke, but one corner of his mouth lifted nonetheless.

"I heard both sides of the conversation. Enough to get the general idea, anyway, and to accept that it was, indeed, your cousin who sold the line proposal to Ignacio Jewelers. Which isn't to say you don't still carry some of the responsibility," he added with a note of severity he wasn't sure he felt.

"What are you saying?" Jessica asked, justifiably suspicious. "That you just…forgive me? Absolve me of guilt for everything I've done since we first met?"

"I wouldn't go quite that far," he replied dryly. "But I'd be a hypocrite—as well as a heel—if I held you responsible for something you didn't technically do. I'll talk to our attorneys, see if there's anything we can do about your cousin's spin at corporate espionage."

He paused to gauge her reaction to that, expecting anything from a heated defense of her family member to hysterical tears and begging for leniency. Instead, her full lips pulled into a taut line and her shoulders went back a fraction.

"I'm sorry," he said, "but we have to at least look into it. Losing those plans cost us millions of dollars."

"No, of course," she responded quickly. "What Erin did was wrong. What *I* did was wrong, but I never would have taken it as far as she did. She made her bed…I guess she'll have to lie in it."

"Strange as it might sound," Alex told her, "I actually believe you."

And he did. Not only because of what he'd heard with his own two ears, but because if she'd made a dime off the Princess Line prospectus, she would have shown at least a modicum of guilt. Or been dancing like a spider on a hot plate trying to wiggle her way out of trouble.

He even had to wonder about his assertion that she'd seduced him that night back at Mountain View to get her hands on company secrets. If that were true, she wouldn't have wasted a moment now trying to seduce him into letting her transgressions slide.

But she wasn't fast-talking, and she didn't have her hand down his pants. More's the pity on the latter. She'd simply admitted her part in the whole ordeal, all but assuming the position and waiting for the cops to slap on cuffs.

That was not the behavior of a liar, a cheat or—quite frankly—a gold digger. The verdict was still out on Henry and her purpose in leaving the baby in his boardroom. But since she'd been telling the truth about the majority of charges he'd leveled against her…well, there was a fair chance she was telling the truth about the rest.

Clearing his throat, he stuffed his hands in the front pockets of his slacks to keep from doing something stupid like reaching out to touch her. And not to console her.

He wanted to brush the lock of loose blond hair dusting her cheek back behind her ear. Maybe slide his hand the rest of the way to her nape, thread his fingers into the soft curls there, tug her an inch or two closer….

And from there his thoughts took a decidedly hazardous turn. Better to keep his hands to himself before he risked complicating matters even more than they were already.

"Just because I believe you about your cousin doesn't mean you're off the hook," he told her in a voice that came out rougher than he would have liked.

That roughness wasn't caused by anger but by the fact that he was suddenly noticing the bounce of her blond curls—sans the blue streak of a year ago. The alabaster smoothness of her pale skin. The rosy swell of her lush, feminine lips. And the slight dusting of gray beneath the hazel brown of her eyes, attesting to the stress she'd been under for...he suspected months now.

He hadn't exactly helped alleviate that stress, either, had he? No, he'd added to it in every possible way from the moment she'd walked into his home.

With good reason, he'd thought at the time. But not such good reason now that he knew she wasn't quite the conniving witch he'd made her out to be.

"At the very least," he intoned, "I'd say you owe me one."

She stared at him with eyes gone dull with wariness. "Owe you one...what?"

Rather than answer that question directly, he shrugged a shoulder and finally reached out to take her hand. "I've got something in mind. In the meantime I think we should get out of here. The jet is waiting, and your parents will probably be back soon."

With more familiarity than he thought she realized she was showing, she grabbed his wrist and turned it to glance at the face of his watch.

"You're right, we should go."

She didn't look any happier about leaving than she had when they'd arrived.

"I'm sorry we didn't find what we came here for," she muttered softly as they headed for the garage's service door.

"That's okay." He let her pass first, then followed, closing and locking the door behind them. "I know just how you'll make it up to me."

Thirteen

Though she asked a handful of times on the flight home exactly how Alex expected her to "make it up to him," he wouldn't give her so much as a hint of his plans. Rather than put her out of her misery, he merely smiled a cruel and wicked smile and let her squirm.

Hmph. He was probably enjoying her suffering. He probably didn't have a single clue yet what he was going to ask of her as so-called "repayment"—he just liked having her dangle like a little worm at the end of his hook.

And there was nothing she could do about it. She was at his mercy.

Hunched in the plush leather window seat, the sound of engines roaring in the background, she tried to hold on to her indignation and put on a full pout. The only problem was, she'd never been much of the pouting type. She also knew she deserved a bit of payback for what she'd done to Alex, both the intentional and the unintentional.

That didn't mean she was going to let him walk all over her. If he said he wanted her to assassinate the president or be his sex slave for a month, she'd know he was a crazy person and wasn't as interested in compensation as simply using and abusing her. But if he just wanted her to eat a little crow, she would do her best to sprinkle it with seasoning and choke it down.

Twenty minutes later the plane landed, and Alex accompanied her onto the tarmac and straight to the shiny black Lexus waiting for them. A private airstrip employee opened the passenger-side door, waiting for her to slide inside before rounding the hood and handing the keys to Alex.

They rode in silence until Jessica realized they weren't headed for Alex's estate. At first she thought she just wasn't familiar enough with the area. And then that he was taking a shortcut…except that it turned out to be a long cut. She remembered the route they'd taken from the house to the airport, and this wasn't the reverse of that.

"Where are we going?" she finally asked, finding her voice for the first time in more than an hour.

"You'll see," was all he said, strong fingers wrapped around the steering wheel.

She didn't sigh, at least not aloud. But she did sit up straighter, fiddling with the safety strap crossing her chest while she studied each of the street signs and storefronts as they passed.

Before long, he slowed, easing effortlessly into a parking space in front of a shop called Hot Couture. Sliding out of the car, he came around, opened her door and pulled her up by the hand.

She began to ask again where they were going, but bit down on her tongue before she started to sound like a broken record. He led her across the wide sidewalk and inside the upscale boutique.

Okay, she had to say something. "What are we doing here?"

Everywhere she looked, headless size-zero mannequins were draped in costly bolts of silk, satin, sequins and a dozen other expensive materials she couldn't begin to identify. She'd been away from this sort of extravagance for too long…and hadn't cared for it all that much when she'd been expected to wear gowns like these on a regular basis.

"This is Step One of your penance," he told her as they were approached by a saleswoman who looked as though she'd had her facial features lifted one too many times. Her eyes were a tad too wide, her brows a tad too high, her lips a tad too pursed.

"Good afternoon," she greeted them, focusing her attention much more firmly on Alex than on Jessica. With good reason—Alex looked like every one of the million-plus dollars he was worth, while Jessica was dressed in a pair of worn jeans and a stylish but nondesigner top. They were Daddy Warbucks and Little Orphan Annie…Richard Gere and Julia Roberts…the Prince and the Pauperette.

She rubbed her palms nervously on the legs of her jeans. "This isn't necessary, Alex," she murmured so that only he could hear.

At full volume, he replied, "Yes, it is." Then to the other woman, "We need a gown for a very important gala fundraiser. Shoes and handbag, as well."

The woman looked positively giddy at the prospect of a large commission.

"Alex…" Jessica began.

"I'll take care of the jewelry," he said over the beginning of her protests.

"What kind of fundraiser?" she asked, wanting to know at least that much before she began trying on a year's worth of dresses in the next couple of hours.

"Sparkling Diamonds," he said, naming the well-known charitable organization founded and run by Washington State's most notable jewelers. Since its inception only a few years ago, Sparkling Diamonds had raised hundreds of thousands of dollars to support a variety of worthwhile causes, from childhood cancer to local animal shelters.

"Tuesday night's benefit is being sponsored solely by Bajoran Designs. Some of Seattle's deepest pockets will be there, and we want to rake in as much as possible for this year's literacy campaign. I was planning to go stag, but now that you're here and—as we established—owe me one," he tacked on with an uncharacteristic wink, "you can be my plus-one."

Jessica wasn't entirely sure how she felt about that. Getting dressed up and going to a swanky party with Alex? Hanging on his arm all night with a smile on her face while they mingled with people who might recognize her as a Taylor Fine Jewels Taylor? Oh, the rumor mills would be rife with chatter after that. Word might even get back to her parents.

She thought she might prefer to undergo an extra hot bikini wax. But then, she didn't have much of a choice, did she? And after her conversation with Erin, the cat was pretty much out of the bag, anyway.

"Literacy is important," she said by way of answer.

"Yes," he agreed, rare amusement glittering in his too-blue eyes, "it is. The event is also a chance to show off a few of the company's latest designs. Ones we've been unveiling instead of the Princess Line."

There it was. Knife inserted and twisted forty degrees clockwise. It pinched, just as he'd known it would.

"You'll be wearing the most significant pieces. Yellow gold and diamonds, so they'll go with almost anything."

Turning his attention back to the saleslady, he said, "I want her to look absolutely stunning. Find a dress that showcases her natural beauty."

Inside her chest, Jessica's heart fluttered, heat unfurling just below the surface of her skin. If she weren't fully aware of the situation and where each of them stood, it would be all too easy to be flattered by that comment. After all, Alex was a very charming man. Isn't that how she'd ended up in bed with him in the first place?

But he wasn't trying to be charming. He wanted her dressed up and pretty to impress donors at his charity event. She was sorely out of practice, but that was something she could definitely do.

"Yes, sir," the woman replied, money signs glowing in her eyes along with her wide smile.

Jessica followed her silently to the rear of the store, listening with only half an ear to the older woman's cheerful chatter. Leaving Jessica in the changing room to strip, she went in search of gowns that would meet Alex's high standards.

An hour later, Jessica felt like a quick-change artist. She was tired and out of sorts, and just wanted to get home to see Henry.

She'd tried on so many dresses, she couldn't remember them all. After viewing the first few, even Alex had seemed to lose interest. He'd made low, noncommittal noises, then told her he trusted her to make a final decision before wandering off to talk on his cell phone.

Another six or eight gowns later, Jessica was pretty sure she'd found one that would pass muster. It was hard to be sure how anything would look with the jewelry he had in mind, since she hadn't actually seen the pieces for herself, but he'd described them briefly and she did her best to imagine them with each of the gowns she modeled.

She needed just the right color, just the right neckline. Just enough sparkle to shine, but not *out*shine the jewelry itself.

She'd forgotten how stressful the whole socialite thing could be. There was a reason she hadn't missed it. Much.

It didn't help, either, that her performance needed to be perfect this time. It wasn't just a public appearance or a high-priced fundraiser. It was one of her only options for redemption with Alex and getting into his good graces. There was still so much he could hold against her. So many ways he could punish her, if he so desired.

Licking her dry lips, she finished putting on her street clothes, then carried the gown she'd decided on—albeit uncertainly—out of the dressing room.

"We'll take this one," she told the sales lady.

"Excellent choice," the woman agreed, taking the gown and carrying it to the counter.

Jessica was pretty sure she'd have said the same thing about a gunny sack, as long as Alex was willing to pay a high four figures for it.

A few minutes, later she had shoes and a matching clutch, all of it wrapped up with tissue paper in pretty boutique boxes, ready to go. When the sales woman recited the total, Jessica's eyes just about bugged out of her head and her throat started to close.

It was almost as though she was having an allergic reaction to spending so much money for *one* night out on the town. She had half a notion to tell Alex that if everybody who planned to attend the fundraiser would simply donate the amount they would have spent on getting dressed up for the evening, they wouldn't need to hold the event at all.

It had been a long time since she'd poured money like that into anything that couldn't be eaten, driven or lived in, but the outrageous total wouldn't make a man like Alex so much as blink.

As though to prove her point, he seemed to appear out

of nowhere, passing his platinum card to the clerk over her shoulder.

The sales woman flashed a delighted grin. Thirty seconds later, Alex and Jessica were headed back to the car, expensive packages in tow.

"You found something you like, I take it?" he said once they were on the road again, finally on their way to his estate.

A knot of eager anticipation tightened in her stomach. She couldn't wait to get there and see her baby. They'd only been gone a day—not even a full day, really—but she wasn't used to being away from him. She'd missed him and wanted to see how he'd fared with the nanny Alex had hired—possibly on a permanent basis.

"Yes," she responded, trying to keep her mind focused on the conversation rather than the fact that Alex was driving the speed limit. He could have gone a *few* miles over without risking a ticket, for heaven's sake.

"I hope it's all right. It was hard to pick something to go with the jewelry you have in mind when I couldn't actually try them on together."

"I'm sure they'll be fine. The fundraiser starts at eight. Dinner will be served around nine-fifteen. Can you be ready to leave by seven?"

"Of course." It wasn't as though she had anything else to do or anywhere else to be aside from wandering around Alex's enormous house and spending time with Henry. She could be ready by seven o'clock *tonight,* if he needed her to be.

And in a way, she wished they were attending the charity function tonight. At least then it would be over and she wouldn't have to spend the next day and a half dreading the evening to come.

Alex stood in his den, one hand braced against the mantle of the carved marble fireplace, the other slowly swirling the ice cubes in his glass of scotch. He studied the empty hearth, lost in thought.

Jessica would be down soon to leave for the Sparkling Diamonds fundraiser. How the evening would proceed wasn't at the forefront of his mind, but Jessica certainly was.

After discovering that she wasn't the mastermind behind the theft of the Princess Line designs, he'd begun to wonder what else he might have been wrong about where she was concerned. Could she be telling the truth about everything?

She wasn't one hundred percent innocent, that was for sure. But for each wrongdoing he knew about or had accused her of, she'd come clean.

So what if she was also telling the truth about Henry being his son? He hoped she was, actually. It was a can of worms just waiting to be opened, but having Jessica and the baby under his roof had turned out to be a unique and surprisingly enjoyable experience.

He was just as attracted to Jessica now as he had been the first time he saw her. No matter what had happened in the year since, he still wanted her. His mouth still went dry the minute she walked into the room. His fingers still itched to stroke her skin and peel the clothes off her warm, pliant body.

And the baby…well, he'd been more than a little put off at first, but now he had to admit he was quite smitten. It was hard as hell to wear a mask of indifference, waiting to find out *for sure* whether or not Henry was his son. Not when he spent every day wanting to shed his suit and get down on the floor to tickle the baby's belly, dangle brightly colored plastic keys or play hide-and-seek behind his own hands just to hear the little boy giggle.

Then at night he lay in his big king-size bed imagining Jessica down the hall, sleeping alone. More than once he'd nearly tossed back the covers and marched over to join her…

or drag her back to sleep with him. Not that he had any intention of letting her fall asleep.

Pushing away from the fireplace, he crossed to his desk, setting aside his drink to flip open the file he'd read once before. He needed time to digest the information inside, figure out exactly what to do about it. But even as he rolled it over in his head, he looked the papers over again and was just as stunned and sickened as he'd been when he'd first seen them.

Jessica had mentioned that her cousin blamed him for the Taylors being driven out of business with Bajoran Designs. To his knowledge the decision had been mutually arrived at by the individual heads of each company. At the time that had been Jessica's father as CEO and her uncle—Erin's father, as it turned out—as CFO on the Taylor Fine Jewels side, and Alex's father as CEO and Alex's uncle as CFO on the Bajoran Designs side.

Both companies had been started separately by brothers—Alex's and Jessica's grandfathers and great-uncles. Then they'd joined together because all four brothers had met, formed a strong bond of friendship and thought Fate was trying to tell them something. And it had been a wonderful, very lucrative partnership for many years.

As far as Alex knew, the Taylors had simply decided to go back to being a separate business. His father had assured him the split was amicable and that everything had been taken care of before he'd retired and Alex had taken his place.

Of course what Alex and his family had learned only *after* his father had stepped down, and a few months before his death, was that the elder Bajoran's memory had started to slip. From the moment Alex had taken over the role of CEO, he'd been putting out small fires that his father had unintentionally set ablaze.

This, though...this wasn't a small fire, it was a damn inferno.

Oh, nothing that would harm Bajoran Designs. On the contrary, Bajoran Designs had come out miles upon miles above Taylor Fine Jewels.

But that made Alex far from happy. The bottom line was not more important to him than honor, integrity and proper business ethics. He didn't feel good about the fact that they'd apparently forced the Taylors out of the partnership and probably screwed them out of millions in profits.

The question now became *who* was responsible for that turn of events. It wasn't his father. The man might not be here to defend himself or even question, but Alex knew in his bones that his father would never have done something like that. Not to a business partner, and especially not to one he also considered a friend.

He highly doubted it had been his uncle, either. The two brothers were cut from the same cloth—honest and trustworthy to a fault.

The company investigators he'd put on the case had turned up these initial records fairly quickly, but they hadn't yet tracked down the name of the person who had put this ball in motion. He expected the information to come through any day now, and then he would have to deal with it.

But that was business. Jessica was personal, and he wasn't quite sure what to do about her or the way this information impacted her, as well as the rest of her family.

At the very least an apology was in order, even though he'd awakened that morning thinking she still owed him one.

A soft tap at his office door had him straightening up, closing the file and slipping it into one of the desk drawers for safekeeping. Then, clearing his throat, he called, "Come in."

Mrs. Sheppard poked her head in and said, "Miss Taylor asked me to tell you she's ready and waiting in the foyer."

"Thank you."

The nanny—who was turning out to be an excellent

choice, despite Jessica's original protests—was already up-stairs with Henry, and his driver had been sitting outside in the limo for the past half hour. Grabbing the jewelry box he'd brought home with him that afternoon and the lightweight camel hair coat he'd had special ordered for Jessica for this evening, he headed toward the front of the house, his foot-steps echoing in the cavernous emptiness.

He saw just the back of her head over one of the main stairwell's newel posts as he rounded the corner. Then, as he drew closer, she heard his approach, turned and took a step in his direction.

His heart lurched, slamming against his rib cage hard enough to bruise, and he faltered slightly, nearly tripping over his own two feet.

This was why he'd had to walk away at the boutique on Sunday. He'd waited while she'd changed into two different gowns, then stepped out of the dressing room looking like a supermodel hitting the end of a Paris runway...or an angel dropped straight from Heaven.

His heart had thudded then, too, threatening to burst right out of his chest, and other parts of his body had jumped to attention. Whether it was a white spaghetti strap sheath or long-sleeved red number, she'd made everything she put on look like a million bucks.

He'd had to feign indifference and use phone calls as an excuse to escape before he'd done something phenomenally stupid, like giving the saleslady a hundred dollars to take off and lock the door behind her so he could push Jessica into the changing room and make love to her right up against the wall. He'd broken into a cold sweat just thinking about it.

And that was before she'd landed on *the* dress, added ac-cessories and done her hair and makeup to match. She was so beautiful, she literally took his breath away. His lungs burned from a lack of oxygen, but he couldn't have cared less.

The dress she'd chosen was a sapphire-blue that leaned toward turquoise and made the hazel of her eyes positively pop. It would have clashed horribly with the rebellious near-navy blue stripe that used to be in her hair. Her now all-blond tresses were swept up from her nape, held in place by invisible pins to leave her shoulders and the column of her long neck bare.

The gown was classically understated. A strapless, slightly curved bodice hugging the swell of her breasts…a wide swath of sparkling rhinestones circling the high waist…and yards of flowing blue fabric falling to the floor, with a sexy slit running all the way up to reveal a mouthwatering expanse of long, sleek leg when she moved.

Though she'd balked, Alex had finally convinced her to go into town for a quick mani-pedi. The pampering had done her good, and he'd been sure to spin the suggestion as part of the payback for her lies and thievery. And now her freshly painted toes peeked out of the strappy, diamond-studded heels that poked out from beneath the hem of the gown.

Alex didn't know how long he'd been standing there, drooling like a dog over a particularly juicy steak, but it must have been a while because Jessica's eyes narrowed in concern and she glanced down the line of her own body, checking for flaws. Of which there were absolutely none.

"What's wrong?" she asked, returning her gaze to his. "Don't you like the dress? I told you I shouldn't be the one to choose. It's *your* fundraiser, you should have—"

He cut her off midrant. "The dress is fine. More than fine," he said, grateful his voice came out only a shade rusty and choked.

Her chest rose as she inhaled a relieved breath, drawing his attention to all that lovely pale skin and the shadow of her cleavage. He couldn't decide if he was delighted or annoyed that he now got to decorate it with some of the shining jewels from Bajoran Designs' most recent unveiling.

He knew they would look amazing on her, even if she outshone them just a bit. But on the downside, draping her neck with shimmering diamonds would drag everyone else's eye to something he preferred to keep to himself.

"Do you have the jewelry you want me to wear?" she asked, seeming to read his mind.

He held out the large leather case, embossed in gold with the Bajoran Designs logo. Flipping open the lid, he let her see what lay on the blanket of black velvet inside.

"Oh," she breathed, reaching out red-tipped fingers to touch the necklace's center gem. "They're beautiful."

And yet they paled in comparison to the woman standing in front of him.

Tossing the coat he'd gotten for her over the banister, he set the jewelry box on the flat top of the newel. "Here, let me put them on you."

He started with the bracelet, slipping it on her wrist, and then the oversize dinner ring on the middle finger of her opposite hand. Her ears, normally glittering with multiple studs and tiny hoops, were completely bare, leaving room for his earrings and his earrings alone. Since he didn't want to hurt her, poking around trying to get the fish hooks into the proper holes, he handed the three-inch dangle earrings to her and let her insert them on her own.

"Spin around," he told her, reaching for the pièce de résistance.

Lifting the necklace up and over her head, he waited for her to arrange it in just the right spot before fastening the latch at the back of her neck. He let his fingers linger on her smooth skin, lightly stroking the tendons that ran from nape to shoulders, down to the delicate jut of her collarbones and then back up to cup her shoulders, stroking all the way down the length of her arms.

Circling one wrist, he lightly tugged her around to face him once again. The diamonds at her throat and ears twinkled in the light of the giant chandelier far overhead. But his gaze wasn't locked on the priceless set of jewels that were supposed to be the focal point of tonight's event. Instead, he was struck mute by the brilliant facets of Jessica herself.

Her fingers fluttered up to touch the netted V-shape of the necklace crossing her chest. Even without seeing them ahead of time, she'd chosen the most ideal gown possible to display the jewelry he'd intended to have her wear.

"Would you be offended if I said this set is much prettier than most of the pieces in the Princess Line?" she asked.

He gave a low chuckle. Leave it to Jessica to speak her mind, even when she thought she was in the doghouse.

"It better be. We really had to scramble to make up for that loss. We needed something to release in its place that would make just as much of a splash. Or so we hoped."

She tugged one corner of her lower lip, glossy with red lipstick, between her teeth. "Are you trying to make me feel worse about that than I already do?"

"Actually, no. I wouldn't give up this moment, seeing you in this dress wearing these particular pieces, for anything in the world."

She blinked at him, eyes round with disbelief. He was a little surprised that the words had come from his own mouth, but he wasn't sorry. After all, it was the absolute truth.

Another absolute truth was that if he'd had a choice in the matter, he'd say to hell with the Sparkling Diamonds fundraiser, scoop Jessica into his arms and carry her upstairs to his bed where she belonged. Or where he wanted her, at any rate. Almost more than his next breath.

His hand tightened on her wrist and he had to make a concerted effort to lighten his grip before he hurt her. Or followed through on his baser instincts.

"We should go," he murmured reluctantly. Lifting his free hand, he brushed the back of his knuckles along her cheek to her ear, pretending to straighten an earring.

She gave a small nod, but didn't look any more eager to move than he was.

"Here," he said, reaching for the ladies' camel hair coat. He was glad now that he'd chosen to order one in black. It went beautifully with her gown, but would have gone with a dress of any other color, as well.

He held it for her and she turned to slip her arms into the sleeves. Pulling the front closed, she lightly knotted the belt at her waist then took his elbow when he offered.

Crossing the polished parquet floor and stepping outside to climb into the waiting limousine, Alex let himself imagine, just for a moment, that this was real. That Jessica was his and that going out with her for a night on the town was the most normal thing in the world.

As would be coming home late, crawling into the same bed together and making love until dawn.

Fourteen

Two hours into the fundraiser, Jessica was ready to go home. Not because it wasn't enjoyable, but simply because she'd forgotten how exhausting events like this could be.

Once the thousand-dollar-a-plate dinner had been served and consumed, it was all about mingling. Rubbing elbows, making polite conversation, promoting your company and raising money for the cause du jour.

To his credit, Alex was a pro at it. There must have been close to two hundred people in attendance, but he acted as though each person he talked to was the *only* person in the room. He was charming and handsome, and positively oozed self-confidence.

Everyone they met was treated to the same suave greeting, which included introductions, questions about the other person's family and/or business, and then idle chitchat until Alex found an opening to bring up both a reference to Bajoran Designs and a request for a healthy donation. Jessica didn't know who was in charge of collecting checks, but she would be willing to bet his or her head was spinning in delight by now.

She was also relieved that even though Alex was introducing her by her real name, and she was sure most of the guests recognized her for exactly who she was, nobody seemed to be giving her curious looks or talking behind their hands about a Taylor returning to the fold on the arm of a Bajoran.

That wasn't to say the grapevine wouldn't be ripe with fresh rumors by morning, but at least no one was making an issue of it this evening.

Breaking away from the latest group of smiling faces, Alex put a hand at the small of her back and led her on their continued circuit of the room.

In addition to key Bajoran Designs executives and board members wearing the latest pieces of jewelry to show off, there were blown-up full-color signboards on easels arranged throughout the large ballroom featuring other Bajoran designs. It was an enticing display. Jessica had noticed more than one woman already decked out in her weight's worth of gold and jewels admiring what Jessica suspected would be her—or more likely, her husband's—next acquisition.

And for some reason she was inordinately pleased. She loved the jewelry business, loved the sparkle of priceless gems and the intricacies of the designs themselves. Hadn't realized just how much she'd missed it, actually. And even though she and her family were no longer involved in it the way they'd once been, she still wanted Alex's company to be successful.

Alex slowed his step when he noticed her studying one of the extraneous designs more closely than the others photographed on a background of bright pink satin.

"Do you like it?" he asked softly.

"Of course. Your company does very nice work."

"Very nice?" he replied.

When she tipped her head in his direction, she saw that one dark brow was notched higher than the other.

"Shouldn't you be swooning and dreaming of the day you can wear that necklace around your own neck?"

She gave a low chuckle. She was already wearing a lovely necklace from Bajoran Designs worth probably twice as much as the one in the oversize photo. Not that either of them would be very practical in her day-to-day life unless she sold them for things like food and diapers.

To Alex she said, "You forget that I used to be around jewelry like this all the time. After a while it loses a bit of its allure."

He leaned down to whisper in her ear. "Shh. Don't let anyone hear you say that or we'll lose customers."

She laughed again. "Sorry," she returned in an equally low, equally conspiratorial voice.

"So why were you studying this one so intently?"

Shrugging a bare shoulder, she turned back to it. "There are just a few things I would have done differently, that's all."

It took a second for Alex to reply. Then he asked, "Like what?"

She worried her bottom lip for a moment, not sure she should say anything. Then with a sigh, she decided she probably couldn't get into any more trouble with him than she already was.

"The metalwork is a bit heavy-handed," she said, pointing to the spots she was talking about. "These stones don't need that thick a setting. If the gold were a bit thinner, more of the emeralds would show and the whole thing would have more sparkle to it."

One beat passed, then two.

"What else?" he asked.

"I might have gone with more slope to the design." She ran

her finger over the outline of the piece to illustrate her point. "This is very boxy, whereas more curvature would lay better against a woman's chest and be more appealing to the eye."

This time, more than a couple of beats passed in silence. She'd counted well past ten and begun to sweat before she twisted slightly to face him.

His expression was inscrutable. The only thing she could tell was that his eyes had gone dark and he was studying her as though he expected her to burst into flames at any moment. And she just might, if her embarrassment grew much hotter.

She opened her mouth to apologize, backpedal as much as possible, but he cut her off.

"How do you know so much about this stuff?"

Caught off guard, she rolled her eyes and said the first thing that popped into her head. "Hello? Jessica Taylor, Taylor Fine Jewels. I told you, I grew up around all of this. Before my family and your family went their separate ways, I was in line to start designing for the company on an official basis. But even before then, my father let me offer suggestions on existing design specs."

She turned toward the crowd, watching until she spotted just the right example. "See that woman standing over there in the too-short red dress?"

Alex followed her line of sight. "I don't think it's too short."

With a snort, Jessica murmured to herself, "Of course you don't." He probably didn't think the dress was too tight for the woman's build, either, considering how much of her breasts were popping out.

Then to him she said, "The earrings and necklace she's wearing are mine. Marquise-cut diamonds in a white gold setting, with a lone ruby as the main focal point. My father made me work with one of the company's design teams, but only to be sure everything was done correctly. Otherwise, he told them to give me free reign."

Jessica could feel that she was smiling from ear to ear, but she couldn't help it. Perfecting and designing those pieces, working at her family's company and having her father show so much faith in her had been one of the happiest times of her life. She'd so been looking forward to doing that every day. Not just on a whim or trial basis, but as a career.

For the first time, she realized she shouldn't have given up on that dream so easily. She'd been so busy starting a new life that she'd lost sight of those goals. Even if it had been in another city, for another company, she should have found a way to continue designing.

Once again the stretch of silence from Alex brought her head around. His sharp blue gaze made her pulse skitter and sent a shiver rippling under her skin.

"The only other time I've ever seen you smile like that is when you're playing with Henry," he told her, his tone so low and intense, her chest grew too tight for her lungs to draw in a breath. "Why didn't I know about any of this before?"

Jessica blinked, her fingers curling into the palm of one hand and around the rhinestone-studded satin clutch in the other. He was moving too fast for her, jumping from business to personal, personal to business, too quickly for her to keep up. Not with the conversation, but with the feelings he was stirring inside of her and with what she *thought* he might be conveying with his suddenly severe expression.

Was the heat of his gaze banked passion or tightly controlled anger? She couldn't tell for sure, but from the arousal coiling low in her belly, she found herself hoping it was the former. As dangerous as that thought was.

Licking her dry lips and swallowing until she thought she could manage clear and normal speech, she said, "I guess my father never told anyone. Maybe he was waiting to see how I performed and whether my pieces actually sold before taking steps to hire me into the company officially."

Reaching out, he brushed a tendril of hair away from her face, letting the backs of his fingers skim her cheek. Sparks of electricity went off in her bloodstream at the contact, raising goose bumps over every inch of her flesh.

"We didn't manufacture very many of that design," he said softly, the words barely penetrating her hormone-addled brain. "But they sold very, very well."

She blinked, pleasure flooding her at his admission.

"I even remember commenting that we needed to put out more pieces like that on a larger scale, but I never thought to ask for more from the actual designer. I simply assumed they were the result of a design team's efforts."

"If you're saying all of this just to be nice or to butter me up for something, please don't tell me the truth yet," she murmured, letting her eyes slide closed on the riot of sensations washing through her. "Let me savor this feeling just a while longer."

Eyes still closed, she smelled Alex moving closer a second before she felt his warm breath fan her face. His aftershave was an intoxicating mix of spicy citrus and sandalwood that she remembered intimately from their single night together. Now, as she had then, she inhaled deeply, wanting to absorb his scent and carry it with her from that moment on.

His mouth pressed against hers. Soft, but firm. Passionate, but not at all inappropriate given their current location and how large an audience they might be attracting.

He pulled away long before she was ready, leaving her cold and lonely. Her eyes fluttered open and she almost moaned with disappointment.

Still standing close enough to draw undue attention, he whispered quietly, "I meant every word. Although I do have a question for you that you might think I *was* buttering you up for."

His thumbs stroked the pulse points at her wrists, which she was sure were pounding harder than a jackhammer.

"For the record, I wasn't. You can say no, even though I sincerely hope you'll say yes."

Yes. Yes, yes, yes! She didn't even know what the question was yet, but the word raced through her mind, anyway, rapidly multiplying like furry little bunnies. She almost didn't care what he asked— Will you marry me? Will you sneak into the ladies' room and let me take you against the vanity? Would you like brown sugar on your oatmeal?—she wanted to say yes.

Her voice cracked as she made herself say, "All right. What is it?"

So many words. And she sounded so reasonable, when inside she was flailing around like a passenger on a tilt-a-whirl.

"Will you come home with me?"

Some fragment of her brain thought that was a silly question.

"I have to," she told him. "You're making me stay with you until the paternity results come back."

His lips curved in a patient smile. "No," he said softly. "You know what I mean. Let me take you home, to my bed. Spend the night with me the way I've been wanting you to since you came."

She nearly wept. Inside she actually whimpered. If he only knew how hard it had been to lie in bed all those nights, alone, knowing he was only two doors away. She'd thought about him, fantasized about him, even cursed him. And then, once she'd fallen asleep, she'd dreamed about him.

"What about your fundraiser?" she asked, needing to buy a little time for her heart to slow its frantic gallop and her

mind to be sure—really, really sure—she could deal with
the consequences of her answer.

"There are others here who can see it through to the end.
And if we don't get out of here soon, it's possible they'll be
in for more of an evening than they bargained for. We're talking full-out, triple-X public displays of affection right here
in the middle of the ballroom."

He emphasized his point by pressing against her, letting
her feel the full state of his arousal through his tuxedo slacks
and the fall of her gown. She leaned into him, reveling in his
palpable desire for her. Though her response wasn't nearly
as noticeable, it was just as intense, just as overwhelming.

She also wasn't sure she'd mind if he threw her down on
the nearest banquet table and had his wicked way with her,
but it might turn into a public relations nightmare for his
people.

"Then maybe it would be best if we left," she murmured.

She felt his chest hitch as he sucked in a breath.

"Is that a yes?" he asked, his voice sounding like sand-
paper on stone.

"Yes," she answered easily. "It's definitely a yes."

She wanted to laugh at the endearing, lopsided grin he
beamed at her. And then they were moving. He spun her
around, keeping her in front of him as he steered her across
the room, making excuses and lining up others to oversee
the rest of the fundraiser in his place. Depending on who he
spoke to, he blamed their premature exit either on *his* early
meeting schedule the next morning or *her* phantom headache.

Finally they were in his limo, pulling away from the hotel
portico and racing toward his estate.

As soon as the chauffeur had closed the door behind them,
Alex was on her, devouring her mouth, running his hand up
and down her leg through the slit in her gown, anchoring her
to him with an arm around her back.

Her fingers were in his hair, loving the silky texture and holding him in place while her tongue tangled with his. The plush leather of the wide seat cushioned them and brushed against the bare skin of her shoulders and back, making her realize they'd left the benefit without a thought for the coats they'd checked at the beginning of the evening or the chill in the late-night air.

Breaking the kiss, Alex panted for breath, his hands never pausing in their rabid exploration of her body through the sleek material of her gown.

"I want to take you right here," he grated, "so I'll never again be able to ride in this car without thinking of you."

Her heart did a little flip. "Then what are you waiting for?" she asked in a soft voice. Thankfully the privacy window was up—and she hoped soundproof.

His teeth clicked together, a muscle throbbing in his jaw. "Not enough time," he bit out. "But soon. Believe me—very soon."

With that, he pulled away, tugging her down to lie almost flat along the wide seat.

"What are you—?" she started to ask, but his hands were beneath her skirt, finding the elastic waistband of her panties.

In one swift, flawless motion, he had them down her legs and off. Then he was pushing aside the folds of the dress, leaving her naked from the belly button down except for the diamond-studded heels strapped to her feet.

Sliding to the limousine floor, he knelt there, a wolfish grin slashing his face and flashing straight white teeth. His hands at her hips tugged her forward, then gently parted her knees.

A quiver of anticipation rushed over her, pooling low in her belly. "Alex—" she whispered in a halfhearted protest, but it was already too late.

Lowering his head, he brushed kisses along the insides of

both thighs, leading upward until he reached her mound and pressed one there, as well. His lips moved over her, nuzzling the sensitive flesh and burrowing between her damp folds swollen with arousal.

He tortured her with long, slow strokes of his tongue that made her back arch and her nails dig into the leather seat cushions. She whimpered, writhed, panted for breath. Alex merely hummed his approval and redoubled his efforts to drive her out of her mind.

He licked and nibbled, flicked and suckled until Jessica wanted to scream. She was pretty sure *that* sound wouldn't remain on this side of the privacy window, however, so she squeezed her eyes shut and bit her lips until she tasted blood.

A second later, the limousine started uphill, rolling them together even tighter and pressing Alex more fully between her legs. His lips and tongue and fingers hit just the right spot with just the right amount of pressure to make her shatter, her insides coming apart in sharp, mind-blowing spasms of pleasure.

When she regained consciousness—because she truly believed she might have fainted from pure physical delight—Alex was hovering over her, smiling like a cat who'd just figured out how to unlock the birdcage. Her legs were demurely draped across his lap, her dress rearranged to cover them.

"We're home," he said quietly, leaning in to brush his fingers through her hair, which she was pretty sure was a tangled mess by now, no longer pinned in the lovely swept-up twist she'd fought so hard to get right only hours before.

With his help, she sat up, struggling to get her bearings and stop her cheeks from flushing bright red with awkwardness. It didn't help that the front of Alex's pants were noticeably tented by the bulge of his erection.

Spotting the direction of her gaze, he chuckled, shifting

slightly to alleviate the pressure behind his zipper. Then he reached down and plucked a scrap of sheer blue fabric from the car floor.

She held out her hand, expecting him to return the lost article of clothing. Instead, he dangled it from one finger, continuing to grin.

"Alex, those are my underwear," she said on a harsh whisper. Not that anyone else was around to hear. "Give them back."

"Nope."

She made a grab for them, but he slipped them into the pocket of his tuxedo jacket before she even got close. Sliding across the seat, he opened the door and stepped out, reaching a hand back to help her out.

"Come on. Let's go inside before Javier asks what all that screaming was about."

Fifteen

"Oh, no," Jessica groaned in utter mortification.

Taking his hand, she followed him to the house as fast as she could, making a concerted effort not to look around for fear she'd make eye contact with Alex's driver and die of humiliation right there on the front drive.

Once inside, he slammed the door shut, then spun her around to press her back flat to the thick wooden panel. His body boxed her in, arms braced on either side of her head, chest and hips and upper thighs pressing against her like a big, warm, heavy blanket.

His mouth crashed down on hers, stealing her breath and reviving every sensual, red-blooded nerve ending in her body, even the ones she'd thought had gotten their fair dose of pleasure for the night. She gripped the lapels of his jacket, hanging on for dear life while their tongues mated and their lips clashed hard enough to bruise.

One minute she was standing upright, pressed to the front

door. The next she was biting off a yelp of surprise as he swept an arm behind her knees, placed another at her back and yanked her off her feet.

Reluctantly, he pulled his mouth from hers and turned to march up the stairs. He carried her as though she weighed no more than Henry, but still she could feel his heart pounding beneath the layers of tuxedo jacket and dress shirt.

She kept one hand flattened there on his chest, the other toying with the short strands of hair at his nape. All the while she pressed light butterfly kisses to his cheek, his jawline, his ear, the corner of his eye, the pulse at his neck.

He growled low in his throat. She gave a long purr in response.

Stopping in the middle of the hallway, he gave a sigh that had her lifting her head. They were standing only a few feet away from the nursery door, which was slightly ajar.

"As much as it pains me," he said, "I don't want you to blame me later for not letting you see Henry before we go to bed. Especially since I intend to keep you there for a very long time. Do you want to run in and check on him?"

Her body might be humming, her blood so hot it was close to boiling her alive, but she was still a mother, and she really did want to see the baby one last time before Alex made her forget her own name.

"Would you mind?" she asked, lips twisted in apology.

He made a face. One that told her he didn't want to waste even a second on anything but getting her naked and between the sheets. But just as she'd always known, he was a good man. A kind, generous, sometimes selfless man.

Without a word, he slowly lowered her to the floor until she was standing none too steadily on her own two, three-inch-heeled feet. Keeping a hand at the small of her back, he walked with her to the nursery door.

Pushing it open, she tiptoed inside. Wendy was sitting

in the rocking chair in one corner, reading beneath the low wattage of the only lamp in the room. She lifted her head and smiled when she saw them.

"How was he tonight?" Jessica whispered, continuing over to the crib. Henry was on his back on the zoo animal sheets, covered almost to his chin by a lightweight baby blanket.

"He was an absolute angel," the nanny said, moving to Jessica's side. "We played most of the evening. I read him a story and gave him a bottle around eight. He's been sleeping ever since."

"That's great," Jessica replied, even though she was a little disappointed he wasn't still awake so she could wish him good-night. Doing the next best thing, she kissed the tips of two fingers then touched them to his tiny cheek. His mouth moved as though starting to smile—or more likely to give an extra suck of his pacifier—and warmth washed through her.

Straightening away from the side of the crib, Jessica thanked Wendy. "You can go to bed now," she told her. "I'm sure he'll be fine for a few more hours, at least."

The nanny nodded and moved back to the rocker to gather her things.

Standing close, having looked into the crib at Henry himself, Alex said, "Keep the monitor with you, if you would, please. We'll be available if you need us for anything, of course, but we'd prefer not to be disturbed tonight, if at all possible."

Jessica was sure that his hand at her waist and the high color riding her cheekbones left nothing to the nanny's imagination.

But she nodded without blinking an eye. "Of course. Not a problem, sir."

"Thank you," Alex murmured, applying pressure to Jessica's waist to get her moving toward the door.

"Thank you," Jessica said again, casting one last glance

over her shoulder at both the nanny and what she could see of the baby through the slats of the crib. "Good night."

And then she was back in the hall, being hustled next door to Alex's bedroom. She laughed at his speed and single-minded determination as he shoved her inside, catching a quick glimpse of dark wood, a masculine color palette and sprawling space before he closed the door, shutting out the light from the hall and locking them in near darkness.

As soon as they were alone, he was on her like a bird of prey, holding her face in both of his hands while he kissed her and kissed her and kissed her, turning her round and round and round as he walked her in circles farther into the room.

"Wait," she breathed between tiny nips and full-bodied thrusts of his tongue. "Turn on the lights. I want to see your room."

"Later."

"But…"

"Later," he growled.

She started to smile in amusement, but then his hands skimmed up the length of her spine, found the miniscule tab of the gown's zipper and slid it all the way down. The billowy, strapless blue material fell away from her breasts and dropped to the floor in a soft whoosh.

Since the dress didn't allow for a bra, and her panties were currently tucked in the pocket of Alex's jacket, the action left her completely naked but for her strappy stilettos and all four pieces of priceless Bajoran jewelry. Cool air washed over her, cooling the diamonds against her skin, raising gooseflesh and pebbling her nipples.

Or maybe it was the anticipation of making love with Alex again after what seemed like forever.

He stepped back, his eagle eyes roaming over her nude-but-bejeweled form from head to toe. Though how he could see much of anything in the dark, she didn't know. Only the faint glow of moonlight shone through the sheer curtains at the windows.

Not that the lack of illumination seemed to bother him. Not letting it slow him down one tiny bit, he shrugged out of his tuxedo jacket and started to undo his tie, collar and cuff links.

One by one, items were discarded, the buttons at the front of his starched white shirt slipped through their holes. Slowly, the hard planes of his chest came into view. Shadows of them, at any rate.

Heart rapping, she closed the scrap of distance between them, covering his hands at the waist of his slacks. His movements stilled and she pushed his hands away entirely.

He let them fall to his sides, giving up so easily. Yet she could feel the tension emanating from his body, in the steel-cable rigidness of his stance and every tightly held muscle.

His chest rose and fell in sharp cadence as she tugged the tails of his shirt out of the waistband of his pants. Pushing the fabric open and off over his shoulders, she let her palms run the full expanse of his wide masculine chest.

Just as she remembered from so long ago, it was broad and smooth, throwing off heat like a furnace. A light sprinkling of hair tickled her fingertips while she explored his flat abdomen; the rise of his pectorals with their rough, peaked centers; the hard jut of his collarbones and the curve of his strong shoulders.

The white material floated to the floor, and she returned her hands to the front of his pants. Sliding them open, she lowered the zipper past his straining erection while he sucked in a harsh breath and held it. She let her knuckles brush along his length through his black silk boxers.

Muttering a curse, he kicked out of his shoes, stripped the slacks and underwear down his muscular legs, and dragged her away from the entire pile of their shed clothing. He walked them over to the large four-poster bed, lifting her onto the end of the high mattress.

He moved in for a kiss, tipping her chin up and cupping her face in both hands. His thumbs gently brushed the line of her jaw while he drank from her mouth. She parted her knees, making room for him in the cradle of her thighs, and he pressed close, brushing every part of her with every part of him.

Her nails dug into the meat at the sides of his waist, then she brought her legs up to hitch her knees over his hips. He groaned, the sound filling her mouth as he leaned into her even more.

A second later she found herself lifted by her buttocks and tossed several inches closer to the center of the bed. Alex came with her, landing on top of her even as she bounced lightly, the glossy satin coverlet cool at her back.

While she wrapped her legs more firmly around him, he buried his face in her neck and began trailing kisses down her throat, tracing the lines of the necklace until it gave way to the bare flesh of her chest and one plump breast. He pressed his mouth dead center, then started to lick and nip all around.

Beneath him, Jessica arched, moaned, writhed. And Alex reveled in every ripple, every soft whimper of sound.

He'd wanted to drape her in his jewels, and now he had. And she was just as glorious as he'd known she would be in nothing but what he'd borrowed from the company safe.

He could hardly believe he actually had her in his bed again.

Different bed. Different city and state. Different year. Maybe even two different people…different than they'd been the first time around, anyway.

But so much was the same. The instant spark between them that quickly turned into a five-alarm fire. The uncontrollable desire he felt for her almost every minute of every day. Her hot, liquid response to his touch.

She humbled him and made him feel like a superhero all at once. And it was quite possible she'd given him a son. An heir. Another Bajoran to someday take over the family business.

That thought made him want to put her up on a pedestal and treat her like a queen. Surround her in swaths of cotton and bubble wrap, and keep her safe for the rest of their lives.

But for now, with her warm and willing beneath him, he most wanted to drive her to the brink and then straight over the edge into mind-bending bliss.

If only he could hold back his own climax long enough to get her there. And the way her legs were wrapped around his hips, her damp heat brushing him in all the right places, was making that more and more impossible.

Her stiff nipple abraded his tongue as he swiped at it over and over again. Around it, her dusky rose flesh puckered and tightened.

With a groan, he moved to her other breast and did the same. Her hands stroked his bare back, his shoulders, through his hair and along his scalp. Her nails scraped and dug and clawed.

Between her legs her warmth beckoned. He burrowed closer, locking his jaw to keep from moaning aloud. Continuing to toy with her nipples and the sensitive area surrounding them, he trailed his hands down her sides, over her hips and the mound of her femininity. She gasped as his fingers found her, and he captured the sound with his mouth.

For long languorous minutes, he explored her feminine core. The soft folds, swollen channel and tight, sensitive bud, all slick with tantalizing moisture.

"Alex, please," she whimpered against his lips, her pelvis rising upward, straining for the pleasure he was so cruelly withholding.

As much as he wanted to keep playing, keep touching and stroking and teasing her for hours on end, he didn't have all that much restraint left, either. Not after a year of celibacy since their last time together and the torturous session in the limousine.

Sliding more closely against her, he let her wet heat engulf him as he slowly pressed forward. He gritted his teeth while she took him inch by inch, her chest hitching beneath him in an effort to continue taking in oxygen. His own lungs burned just like hers, every muscle bunching tight.

"I remember this, you know," he grated, nostrils flaring and mind racing while he tried desperately to distract himself from the incredible sensations threatening to make him come apart at the seams.

She made a sound low in her throat. Part agreement, part desperation.

"I never forgot," he told her, "even though I tried hard to do just that."

Jessica's breath blew out on a shuddering sigh. "Alex?"

"Hmm?"

"Let's talk later, okay?"

She panted the words, her nails curling into his shoulder blades and making him shudder from the top of his scalp to the soles of his feet.

He chuckled. "Okay."

Grasping her about the waist, he yanked her toward him as he thrust, driving himself to the hilt. She gasped, and Alex ground his teeth to keep from doing the same.

Rolling them both to their sides, he held her there, moving inside of her, kissing her while temperatures rose, sensations built and the air filled with the sounds of heavy breathing and needy mewls. Jessica's hands on his body licked like flames. Tiny flicks of pleasure that shot straight to his center.

They rocked together on the soft, wide mattress. Side to side. Forward and back. Tongues mingled while bodies meshed, slowly becoming one. Her hips rose to meet his every thrust, her breasts rubbing his chest.

"Alex," she whispered, pulling her mouth from his to suck in a heartfelt breath. "Please."

She didn't need to beg. He was right there with her, desperate and so close to going over, his bones ached.

Clasping her smooth, bare buttocks, he tugged her closer, then rolled them again so that she was on her back and he was above her, covering her like a blanket. Faster and faster they moved until she was clenching around him and he was straining not to explode.

Which would have been a lot easier if she weren't grabbing at his hair and murmuring, "Yes, yes, please, yes," over and over again in his ear.

"Jessica," he bit out, not sure how much longer he could hold out.

"Alex," she returned with equal urgency. "Alex, please. Now."

"Yes," he agreed, forcing the word past his locked jaw. "Now."

And then he was breaking apart with Jessica spasming around him, her cries of delight filling the room and echoing in his ears.

Sixteen

Jessica stretched and rolled to her opposite side, surprised to find herself alone in the wide king-size bed. All through the night, Alex hadn't let her get more than half an inch from him except to run to the bathroom or peek in on Henry.

He'd wrapped his arms around her, tugged her snug against his long solid frame and held her while they slept. Then he'd woken her with kisses and the light caress of his hands on her skin to make love to her again. And once she'd awakened him the same way.

As nights went, it had been just about perfect.

Finding herself alone with the midmorning sunlight shining through the curtains put a bit of a damper on that perfection, though. It made her wonder if the entire evening had been as wonderful as she remembered. If the feelings she'd felt for Alex and *thought* he might return were real.

Insecurities flooding her, she slipped from the bed, pulling the rumpled coverlet along to tuck over her breasts, letting it trail behind her like a long train. She gathered her dress and shoes and other personal items from the seat of a chair where Alex had apparently collected them from the floor. Checking the hall, she tiptoed to her room and dressed in something other than an evening gown and three-inch heels.

With her hair pulled back in a loose ponytail and her body encased in comfortable cotton and denim, she headed for Henry's nursery only to find the crib empty. Far from being worried, she simply assumed he was with the nanny.

Making her way downstairs, Jessica checked Alex's office first, wanting to see him again, even though she wasn't entirely sure how he would respond to her in the bright light of day. But the room was empty, the door standing wide open and Alex's chair pushed back from his desk.

Turning toward the other side of the house, she trailed along to the kitchen, deciding that even if she didn't find Alex or Wendy and Henry there, she could at least grab a bite of breakfast.

As soon as she stepped into the deluxe gargantuan room, she heard the sounds of her son's giggles over the gentle din of pots and pans, spoons and spatulas. Alex sat in the breakfast nook before the wide bank of tall windows with Henry balanced on one strong thigh.

He was dressed more casually than she'd ever seen him in a pair of simple tan slacks and a white dress shirt open at the collar. Henry had a bib tucked under his chin, and there were small dishes of assorted baby foods on the table in front of them. Alex was obviously attempting to feed him, but he must have been teasing too much because Henry couldn't stop laughing and wiggling around.

Slipping her fingers into the front pockets of her jeans, Jessica strolled to the table. She was a little nervous after what she and Alex had shared last night, but happy, too, to see him so friendly and comfortable with the baby.

"What are you two up to?" she asked in a near singsong voice, sliding onto the bench seat across the table from them.

Raising his head, Alex shot her a wide grin, a spoonful of orange goop—peaches, she assumed—hanging from his free hand.

"Just letting you sleep a little longer," he replied. "And getting to know my son a bit better."

He said it so easily, so casually that she almost didn't catch his meaning. Then the words sank in and her eyes snapped to his.

Her sharp gaze must have been questioning enough, because he gave an almost imperceptible nod. "The doctor called this morning. The test results are positive—Henry is most definitely mine."

Jessica almost couldn't hear for the sound of her heart pounding in her ears. She'd never doubted Henry's paternity, of course—she *knew* Alex was the father for the simple fact that there'd been no other men in her life at the time of his conception…as well as long before and after. But she'd nearly forgotten Alex's doubts, and that DNA results were what they'd both been waiting around for.

Taking a moment to mentally slow her rampant pulse, she swallowed and then cocked both her head and a single brow. "Am I allowed to say *I told you so?* Because I *did* tell you so."

To her surprise, he chuckled, a genuine smile breaking out across his normally stern features. "Yes, you did." His smile slipping a couple of notches, he added, "I hope you know I wanted to believe you. I wanted it to be true, I just… I had to be sure."

His heavy-lidded eyes were storm-cloud blue and almost— she could have sworn—apologetic. She did understand. Alex alone was worth millions of dollars, his family as a group likely worth hundreds of millions. For all she knew, dozens of women had shown up on his doorstep claiming he was the father of their children.

Her own father had run off many a young man he suspected was more interested in the Taylor fortune than in her. It had made dating in high school an adolescent nightmare.

"So what do we do now?" she asked quietly.

Before Alex could answer, Mrs. Sheppard appeared at her elbow, sliding a plate of scrambled eggs and toast in front of her. She added a glass of orange juice and then disappeared again to the other side of the room, well out of earshot.

"Are you going to eat?" Alex asked after she'd sat there a few long minutes staring at the meal but making no move to touch it.

Taking a deep breath, she picked up her fork and stabbed at the eggs but turned her true attention to him instead.

"I'm a little distracted right now," she told him.

"For good reason, I suppose," he said, inclining his head and taking a moment to feed Henry another spoonful of pureed baby breakfast.

"I need to run into the office for a while this morning, but was hoping you'd meet me there later. Do you think you could do that—and bring Henry with you?"

"A-all right," she stuttered, confused by his nonchalance and focus on a topic unrelated to the recent discovery that he was, indeed, Henry's father. "But what about—"

Pushing to his feet, he carried Henry over to her and deposited the baby into her arms instead. Henry giggled, kicked and wiggled until she got him arranged on her own lap. Alex moved the jars of baby food to her side of the table and handed her the tiny peach-caked spoon.

"Just meet me at my office in a couple of hours, okay? Around one o'clock."

He leaned down and pressed a kiss to the crown of her head, ruffling the top of Henry's at the same time.

"Trust me," he added.

Calmly, competently, completely at ease while her insides were jumping around like seltzer water.

Two hours later, almost on the dot, Jessica walked into the Bajoran Designs office building. She wasn't sneaking around this time, hoping to get in and out without being spotted by security. Instead, Alex had made sure a car and driver were available to bring her into the city and drop her off at the front door.

She'd also changed from jeans and casual top to a short burgundy wraparound dress, and put Henry into a long-sleeve shirt covered in cute yellow ducks with a pair of brown corduroy overalls. She didn't know what Alex's intentions were for asking her to come to his office with the baby, but she wanted to be prepared. And knowing she looked good helped to boost her self-confidence.

At least that's what she told herself as she made her way up to the twelfth floor in the main elevator. The doors slid open and she stepped out.

She was a little surprised to find the reception desk and hallway completely empty on a Wednesday afternoon. Not even a receptionist behind the main desk. If the place had been this deserted when she'd left Henry on Alex's boardroom table, she wouldn't have had nearly as much trouble sneaking in and out or been half as nervous about getting caught.

Since Henry's carrier—with Henry strapped safely inside—was getting heavy, she set him on the low coffee table in the waiting area, wondering if she should stay here or go in search of Alex.

Before she could decide for sure, a door opened at the end of the long hallway and voices filtered out. A minute later Alex stepped into view, standing aside while several other men, also dressed in expensive, conservative suits, filed out. The last man exited the room, flanked by two security officers.

He wasn't handcuffed. In fact, they weren't touching him at all. But it was clear they were escorting him, and he looked none too happy about it.

Jessica stayed where she was, watching as the group of men made their way to the elevators, waited for the car to arrive and stepped on. The second elevator carried the angry man and the two security guards to the lobby.

After both sets of doors slid closed, she turned her head to find Alex striding toward her, a warm smile softening the strong lines of his face. From the moment he'd issued the invitation, she hadn't known what to expect. That look encouraged her, made her think they might be here for something other than bad news.

"You came," he said, leaning in to press a light kiss to her mouth. He stroked a hand down her bare arm to thread his fingers with hers at the same time he patted Henry's leg and sent the carrier rocking back and forth.

"You asked us to," Jessica replied carefully, not quite sure what else to say.

"And you trusted me enough to do it, even though I didn't tell you why I wanted you here."

He seemed infinitely pleased by that fact, and she found herself returning his near grin.

"I have a surprise for you," he said. "But first we need to talk."

"All right."

He gestured for her to take a seat on the low leather sofa, then sat down beside her. Their knees brushed, and he reached for her other hand so that he held both of hers in both of his, resting on his upper thigh.

Inside her chest, her heart bounced against her ribs, her

diaphragm tightening with nerves. She had no idea what he was going to say, but she felt like a teenager about to be reprimanded for missing curfew.

"I looked into the problem you mentioned about your family," he told her. When her brows came together in a frown, he clarified. "The belief that Taylor Fine Jewels was forced out of partnership with Bajoran Designs."

She understood what he was talking about, but was no less confused.

"It turns out you were right. For the record," he was quick to point out, "I knew nothing about it. All of that was over and done with before I took over the position of CEO, and behind my father's back. But my cousin George apparently decided he could rise higher and bring in more money for the Bajorans if our two families were no longer in business together."

Jessica's eyes widened. She wasn't all that stunned by Alex's pronouncement, considering she'd known the truth all along. Maybe not the details—about his cousin being the impetus for her family's ruin—but she'd certainly known the rest.

What surprised her was that Alex had listened to her and looked into her claims rather than automatically taking his family's side and dismissing her as crazy or scorned.

"Thank you," she said with a small hitch in her voice.

Knowing what Alex had done—that he'd discovered the truth and was man enough to admit it—suddenly meant the world to her.

It was so much more than she would have expected of anyone...but especially Alex.

"Don't thank me," he said with a shake of his head. "Not when I owe you an apology. What my cousin did was wrong and is what started all the bad blood."

Jessica gave a watery chuckle. "It seems we both have evil cousins hiding in the branches of our family trees. What I did to you back in Portland thanks to *my* cousin was wrong and unfair to you, as well. If you can forgive me for that, I think I can forgive you for something you had absolutely nothing to do with."

Lifting a hand to his lips, he kissed her fingers. "I forgive you," he murmured in a tone so resolved she could never doubt his sincerity.

"I forgave you long ago," he continued, "though I'm not sure I realized it until recently. But I owe you—and your family—more than that."

She started to shake her head. "You don't owe me—" she began, but he cut her off with a smile and the pad of one index finger pressed to her lips.

"It's already done, so just sit there for a minute and let me tell you how I'm making this right."

She swallowed hard, taken aback by his determination on the subject. But she did as he asked, sitting back and giving a short nod to let him finish.

"The man you saw being led out by security…that was my cousin George. The others were board members who came in for an emergency shareholders meeting. Once I explained to them what George had done and showed them definitive proof, they agreed to his immediate termination."

His lips twisted at her shocked gasp. "He only went quietly under threat of having criminal charges leveled against him."

"I can't believe you would fire your own cousin," she whispered.

Alex scowled. "He's lucky I didn't throttle him. I might yet. But that doesn't do much to help your family, so I want you to know that I intend to approach them about going into business with us once again."

Jessica's lungs hitched, her pulse skipping a beat. "Oh, Alex," she breathed.

"Do you think it's something they'll go for?"

"There may be hard feelings at first," she said with a laugh. "The Taylors can certainly be stubborn at times. But once they've had a chance to consider your offer and realize it's genuine, I think they'll be delighted."

On a burst of pure gladness she bounced off the sofa cushion and threw herself against Alex's chest, hugging him tight. "You really are a wonderful man, Alexander Bajoran. Thank you."

His arms wrapped around her, squeezing her back. He cleared his throat before speaking, but even then his voice was rough.

"You're welcome. There's more, though," he said, giving her one last embrace before setting her away from him and taking her hands again.

His chest swelled as he took a deep breath. This next part was delicate. She was either going to be thrilled with him and throw herself into his arms again, or she was going to be furious and possibly slap him a good one.

"Your parents are here," he announced quickly—almost too quickly, like tearing off a bandage. He saw the question in her eyes, the incomprehension on her face.

"What? Why are they... What?"

Mouth dry and pulse racing, Alex tightened his grip on her fingers. "I'm hoping you'll consider sticking around Seattle for a while longer, preferably staying with me so that we can see if this...*thing* between us is as real and as strong as it feels. And in order to do that, your parents need to know where you are—and that they have a grandson."

He'd crossed the line in contacting Jessica's parents behind her back and without her permission, but he hadn't known how else to get all of their problems ironed out and taken care of in one fell swoop. And for some reason it was important to him to get everything out in the open and dealt with *right now*.

There had been too many secrets, too many lies already. Starting years ago with his cousin's slimy, despicable actions toward her family on behalf of his, to as early as this morning when the doctor had called and announced that he *was* indeed Henry's biological father.

That phone call had both elated and disgraced him.

Elated him because he couldn't imagine anything that would make him happier than knowing Henry was his. Especially after last night when he'd pretty much decided he didn't care one way or the other.

Being with Jessica again, in and out of bed, had reignited the same powerful feelings he'd felt for her a year ago, and he'd known he wanted to keep her in his life. Jessica and Henry both, regardless of DNA.

But the test results had shamed him, too, because they reminded him that he'd doubted Jessica to begin with. Doubted her word, doubted her integrity, let pride and suspicions cloud what his heart and gut had been trying to tell him.

Hadn't he known as soon as he'd seen her again that he was in love with her? Hadn't he known the minute she'd told him Henry was his son that she'd been telling the truth?

She'd made some bad decisions, but he had some making up to do, that was for sure. And today's business was a step in that direction.

Still clutching Jessica's hands in his lap, he stroked her long slim fingers distractedly.

"I told them everything. Explained how we met last year, how you tried to steal company secrets to avenge the wrong that had been done to your family. And I told them about Henry."

With each word he uttered, Jessica's eyes grew wider, her expression panicked while the color leeched from her skin. On his lap her hands started to quiver.

"I'm sorry," he told her quickly. "I know it was probably

your place to tell them about the baby and why you disappeared on them, but I didn't want them to feel ambushed once they arrived. And I sort of hoped that having time to think during the flight—" he'd sent his own jet to pick them up "—would help them absorb the turn of events more easily."

"Oh, God," Jessica groaned, dropping her head to rest on their clasped hands. She was breathing fast and shallow... he hoped *not* on the verge of hyperventilating.

"Oh, God, oh, God. What did they say?" she asked in a muffled voice. "Were they angry? Do they hate me? Did my mother cry? I can't handle it when my mother cries. Oh, they must be *so* upset and disappointed in me."

Her hysterics were enough to make him chuckle, but he very wisely held back. Instead, he freed a hand to rub his wide palm up and down the line of her spine.

"Your mother did cry," he said, remembering his meeting with them in his office before he'd crossed the hall to deal with his cousin and the board.

"But I'm pretty sure they were happy tears. She's delighted to have a grandson, and can't wait to see him. They're eager to see you again, too, though your father did admit that if you'd shown up pregnant with my child, they probably would have been none too pleased. Realizing how they likely would have reacted to the news helped them to understand why you've stayed away these past months, I think."

Taking a deep, shuddering breath, Jessica raised her head and met his gaze. Her eyes were damp and worried.

"Do you really think so?"

He gave her a reassuring smile. "I do. Your parents are very nice people," he added. "I liked them, and am looking forward to working with them if they agree to partner with Bajoran Designs again."

The anxiety in her features seemed to fade as she reached

up to stroke his cheek. "You're something else, you know that?"

Alex quirked a brow. "In a good way or a bad way?"

"Oh, a very good way. I might even go so far as to say amazing, but I don't want you to get an inflated opinion of yourself. Or more of one, at any rate," she teased.

Then she sobered again. "I mean it, Alex. What you've done, all of it, it's…wonderful. And you didn't have to. You didn't have to do any of it. I'd have told my parents everything eventually. And what happened between our families, with the company… It was so long ago, and you had nothing to do with it. You could have let it all go on just as it has been."

"No," he said with a sharp shake of his head and the beginning of a scowl, "I couldn't. I don't want either of us to go into this relationship with baggage."

Jessica licked her lips, eyes darting to the side before returning to his.

"Relationship?" she asked in little more than a whisper.

"Yes." His tone was low, serious. Because this was possibly the most serious, important conversation of his life.

"I meant what I said," he continued, being sure to hold her gaze. "I want you to stay. Move in with me officially, as more than just a temporary guest. I'd really like to see if we can make this work. As a couple. As a family."

For several tense seconds she didn't respond. Except to blink, her thick lashes fluttering over wide eyes.

She was silent for so long, Alex nearly squirmed. Maybe this had been a bad idea. Maybe he was pushing for too much too soon.

As usual he'd forged ahead with his own plans, his own desires, expecting everyone and everything to fall into place just as he wanted it. After all, wasn't that how it had been his entire life?

This was so much more important than anything else

had ever been, though. And it wasn't only about what he wanted—it was about what Jessica wanted, and what was best for both her and Henry.

His ideal would be for them to stay with him. He didn't know if they were ready for forever just yet, but he certainly wouldn't mind if they moved in that direction.

If Jessica wanted something different, however, if her ideal was something else entirely, then he would have to accept that. He would still be in Henry's life, there was no doubt about that. And he didn't think Jessica would ever try to keep him out of it.

When the near-static buzz of intense silence became oddly uncomfortable, Alex cleared his throat and made a concerted effort to loosen his grip on Jessica's fingers. As romantic and sweeping as he'd hoped his actions and this gesture would be, it was a lot to digest. He couldn't blame her for being wary and needing time to consider her options.

"It's all right if you're not ready for something like that," he told her. He kept his tone even, devoid of the disappointment churning in his gut. "I shouldn't have sprung everything on you quite so quickly. I understand if you need time to think it through. And maybe last night was just one of those things. It didn't have to mean anything—"

The pads of two fingers pressed to his lips stopped him midsentence.

"It meant something," she said, barely above a whisper. "And I don't need time to decide anything. Yes—Henry and I would love to move in with you. Your house—mausoleum that it is—" she added with a grin "—is starting to feel like home already. I'm just…surprised you're asking. I'm shocked by all of this," she admitted, leaning slightly away from him and sweeping her arms out to encompass the waiting area and beyond.

Turning back to him, her eyes were warm, her expression

open and inviting. It made his heart swell and his own blood heat to a healthy temperature as it pumped through his veins.

"But, Alex," she began, her voice quietly controlled, "are you sure about this? You were so unconvinced of Henry's paternity, so suspicious of me. I didn't think you felt...*that way* about me."

She wasn't trying to make him feel like a heel, but he did. And if he'd ever needed confirmation that she was one of the most honest, genuine women he'd ever met—*not* a gold digger after his or his family's fortune—her cautious protests would have done it.

With a grin he felt straight to his bones, he brought her knuckles to his lips and kissed them gently. "Maybe I wasn't convincing enough last night."

"Oh, you were plenty convincing. But that's just sex, Alex. What you're talking about is...more. At least if you're saying what I think you're saying."

"I am," he told her. No hesitation, no mincing words. "It was definitely more than just sex between us. Last night and a year ago—I think you know that. From the moment we met," he murmured, alternately brushing the tops of her fingers and the underside of her wrists, "there was something between us. I'm just asking now for a chance to make it work. To see if we have a future together."

A short, shaky laugh rolled up from her throat. "I'd like that. More than you can imagine."

Yanking her to her feet, he held her close and kissed her until they were both gasping for breath.

"I'd like to take you home right now and celebrate properly," he told her, hands tangled in the hair at either side of her head while he cradled her face. "But your parents are still waiting in my office, no doubt growing more agitated by the minute. I know they're eager to see you...not to mention meet their grandson for the first time."

She inhaled deeply, then let the air slip from her lungs in a quavering sigh. "Will you come with us? I don't want to do this alone."

Rubbing his thumb along the full swell of her lower lip, he smiled gently. "You don't ever have to be alone again."

Epilogue

One Year Later...

The ballroom was brimming with guests dressed in tuxedos and designer gowns. Their voices were a loud din, interspersed by laughter and the clinking of glasses.

Beside her, Alex smiled and nodded as an associate droned on about his recent vacation in Milan, while the butterflies in Jessica's stomach fluttered violently enough to break through and fly away.

She tried to pay attention, really she did. And her cheeks hurt from trying to keep such a pleasant smile on her face. Inside, though, she was shaking, her fingers cold and stiff around her flute of champagne.

Apparently noticing her silent distress, Alex wrapped up his conversation with the couple before them and took her elbow to lead her several feet away. There weren't many quiet corners in the overflowing ballroom, but he managed to find one.

"You look like you're going to pass out," he remarked, clearly amused. His hands moved up and down her bare arms, rubbing warmth back into them along with a semblance of normalcy.

"Take a deep breath," he commanded. "Now slow and easy. Relax. You're the guest of honor tonight...you should be walking on air."

She followed his instructions, *tried* to relax and was relieved to feel her pulse slow by at least a couple of beats per minute.

"What if they hate it? What if you lose money? What if they hate *me* and start hating Bajoran Designs? You know the rumor is that I trapped you for revenge, and blackmailed you into bringing my family back into the company."

He had the nerve to chuckle, which earned him a less-than-ladylike scowl.

"Only a few very shallow, catty and jealous people think that. Everyone else—everyone who counts, at any rate—thinks you're delightful and knows how lucky I am that you and your family gave me a second chance."

Continuing in her downward spiral of unladylike behavior, she snorted with disbelief.

Alex lifted a hand to her face, brushing his knuckles lightly along one cheek and into her hair, which was currently loose around her shoulders, streaks of cotton-candy-pink spiraling through the otherwise blond curls.

Another bit of ammunition the gossips relished using against her, but she liked it and Alex claimed it was "hot."

"It's true," he told her. "Just as it's true that you're magnificently talented, and your True Love Line is going to be hugely successful."

Dropping her head to his chest, she inhaled the spicy masculine scent of his cologne and fought not to cry. "I just don't want to embarrass you or make anyone at your company mad for taking a chance on me."

Thumbs beneath her jawline, he raised her gaze to his. "First, you could never embarrass me. And second, it's not *my* company. Not anymore. It's *our* company, which means you have just as much say in what takes place there as I do. Besides, everyone at Bajoran Designs knows incredible natural talent when they see it. Giving you your own line was, as they say, a no-brainer."

That brought a smile to her face, the first honest one of the evening.

"Your family is here," Alex continued. "My family is here. Even Henry is here."

He cast a glance over his shoulder to where their fifteen-month-old son—the only child in attendance—was perched on his grandmother's hip in his adorable miniature tuxedo. He was starting to pull himself up and toddle around now, eager to learn to walk so he could become even more independent and keep up with the adults in his life. Until he managed that, however, he spent his time alternately napping, charming the world or getting into trouble as only a rambunctious toddler could.

But she and Alex both adored him more each day. Even the days they fell into bed utterly exhausted from chasing him around Alex's sprawling estate.

She'd been surprised, actually, when Alex had insisted they bring the baby along tonight, despite the fact that it was well past Henry's bedtime and they were inviting public crankiness by keeping him awake. But Alex had wanted—in his words—his "entire family" there for the debut of Jessica's True Love Line. A gesture that had both touched her and filled her with added anxiety.

"All to show how proud they are and how much they support you."

Chest finally beginning to loosen, she gave a peaceful sigh. "You're better than a full body massage, do you know that?"

Alex made a low, contented sound at the back of his throat. "I'll remind you that you said that—later, when we get home."

Leaning into him, she let his warmth and love surround her, calm her, remind her why she'd been inspired to name her debut jewelry line True Love to begin with. The wisdom of that decision was only underscored when he pressed a kiss to her brow.

"At the risk of sending you into a near faint again," he murmured against her skin, "I have one more thing I need to discuss with you before we unveil your designs."

A shimmer of tension rolled through her, but nowhere near the level of moments before.

Reaching into his pocket, Alex drew out a small velvet jewelry box with the Bajoran Designs logo stamped on the outside.

"We've been together a year now. Living together, raising Henry, loving each other like a real family. And I, at least, think it's working."

Popping open the lid of the box, he held it out to her. Inside was the most beautiful, sparkling diamond engagement ring she'd ever seen. Her heart lurched and the air stuck in her lungs.

"So how about we make it official?" he asked. "I love you, Jessica. I have almost since the moment we met, even if I didn't quite realize it. You getting pregnant with Henry that first night together was the greatest miracle of my life, because it brought you back to me when I might have lost you otherwise."

Moisture prickled Jessica's eyes as emotion filled her with a wave of unadulterated joy, tightening her chest.

"Oh, Alex," she breathed. "I love you, too. And I'm so glad you saw Henry and me as a blessing rather than a burden."

He tugged her close once again, framing her face with both hands, placing a hard kiss on her lips this time. When he spoke, he had to clear his throat, and even then his voice was rough and deeper than normal.

"The only burden you or Henry could ever cause me is making me hold this ring much longer. Will you marry me, Jessica? Be my wife, my lover, my partner both at home and at the office, and the mother of not just the child we already have, but any others who might come along?"

It was the easiest question she'd ever had to answer.

"Oh, yes." A tear slipped down her cheek, and she couldn't have cared less that it might mar her perfectly applied makeup.

He took the ring from its nest of velvet and slipped it on her left hand. The stone, roughly the size of a dime, glittered in the light of the room. She turned her hand one way, then another, taking pleasure in every facet and detail that caught her eye.

"It's beautiful, Alex, thank you."

It was also huge and quite heavy. She would need a little red wagon to cart it around with her all day, every day.

"I designed it myself," he told her, chuckling when she shot him a surprised look. "I may not be as talented as you, but I knew what I wanted. I also know what you like."

Taking her hand, he slid the ring back off her finger. "I know you think it's too big, too ostentatious, even though secretly, you adore how large and showy it is."

Well, he had her there. Didn't every woman want an engagement ring the size of a compact car to show off and use to impress their friends?

"Which is why it's actually two rings that come together to form one."

He wiggled things around with a little click, and suddenly he held a piece in each hand. They were both gorgeous and still quite remarkable, while also being a bit more manageable.

"You can choose which to wear on a regular basis, or switch back and forth, if you like. And when you want to flaunt your wealth or show off just how much your husband adores you, you can put them together and cause temporary blind spells everywhere you go."

She laughed, amazed at his ingenuity and how much thought he'd put into it when he could have pulled any ring from the Bajoran Designs collection instead, and she wouldn't have known the difference.

"I'm *very* impressed," she admitted as he clicked the two bands into place and slipped all umpteen carats back on her finger.

Going on tiptoe, she wrapped her arms around his neck and pressed a soft kiss to his waiting lips. "I also love it. And I love you. Coming to Seattle was the best decision I ever made, even if we got off to a slightly rocky start."

His own arms came up to circle her waist, holding her close while he nibbled lightly at the corners of her mouth and jaw.

"Ah, but don't you know that the rockiest paths sometimes lead to the very best destinations?"

With a perfectly contented sigh, she leaned back to stare deep into his crystal-clear sapphire eyes.

"Yes, I guess I do," she whispered as everything else faded away, leaving them the only two people in the world, let alone the crowded ballroom. "Because my rocky path led me to you."

* * * * *

TO SIN WITH THE TYCOON

CATHY WILLIAMS

To my beautiful daughters for all their support

Cathy Williams is originally from Trinidad, but has lived in England for a number of years. She currently has a house in Warwickshire, which she shares with her three daughters, Charlotte, Olivia and Emma, and their pet cat, Salem. She adores writing romantic fiction, and would love one of her girls to become a writer – although at the moment she is happy enough if they do their homework and agree not to bicker with one another!

CHAPTER ONE

ALICE MORGAN WAS growing more annoyed by the second. It was ten-thirty. She had now been sitting in this office for an hour and a half and no one could tell her whether she would be sitting there, tapping her foot and looking at her watch, for another hour and a half, two hours, three hours or for the rest of the day.

In fact, she seemed to have been forgotten. Mr Big played by his own rules, she had been told. He came and went as he pleased. He did as he wanted. He was unpredictable, a law unto himself. All this had been relayed to her by a simpering, pocket-sized blonde Barbie doll as she had been ushered into her office to find that her new boss was nowhere to be found.

'Perhaps he has a diary?' Alice had suggested. 'Maybe he had a breakfast meeting and forgot that I would be coming at nine. If you could check, then at least I would know how long I can expect to be kept waiting.'

But, no. Mr Big didn't run his life according to diaries. Apparently he didn't need to because he was so clever that he could remember everything without the benefit of reminders. Besides, no one was allowed into his office when he was absent—although the Barbie doll had worked for him for four days a few months ago and knew for a fact that he didn't use any diaries. Because he was brilliant and didn't need them.

The Barbie doll had since peered into the office twice, smiled apologetically and repeated what she had previously said—as though lateness and discourtesy were winning selling points that the entire staff happily accepted and so, therefore, should she.

Mouth tight, Alice looked around her, from her smaller office through the dividing glass partition into Gabriel Cabrera's much bigger, much more impressive one.

When she had been told where she would be temping, Alice had been thrilled. The offices were situated in the most stunning building in the city. The Shard was a testimony to architectural brilliance with magnificent views over London. People paid to go up it. The bars and restaurants there were booked up weeks in advance.

And now she would be working there. True, her contract was only for six weeks, but she had been told that there was a chance of being made permanent if she did well. He had a reputation for hiring and firing, the woman at the agency had added, but Alice was good at what she did. Better than good. By the time she'd arrived at the building at precisely eight-forty-five that morning, she had made up her mind that she would do her damnedest to secure a permanent position there.

Her last job had been pleasant and reasonably well paid, but the surroundings had been mediocre and the chances of advancement non-existent. This job, should she manage to get it, promised a career that might actually move in an upward direction.

Right now, she thought that she wouldn't be going anywhere if her new boss didn't show up, except back to her little shared house in Shepherd's Bush with one wasted day behind her. She probably wouldn't even be paid for her time because no one would sign off her work sheet if she didn't actually do any work. She wondered whether his reputation as a hirer and firer wasn't actually a case of him being left in the lurch every three weeks because his secretaries got fed up dealing with his so-called brilliance. Not so much a case of him firing his secretaries as his secretaries firing him.

She caught a glimpse of herself in the mirrored wall that occupied one section of her office and frowned at the image reflected back: her neat outfit and unremarkable looks did not seem to gel with the glossy, snappy image of the other employees she had seen as she had been channelled onto the directors' floor. She could have landed on a film set. The guys all wore snappy, expensive suits and the women were largely blonde and achingly good-looking in a polished, well-groomed way. Young, thrusting, career graduates who all had the full package of looks, ambition and brains. Even the secretaries and clerks who kept the wheels of the machinery oiled and running were just as glamorous. These were people who dressed for their surroundings.

She, on the other hand…

Brown eyes, brown hair falling straight to her shoulders, and she was far too tall, even in her flat, black pumps. Something about her grey suit and white blouse screamed lack of flair, although when she had stuck it on that morning she had been quietly pleased at the professional image she projected. It had certainly made a change from the more casual gear she had become accustomed to wearing at her last job. Now, here, she just looked vaguely…*drab*.

For the first time she wondered whether the gleaming CV in her handbag and her confidence in her abilities were going to be enough. An eccentric and insane employer who

surrounded himself with glamour models might just find
her a little on the boring side.

She swept aside the nudge of insecurity trying to push
itself to the forefront. This wasn't a fashion parade and she
wasn't competing with anyone in the looks stakes. This
was a job, and she was good at what she did. She picked
things up easily; she had an agile brain. When it came to
work, those were the things that mattered.

She hunkered down for the long haul.

It was nearly midday, and she was bracing herself for an
awkward conversation with one of his employees about his
whereabouts, when the door to her office was pushed open.

And in he came. Her new boss, Gabriel Cabrera. And
nothing had prepared her for him. Tall, well over six foot,
he was the most sinfully good-looking man she had ever
set eyes on. His hair was slightly too long, which lent him
a rakish air, and the perfection of his dark, chiselled features was indecent. He emanated power and a sort of restless energy that left her temporarily lost for words. Then
she gathered herself and held out her hand in greeting.

'Who are you?' Gabriel stopped abruptly and frowned
at her. 'And why are you here?'

Alice dropped her hand and bared her teeth in a polite
smile. This was the man she would be working for and she
didn't want to kick things off on the wrong foot—but, in
her head, she added to the list of pejorative descriptions
which had been growing steadily 'rude and fancies himself'.

'I'm Alice Morgan…your new secretary? The agency
your company uses got in touch with me. I have my CV…'

'No need.' He stood back and looked at her intently,
head tilted to one side. Arms folded, he circled her, and
she gritted her teeth in receipt of this insolent, arrogant
appraisal.

Was this how he treated his female staff? She had got the message loud and clear that he did what he wanted, irrespective of what anyone had to say on the matter, but this was too much.

She could leave. Walk out. She had already been kept waiting for over two hours. The agency would understand. But she was being paid over the odds for this job, way over the odds, and it had been hinted that the package, should she be made permanent, would be breath-taking. The man paid well, whatever his undesirable traits, and she could do with the money. She had been renting for the past three years, ever since she had moved to London from Devon, where her mother lived. There was no way she could afford to leave rented accommodation but she would love to have the option of not sharing a house. And then there were all those other expenses that ate into her monthly income, leaving her with barely enough to survive comfortably.

Practicality won over impulse and she stayed put.

'So...' Gabriel drawled, eyebrows raised. 'My new secretary. Now that you mention it, I *was* expecting you.'

'I've been here since eight-forty-five.'

'Then you should have had ample opportunity to read and digest all the information on my various companies.' He nodded to the low ash sideboard which was home to various legal books and, yes, an abundance of financial reports on his companies. She had read them all cover to cover.

Alice felt her hackles rise. 'Perhaps,' she said, keeping her voice level, 'you could give me a run-down of my duties? Normally there's a handover from the old secretary to the new one but...' *But the last one obviously ran for cover without looking back...*

'I don't actually have time to run through every detail of what you're expected to do. You'll just have to pick it up as you go along. I'm assuming the agency will have sent me someone competent who doesn't need too much hand-holding.' He watched as delicate colour invaded her cheeks. Her eyes were very firmly averted from him and she was as stiff as a piece of board.

All told, it was not the reaction Gabriel usually expected or received from the opposite sex, but perhaps the agency had been right to send him someone who wouldn't end up with an inappropriate crush on him. Miss Alice Morgan— and she looked every bit a 'Miss' even if he hadn't known she was—clearly had her head very firmly screwed on.

'Item number one on the agenda is…a cup of coffee. You'll find that that's an essential duty. I like mine strong and black with two sugars. If you unbend slightly and turn to the left, you'll notice a sliding door. All coffee making facilities are there.'

So far, everything the man was saying was getting on her nerves, and she hadn't missed the amusement in his voice when he had told her that she could 'unbend'.

'Of course.'

'Then you can grab your computer and come into my office. Fire it up and we can get going. I have some big deals on the go. You might find that you're being thrown in at the deep end. And you can relax, Miss Morgan. I don't eat secretaries for breakfast.'

Her legs finally started moving as he disappeared into his office. Duty number one : coffee making. She had not made coffee for her boss in her last job. There, everyone had chipped in. Quite frequently, Tom Davis had been the one bringing *her* a cup of coffee. It was clear that Gabriel Cabrera did not operate on such civilised lines.

By nature, Alice was not confrontational. There was, however, a streak of fierce independence in her that railed against his dictatorial attitude. She simmered and seethed as she made the coffee for him.

His image still swam in her head with pressing insistence: that ridiculously sexy face; the casual assumption that he was the big boss and so could do precisely as he pleased, even if his behaviour bordered on rude. He was rich, he was drop-dead good-looking and he knew the full extent of the power he wielded. When he had stood in front of her, she had felt as vulnerable as a minnow in the presence of a shark. Something about him was suffocating, larger than life. He was dressed in a suit, charcoal-grey, but even that had not been able to conceal the breadth of his shoulders or the lean muscularity of his physique.

He was a man who was far, far too good-looking, far too overpowering.

'Sit,' was his first word as she entered the hallowed walls of his office.

It was a vast space. Floor-to-ceiling panes of glass flooded the room with natural light which was kept at bay by pale-grey shutters. Beyond the immediate vicinity of his working area was a sectioned-off space in which low chairs circled a table and tall plants created a semi-private meeting space.

'You'd better brief me very quickly on what computer systems you're familiar with.' He drummed a fountain pen on his desk, which was chrome and glass, and gave her his undivided attention.

A sparrow. Neat as a pin, legs primly pressed together, eyes tactfully managing to avoid eye contact. Gabriel wondered whether he should send her back in exchange for something a little more decorative. He liked decorative, even though he knew the drawbacks always outweighed the advantages. But, hell, he was a man who could have anything he wanted at the click of a finger and that included interchangeable secretaries. Ever since Gladys—his sixty-year-old assistant of seven years—had inconsiderately emigrated to Australia to be with her daughter, he had run through temps like water. He knew that any agency worth its salt would have scratched him from their books if he'd been anyone else, just as he knew that they never would with him. He paid so well that they would be saying farewell to far too much commission and, in the end, wasn't greed at the bottom of everything?

His lips curled in derision. Was there nothing he couldn't have? There were definite upsides to being able to get whatever he wanted... Women flocked to him; heads of business fell silent when he spoke; the press followed him with bated breath, waiting for a hint of the next financial scoop or for a glimpse of his very active private life. He was at the very peak of his game, the undisputed leader of the pack, and there were no signs that he would be relinquishing the position any time soon. So why did life sometimes feel so damned *unsatisfying*?

He sometimes wondered whether he had used up his capacity for any genuine emotion in his tenacious climb to the top. Perhaps battling against the odds had actually been the great adventure. Now that the game had been played and he had emerged the winner, was the adventure over? Not even the brutal, frenetic push and shove of work could provide him with the adrenaline it once did. What was the point of trying when you could have it all without effort? Was *trying* just something else that had once mattered but now no longer did in the same way?

The sparrow was in full flow, telling him about her last job and giving him a long list of her responsibilities there. He held up one imperious hand, stopping her mid-sentence.

'You can only be an improvement on the last girl,' he drawled. 'I think somewhere along the line the agency lost track of the fact that I actually wanted someone who knew how to type using more than one finger.'

Alice smiled politely and thought that maybe the agency was in the dark as to whether he cared one way or another, given that his priorities seemed to lie with how good-looking the candidates were.

Gabriel frowned at that smile; it seemed at odds with the meek and mild exterior projected. 'You'll find the file on the Hammonds deal on your computer,' he said, focusing now. 'Call it up and I'll tell you what you need to do.'

Alice didn't surface for the next four hours. Gabriel kept her pinned to her computer. There was no lunch break, because it had been practically lunchtime when he had eventually strolled into the office, and he clearly assumed that she would not be hungry. He wasn't, after all, so why should she be?

At four-thirty, she looked up to find him standing in front of her.

'You seem to be keeping up. New broom sweeping clean, or can I expect this show of efficiency to be on-going?'

Under the full impact of his rapid-fire instructions, Alice had forgotten how objectionable she found him. If that was his way of telling her that she had done a good job on day one, then surely there had to be more polite ways of delivering the message?

'I'm a hard worker, Mr Cabrera,' she told him evenly. 'I can usually handle what's thrown at me.'

Gabriel sat down in the chair facing her desk and extended his long legs to one side.

Every inch of him breathed self-assurance and command. Okay, so she had to admit that the man was clever. He had the astute brain of a lawyer and an ability to pick through the finer details until he found the essential make or break one that was the difference between success and failure. On the telephone, he was confident and authoritative. From every pore of his body, he radiated the self-assurance that what he wanted, he would get.

'Highly commendable,' he said drily.

'Thank you. Perhaps you could tell me what time I shall be expected to work until today?' *Considering he had kept her waiting for hours for reasons he had not bothered to share.*

'Until I'm satisfied that your job for the day is done,' Gabriel said coolly. 'I don't believe in clock watching, Miss Morgan. Unless, of course, you have some pressing need to go by five? Have you?'

Alice smoothed her skirt with nervous hands. She had read all the promotional literature on offer during the three-hour wait in her office, and within a few seconds had known that the man was beyond influential. He was a billionaire with killer looks and she had seen from the way he had dealt with various interruptions by staff members during the day that, as the little Barbie had informed her, he did exactly as he pleased. One poor woman, the head of his legal department, had been told very firmly that she would be required to work the following weekend without a break because they were closing an important deal and would therefore be required to miss her best friend's wedding. He hadn't even bothered to pay lip service to an apology.

Gabriel Cabrera paid his employees the earth and in return they handed over their freedom.

That was a bandwagon Alice had no intention of jumping on. Right now, she was nothing more than a lowly temp, so could speak her mind and lay down some boundaries. Because should—and it was a big should—the job be offered to her on a permanent basis, then she would no longer have the freedom to tell him what she was willing to do and what she wasn't. And working weekends was definitely not on the agenda. Not given her mother's current situation.

'I'm not a clock watcher, Mr Cabrera, and I'm more than happy to work overtime if necessary. But, yes, I do value my private life and I would have to know in advance if I'm expected to sacrifice my leisure time.'

Gabriel looked at her narrowly. 'That's not how my company operates.' Indeed, that was not how *he* operated. Doling out long explanations for what he did was not part of the package. He did as he pleased and the world accepted it. He felt another tug of weary cynicism which he swatted aside. He had earned his place at the head of the table by fighting off the competition. He had started from nothing and now had everything...and that had been the object of the game: to have it all. He was accountable to no one, least of all a secretary who had been with him for two minutes!

'If I understand correctly, you're being paid double what you would normally get doing the same job in another company.'

But with a different boss, Alice was tempted to insert. *A normal boss.*

'That's true,' she admitted.

'Are you going to tell me that you don't like the nice, juicy pay packet? Because I can, of course, slash it if you want to start imposing conditions for your working hours. You've been here for five minutes and you think that you can start dictating terms?' He gave a short, incredulous laugh and shook his head. 'Unbelievable.'

'The agency implied that there might be a permanent job on offer if I made it through the probation period. I understand you haven't had a great deal of success with the previous secretaries who were sent to you.'

'And, because you've had a good first day, you somehow think that you have leverage?' But he had had a bad time of it when it came to his secretaries. Perhaps he should have been hunting down a Plain Jane like the one sitting in front of him, but you should be able to get along with the person in whose company you usually ended up spending most of your day. That seemed a sensible conclusion. He was forced to concede that his theory fell down slightly given the fact that some of the girls he had employed had wanted to get along a little too well with him for his liking.

'You seem to be getting a little ahead of yourself here,' he remarked, watching her closely. 'Wouldn't you agree?'

'No.' Alice took a deep breath, prepared to stand her ground, because she could see very clearly how the land lay with this guy.

Dark eyes clashed with hazel and she felt a tremendous whoosh go through her, as though the air had been sucked out of her body. She found him unnerving, yet today had been the most invigorating she had spent in a long time. She had blossomed under the pressure of her workload, had even seen areas where she might be able to branch out and assume more responsibility.

Was she willing to jeopardise six weeks of a sure thing in favour of laying down ground rules for a permanent job that might not even be hers?

Even as she asked herself that question, she knew the answer. She wasn't going to let anyone, however much they were paying her, dictate the parameters of her life, and not just her working life. No one in his company seemed to mind. Half the women were probably besotted with him, but not her, and she needed her time out. Life was difficult enough as it was, with her weekends taken up going to Devon to visit her mother. The last thing she needed was to have her precious week-day evenings sucked away, even if it meant forfeiting paid overtime.

'I beg your pardon?' Gabriel couldn't actually recall the last time anyone had ventured an opinion that was obviously unwelcome. Great wealth gave great freedom, and commanded even greater respect, and hadn't that always been his driving goal in life—to jettison the dark days of growing up in foster homes, where his opinion had counted for nothing and his life had been in the control of other people?

'I've only been here for one day, Mr Cabrera, and on my first day I waited for nearly three hours until you arrived. Yes, that *did* give me ample time to read your company literature, but I wasn't aware that that would be how I would spend my morning.'

'Are you asking me to account for my whereabouts this morning?' He looked at her with blatant incredulity.

At this juncture ordinarily, she would have ambushed all her chances of having another day in his company, much less the permanent position she seemed to think might be hers. But he was galled to discover that the thought of another line of inept secretaries inconveniently fancying him was not appealing, even if he *did* enjoy the pleasant view from his office they provided.

He was also weirdly fascinated by her nerve.

'Of course I'm not! And I do realise that it's not my place to start laying down any terms and conditions...'

'But you're going to anyway?' Blazing anger was only just kept in check by the fact that she had done damn well on the work front, too well to dismiss without a back-up waiting in the wings.

'I'm afraid I can't sacrifice my weekends working for you, Mr Cabrera.'

'I don't believe I asked you to.'

'No, but I saw you cancel that poor girl's weekend. Her best friend's wedding, and you told her that she had no choice but to work solidly here on both days.'

'Claire Kirk makes a very big deal about being one of the youngest in the company to head a department. She's good at what she does, and it would be a mistake to encourage her into thinking that she'll go places in this company if she isn't prepared to go the extra mile.'

Alice didn't say anything but she wondered whether he knew that there was 'going the extra mile' and then there was sacrificing your life for the sake of a *job*.

'I wouldn't have made a big deal about any of this,' she said quietly, 'But I thought you ought to know how I feel about my working conditions from day one rather than not say anything and then find myself expected to work hours I'm not willing to work. I'm not saying that I won't do overtime now and again, but I'm a firm believer in separating my personal life from my working life.'

'Tell me something, did you lay down similar boundary lines for your last boss?'

'I didn't have to,' she replied.

'Because he was a nine-to-five-thirty kind of guy? Thought so. Well, I'm not a nine-to-five-thirty kind of guy and I don't expect my employees to be nine-to-five-thirty kind of people.' It would be a shame to lose someone who showed potential but he had humoured her for long enough. 'Employees like Claire, who want to aggressively climb career ladders, work weekends when they don't want to because they understand the rules of the game. The prize never goes to the person who doesn't realise that a little sacrifice is necessary now and again if something important arises. Granted, you're not the head of a department, and you may not want any kind of career to speak of—'

'I *do* want to have a career!' Bright patches of colour appeared on her cheeks.

'Really? I'm all ears, because you're not selling it...'

Alice licked her lips nervously and stared at him. There was a brooding stillness to him that was unsettling. Nerves did their best to launch her into mindless chatter but a deeply ingrained habit of keeping her private life to herself held her back and she composed herself sufficiently to flash him another of her polite smiles.

'That was why I left my last job. I liked it there but Tom, the director of the company, was going to hand the reins over to his son, and Tom Junior wasn't a strong believer in women in the workplace, especially not in the haulage business.'

Gabriel cocked his head to one side, listening to what she was saying and what she wasn't. She talked like a prissy school-marm but there was nothing prissy or school-marmish about the way she had stood up for herself. She claimed to want a career but, when pressed, could only tell him something vague about why she had left her last company. Given half a chance, most women couldn't wait to involve him in long stories about themselves, especially long stories that were slanted in their favour, but this one... He got the feeling that she only said what she wanted someone to hear and that included him.

He glanced over her, his eyes taking in the unimaginative get-up, the long, slim frame, the uninspiring haircut.

His employees were all given a generous clothes allowance. They could afford designer gear, and this worked in particular favour of his staff lower down the pecking order, whose salaries were less enviable. Everyone, whatever their ranking, projected a certain image and he liked that. Compared to them, the little sparrow in front of him lacked polish, but there was something about her...

'So what were you planning your career to be there, had little Tommy Junior not come along to fill Daddy's shoes...?' Gabriel had virtually no respect for anyone gifted a business. He had had to find his way by walking on broken glass and he was fundamentally contemptuous of all those well- groomed, pampered boys and girls born with silver spoons in their mouths. He was a hard man who had travelled a hard road. It had worked well for him, had put him where he was today, able to do precisely as he pleased.

'I thought I might be able to get funding for an accountancy course...' She thought wistfully of the dreams she had once had to get involved in finance. She had always had a thing for numbers and it had seemed a lucrative and satisfying road to go down. Dreams, she had discovered, had a tendency to remain unfulfilled. Or at least, hers had.

'It wasn't to be,' she said briskly. 'So I thought that perhaps joining a bigger, more ambitious company might be a good idea.'

'But, before you got too accustomed to the job, you felt it necessary to tell me that your working schedule is limited.'

'My weekends are accounted for.' Alice was beginning to wish that she had decided never to say anything. She should have just kept her head down and then crossed whatever bridge she had to cross when she came to it. Instead, she had made assumptions about the way he ran his company and had decided to act accordingly.

'Boyfriend?'

'I beg your pardon?'

'Or maybe husband, although I don't see any wedding ring on the finger.'

'Sorry, but what are you talking about?'

'Isn't it usually the boyfriend in the background who

ends up dictating the working hours?' Gabriel asked, intrigued by her outspokenness, her sheer gall in laying down ground rules on day one—as though she had any right—with *him*. Intrigued, too, by that air of concealment that was so unusual in a woman. At least, in the women he knew.

'Not in this case, Mr Cabrera,' Alice told him stiffly.

'No boyfriend?'

Alice hesitated but, perhaps having misjudged her timing to start with, why not go the whole hog and expand on her conditions? He would probably chuck her out on the spot. She would return to the agency, who wouldn't be surprised to see her, and they would find her another job—something with a normal boss, working normal hours in a normal environment. It sounded unappetising.

'I should mention...' She heard the wooden formality in her voice and cringed because she was twenty-five years old, yet she sounded like someone twice her age. 'I also do not appreciate talking about my personal life.'

'Why not? Have you got something to hide?'

Alice's mouth fell open and, in return, Gabriel raised his eyebrows without bothering to help her out of her awkward silence.

'I...I do a very good job. I take my work very seriously. If you decide to keep me on, you won't regret it, Mr Cabrera. I bring one hundred and ten percent to everything I do in the working environment...'

Gabriel didn't say anything. He watched her flounder and wondered whether she brought one hundred and ten percent to whatever it was she did in the leisure time that she was so stridently protecting.

'Accountancy courses require weekend time... What would you do about those precious weekends of yours that you can't possibly sacrifice?'

'I can do the work in my own time,' Alice said promptly. 'I've checked it out. And I would pass the exams. I have a good head for figures.'

'In which case, remind me why you didn't go into that field of work when you left school…college…university? In fact, now that you seem to be campaigning for a permanent job with me, why don't you hand over the CV which I am sure is burning a hole in your bag…?'

Alice hesitated fractionally and Gabriel looked at her, his dark eyes cool and assessing.

His mobile phone rang; he glanced down at the caller ID and then he, too, hesitated, fractionally, but this time there was a smile hovering on his lips as he disconnected the call.

'Here's the deal, Miss Morgan.' He sat forward, invading her space, and rested his elbows on her desk.

Alice automatically inched back and her breathing quickened as their eyes clashed. Suddenly, she was aware of every inch of her body in ways she had never been before. She felt hot all over; her breasts felt prickly and sensitive, her skin tight and tingly. She took a deep breath and shakily told herself that she would have to subdue reactions like that if she was to be offered the job of working with this man full-time. She might not like the guy but she couldn't afford to let that dislike control her responses.

'Yes,' she said, grateful that her voice was steady and cool.

'I'm going to read your CV and, provided I don't discover any…suggestion of little white lies in it, and provided your references check out, I'm going to offer you a full-time job working with me…'

'You *are*?'

'And I'm going to go the extra mile. After all, don't

preach what you can't practise. I'm going to open the door for you to do that accountancy course you want to do.'

'Really?' A thousand jumbled thoughts were flying through Alice's head but the one that was winning the race was the one that was telling her that her life might finally start moving forward, that she might finally have enough money to start saving a little bit...

'And, naturally, you won't be called upon to sacrifice your weekends unless imperative. In return...'

'You'll find that I'm up to anything you can throw at me.'

'In that case...' He reached over for the telephone on her desk and dialled a number then, before the line connected, he said with a slow smile, 'You'll find that there are times when you do need to involve yourself in my personal life, Miss Morgan.' He handed her the phone. 'I won't be in touch with this particular woman again, so maybe you can set her straight on that score. And let's see whether you're really up to anything I can throw at you...'

CHAPTER TWO

GABRIEL SAUNTERED INTO his office and closed the door behind him. He felt energised, pleased with his decision to hire the new woman on the spot. Normally, something as trivial as this would be left to his Personnel department but the impulse had felt right.

On the spur of the moment, he telephoned the company where she had last worked and spoke for five minutes to the boss, who gave her a glowing reference.

So, he had had an interminable string of relatively competent secretaries. They had all looked good, and why shouldn't he have gone for that? Some of them could even have been brought up to the standard he wanted had they not ended up becoming inconvenient. Lingering looks, offers to work as much overtime as he wanted, skirts that seemed to get shorter and tops more plunging as the days went on... All in all, pretty annoying in the end.

He wondered how this new one was dealing with the latest woman to have been dispatched from his life and he half-smiled when he imagined her tight disapproval.

Georgia had been exciting at the beginning. She had been enthusiastic and innovative in bed and, more importantly, had seemed to really take on board the ground rules for any relationship with him—namely, forget about looking for long-term commitment. So why had he got bored with her? She had certainly been eager to please and what man didn't want a woman willing to bend over backwards for him? He wondered whether there were just too many women willing to bend over backwards for him: gorgeous, sexy, voluptuous women whose vocabulary largely centred on the word 'yes'. In his high-octane, high-pressured life, the word 'yes' had always been a soothing counterpoint. Although of late...

He scrolled through the report in front of him and acknowledged another successful takeover that would allow him to expand certain aspects of one of his technology companies into Europe. In a rare moment of introspection, he grimly congratulated himself on the distance he had travelled from the foster-home kid with zero prospects to a man who ruled the world. He was sure he had felt more pleasure in the past when he had occasionally contemplated his achievements.

He had started on the trading floor, a sixteen-year-old gofer with an uncanny ability to read markets and predict trends. His first real kick had come when he had realised that the guys with the cut-glass accents and the country estates had begun to take him seriously when he spoke. They had started seeking him out and, with the instincts born of someone from the wrong side of the tracks who was hungry and ambitious, he had learnt how to ruthlessly use and eventually channel his talents. He had learnt when to share information and when to withhold it. He had learnt that money was power and power brought immunity from ever having to do what anyone else told him to do.

He became the man who gave the orders and he liked it that way. Thirty-two years old and he was untouchable.

The firm knock on the door snapped him out of his thoughts and he sat back in his chair and summoned her in.

This, Alice was thinking as she walked into his of-

fice, was why she could never like this guy. He had dialled a number and then left her to it and, from what she
had gleaned during that conversation with Georgia of the
husky voice, he was just the sort of inveterate playboy she
despised.

But the job was going to be hers and she wasn't going
to let this type of challenge kill her chances. He seemed
to have accepted her request for her weekends to remain
sacrosanct and had hired her without the usual bank of interviews. She got the feeling that this was a departure for
him. So she could bend a little in this area…

Her face, however, was rigid with disapproval as she
sat in the chair indicated.

'I assume,' she began stiffly, 'that you would want to
see me to find out how my conversation went with your…
girlfriend…'

'Ex—ex-girlfriend. Hence the point of the conversation.
So that she could be left in no doubt as to where matters
stood.' The waves of disapproval emanating from her were
palpable. She looked as though she'd swallowed a lime and
was painfully having to digest it. 'I spoke to your ex-boss.
Sounds like a nice man. I'm thinking you were never required to step up to the plate and have any awkward conversations with his ex-lovers…'

Was he being deliberately provocative? The lazy intensity of his gaze and the suggestion of a smile on his lips
sent the blood rushing to her head and she tightened her
jacket around her and sat up a little straighter. Her crossed
legs felt as stiff as planks of wood, yet there was a curling
sensation low down in her pelvis that she chose to ignore.
Top of her mind right now was counting the ways she dis-
liked her new boss. Good-looking he might be…*stagger-
ingly good-looking*…but she decided on the spot that his
personality left her cold.

In a way, it would make for an excellent working relationship. She had already gleaned from her phone call with the unfortunate Georgia that the problem with his past few secretaries, apparently, had been with them all developing inappropriate crushes on him.

'I can't believe he's got one of his secretaries to do the dirty work for him!' Georgia had wailed down the line. 'Well, if you're like the other one...' she had sobbed, 'Showing off your boobs and thinking you can snap him up, then you're making a mistake! He's never going to go there! He doesn't like to mix work and play. He told me! So you can forget it!'

Georgia had lasted a mere two months, one week and three days. Was that the average duration of his relationships with women—a handful of months before he got bored and moved on to the next toy?

Thoughts that were usually deeply buried rose swiftly to the surface and she thought about her father—the years spent watching from the sidelines as he'd failed to return home, failed to pretend that he hadn't been playing away, failed to pay lip service to a marriage he'd wanted to ditch but couldn't afford to. She killed that pernicious, toxic trip down memory lane and dragged her wayward mind back to the present.

'Tom was and is a very happily married man,' Alice intoned. 'So, no, there were no awkward phone calls to women.' *And you should make your own phone calls,* she wanted to snap.

'I gather from your expression that I'm not winning a popularity contest at this moment in time?' Did he care one way or another? No. But if they were going to work together then there was no point in pretending to be a saint. Soon enough she would come into contact with the women who entered and left his life, barely producing a ripple.

She would have to get used to fending off the occasional uncomfortable phone call and, if her moral high ground didn't allow for that, then he needed to know right now.

'She was very upset,' Alice informed him, trying hard to avoid the trap of sounding judgemental, because what he got up to in his private life was none of her business. If he didn't care who he shared it with, then that was up to him.

And yet, she couldn't help feeling that there were sides to him that he shared with no one, and she couldn't quite work out what gave her that impression—something veiled in his eyes that belied the image of a man who laid all his cards on the table. He didn't give a damn whether she knew about his women or not but, yes, he *did* give a damn about other things, things she suspected he kept to himself.

Of course, it was fanciful thinking, because it didn't take a genius to work out that a man who had reached the meteoric heights that he had would not be the open, transparent type. He would be the type who revealed only what he wanted to and only when it served his purposes.

'I have no idea why,' Gabriel said wryly. 'I'd already informed her that I was pulling the plug on our relationship. Unfortunately, I think Georgia found it harder than she thought to accept the breakup.'

'Do you usually farm difficult conversations out to your secretaries?'

The edge of criticism in her voice should have got on his nerves but Gabriel found that it didn't. For once, he was in the company of a woman who seemed in no danger of developing a crush on him. Nor was she his type. He liked them small and curvy with an abundance of obvious charm. Prickly and challenging didn't work for him. Prickly and challenging smacked of an effort he had no enthusiasm for giving.

'I can't say the opportunity has arisen in the past few months,' Gabriel drawled.

And it wouldn't have happened now, Alice deduced, except for the fact that he had wanted to put her to the test. Maybe he thought that she would not be up to the task—too prim and proper. She didn't have to hear him say that to know that it was what he had been thinking and she bristled even though a part of her knew that, yes, she took life seriously. She had always had to. There had not been much scope to develop a frivolous side when she had spent so much of her youth supporting her mother through the innumerable bouts of her father's indiscretions.

Pamela Morgan had never seemed to have the strength to stand up to her bullying, philandering husband, so she had turned to Alice for moral support. By the time Rex Morgan had died, in a car accident, his wife had become a shadow of the girl who had married him in the false expectation of living happily ever after.

Alice's dreams had been put on hold and, when she looked back, she could see that she had spent her teenage years laying down the foundations for the person she would later become: reserved, cautious, lacking in the carefree gaiety that might have been her due, given a different set of circumstances.

Her one experience with the opposite sex had merely served to drive home to her that it never paid to think that anything good was a foregone conclusion.

'Is there anything else you'd like me to do now, and what time might I expect you to be in tomorrow morning? I don't know what your diary is.' The diary he never used.

'I keep my diary on my phone. I'll email you the contents. And tomorrow? I expect I'll be in…at my usual time. Then I'm away for the next three days. Think you can handle being on your own?'

'As I said, Mr Cabrera, I will do my utmost to deal with anything you can throw at me...'

Disgorged from the jumble of people on the tube three weeks later, it occurred to Alice that whatever had been thrown at her had obviously been full of all the right vitamins and proteins because she was enjoying her job. No, more than enjoying it. She got up early with a spring in her step, looking forward to the workload ahead of her and the slow creeping of responsibilities that were landing on her plate.

Her brain was being challenged in all sorts of ways. She was personally responsible for three large accounts. She had enrolled for her accountancy studies. And, by her standards, she was being paid a small fortune.

It was amazing, given the fact that she disapproved of much of what Gabriel stood for. She disapproved of his blatant womanising; she disapproved of the way he picked up lovers and then discarded them. He made no secret of the fact that he was as ruthless in his private life as he was in his working one. She disapproved of his supreme certainty that whatever he wanted would be his. She disapproved of the way every female employee, almost without exception, practically went down on bended knee whenever he deigned to address them. She disapproved of his ego.

On a daily basis, she fielded calls from women who wanted to talk to him and she could gauge from their hopeful, breathless voices that talking was not the only thing they wanted.

She disapproved of all of that.

The guy clearly didn't have to try when it came to the opposite sex, so he didn't. He was pursued and presumably, when he felt like it, he took one of his pursuers up on her offer and established something that couldn't even really be called a relationship.

He was lazy.

But so beautiful, a little voice in her head absently pointed out, and Alice halted for a second so that the crowds parted around her, some of them muttering impatiently under their breath.

She wouldn't deny that he had looks. The strong, aggressive lines of his lean, dark face were imprinted in her head with the force of a branding iron. She thought about him in passing more than she liked, then justified her lapses by telling herself that of course she would think of him—he was an exciting person to work for and she was only new to the job, hadn't had time to get used to him yet.

Which was why she knew just how long his dark lashes were and the way they could conceal the expression in his eyes... Which was how she knew that the second he entered the office, bringing all that force and vitality behind him, he would roll up the sleeves of his shirt, walk past her and immediately ask for his coffee.

She doubted that he even really noticed her. She was his über-efficient secretary who did as she was told faster than the speed of light. For long periods of time, he barely glanced in her direction at all.

She picked up speed, suddenly irritated for allowing her thoughts to stray down forbidden paths. He didn't notice her because she wasn't his type.

His type was...

No, she wasn't going to let her mind start speculating.

By now familiar with the impressive entrance foyer and well used to the hordes of workers and, later in the day, the tourists who were always milling about, Alice blanked everyone out as she strode purposefully towards the lift.

It was not yet eight. The three floors occupied by his

company would only be partly peopled. She liked the relative quiet as she was transported upwards…and upwards and upwards…

She felt a curl of excitement as she exited the lift. She barely recognised the emotion. Her head was full of what she had to do that day. The last thing she was expecting was to enter her office to the sight of two figures having an argument in Gabriel's office.

Through the slender panes of glass, Gabriel's face was dark with anger. She couldn't make out what was being said but his voice was low and deadly. The woman's, on the other hand…

She should interrupt. She should try to manage this situation because it was just the glorified version of what she occasionally had to do on the phone.

He didn't seem to care whether women chased him or not, or even whether they threw hissy fits down the end of the line, but he kept sharp dividing lines between work and play.

Obviously some poor woman had failed to pay attention to that dividing line and was paying the price.

And doesn't it serve him right?

The thought sprang from nowhere but, once it took hold, it couldn't be budged.

She had no idea who this woman was but why shouldn't he sort this situation out himself? Just because he had all the money and power in the world, it didn't mean that he could take the easy way out when it came to the situations he engendered with his women!

She calmly removed her lightweight coat and hung it up in the sliding cupboard. Then she made herself a cup of coffee and, with mug in hand, she sat at her desk and switched on her computer.

But she couldn't focus. Her eyes kept sliding from her

computer screen to the sketch being enacted behind Gabriel's closed door. That said, she was still shocked when the closed door was banged open and out flew a woman with waist-length dark hair and a porcelain-white complexion. Her red dress was skin-tight, her heels were five inches high at the very least and she was trailing a pink-and-black-checked summer coat over her shoulder.

She looked furious. Furious and upset. She paused just long enough to glare at Alice through tear-filled eyes.

'He's a pig!' She glared over her shoulder to where an impassive Gabriel was watching them both with steely-eyed coldness, then fixing enraged dark eyes on Alice. 'But at least he hasn't got one of those dolly birds working for him this time!'

'Georgia…' Gabriel's voice silenced what promised to be a tirade. He spoke very quietly and with such contained menace that Alice felt sorry for the poor woman. 'If you don't leave my premises immediately, I will call security and have you thrown out. And you…' He directed this at Alice who tilted her head to one side in perfect secretarial mode. 'Kindly escort Georgia out of the building and then come into my office…'

She was barely aware of Georgia talking non-stop on the way down in the lift. The diminutive brunette was angry, bitter and, reading between the lines, humiliated because she had never been dumped in her life before. Men chased *her* and *she* was the one responsible for doing any dumping.

Alice could have told her that she had taken on far more than she could ever have hoped to chew with a man like Gabriel.

'Well, at least you'll be safe as houses,' the other woman sniped as her parting shot. 'Gabriel would never look twice at someone like you. And tell him from me—I hope he rots in hell!'

The spurt of courage that had prompted her to stay put in her office twenty minutes earlier had evaporated by the time Alice returned there, having successfully deposited Georgia on the street outside. Still, there was no way that she intended to apologise for not having interrupted the scene in his office.

With any luck, he would simply brush over the whole incident and the day would commence as it always did, at full tilt.

'What the hell do you think you were playing at?' were his opening words as she walked into his office with her tablet in her hand, ready for the day to begin.

'I beg your pardon?' She started as he swooped round his desk to perch on the edge so that he was looming over her, face as dark as thunder.

'And don't give me that "butter wouldn't melt in your mouth" look! I saw the way you sneaked into the office and hid behind your computer!'

'I did not *sneak* into my office, Gabriel...' It always felt odd to call him by his Christian name but after three days of 'sir' and 'Mr Cabrera' and 'Mr Cabrera, sir' he had impatiently insisted that she drop the titles and call him Gabriel. It was one of those names that did not happily roll off the tongue. It was just too...*sexy*...

'Nor,' she asserted firmly, 'did I *hide* behind my computer!'

'You did both. You knew that I was trapped there with that woman and instead of offering to escort her out you ducked for cover and watched from the sidelines!'

'*That woman...?*'

Gabriel flushed darkly and raked long fingers through his hair. 'I'm not in the mood for your sermonising,' he growled, glaring at her.

'I didn't realise that I sermonised,' Alice said truthfully. She had her thoughts, but those she kept very much to herself.

'You don't have to! I know exactly what goes on in that head of yours whether you voice your opinions or not!'

Alice didn't say anything. His proximity was having a weird effect on her. If she looked directly at him, the glittering intensity of his dark eyes was unnerving. But if she looked a little lower, then she was confronted by his thigh, the taut pull of fine fabric over muscular legs, and that was even more unnerving. She could almost hear the steady drum roll of her heart and the rush of blood in her ears. He rarely invaded her space like this and she didn't have the resources to withstand the impact he had on her nervous system.

'Explain that remark.'

Alice had subtly pressed herself into the back of her chair. She wished he would let this conversation go because she could feel it teetering on the brink of getting too personal, and getting personal was something he had studiously avoided over the past three weeks. He never even asked her how she had spent her weekends.

'What remark?' she asked warily and he gave her another of those piercing looks that seemed to imply that he was perfectly aware that she was trying to dodge the conversation.

'You should try to avoid doing that as much as you can, you know,' he murmured softly.

It was like having her skin lightly brushed with a feather; the lazy speculation in his voice was even more disconcerting than the full-body impact of his towering presence so close to her.

'Aren't you going to ask me what I mean by that?' Gabriel continued into the lengthening silence, and Alice tried her best to dismiss the prickles of sensation racing through her body like tiny sparks of fire. 'No, of course you won't, but I'll tell you anyway. You should never try and wriggle away from a direct question. It makes me all the more determined to prise a suitable answer from you. The rule of thumb is that there's nothing more challenging to a man like me than a gauntlet that's been thrown down—and your silences count as gauntlets.' He didn't normally like challenges when it came to women but, hell, he liked *this* one…

A man like him?

Alice steeled herself to look him squarely in the face. 'I don't think it's very nice of you to throw your ex-lover out of the building because she happened to be upset with you.' There was a lot more she could have said on the subject but she chose to keep that to herself.

'It wasn't,' Gabriel grated, '*very nice* of my ex-lover to descend on me, in my office, so that she could throw a tantrum.' He vaulted upright and prowled through the office which she had somehow managed to make her own in the handful of weeks she had been working for him. There were two plants on the bookshelf, another on her desk and a discreet Buddha figurine which she kept next to the telephone. Having circled the room, he returned to stare down at her, hands thrust into his pockets.

'I don't suppose that was her intention,' Alice told him calmly. 'I don't think she came here planning to have a yelling fit at you. I think if she'd planned on screaming she could have done it down the telephone rather than come here and risk the humiliation of being ushered out of the building like a common criminal.'

'But then, if she'd used the telephone, she would have had to get past my faithful and extremely proficient secretary, wouldn't she?'

Alice blushed and wondered how two perfectly flattering adjectives could end up sounding so unappealing.

'Maybe,' he mused, leaning down, palms of his hands on her desk, 'she was overcome with a pressing need to vent. Do you think that might be it?'

Alice shrugged and for a few seconds their eyes tangled. Her mouth went dry and her brain seemed to seize up completely so that she had to suck in air and force herself to breathe evenly.

'Have *you* ever experienced that before, Alice?'

'Experienced what?' Alice asked in a hoarse whisper, and he laughed under his breath.

'The grip of passion that makes you behave irrationally…'

'I prefer to trust reasoning and logic,' she managed to say.

'So that's a *no*…'

'If you recall…' She was close to snapping because not only was he making her feel uncomfortable but he was enjoying himself. 'I *did* say to you when I took this job that I didn't want to talk about my private life!'

'Was that what we were doing? Talking about your private life?' He stood up, flexed his muscles, debated whether to let this conversation go and just as quickly decided not to. Georgia's untimely visit had dented his concentration and he was finding it strangely enjoyable to offload on his secretary. Offloading was not something he normally did. In his formidably controlled life, there was seldom any reason to, and he had to concede that, had Alice not been there, not been his secretary, he wouldn't have felt tempted.

But, hell, why deny it? She roused his curiosity. She was so contained, so secretive whilst giving the impression of being straightforward, so unwilling to share even the smallest of confidences, such as what she did on those precious weekends of hers that couldn't possibly be interrupted…

He would stake his fortune on 'nothing' and he wondered whether his curiosity was sparked by the mere fact that she never mentioned it. When you could have anything you wanted, including access to people's thoughts and emotions, what price for the person who withheld everything?

'You may think it's okay to treat women exactly how you like, but everyone has their story to tell, and you have no idea what sort of collateral damage you could be inflicting!' Her eyes skittered away from his narrowed gaze and she knew that she was beetroot-red and angry with him for encouraging an outburst that was inappropriate.

'Collateral damage…?' he asked thoughtfully.

'I apologise. I shouldn't have…said anything.' She offered him a weak smile which he chose to ignore.

'We work closely together,' he murmured. 'You should always feel free to speak your mind.'

'You like women speaking their minds, do you?' Alice asked tartly and was rewarded with one of those rare smiles that always knocked the breath out of her body.

'Touché… It can occasionally be a little tedious, but then I never encourage the women I date to ever think that it might be a good idea to give their thoughts an airing.'

Why not? Alice was tempted to ask. She didn't dare look at him because she had a sneaking suspicion that he might be able to read her mind.

Besides, didn't she know why? Why go to the bother of working at something meaningful if you could have whatever you wanted without putting the effort in? People got where they were because of circumstances shaping them over the course of time and, whatever the circumstances that had shaped Gabriel Cabrera, they had left him in a place where he just couldn't be bothered.

'What do you encourage them to do?' She asked her reluctant question, which was motivated by a burning curiosity she was desperate to kill whilst being unable to resist.

'I don't.' Gabriel gave her a slashing smile of satisfaction. 'And, now that we've plumbed the depths of my psyche, why don't we get down to doing something productive?'

It was nearly six by the time she surfaced. He had spent a good part of the day involved with high-level meetings, giving her the chance to quell the sludgy, disturbing feelings that had come to the fore during their conversation, when he had strayed beyond their normal boundaries like an invader testing a solid wall for cracks through which unwelcome entrance might be possible.

As she began clearing her desk to leave, she succumbed to a little smile at what an overactive imagination could produce. He didn't want to find out about *her*. He wasn't interested in whether there were cracks in her armour or not. He enjoyed pushing against barriers because that was the way he was built and, if the barriers happened to be around *her,* then push against them he would if the inclination took him.

As a woman, she held no interest for him.

She thought of Georgia of the husky voice and imagined that *that* was the sort of woman that interested him. Men always went for the same *type,* didn't they?

An image of Alan sprang uninvited into her head. Alan of the floppy blond hair and the brown eyes, who had ditched her for a version of womanhood not a million miles removed from her boss's ex. Flora was small and curvy as well. Not as stunning, and probably not as breezily self-confident about the power she had over the opposite sex, but, yes, fashioned from the same mould.

'You're smiling.'

She hadn't even been aware of Gabriel entering the office behind her as she shrugged on her jacket and she started and blushed.

'It's nearly the end of the week,' she responded automatically, although, thinking about it, her week days were more relaxing than her weekends, which were consumed with long trips down to visit her mother.

'Is working for me that much of a trial?' She had been awarded the same clothes allowance as the other employees on her level yet she still wore the same dreary suits to work. Black and shades of black seemed to be the preferred, professional option with his staff, yet her suits, although the requisite colour, didn't seem to fit with the same snug panache.

The errant thought occupied his mind for a few seconds and he frowned and pushed it away.

'Of course not. I...I love it, as a matter of fact.' He was lounging against the doorframe, as dramatically good-looking at the close of day as he was first thing in the morning. Where most people occasionally looked harried, he always seemed to be brimming over with vitality, however frantic his day might have been.

'That's good to hear because I haven't got around to having any kind of appraisal with you.'

Alice doubted he had ever done an appraisal in his life. If his employee didn't fit the bill, then he simply dispensed with them.

'Not,' he said, reading her mind with unnerving accuracy, 'that I make a habit of conducting appraisals of my secretaries.'

'Is that because they usually only last two minutes?'

A tingle of pure pleasure raced through her when he burst out laughing, which subsided eventually for him to cast appreciative eyes over her.

'Something like that,' he murmured. 'Seems a little pointless to give them an appraisal when they've already got one foot through the back door and their desk has been cleared.'

'Well...' He was blocking her way out and she dithered uncomfortably. Standing by him, it was brought home sharply just how tall he was. She was tall but he positively towered over her.

'Well, of course, you're on your way out. Is that what had you smiling?'

'I beg your pardon?'

'Your plans for the evening. Is that what put that smile on your face?'

If only you knew... If only you guessed that I was smiling at the notion that you would never look twice at me; smiling for being an idiot even to think about something like that.

His plans had been for the theatre, followed by dinner at one of the most exclusive restaurants in London.

The theatre, followed by dinner out—at a haunt for the paparazzi because the clientele was usually very high-profile—followed by...

Heat flooded her as she contemplated after-dinner sex with the man standing in front of her, still blocking her path. His hands on her body, his mouth exploring her, that dark, sexy voice whispering in her ear...

Her body jack-knifed into instant, crazy reaction. Liquid pooled between her legs and the unfamiliar tug of desire hit her like a ton of bricks, shocking in its intensity and as destabilising as the sudden onslaught of some ferocious disease. She couldn't move. Her legs were blocks of cement, nailing her to the floor as her imagination took flight in forbidden directions.

And, all the while, she could feel those dark, dark eyes pinned to her face.

'I have to go,' she said tightly. She went to push him aside and more heat flared inside her, making a mockery of her attempts to harness her prized composure.

He was a man she might respect but didn't like! A man whose brilliance she could admire whilst being left cold by his detachment!

Once out of the office, she fled…

CHAPTER THREE

ALICE WOKE WITH a start. In her dream, she had been running down an endlessly long corridor, chasing Gabriel who would occasionally glance over his shoulder, only to turn away and continue running. In the dream, she had no idea what lay at the end of that corridor, or even if there *was* an end to it, but she was filled with a sense of terrifying foreboding, wanting to stop and yet propelled forward by some power greater than her own.

She was slick with perspiration and completely disoriented and it took her a few seconds to realise that her mobile was ringing. Not the sharp, insistent buzz of her alarm but actually ringing.

'Good. You're awake.'

Hard on the heels of her disturbing dream, Gabriel's voice cut through the fog of her sleepiness as effectively as a bucket of ice-cold water, and she sat up in bed, glancing at the clock on her bedside table which showed that it wasn't yet six-thirty.

'Is that you, Gabriel?'

'How many calls do you get from men at this hour of the morning? No, don't answer that.'

'What's wrong with your voice?' This was the first time he had ever called her at home on her mobile and she looked around her furtively, as though suspecting that at any second he might materialise from the shadows.

Thankfully, her bedroom was as it always was—small with magnolia walls, some nondescript curtains and two colourful pictures on either side of the dressing table, scenes of Cornwall painted by a local artist whom Alice knew vaguely through her mother. An averagely passable room in a small, uninteresting house whose only selling point was its proximity to the tube.

In the bedroom next to hers, her flat mate, Lucy, would still be sleeping.

'It seems I'm ill.'

'You're *ill*?' The thought of Gabriel being ill was almost inconceivable and she felt a sudden grip of panic.

Whatever was wrong with him, it would be serious. He was not the sort of man to succumb to a passing virus. He was just too...*strong*. She couldn't imagine that there could be any virus on the planet daring enough to attack him.

'Ill with *what*?' She brought the decibel level of her worried voice down to normal. 'Have you called the doctor?'

'Of course not.'

'What do you mean *of course not*?'

'Are you dressed?'

His impatient voice, which she had become accustomed to, sliced through her concern and she glanced in the dressing-table mirror facing her to see her still sleepy face staring back at her.

Her straight hair was all over the place and the baggy tee-shirt, her bedtime attire of choice, was half-slipping off her shoulder, exposing the soft swell of a breast.

Self-consciously, she hoiked it up and then lay back against the pillow.

'Gabriel, my alarm doesn't go off for another forty-five minutes...'

'In that case, switch it off and think about getting up and out of bed.'

'What's wrong?'

'Sore throat. Headache. High fever. I've got flu.'

'You've phoned me at…at *six-twenty* in the morning to tell me that you've *got a cold*?'

'I think you'll find that what I have is considerably more serious than *a cold*. You need to get up, get into the office and bring the two files I left on my desk. Not all of the information is on my computer and I need to access it in its entirety.'

She had worked with him long enough to know that he dished out orders in the full expectation that they would not be countermanded, but she was still outraged that he had seen fit to yank her out of sleep so that he could…

What, exactly?

'Bring your files?'

'Correct. To my house. And bring your computer as well. You'll have to work from here. It's not ideal but it's the best I can come up with. I can't make it into the office today.'

'Surely you can just take the day off if you're not feeling well, Gabriel?' *Like any other normal human being,* she was tempted to add. 'If you tell me what you want me to work on, I can do it in the office and I can scan and email the files over to you, if you really think that you're up to working.'

'If I'd wanted you to do that, I would have said so. And I can't keep talking indefinitely. My throat's infected. If you head for the office now, you can be with me within an hour and a half. Less, if you get your skates on. Got a pen?'

'A pen?' Alice parroted in dismay as this new unfolding of her day ahead began to take shape in her head.

'A pen—instrument for writing. Have you got one to hand? You'll need to write down my address and postcode. And for God's sake, take a taxi, Alice. I know you're fond of the London public transport system, but we might as well get this show on the road as quickly as possible. There's a lot to get through and I won't be up to much beyond six… It's ridiculous. I haven't been ill in years. I must have caught this from you.'

'You haven't caught anything from me! I'm fighting fit!'

'Good. Because you have a lot to get through today. Now, let me give you my address.'

She got a pen and wrote down his address and then listened as he rattled off a few more orders and then… dial tone.

She had no time for breakfast. She could have grabbed something but for some unaccountable reason she found herself rushing to have a shower, rushing to get dressed, rushing to head for the tube and then, on the spur of the moment, hailing a black cab—because she could almost feel those dark eyes peering at her from wherever he was.

The man was utterly impossible. He really and truly didn't care what discomfort he caused for other people. He took it as his God given right to disrupt other people's plans and then excused himself his own arrogance by giving one of those elegant shrugs and waving aside all objections because, after all, comparatively he paid them the earth. He was brilliant, he did as he pleased, and why on earth would anyone not want to fall in line?

She made it to his house within the hour and only when the taxi had deposited her there did her nervous system kick back into gear.

This was unknown territory. Had anyone in the office ever been to his house? Company entertaining was all done in restaurants, or expensive venues in the City, and he certainly wasn't the avuncular sort of boss who hosted little parties so that his employees could bond with one another.

She stared at the impressive Georgian facade and hesitated. What had she expected? She didn't know. Something far less grand—a penthouse apartment, perhaps. There was, after all, only *one* of him, even if he had all the money in the world to play with. Why did he need a London mansion?

Black brass railings cordoned off the house and matched all the other black brass railings of the mansions alongside it. Standing here, gazing up with her little handbag, her company case full of files and her computer, she felt as though she might be arrested at any moment for the crime of just not quite blending in.

Inhaling deeply, she rang the buzzer and his disconnected voice came on the line.

'I'll buzz you in. You'll find me upstairs.'

'Where...?' But the door had popped open; as to his whereabouts...she assumed she would have to locate him through sheer guesswork.

Her heart was beating madly as she stared around her. The hall was absolutely enormous, almost as big as the entire ground floor of her shared house. Victorian tiles were broken by a pale Persian rug and ahead of her a staircase wound its elegant way upwards.

What was he doing upstairs? Was his office there?

She smoothed down her skirt with perspiring hands. She could have worn something more casual— could have worn her jeans and a tee-shirt, considering she wouldn't actually be in the office—but she hadn't. She had dressed as she always did, in a neat black skirt, her white short-sleeved blouse and her little black jacket. She was very glad she had gone for the formal option.

It was harder to locate him than she would have thought possible because the house was huge, split into three storeys with myriad rooms to the left and right of the staircase. She peered into two sitting rooms and several bedrooms before she eventually hit the right one at the very end of the wide corridor.

Through the half-open door, she glimpsed rumpled covers on a bed and she hesitantly knocked.

'About time! How long does it take one person to make her way through a house?'

Gabriel was propped up in bed. The rumpled duvet had been shoved to one side and he was in a black dressing gown, legs bare, sliver of chest exposed, black hair tousled. Next to him was his computer, on which he had clearly been working.

Alice averted her eyes and felt a tightening in her chest, almost as if she was in the grip of an incipient panic attack.

'Are we going to be…er…working *here*?'

'Stop hovering by the door and come inside. And where else do you suggest we hold proceedings?'

'I passed an office…'

'I can't get out of bed. I'm ill.' This was the first time in living memory that he had been in his bed and the woman standing in his bedroom looked as though the last thing she wanted was to be there. 'And, as you can see, this isn't a bedroom. It's a suite.' He nodded to the sofa which was by the tall windows and the long coffee table in front of it. 'Does it make you uncomfortable, Alice?'

'Of course not.' But there was a wicked gleam in his eyes which *did* make her uncomfortable. Gabriel would not be happy with being bed-ridden for whatever reason. He was not the sort of man whose restless energy could be contained without it emerging somewhere else. The Devil worked on idle hands and for him his hands would be idle…

'I just think that it might be more suitable if we were in an office environment.'

'Why? Everything I need is right here. Where are the

files? And for God's sake, sit down! How are you going
to work if you keep standing by the door?'

He shifted impatiently and Alice gulped as yet more of
that hard, bronzed torso was revealed.

He should be in his suit. He should be properly attired.
There was an intimacy here that had her nerves all over the
place and she was so keen to make sure that he didn't see
that, her movements were stiff and awkward, her mouth
more tightly pursed, her hands white as they gripped the
case she had brought with her.

She felt horrendously uncomfortable in her knee-length
black skirt, and her sheer black tights were itchy against
her legs.

'Have you…taken anything for your cold?' she asked
as she sat gingerly on the sofa and tried not to look at him
without actually looking away; tried to mentally blank him
out, which was next to impossible. 'Sorry, I meant *flu*?'

'Of course not.'

'Why ever not?'

'What good would that do? The thing just has to run
its course.'

'I'll get you some paracetamol.'

'You will sit and start going through the Dickson file
with me.'

'Where is your medicine cabinet?'

'I don't have one.'

Alice shot him an exasperated look and walked across
to stand over him with her arms folded. 'You look terrible.'

'Good. You're waking up to the fact that I'm seriously
ill.'

'And you look terrible because you're refusing to help
yourself. You are *not* seriously ill, Gabriel. You have a
spring cold. You're just not accustomed to being under
the weather.'

'What do you mean, I'm *refusing to help myself*?' Gabriel growled. 'You're a woman! Where's your milk of human kindness? Do you know how many women would kill to be in this position—to be able to prove that they're domestic goddesses by cooking me something to eat and playing at Florence Nightingale!'

'In which case…' She handed him his mobile phone. 'Please feel free to call any one of them. I'm more than happy to be replaced.'

'Sit down!' he roared, before spluttering into a coughing fit which Alice observed without budging, arms still folded, cool as a cucumber and grudgingly amused at seeing her all-powerful boss losing his control because he was in the grip of nothing more serious than a simple passing cold.

He could be vulnerable. In a way least expected, he was showing her that he could be petulant, utterly exasperating in a very human way and…

Stupidly endearing with it.

'I have some tablets in my handbag. I'll fetch you a glass of water and you're going to take them. They might not cure your cold but they'll relieve your symptoms.'

'Does that include my roasting fever? I'm burning up. Feel me if you don't believe me.'

Alice sighed and felt his forehead and, as she did so, she felt a throbbing ache rip through her, scattering her self-composure for a second or two.

'You have a slight temperature.' She yanked her hand back and surreptitiously wiped it on her skirt, hoping to rid herself of the spark that had flared between them, dangerously, electrifyingly alive and as threatening as her dream had been to her peace of mind.

Why the sudden *awareness* of the man? she wondered. She disapproved of him as much now as she had done when she had first met him. So, they worked well together. So, maybe there were different sides to him; he wasn't the one-dimensional guy she had chosen to categorise him as...

But why was it that the minute he was within touching distance of her she became as jumpy as a cat on a hot tin roof?

It was galling to think that she might have fallen into the same pathetic trap as all his other secretaries and she instantly killed that notion by telling herself that she hadn't. He was fabulously good-looking and she was only human, after all. What reaction he evoked was one she could squash without any difficulty.

Although right now, having to sit in the same room as him when he was, quite frankly, indecently under-dressed...

She strode out of the room into the adjacent *en suite* bathroom, ignoring the slightly damp white towel carelessly slung on the heated towel rail, and emerged with a glass of tap water and the tablets which she had extracted from her bag.

'Take them.'

'You're extremely bossy.' But he took the tablets from her and swallowed them with a gulp of water. 'Not a feminine trait.'

Alice blushed, hot, flustered and irritated. 'I'm not here to be "feminine",' she retorted tartly. 'I'm here to go through some files which couldn't possibly wait until next week. You have your string of girlfriends to distract you with their feminine wiles.'

'I'm a girlfriend-free zone at the moment, as it happens. Although I'm sure you're already aware of that, considering you're the one who's responsible for booking the venues I go to with them.'

The unfeminine, drab-but-efficient secretary who an-

swers to your beck and call and books all the exciting places you take your women to...

So far, she had just booked the opera, but he was still fresh out of his relationship with Georgia and perhaps not quite there when it came to diving into a brand new relationship with another woman. The opera for two...

'What happened to your opera companion?' She allowed herself to be distracted, swept away on the disagreeable thought that life was passing her by as she stood on the sidelines, somehow waiting for it to happen.

She had never felt this way before. She had been happy to settle into a routine and to accept that, if things hadn't turned out the way she had planned, then they could be worse. This was her lot and so be it.

Was it Gabriel's overwhelming vitality that made her feel slow and sluggish in comparison? Was it the fact that she was the dullard behind the computer who booked the exciting events for exciting women?

'Turns out she didn't have what it takes. Admittedly, she was sexy as hell,' he mused lazily. 'But sadly the legs, the curves, the winning pout...weren't enough to save her from being interminably boring.'

Alice's rictus smile felt strained at the edges. *Another one bites the dust*, she thought with simmering resentment. Time to move on to another model and, fingers crossed, the legs, the curves and yet another winning pout might be combined with half a personality. While other *normal* people stuck things out because life was just not one long array of delectable dishes to be sampled and discarded, the Man Who Had It All just couldn't be bothered with little niceties like that.

'Maybe,' he continued in the same musing, sexy voice, 'I should incorporate that into your job description... Maybe I should delegate you to finding me someone who won't prove tiresome after five seconds. Think you can handle it?'

Anger replaced resentment and, suddenly, Alice saw red. Who the heck did he think she was? Some kind of facilitator to ensure that even less effort was required by him when it came to finding a woman? Did he have any idea how condescending he sounded? How terminally *dull* he made her feel? Did he even *care*?

'You…you…you have to be the *laziest man* I have ever met in my *entire life*!'

'Come again?'

'You heard me, Gabriel. You're lazy!' Hot, angry eyes raked over that sexy, prone body with the silk dressing gown allowing her far too wide-ranging a view of hard muscle and sinew. 'You may work like the Devil, and you may have the Midas touch, but you can't even be bothered to sort your own emotional life out! Why don't you put some thought into booking the stuff you decide to do with your women? Why don't you field your own calls and make your own excuses when you don't want to see someone? You even got me to *choose* a parting gift for Georgia after she stormed out of your office! Something conciliatory, you said, money no object—and you never even bothered to find out *what* I'd chosen! How lazy is that?'

She had picked out a huge bouquet of flowers and a designer scarf in the colours of the coat the other woman had been wearing when she had had her hissy fit in his office. It had been eye-wateringly expensive but she doubted he would even raise an eyebrow when it showed up on his statement.

'You're going beyond your brief,' Gabriel told her coolly. *Lazy? Him? Hell, he worked all the hours God made! He had climbed the ladder no one thought he could and he had climbed it to the very top and built a castle there!*

But she hadn't been referring to his unparalleled success on the work front, had she? She had gone straight to the emotional side of his life. Typical of a woman, he told himself without the slightest inclination to analyse what she had said. As far as he was concerned, he had come from nothing and now had everything. He could have any woman he wanted. They flocked to him and he was astute enough to suspect that his sizeable bank balance had a lot to do with it. Would they still have flocked in their droves if he had never climbed that ladder? If the foster-care kid had become the welfare-dependent adult? Somehow, he didn't think so.

No, the only thing he could rely upon was his ability to make money and to use his wealth to buy himself absolute freedom. Everything else fell by the wayside in comparison.

But the description still left a sour taste in his mouth.

'I'm sorry,' Alice told him without hesitation. 'I didn't mean to be critical.'

Gabriel could have taken her up on that insincere assertion. He didn't. Instead, he turned to the reason she was there in the first place and the next three hours were spent poring over the files she had brought with her.

She had a good brain. She had creative and different ways of looking at potential problems. She could quickly do the maths when it came to sounding out the viability of certain tricky areas.

She had obviously forgotten her outburst but he still caught himself staring at her every so often, her down-bent head, her slender fingers tapping expertly on the keyboard as she amended documents.

And the damn woman had been right about the tablets. By midday, he was feeling better.

'Right.' He swung his legs over the side of the bed and

Alice, ensconced on the sofa by the window, looked at him in alarm.

'What are you doing?' She had just about forgotten that she was working with him in his bedroom and that he was wearing nothing but a flimsy black robe which he was at no pains to pull tightly around him. She had told her wayward eyes to get a grip and thankfully, under the onslaught of work, they had. She had established their routine of sorts. And now he was standing up and tying the belt of the bathrobe only after she had glimpsed boxer shorts and brown thighs speckled with fine dark hair. He had amazing ankles. She kept her eyes firmly riveted on that fairly harmless section of his body as he strolled towards the bathroom and informed her that he was going to have a shower.

'Why don't you wait for me in the kitchen? We can grab something to eat before we carry on.'

'You seem a lot better,' Alice ventured. 'Are you sure you wouldn't rather wrap up what we've been doing and really…um…harness your energies? They say that the best way to get rid of a cold—sorry, flu—is to just take it easy and rest.'

'That might work for some people but not for me. Taking it easy isn't my style. Now, unless you want to follow me into the bathroom so that we can continue discussing the situation with the electronics subsidiary, I suggest you stretch your legs and head downstairs. In fact…' He paused by the door and looked at her, his eyes showing just the merest flicker of amusement even though his tone of voice remained bland. 'You could always make yourself useful and cook us something to eat. You'll find the fridge and the cupboards well-stocked. In keeping with my laziness, I have someone who makes sure that they are…'

With which he disappeared into the bathroom, not bothering to lock the door, leaving her with the frustrated feeling that somehow the rug had been neatly pulled out from under her feet.

Since when did her secretarial duties encompass cooking for the boss? Did the man know how to do anything but take advantage? Since when had it been written into her contract that she would have to fly over to his house, faster than the speed of light, so that she could plough through endless files with him because he happened to have caught a passing bug?

And why on earth hadn't she objected more than she had? Why on earth did she feel so *alive* even when she was around him?

Downstairs, she looked around a kitchen where everything, from granite counters to gadgets, was polished to a high shine. She guessed that the person responsible for making sure that the fridge and cupboards were stocked with food was also responsible for making sure that dust and dirt didn't find a foothold.

There was bread, ham, eggs and all manner of delicacies in the fridge and, after several attempts, she located the whereabouts of the tea, various kinds, and also various kinds of coffee.

'I could always order in…' His voice drawled behind her and Alice spun round, skin burning as though she had been caught red-handed with her hand in the till.

Gabriel wandered towards her, freshly showered and thankfully out of his bathrobe and in clothes—although his clothes were no less disconcerting, because he was in a pair of black jeans and a baggy rugby shirt. She couldn't expect him to get dressed in his usual suit to stay home, but she wished that he had, because it would have cemented the boss-secretary line between them, would have reinforced their respective roles.

He was the essence of the alpha male—tall, dominant, with the sleek, latent power of a predator. In fact, there were times when she felt distinctly like prey when she was around him. This was one of those times, although she didn't know why. She just knew that watching him pad through the kitchen barefoot, in jeans that delineated every powerful line of his body, was horribly unsettling.

'You should be wearing something on your feet,' she said inanely as he joined her by the kitchen counter so that he could help with the tea making. 'You might be feeling better thanks to the tablets, but you don't want to get a relapse.'

'Underfloor heating in the kitchen. If you'd take those black pumps off, you'd find that the floor is very warm.' She hadn't so much as undone the top button of her very neat white shirt, he thought. She was out of the office, and there had been no need to wear office garb, but pre-dictably she had not deviated from her strict dress code. She hadn't even kicked off her sensible patent shoes for the entire time she had been sitting on the sofa in his bedroom taking notes and amending reports on her computer.

She was the stiffest, least relaxed woman he had ever met. Yet, when she had exploded, he had glimpsed a side to her that was as volatile and as fiery as a volcano. It made sense. She was smart, she had a good brain. That in itself would indicate that there was more to her than the dutiful secretary who spoke her mind, but politely, and always managed to leave the impression that there was a lot more to her than met the eye.

He wondered *what*.

Having grown accustomed to a diet of very willing and very beautiful women, he let his mind wander over the very prickly, very proper and very average Miss Alice

Morgan. And, once there, his mind showed every inclination of staying put.

Her dress code was so damned bland that it positively encouraged the eye to look away with boredom, but there was a pale delicacy to her face and a fullness to her mouth that hinted at a sensuality he suspected she was not aware of.

And just like that he felt himself harden.

'I would rather finish what we're doing and then head home.' Alice was uncomfortable with this domestic game they seemed to be playing. She hadn't signed up for this and she didn't know how to deal with being yanked out of her comfort zone.

Gabriel scowled. Without warning, he imagined her taking it between those cool hands of hers, lowering her mouth to it and licking it with her very delicate pink tongue. The graphic clarity of the image shocked him.

'Too bad,' he snapped. 'You're not being paid to skive off early just because I'm not fighting fit.'

What had brought *that* on? Alice wondered. Maybe he was getting to the end of his tether being cooped up in his house with a woman who wasn't his temporary bed partner. He was probably used to sharing his kitchen with a Georgia lookalike, except one in even less clothing. A Georgia lookalike wearing nothing but an apron and waving a spatula about with a come-hither grin.

'That's not fair,' she told him quietly. 'I'm just not very hungry; please don't think that you have to break off because of me.'

'I'm not,' Gabriel said shortly. He was still aching, his erection still hard and throbbing, and his imagination was still galloping merrily on a free rein. Without a trace of vanity, he knew that most women would kill to be in her position—in his kitchen with him, cooking. He had yet to allow any woman to cook for him. Why give them the wrong ideas? No, he entertained them in the relative safety of expensive restaurants. That way they couldn't start harbouring unrealistic ideas of domesticating him.

Yet here she was, standing with her back pressed against his kitchen counter, trying to find excuses to leave.

It was ludicrous to let that get under his skin but, coming hard on the heels of the erotic thoughts that had taken root in his head, it did.

He fished his mobile phone out of his pocket, called his friend and head chef at one of the top restaurants in the city and ordered a meal for two, menu unspecified. As he spoke, he kept his eyes pinned to Alice's face and she angrily wondered whether this was an attempt to generate some sort of guilt complex in her because she hadn't jumped at the chance of cooking a meal for him.

The more she thought about Gabriel, the more she realised just how lazy he was in his personal life. But, if he thought that he could make inroads into *her,* somehow turn her into one of his followers who did every single thing he wanted with a smile on their face, then he was in for a shock.

'You do realise that there's still a hell of a lot of work to do on Trans-Telecom,' he grated, sitting on one of the chrome and leather chairs by the kitchen table. He could feel the temperature he had managed to keep at bay with the tablets begin to rise as the pain killers wore off. 'You don't have to stand over there!' he snapped. 'If you're going to catch anything from me, then chances are you will have caught it already!'

'I thought you had covered most of the technical details on that.' Alice walked towards him and perched facing him. The thought that he might be infectious hadn't even crossed her mind. She had been far too busy just fretting about being in his house with him! He obviously hadn't shaved this morning and the darkening of stubble on his face was sinfully, extravagantly attractive.

'There's a deadline on this deal. The lawyers have pored over it with a fine-tooth comb but I still need to make sure that all bases are covered. I can't afford to have a comma in the wrong place or else there's the chance the whole thing will be called off. It's taken long enough for me to get the family on board with the concept of selling. I don't want any delay to have them getting cold feet at the last minute.'

Alice nodded. She was mesmerised by the intensity of his eyes, the perfect command he had when he was in work mode; the sheer, unadulterated sexiness of him in casual clothes. When it came to business, he was a machine. He could focus for hours on end without losing concentration. He could tackle a problem at eight in the morning and not let up until he had solved it, whether it took him two minutes, two hours or two days. She watched his hands as he gestured, her brow creased in a small frown which she hoped would convey a suitable level of concentration.

'And I'm afraid you have no choice in the matter…'

Alice started as she caught the tail end of his sentence.

'Have you been listening to a word I've been saying, Alice?' Just at that point, the doorbell rang and he returned a minute or two later with two bags filled with beautifully packed gourmet food.

'I'm sorry. Of course. You were talking about Trans-Telecom…'

'And informing you that you might get away with avoiding work duty this weekend but I'm giving you advance warning from now that, whatever plans you have for next weekend, you're going to have to cancel because you're coming to Paris with me to sign off on this deal. I'll need you there to transcribe everything that's said and agreed, word for word.'

'Next weekend...'

'Next weekend. So you can spend next week getting your head round it.'

Of course her mother would be fine for one weekend. Alice knew that but she still felt a stab of guilt. She knew that she could have just told him what her weekend plans were, confided the situation about her mother with him, but somehow that would have felt like another line being crossed and she didn't want to cross any more of those lines.

Besides, Gabriel Cabrera was many things, but a warm and fluffy person who encouraged girlish confidences was not one of those things.

Nor was she the fluffy, girlish type to dispense them.

'Of course,' she said brightly. 'I'll make sure that I... rearrange my weekend plans...'

Which were what, exactly? Gabriel wondered.

'Good. In that case, twenty minutes to eat, and then let's carry on...'

CHAPTER FOUR

ALICE HAD NOT been out of the country on a holiday for a while. She knew that this wasn't going to be a holiday—the opposite. But she would still be leaving the country and how hard would it be to take a little time out and explore some of the city on her own? Even if it meant grabbing an hour or two when they weren't entertaining clients or working.

And her mother had taken it well—better than Alice had expected, in fact.

She had been down in Devon, as usual, at the weekend and had decided, before she had even stepped foot in her mother's little two-bedroom cottage in the village, that she would break the news when she was about to leave.

Pamela Morgan lived on her nerves. A highly strung woman even in the very best of times, she had become progressively more neurotic and mentally fragile during the long course of her broken marriage.

Still only in her mid-fifties, she remained a beautiful woman, beautiful in a way Alice knew she never could be. Her mother was small, blonde, with a faraway look in her big blue eyes. She was the ultimate helpless damsel that men seemed to adore.

But that ridiculous beauty had been as much of a burden in the long run as it had been a blessing. Growing up,

Alice had watched helplessly from the sidelines as her mother had floundered under the crushing weight of her husband's arrogant, far more flamboyant personality. She hadn't seemed to possess the strength to break free. She was the classic example of a woman who had always relied on her looks and, when the going had got tough, had had nothing else upon which to fall back.

When Rex Morgan had begun to lose interest in his pretty wife, she had not been able to cope. She had desperately tried to make herself prettier—had done her hair in a thousand different styles, dyed it in a hundred different shades of vanilla blonde, had dieted until her figure made men stop in their tracks—but none of it had ever been enough. In the end she had given up, choosing instead to remain passive as her husband's philandering had beome more and more outrageous.

She had cowered when he had bellowed and waited without complaining when he had disappeared for days on end, reappearing without a word of explanation but reeking of perfume.

She had sat quietly and in fear as he had sapped every ounce of her confidence so that she could no longer see a way out, far less find the courage to look for it. And she had not complained when he had told her that, if it weren't for the money, he would have walked out on the marriage a long time ago.

The fact was that he'd been financially tied to her. There was still a mortgage on the house, too many bills to pay, and if they divorced and she got her fair share he would have ended up living in something ugly and nasty, no longer able to live it up with his various women.

So he had stayed put but he had made sure to make life as unpleasant for his fragile wife as he could.

Whenever Alice felt a little insecure about the way

she looked, she would sternly tell herself that good looks brought heartache. Look at her mother.

And look at those girls Gabriel dated, the Georgia look-alikes. Who said that a woman with beauty had it all?

Rex Morgan was dead now, in a car accident that had released his wife from her captivity, but he had left a telling legacy behind him. Pamela Morgan was housebound and had been for a while. The thought of leaving the four walls around her and venturing outside terrified her. Over time, and in small but significant stages, she had gradually become agoraphobic and was fortunate now to live in a small village where people looked in on her during the week to make sure that she was okay. In a city, where their house had been, she would have been completely lost.

At weekends, Alice would gently try to ease her out into the garden and, a couple of times recently, actually down to the nearest shop, although that had been a lengthy exercise.

She paid for professional help, which cost an arm and a leg, but recovery was tortoise-slow and uncertain.

Weekends, Alice suspected, were her mother's favourite times, so Alice made sure to reserve those weekends for her, whatever the personal cost.

And, after a year and a half of treatment and regular weekend visits, Alice felt like she was beginning to see a slightly different woman in her mother. She seemed less tentative, more open to a short walk. Of course, the treatment would continue. In conjunction with the occasional pep talk, Alice felt confident that at some point in time she would be able to have more than just the odd weekend away from her mother's side.

To do what, she had no idea. Her love life post-Alan was non-existent and, whenever her mother gently asked her about that, she was always quick to point out that she didn't need a guy.

The unspoken message was: *why would I? Just look at Dad...look at Alan... Men are trouble...*

She had told her mother bits and pieces about Gabriel as well, which cemented that unspoken message.

But things seemed to be progressing and so, when Alice had sat her down and told her that she wouldn't be able to make it the following weekend because of work, she was pleasantly surprised by her mother's reaction.

'That's absolutely fine,' Pamela had said with a smile. 'I need to know how to be a little more independent.'

Which, Alice thought, meant that the very costly professional whose services she was paying for was actually beginning to make a difference.

So, yes, she was looking forward to Paris.

They had spent the past week working flat out on every single aspect of the deal that could go wrong. In between, there had been the usual high-volume work load. She had been rushed off her feet and had enjoyed every minute of it.

And Gabriel's so-called flu had disappeared as quickly as it had come, although he hadn't failed to remind her that she was probably the one who had given it to him, which had made her lips twitch with amusement.

They had arranged to meet at the airport and now, waiting for her taxi to arrive, Alice once again ticked off the mental checklist in her head.

All necessary work documents, including her work laptop, would be in hand luggage. She had her mobile phone and all the necessary work clothes packed.

They would be going for four days and she had managed to fit everything into one average-sized suitcase with room to spare.

Outside, the weather was cool but sunny, and she gave in to a heady feeling of complete freedom. The feeling was so unusual that for a second or two she felt a painful pang that this was something she should have more of; that this was something most girls her age would take absolutely for granted and yet here she was, savouring it like a tasty morsel that would vanish all too soon.

Tasty morsel! She would be in the company of Gabriel most of the time!

Like a runaway train, her mind zoomed off at speed to the memory of him in his bathrobe—the sight of that bare chest, those strong, muscled legs, the way he had been prone on his king-sized bed, macho, dominant and oozing raw sex appeal.

She uneasily shoved aside the unacceptable thought that part of her excitement might have to do with just being with him for four uninterrupted days in Paris, of all places.

Her phoned beeped with the taxi announcing itself outside and, ready for the short trip to Heathrow, Alice focused on practical issues.

Her mother was fine. She hadn't forgotten anything. Another big deal was brewing on the sidelines and she had thought to read up on the company in question and download relevant facts that Gabriel might find useful.

She made it to the airport to find Gabriel already there and waiting at the designated spot by the first-class check-in counter.

He eyed her case sceptically.

'Is that all the luggage you've brought with you?' Annoyingly, she had been on his mind more than usual. He didn't know what he expected when she joined him at the airport but, unsurprisingly, she was in her usual work uniform of nondescript grey suit, a lighter one to accommodate the milder weather, and her neat black patent leather pumps.

'We'll only be gone for four days.' Alice's eyes skirted around him. He was elegantly casual in some cream trousers and a cream jumper under which he was wearing a striped shirt. He looked expensive, sophisticated and drop-dead gorgeous, the sort of man who wouldn't be travelling anything other than first class.

'I've dated women who have packed more than you have for an overnight stay in a hotel,' Gabriel remarked drily. He was discovering that he enjoyed the way she blushed, enjoyed the way her eyes never quite met his whenever she felt that something he said might have been a little too provocative.

He checked her in, holding up her passport so that he could examine the unflattering picture of her, and then they headed to the first-class lounge.

Excitement rippled through her.

'I've never been to Paris,' she confided, impressed with the first-class lounge with its comfortable seating, waiter service and upmarket lounge-bar feel.

Gabriel tilted his head to one side, pleasantly surprised, because she so rarely said anything to him of a personal nature.

In any other woman, that would have been a definite plus point. In her, he found it weirdly irritating. It was as if the more she failed to tell him, the more he wanted to find out.

'Never?'

'Never.'

'I thought school trips over here always involved at least one compulsory trip to France…or have you been to other bits of France?'

Alice thought of her school days. The state school she had attended hadn't been great and she had had next to no supervision at home. Her father had been absent most of the time, either physically or mentally, and her mother had increasingly removed herself from the normal day to day things that most mothers did, burrowing down in her own misery.

'I went to Spain once.' She detoured around his direct question. 'One of my school friends asked me over with her for two weeks over summer when I was fourteen. It was the nicest holiday I can remember having.'

'What about family holidays?'

'There weren't many of those,' Alice said abruptly.

'I know the feeling.'

She looked at him, startled. She knew next to nothing about his past. He came to her as the man already formed, the billionaire with no emotional ties and no desire to form any. He was the brilliant, talented, driven guy who worked hard and played hard; who snapped his fingers and expected the world to jump, but who rarely seemed to put himself out for anyone.

She teetered on the brink of asking him for details. Curiosity clamped its teeth into her but for some reason the thought of stepping over that brink terrified her and she changed the subject, asking him about the places he had been and the countries he had visited.

Besides, would he even share personal details with her? He was intensely private and guarded in what he revealed.

Gabriel noted the way she had backed away from following up on his remark. He wasn't too sure why he had said that in the first place. He had never felt inclined to let any woman into his past. Would he have told her about his foster-home background? Doubtful, although in fairness he couldn't imagine her exclaiming with false sympathy or using it as leverage to try to prise him open like a shell.

His interest spiked and he looked at her with cool, guarded eyes.

The four-day trip to Paris suddenly seemed ripe with all sorts of possibilities. He wondered whether she had ever let her hair down, gone wild, got drunk, danced on tables. He couldn't see it. He wondered what she was thinking, what was going through her head.

What she did on those weekends.

He caught himself wondering whether there was a man in her life, despite protests to the contrary...

The questions settled into vague background thoughts as their flight was announced and soon they had left the country.

Predictably, she talked about work on the trip over. She had shown a great deal of commendable initiative with one of his deals, presenting him with a list of facts and figures on a company he was in the middle of acquiring.

But she was awed by the whole first-class travelling experience. Gabriel was picking that up with antennae finely tuned to women and their responses. She wanted to play it cool, to keep that work hat firmly pinned in place, but she also wanted to stare around her at the plush surroundings, the muted subservience of the airline staff, the luxury...

They would be staying at one of the most expensive and high-profile hotels in Paris, a hotel that took luxury seriously. It was the only hotel in which he stayed when he was in the city and they knew how to look after him.

He felt a kick of pleasurable anticipation at seeing her face when they walked in.

He was a teenager again, trying hard to impress a girl...

Except, his teenage years had been a little too busy for such distractions. Escape had taken priority over making out with girls, not that that had been a problem for him. Besides, he wasn't in the business of impressing anybody. He didn't have to.

The limo that would be driving them wherever they wanted to go while they were in Paris was waiting for them at the airport when they arrived and Alice glanced over to him with a dry smile.

'Don't you *ever* do things the way most normal people do?' The question was directed more at herself than it had been to him, although he picked up the half-murmured remark and chose to answer as soon as they were in the back seat of the car.

'Why would I do that?' he asked with a careless shrug, angling his big body so that he was facing her. She had tucked her hair behind her ears and was wearing ear rings, little pearl studs that were a far cry from the wildly extravagant costume jewellery most girls her age would probably have worn.

Infused with silly holiday excitement, and guiltily feeling a bit like a princess after her first-class experience, now in this chauffeur-driven limo, Alice laughed.

'You don't do that enough,' Gabriel said gruffly, surprising himself with that observation, but meaning every syllable of it.

'Do what?' Alice rested back against the seat and looked at him through half-closed eyes.

'Laugh.'

'I didn't realise that being at work was a laugh-a-second experience,' she said, but there was no sarcasm in her voice which was lazy and relaxed. 'Do you do anything for yourself at all, Gabriel?' she mused aloud and he gave her a toe curlingly slow smile.

'I make money. A lot of it. Beyond that, I pay people to take care of everything else.'

'But surely that can't be satisfying all of the time?'

'Are you going to give me a mini-lecture on all the great things money can't buy?' He thought back to his fractured, troubled past. Money would have bought a hell of a lot for him back then, which was probably why he had become so intensely focused on making lots of it. 'Because, if you are, there's no way you can sell it to me.'

'Money can't buy love.'

This time Gabriel laughed out loud but there was an edge to his laughter that Alice picked up and her brown eyes were curious as they rested on his handsome face.

'Oh, but I've found just the opposite.'

'That's not love…' How had they ended up having this very personal conversation? She sat up and leaned against the car door.

'No, but it works for me,' Gabriel told her drily. He hadn't taken her for a romantic, but was she one at heart? Perhaps all women were. Or at least, they were in love with the idea of being in love: the excited trip to the jewellers; the wedding planning; the meringue of a white dress on the big day; the happy-ever-after, as if such a thing existed. The fact was, the relationships didn't last. They all collapsed in varying degrees. He was a prime example of that, although in his case the degree of collapse had been severe, if the two people who had stupidly had sex and produced him had ever had a relationship at all. It was doubtful, although that was something he would never know. He had been dumped as a baby, taken into care and his life had been kick-started from that point.

'What about marriage? Settling down?' She couldn't resist giving in to her curiosity and he raised his eyebrows questioningly.

'What about it?'

'Aren't you tempted at all…?'

'Not that I've ever noticed. I long ago came to the conclusion, my dear little secretary, that the one thing I can rely on is money. I know how to make it and I'm fully aware of the uses I can put it to. There are no unpredictable variants when it comes to money. It might be hard and cold but it doesn't make demands, it doesn't nag and it doesn't want what's not on the cards. It also…as you have experienced…buys me exactly what I want, when I want it.'

Alice had no illusions about love either, but neither was she steeped in cynicism, and she shivered involuntarily at the ice-cold centre she glimpsed inside him.

Not only did he not believe in love, he would never bother trying to find it. As far as he was concerned, it didn't exist. He made money, he paid people to take care of life's little inconveniences and he slept with women for physical release.

He was not one of life's good guys and how fair was it that, despite that, his raw sexuality made him a magnet that few could resist?

She turned away and stared out of the car window. It was a beautiful day with skies as clear and as blue here as they had been in London.

'Perhaps you could tell me what the plans are for today,' she suggested, pulling back from the conversation, although it lingered in her head like a song being played on a loop.

'Hotel. A few hours' respite. Then we will be taking the client out tonight.'

'I haven't booked anywhere.'

'Francois and Marie are entertaining us,' Gabriel informed her. 'At their home. Hence arriving today rather than Monday. The entire family will be there. I thought it might be an opportune moment to hear their various opinions on the company sale so that we can squash any last-minute nerves.'

'At their *house*?'

'Rumour has it that the place is palatial. I've been told by Francois that various important dignitaries will be there. They are celebrating their fortieth wedding anniversary; we're honoured to have been invited.'

Alice looked at him, alarmed. When it came to the client entertainment side of their stay in Paris, she had been thinking more along the lines of one or two stuffy restaurants where she could easily fade into the background—the ever-professional secretary tagging along to make notes.

She hadn't banked on anything too elaborate. Frantically trying to think what she could wear to somewhere palatial with circulating dignitaries, all thoughts left her head as the limo pulled up outside their hotel.

Lacking in money and poorly travelled as she was, Alice had still heard of this hotel. She paused and stared at the impressive building facing her and was even more impressed when she followed Gabriel inside.

Marble, chandeliers and stunning paintings and tapestries announced its enviable status as the very best anyone could get for their money.

'We're staying here?' she breathed, and Gabriel turned to her with a slight smile.

'If you can afford the very best, why not have it? You know by now that that's my mantra.'

Alice glanced at him. He was the very epitome of a man at ease in his surroundings. He accepted the sudden flurry of activity around him as his due. No one could bow too low or scrape too hard and she felt a thrilling little flutter at being the woman at his side.

Even if she was only here in her role as his valuable secretary.

'There's something I need to ask you,' she whispered as they were shown up to their adjoining suites.

'No need to whisper,' Gabriel whispered back. 'I very much doubt the bellboy is interested in anything we have to say. A poker face is essential in places like this. The truly wealthy seldom like to be gawped at.'

Alice's eyes flashed and he laughed. 'Should I apologise for my arrogance?' He briefly turned away and spoke fluently to the bellboy in French, who faded away with a slight bow and an ingratiating smile at the huge tip placed in his hand.

'I guess you're only being honest,' she reluctantly conceded. From what she could glimpse behind him, the room was spectacular. Huge, big enough for a separate little sitting room, and everything was decorated with decadent opulence.

'One of life's few true virtues: honesty. You said you had something to talk to me about...' He walked into the room, paying no attention at all to his surroundings, leading her to assume that he had been there many times before. 'Come in and spit it out.'

Alice hovered by the door as he pulled his jumper over his head and flung it on the bed which, like the room, was super-sized. In the process, his shirt was tugged out of the waistband of his trousers and she glimpsed a tantalising sliver of bronzed stomach, as flat and as hard as a washboard.

'Well?' Gabriel prompted. 'Don't just stand there.' He turned away and began scrolling down his Blackberry, frowning at emails as Alice tentatively walked into the room.

The presence of the bed was disconcerting. It brought back memories of the last time she had been in a bedroom with him, which was not what she wanted to think about.

When she was stranded in the middle of the room, he eventually glanced up and indicated one of the chairs which formed a little cluster by the window.

'I'm afraid I hadn't banked on us doing anything as fancy as dining out with...dignitaries,' she said without beating around the bush. 'I was under the impression that this was going to be all about work.'

'So you packed your grey suit, a couple of white blouses, some black tights and your black patent shoes...'

'I know it's boring, Gabriel, but I don't see work as a fashion parade!' Her face stung from the implied insult. 'If you had told me that—'

'You knew we would be entertaining this client,' Gabriel pointed out flatly. 'Surely you wouldn't have assumed that your work suits would do the trick?'

'Why not? They're smart and professional—'

'They're bland and drab.'

'I don't think that's fair at all!'

'You get exactly the same clothes allowance as the rest of my employees on your level, yet you don't appear to have spent a penny on clothes.'

Because she spent the money paying a professional to help her mother with her problem. Because, however much she was paid, by the time that money left her hands, given all the other bills, plus the little nest egg she was slowly accumulating, there was precious little left and none at all for jackets that cost five hundred pounds and designer shoes that could run to more.

'How do you know I haven't?'

'Well, unless you're throwing money at an exotic out of work wardrobe, it shows.'

'I didn't realise that there was a certain dress code to work for you.' But it was apparent all around her. She had noticed it on day one. 'And I don't think I should be channelled into wearing stuff I don't like because you say so.'

'Before this conversation starts drifting into territory I know I won't like,' Gabriel informed her coolly, 'I suggest you use what remains of the day to go shopping.'

Alice thought about the paucity of her funds and blanched. 'I...I would have to dip into my savings...'

Gabriel waved aside her faltering objection with an impatient wave of his hand.

'I will transfer money into your account today. Use it. Buy enough designer clothes to last the duration and feel free to make use of the spa centre here. Do whatever it takes.'

'Do whatever it takes…for what?' Alice said stiffly. If the ground had opened up, she would have dived in head first and emerged somewhere very far away from where this man was sitting, telling her in not so many words that she was an embarrassment.

'Alice,' Gabriel told her bluntly, 'you're a young girl in your twenties and I have yet to see you in something frivolous.'

'I would never come to work in anything frivolous.'

'Do you possess anything that isn't sober? Serious? *Grey*?' He knew he was being harsh but he had seen a hint of someone fiery lurking underneath the proper exterior and he wanted to see that person on the outside.

'Francois and Marie are rich and they're French. Put the two together and what you have is elegance. They will be startled if you appear at my side wearing off-the-peg cheap, ill-fitting grey suits. What you wear might not be a deal breaker, but it will help if you blend in. Do you really think that you can show up to tonight's event in a *suit*?'

Cheap, off-the-peg, ill-fitting… The words reverberated in her head until she was giddy with anger.

'I did think to bring my black dress.'

'I'm imagining it's along the same lines as the suit…?'

'By which,' Alice said tightly, 'you mean cheap, off-the-peg and ill-fitting?'

Gabriel raked long fingers through his dark hair and sighed heavily. 'I could have skirted round this,' he told her bluntly. 'I could have wrapped up what needed to be said in lots of pretty packaging, but that's not my style. If you wear one of those suits of yours, you will feel desperately uncomfortable the minute you step through their front door. I'm sparing you that ordeal by being honest. They will wonder what sort of employer I am if I don't pay my staff enough for them to afford decent clothing...'

'Do you have any idea just how *insulting* you're being right now?' She was close to tears but there was no way that she would allow them to spill over.

'Do you have any idea just how awkward you will feel if you arrive there and find that you're not blending in? That you're sticking out like a sore thumb?' His dark eyes challenged her to continue an argument which he knew he would win.

'And what exactly do you suggest I waste your money buying?'

'You're treading on thin ice here, Alice. I could suggest that you buy something dressy...colourful. Or else I could just tell you to—'

'I apologise if you think I'm being ungrateful or rude, Gabriel, but I resent being told what I can and can't wear!' But when she thought about entering a room full of elegant French people who were dressed to kill, in one of her suits or her very simple black dress, she knew that he had a point.

She just hated the way he felt free to tell her with no regard for her feelings at all. She resented the way he felt that he didn't even have to make a pretence of trying to be diplomatic.

'It is what it is.' But for once he was annoyed with himself for doing what he always did, for speaking his mind without window dressing what he had to say.

'Fine!'

She glowered at him and Gabriel was sorely tempted

to tell her that there wasn't a woman on the face of the earth who wouldn't have jumped at the chance to go out and have a shopping spree at his expense. Yet she had that 'just swallowed a lemon' look on her face as though he had somehow humiliated her in public. Hell, he was trying to *spare* her from being humiliated in public! People were shallow and one of the first things he had learnt in his climb up that swaying ladder was that they judged according to what they saw; forget all that claptrap about what was underneath. Dress and act like a king, and they would treat you like one.

Yet he was further annoyed when he felt another wave of guilt wash over him. She had been insulted, even though what he had said had been perfectly true.

He wasn't about to apologise even if she stood there glowering until kingdom come. He pointedly looked at his watch and told her that she should get her skates on if she intended to get through some shopping, then he recommended a couple of districts where designer shops lined the streets. He even told her she could take the limo

'And what time shall I meet you?' Alice could barely get the words out. She hadn't sat down, but had remained standing, and her legs were unsteady with sheer anger.

'The do kicks off at eight. Meet me in the bar here at seven-thirty. We can have a drink first and then get there around eight-thirty.'

Because, she sniped to herself, the great man could arrive late if he wanted. Forget about currying favour with the person whose company you wanted to buy! Currying favour was something only lesser mortals did! Gabriel Cabrera didn't feel he had to do that, so he didn't.

'And will we be doing any work before we leave?' she asked with wooden politeness.

'It's Saturday. I think I can spare you.'

'Fine.' She galvanised her legs into action and walked towards the door. She would have a shower, unpack some of her drab grey clothes to wear out and then she would hit the shops and spend that money he had made no bones about telling her she should spend—so that she could get herself up to scratch and blend in! 'I'll see you in the bar at seven-thirty. Perhaps you could let me know if there's a change of plan.'

She let herself out of the room without a backward glance. She had over-reacted, she knew that, but she had just lost her cool at the sheer arrogance and superiority of the man.

She showered quickly, barely paying any attention to the stunning bedroom she had been allocated, which was a mirror reflection of his, then out she went.

He wanted his drab secretary to do something about her appearance so that he didn't flinch when he looked at her?

Well, she would make sure she did her very best to do as he had asked!

CHAPTER FIVE

ALICE HAD NEVER, ever had anything that could possibly be called an unlimited budget when it came to buying clothes. Or buying anything, for that matter.

Growing up, her father's job had been good enough. He'd been a middle-management man who had paid the bills, given his wife just enough to get by and spent the remainder on pleasing himself. Holidays had just not happened. Or maybe they had, in the early days before she had come along, and perhaps when she had been a baby, too young to remember them. Maybe they had happened when her parents had been a happily married statistic instead of two opponents fighting their private cold war.

Pocket money for clothes had been thin on the ground. Her mother had passed her some, whatever was left from the housekeeping money at the end of the month, but Alice had never known what it was like to spend cash on things that weren't strictly necessary.

So it took her a little while to get her head round the fact that that was exactly what she had now been ordered to do.

She had brought a little pocket guide-book with her and, instead of rushing instantly to the shops, she took the limo to the Champs-Elysées, which was hardly necessary, considering how close their hotel was to it.

She wandered. She mingled in the glorious weather with the rich fashionistas. She walked past the expensive restaurants and cafés. There was no time to visit any of the museums but she could admire the architecture of some of the grand buildings and submerge herself in the airy affluence. She stopped to have a coffee and a croissant in one of the cafés and sat outside so that she could people watch.

In her head, she replayed every word Gabriel had said to her and relived the hurt she had felt at being dismissed as someone inferior. It didn't matter whether he praised her work skills to the skies. It didn't matter if he complimented her on her initiative in digging out bits of useful information on companies he was interested in acquiring. It didn't matter if he now trusted her to flesh out reports which he gave to her in skeleton format.

She was the drab, grey little person who didn't know how to dress.

She had a flashback of Georgia in the office, in her tight red dress and her high, high shoes, with her dark hair everywhere and her long nails painted scarlet.

There was no way that Alice would want to replicate that look. As far as she was concerned, the other woman had embodied everything that was obvious and way too out there.

But she wasn't going to be a mouse.

It took her a little while, but by the time she hit the fourth shop she was in her stride. She cruised through all the designer shops, growing in confidence as the afternoon wore on, and by five o'clock she returned to the hotel clutching several bags. She could have summoned the limo again but the walk had been tempting, if tiring.

And what better place to soothe a weary body? She dumped the bags in her bedroom, inhaled the gorgeous opulence of a hotel room the likes of which she would never stay in again for a few heady minutes and then phoned through to make an appointment at the hotel pa.

By six-thirty, Alice was fully rested and relaxed. Back in her room, she looked at her nails, her feet, her hair.

Vanity had never been a problem for her. As a teenager, when all the other girls had been preening in front of mirrors and whispering about boys she had been busy keeping her head down, studying and wondering what the following day would bring; wondering what sort of mood her mother might be in or whether her father might be on one of his many 'time out' trips.

The years had passed her by without her taking time out to pay much attention to her appearance.

Besides, her learning curve had been subtle but powerful. Beauty came with a price. She wasn't beautiful and she had no interest in making herself try to be.

But now…

She had a long, lingering bath in a bathroom that was ridiculously luxuriant and emerged twenty minutes later feeling refreshed and…weirdly excited.

She wasn't Cinderella going to the ball—not exactly— but she would leave behind serious, composed, take-no-risks Alice Morgan for the evening.

She had bought four dresses, one for each evening they would be in Paris, but the dress she had bought for tonight's affair was the dressiest.

It was a long dress, in the palest of pink, with a scooped neck and was figure-hugging. Her long body, which she had always considered far too thin and far too flat-chested, filled it out perfectly and her height was accentuated by four-inch stilettos. She had bought a matching cashmere throw, iridescent with little pearls, to sling over her shoulders. Her nails matched the outfit and her hair…

Her brown hair, always *au naturel*, had been highlighted

while she had had her hands and feet done. Shades of warm chestnut and caramel streaked through it, giving it dazzling life, turning her into a person she barely recognised as herself.

On the spur of the moment, she took a picture of herself and messaged it to her mother, and grinned when her mother returned a message which was just several exclamation marks.

She was a different person, at least on the surface, and she left her bedroom at precisely seven-thirty to make her way downstairs to the bar.

People turned to stare.

That had never happened to her in her life before. She wasn't sure whether she liked it or not but it was certainly an experience.

Was this what it was like for Gabriel? she wondered. Was that why he had become so lazy? Why he picked what he wanted from life and discarded the rest without a backward glance? Was he so accustomed to walking into a room and finding himself the focus of attention that he no longer saw the point of trying any more? Why seek people out when they sought *you* out? Why make an effort with a woman if the woman was happy to do all the chasing? Why commit to a relationship when you could treat life like a great big candy shop where you could pick and choose the candy you wanted before moving on to sample something else?

She wondered whether he got pleasure from making money. He had made so much already and at such a young age, more than enough to last several lifetimes. He threw himself into his work, there was no denying that, and the man was a genius with a knack of knowing the markets—but did it still give him a kick? When you could have whatever you wanted without trying, was there *anything* that was still capable of giving you a kick?

She had to ask directions to the bar and, when she got there, she paused and frankly gaped.

It was carpeted, the carpet pale, patterned and very old. On the walls, deep, rich tapestries left you in no doubt that this hotel was old and proud of its age. Rich velvet curtains hung at the long windows and the chairs were regal, blending in with the air of expensive antiquity. There were no modern touches, nothing to indicate that outside the bustling twenty-first century was happening.

It was fabulous French decadence. It recalled the days of aristocracy and noblemen.

At which point, she scanned the room and there he was, sitting at one of the tables, frowning in front of the newspaper.

Temporarily lost in the financial section of the newspaper he was reading, absently drinking a glass of red wine from the bottle that had been placed on the table in front of him, Gabriel was unaware of her entrance.

And of the heads turning in her direction as she stood by the door looking at him.

But gradually he picked up that there was a certain silence. His eyes unerringly found her and for a few seconds he found that he was holding his breath.

He half-stood, which she took as a signal to move forward to join him, and although his breath returned he couldn't tear his eyes away from her slowly approaching figure. He was aware of men turning to stare.

'So…' he drawled when she was standing in front of him. 'You obeyed my instructions to the letter.' She was exquisite. How had he failed to notice that before? The pale delicacy of her features was a revelation, as was the slender column of her neck, the graceful elegance of her body. Her presence dominated the room even though what she had chosen to wear was simple, unrevealing and refined.

'You told me to get rid of my drab, grey clothes...'
Was that all he could say? she thought with a stab of disappointment.

'Glass of wine?' He sat back down, inwardly marvelling that she had managed to puncture his composure. 'Where did you go shopping?'

Alice sat and gave him a little run-down of how she had spent her afternoon. Had he been staring at her as she had walked towards him? Or had he only been just looking to make sure that she could pass muster? His expression had been unreadable and she had a fierce longing for him to tell her that she looked beautiful.

He, of course, looked as stunning as he always did. He was dressed semi-formally in a charcoal-grey suit that looked hand-tailored and lovingly accentuated his physique.

'Your hair...' he murmured. 'Very effective.'

Alice blushed, no longer feeling like his secretary but feeling, weirdly, like his date, even though she recognised the foolishness of letting herself get swept away by such a silly notion.

'I had it dyed,' she confessed self-consciously. 'I hope it's not too much.'

'It's...' Gabriel was momentarily lost for words. 'It's... It suits you.' He fought the temptation to reach out and run his fingers through its silky length.

'Should we perhaps run through what sort of questions we might get asked about this buy-out?'

Gabriel found that he couldn't care less about the buy-out. For once, business could not have been further from his mind. Those little snippets of wayward thoughts that had flitted through his mind now and again—little snapshots of her released from her armour of the perfect little secretary—coalesced into one powerful image of her without that dress on, naked and sprawled on his bed…

And where was he going with that thought, exactly? He had always made it his business never to mix work with pleasure—that was a sure-fire recipe for problems. The sexy little thing in the accounts department might display her wares but those were offers he had always avoided like the plague.

But this woman…

'Yes,' he murmured. 'We should do that—discuss potential problems; try and cut them off at the pass…' He drained his glass and poured himself another. Potential problems? Who cared? He had it covered. His mind wanted to think about other intriguing possibilities…

He half-listened as she launched into a summary of the company and the technicalities of buying something that was rooted in a family.

'Especially when there are…how many children did you say…? Three? All involved in the decision-making process…?'

'Three children, yes,' Gabriel murmured, sitting back and sipping his wine. It took extreme will power not to let his eyes rove over her pert breasts. She was so unlike the women he'd dated who had all been universally proud of the fact that they spilled out of bras. Since when, he mused, was that such a great selling point anyway? 'Two boys and a girl,' he added, because she seemed to expect him to expand on that succinct statement. 'And I gather the daughter doesn't really care one way or another. She travels, it would seem, spreading peace and love and playing at being a trust-fund hippy. What about you? Any siblings?'

'I beg your pardon?'

'We're sitting here, having a drink. We don't have to spend our time discussing work.' He topped up her glass, gently pushing aside her hand which she had raised to stop him. 'Tell me about your family. Brothers? Sisters? Usual assortment of nieces and nephews, cousins and aunts and uncles wheeled out on high days and holidays?'

Alice felt the little pulse at the side of her neck beating steadily. Her mother was an only child and her father had a brother in Australia whom, he had always been very proud to say, he loathed. When she had been younger, she had longed for a brother or a sister. As time had gone by, she had ditched those dreams. What if a brother had turned out like her father? No, theirs had always been an unhappy little family unit, marooned on open water without the benefit of a neighbouring craft to help pick up the pieces should anything happen. As it had.

He was simply being polite, and she was hardly confessing to state secrets, but it still felt awkward to start talking to him about her private life. She needed those boundaries between them to be kept in place or else it would be so much more difficult to keep the attraction she felt towards him at bay.

Hadn't she already fluttered like a girl on her first date? Hadn't she wanted him to *notice* her, and not just as his efficient secretary? She was in dangerous territory and control came from not forgetting their respective roles.

But if she dodged his question she'd stir his curiosity and he was tenacious, a dog with a bone, when it came to finding out things he wanted to find out.

'I'm—I'm an only child,' she told him haltingly. 'My father's dead. A car accident.'

'I'm sorry.' Though the way she had said that… 'And your mother?'

'Lives in Devon.' She took two small sips of wine and offered him a bright, brittle smile.

'Has the polite conversation come to an end?' he asked.

'I've just had a look at the clock behind you and it's time for us to go.' She stood up and carefully avoided looking at him as she smoothed down her dress. When she raised her eyes, it was to find his on her and he didn't look away. He just kept looking until colour crawled into her cheeks, her mouth went dry and her brains turned to cotton wool.

Confusion paralysed her. Was he looking at her *that* way? The way she tried hard not to look at him?

'You look quite…stunning,' he murmured, extending his arm and then tucking her arm into the crook of his.

'Thank you,' Alice croaked. She wasn't sure what she was finding more disastrous on her nerves, the fact that she had her arm looped through his or the fact that he had just delivered the compliment she had been desperate to hear with a look in his eyes that had made her whole body tingle with forbidden awareness.

Maybe it was a look that he pulled out of the box whenever he saw any woman who didn't look half bad.

'Even though,' she continued, weakly asserting her independence, 'I still disapprove of you telling me what I can or can't wear.'

'Even though you're surely going to be the belle of the ball?'

'Oh, please!' She tried to dismiss that husky compliment with a laugh.

'You don't believe me?' They were at the limo, which had appeared as if by magic, and the chauffeur swooped round to open the door for her.

'I…no…maybe. I don't know.' Her voice was low, breathless and husky. Nothing at all like how she usually sounded. It was a voice that matched her beautiful Cinderella dress. Her eyes were wide, her pupils dilated as she stared at him, riveted by the beautiful, hard planes of his face and by the way he was still looking at her.

She heard something come from her, something soft and low, and recognised with horror that it was a moan, barely audible, but as loud as clanging bells in her own ears.

Gabriel knew this moment for what it was. Her pliant, warm body was inches away from his. They were leaning into one another, driven by some unseen current. If he turned away right now he would break the spell and that would be the best thing to do.

She was his secretary! And a damned good one. Did he want to jeopardise that by starting something he would not be able to finish? Something that would end in her being hurt, in walking out on him? Wasn't this the very reason there was such a thing as lines that should never get crossed?

He kissed her.

Long, slowly, lingeringly, his tongue probing into her mouth, tasting her sweetness and hardening as she moaned back into his mouth.

Hell, they were in the back seat of a car! He was not cool or controlled, but he couldn't help himself as he cupped one small, rounded breast and rubbed his finger over the nipple which he could feel pressing against the fabric.

'You're not wearing a bra…' He was turned on beyond belief. Her nipple was hard and he was gripped with an insane urge to tell the driver to turn around so that he could take her back to his hotel room and…have her. Rip the dress off her, get her down to her underwear and take her as fast and as hard as he could.

'The back of the dress is too low…' She didn't want him to talk. She wanted him to carry on kissing her. Her whole body was on fire, as though she had been plugged into a live socket. Her nerve-endings were charged, her thoughts sluggish, the blood hot in her veins.

She felt the heaviness of his hand resting on her thigh,

gently pressing, edging between her legs, and sanity shot through her. She pulled back and made a show of straightening her dress, giving herself time to come to her senses.

Her breasts were tingling and her nipples pinching from where he had touched her.

What the heck had she done?

'What's the matter?' Gabriel was so turned on that he could hardly string that simple sentence together. He wasn't sure whether it was the taste of the forbidden, or the fact that she was a novelty after a steady diet of Georgia clones, but he had never been so turned on in his life before.

'*What's the matter?* What do you *think* the matter is, Gabriel?' She glanced furtively at the chauffeur but he was seemingly indifferent to what had taken place in the back seat of the limo. Gabriel was right—underlings knew the wisdom of playing dead when it came to the shenanigans of their wealthy employers.

'I have no idea,' Gabriel drawled, settling back against the car door to look at her calmly. 'One minute you were kissing me and the next minute you'd decided to play the outraged virgin. What blew the fire out?'

How could he sit there and look at her as though she had made a mistake with her typing, misfiled something or put through the wrong call? How could he be so...*cool*?

'That should never have happened,' Alice told him tautly. 'And it wouldn't have happened if I hadn't had two glasses of wine.'

'One and a half, and if you kiss men after a glass and a half of wine what do you do after a bottle? There's nothing worse than a woman who blames alcohol for doing something she actually wanted to do but then had second thoughts about doing.'

Alice reddened. 'Well, it won't happen again. I made

a mistake and I won't be repeating it. And I don't want it mentioned ever again.'

'Or else…?'

'Or else my position with you will become untenable and I don't want that to happen. I like my job. I don't want one small, tiny error of judgement to end up spoiling that.'

Gabriel allowed the silence to lengthen between them until she was compelled to look at him, if only to find out whether he had heard what she had just said.

One small, tiny error of judgement, he thought, amused at her naivety in assuming that she could shut the door on what had happened and pretend it hadn't happened. She had wanted him. Her warm body had curved into his and he had felt her desire throbbing through her, hot, wet and feverish. If he had slipped his hand under that long dress, if he had found the bareness of her thighs, he would have found her ready for him.

'I don't suppose you've ever had any woman say that to you before.' Alice broke the silence which was driving her crazy. 'And I don't want to offend you, but that's how it has to be.'

'In response to that statement, you're right. I've never had a woman say that to me before. I'm not offended.' He raised both his hands in a gesture that was rueful but accepting. 'And of course, if you decide that denial is the right course of action, then that's not a problem. We'll pretend it never happened.'

'Good.' She felt a hollowness settle in the pit of her stomach.

'There's our destination straight ahead.' Gabriel pointed to the bank of lights leading up a tree-lined avenue towards a manor house that resembled the Place des Vosges. Expensive cars were dotted around the courtyard and along the avenue, half on, half off the grass verge. He began giving her a potted history of the place, which had been in the family for generations.

But he was alive to her presence next to him. She had opened a door and he had walked through; did she now expect him politely to turn around and walk back out because she'd had a change of heart?

Frankly, if he believed for a second that her response had been wine induced, he would not have hesitated to put their five-minute interaction down to experience.

But she had wanted him and she still did. He could feel it in the way she wasn't quite managing to look at him, in her breathing which she was trying to control, in the way she was ever so casually pressed against the car door. It was almost as though if she got too close to him she would burst into flame. All over again.

Any thoughts about walking away from this challenge vanished in a puff of smoke. The predator in him prowled to the fore, leaving no room for questions about the foolhardiness of what he wanted to do.

For once, there was something in him that wasn't in control and he liked it. It made a change and a change was as good as a rest.

The party was in full swing when they walked in. Beautiful people were circulating, chatting in groups, drinking champagne and picking off the canapés that were being paraded from group to group by a selection of very attractive waitresses. They were all dressed in just the sort of sexy uniform associated with the French waitress: short skirt, tight black top, high black shoes and sheer black stockings.

Gabriel barely noticed them. Alice was the sole recipient of his brooding attention.

She did him proud, it had to be said. Men looked, as did the women. She shone. And, if her grasp of French was classroom, she charmingly made the most of what was at her disposal as she was adopted by groups of people and encouraged to join their conversations.

And the deal was cemented. The family, Francois told him, taking him to one side towards the end of the evening, was behind him all the way. There were some regrets about losing the business but he intended to join his sons in a new start-up, completely different, in the leisure industry.

Gabriel had expected nothing but a positive outcome and he was ready to make his exit when he scanned the room to see Alice laughing, deep in conversation with a man. A tall, blond man who was watching her over the rim of his flute as he drank his champagne in a way that Gabriel recognised all too well. She was laughing.

Rage tore through him.

He made his way through the thinning crowds. The noise level was high. People had had a lot to drink. Hell, *she* had had a lot to drink!

He descended on them like an avenging angel and cupped her elbow in the palm of his big hand.

'Time to go, Alice.'

'Already?' There was still that laughter in her eyes as she turned to look at him. Her face was flushed, her full mouth parted, inviting…

'Already,' Gabriel gritted. He spoke to the blond guy in rapid French and then waited in silence as the other man replied and then, when nothing further was forthcoming, made his apologies, taking her hand and kissing it in a way that smacked of unwelcome intimacy.

'We're going to bid our farewells to our charming hosts.' He still had his hand on her elbow and was channelling her towards Francois and Marie who were standing in the centre of the room, surrounded by their friends and family. 'And then we're going to head back to our hotel.'

'Hasn't it been a fantastic affair?'

'Who the hell was that loser you were talking to?' He plastered a polite smile on his face as they approached their hosts, and kept smiling as he thanked them for a wonderful time, to be repaid in full when they were next in London. Arrangements were made for meetings on Monday. He didn't take his hand away from her.

'That,' he said, dropping her elbow as they walked out into the cool late night air, 'was not what I brought you here to do.' In his mind's eye, he saw her laughing face as she looked up at Prince Charming of the floppy blond hair.

Alice laughed. The champagne had gone to her head, as had the fact that she had only had a handful of the delicious canapés being passed around. The memory of that searing kiss in the back seat of the limo, her confusion at what had promoted it and sheer nerves at being somewhere so utterly out of her comfort zone had combined and she had drank far more than she usually did.

'You wanted me to dress the part and mingle…'

'I wanted you to stay by my side and listen so that you could make mental notes of what was said about the deal!' He waited until she was in the passenger seat, indicating to the chauffeur to remain where he was, and slammed the door behind her.

'I did *not* expect you to drink like a fish and start cosying up to random men!'

Alice swivelled to look at his hard, unyielding profile. 'I wasn't *drinking like a fish* or *cosying up to random men*,' she protested. She sensed the tension in his bunched shoulders and sat on her treacherous hands, because more than anything else she wanted to touch him and that wasn't going to do.

'Who was that guy? Did he have anything to contribute on my acquisition of Francois' company?'

'Well, no...' She stifled a yawn and was treated to a thunderous glare.

'Am I keeping you awake? Maybe you've forgotten that you're being paid a hefty amount of money for the inconvenience of losing your weekend.' He knew he sounded like a tyrant but he wasn't about to back down. She looked sleepy-eyed and just so damned sexy...

'I would have stuck to you like glue if you had made it clear that that was what you wanted, but I gathered...' she stifled another yawn, which didn't go unnoticed '...that this was a social event. Besides, I didn't notice you in any tête-à-têtes with Monsieur Armand or I would have come over. I know I'm being paid a lot for my overtime here. You don't have to remind me.'

Gabriel couldn't care less about the money and she wasn't saying anything he wanted to hear. Who was that guy? Had she answered *that* question? No. Had telephone numbers been exchanged? Had some kind of date been set up?

'So who was he?' he asked through gritted teeth.

'Are you...*jealous*?' Her lips parted and she was suddenly as sober as a judge.

'Did you exchange numbers? Set up a hot date for later in the week? If so, you can forget it. You're going nowhere on company time.' He raked his fingers though his hair and stared at her with frowning intensity.

He had never been jealous in his life before. He didn't do jealousy. Why would he? Women came and they went and, whatever the pasts were, whoever they had been out with or spoke to, well, he had never cared. Nor had he ever doubted that once they were in his bed they were utterly faithful.

He was jealous now and he didn't like the sensation.

'Of course I didn't give Marc my telephone number,'

Alice muttered, half-resenting that she had been called to task like a kid, half-thrilled because, whatever he said or didn't say, he *was* jealous. It made her feel better about fancying him. At least she knew that he wasn't as casual about it as he had pretended.

Not that it mattered, one way or another.

'And there are no hot dates lined up. He was just a nice man who didn't mind talking to me in pigeon French.'

Gabriel thought that there was a lot more the guy wouldn't have minded doing, given half a chance, but no numbers had been exchanged, no hot dates lined up. She seemed blissfully unaware that looking the way she did and laughing the way she had would be considered flirting in any language, pigeon or not.

'You asked me if I was jealous,' Gabriel murmured, keeping his distance but looking at her with dark intensity. 'I was jealous.'

The atmosphere between them shifted and changed into something so charged that it was almost tangible. Alice drew her breath in sharply and then exhaled it in a shudder. Wild horses wouldn't drag this out of her, but she had been keeping an eye on him throughout the evening, waiting to see if he looked at any of the glamorous women there or any of the pretty young waitresses. He had garnered enough attention, although if he had noticed any of it he hadn't shown it.

'Why?' She strove to remember the boundary lines between them and to summon up the will power she had shown earlier when she had told him that that one kiss had been a mistake, never to be repeated.

'Because I want you.' His body language was a heady turn-on; he was leaning indolently against the car door while he continued to watch her with still, lazy eyes.

'We can't do anything,' she said huskily. 'It would be a terrible mistake. I'm just not that type of girl.'

'The type who sleeps with a man if she wants to? And don't try telling me that you don't want to.'

'We shouldn't be having this conversation.'

'And your vocabulary shouldn't be littered with so many shoulds and shouldn'ts...'

'You're accustomed to women dropping at your feet.'

'And yet I haven't noticed you dropping at mine.'

The limo pulled up outside the hotel. He hadn't even noticed the journey. Every nerve and fibre in his body had honed in on the woman sitting as far as she could away from him.

He leaned forward to have a word with the driver and then they were walking up to the hotel entrance, several feet between them. He had his hands in his pockets and she was clutching her pink pearl throw and little handbag for dear life.

He was jealous...a first.

He was in pursuit...also a first.

And he would have her...but she would come to him.

CHAPTER SIX

ALICE COULD HEAR the beating of her own heart as they headed for their respective bedrooms. It was still relatively busy in the foyer, but once they left that behind the silence between them was deafening.

In fact, she wondered whether she had imagined the bizarre conversation they had just had. She couldn't bring herself to look at him, but it didn't matter, because in the quiet of the lift his image was reflected back at her whether she liked it or not.

She, standing by the door, arms wrapped round her body... He, leaning against the mirrored wall, hands in his pockets, dark, lean face sending shivers up and down her spine.

The doors pinged open and she leapt out. Her feet were aching from wearing high shoes and on the spur of the moment she stooped and took them off so that the long dress pooled on the ground.

'Undressing already?' Gabriel murmured in a sinfully seductive voice.

'My feet are killing me. I'm not used to wearing heels.'

'Well, give them a good night's rest and I shall see you in the morning.' He inclined his head politely, spun round on his heels and started walking towards his bedroom which was a little further up from hers.

And tomorrow, Alice thought feverishly, all this would be forgotten. That kiss in the back of the limo…the way he had looked at her…their conversation after the party: it would all be forgotten in the cold, clear light of day because that was just how things were.

She was the perfect secretary and if, by some weird twist of fate, he made her feel young and alive and filled with possibilities then that was something she would have to set to one side.

Maybe even to learn from it.

If a man whose value system left her cold managed to rouse her the way he did, then it was time for her to do something about getting her toes wet in the dating game instead of gathering cobwebs on the hard shoulder.

Shoes in hand, she watched as he fished into his jacket pocket for the key to his door. He wasn't even looking at her. He was going to shut that door behind him and…

She would never know.

'Wait!'

Gabriel turned slowly and smiled. Had he known that she would stop him? For once, he had been faced with an unpredictable outcome and he really wasn't sure what he would have done if she had struck off to her own room, shoes in hand, to get a good night's sleep and rest her feet.

He wasn't sure whether a few cold showers would dampen his raging libido.

'Yes?'

Alice sprinted towards him. It was funny but she hadn't realised how old she was in her behaviour, in her whole outlook on life, until he had come along and shaken her up so that everything had gone topsy-turvy and then re-settled, but in different positions.

She was twenty-five years old—when was the last time she had had an adventure?

She stood in front of him and looked up. 'Okay.'

'Okay…?'

'You know what I'm talking about. I…I'm attracted to you and I really don't understand why. You're not my type at all.'

'Promising start. That way, you won't start getting ideas.'

'What sort of ideas? Oh, forget I asked. Georgia-type ideas about having you around for longer than five seconds and getting attached and projecting into a non-existent future.' She laughed edgily. 'I work for you, remember? I'm not that stupid.'

'What's brought about the change of mind? I thought after we kissed that I was under instructions to forget about it immediately and pretend it had never happened.' He pushed open the bedroom door and stepped inside, switching on the light at the same time, then immediately dimming it to a mellow glow.

The bed had been turned back, not that there had been any need, and her pulses picked up their tempo as she looked at it—king-sized and beckoning her like a dangerous dare.

'Well?' he prompted, walking towards the sofa and flopping down on it, legs apart, arms resting loosely along the back.

'I…I suppose this is a one-off for me, and I know it's not a good idea, but…'

'Life is always full of *buts*,' Gabriel agreed. 'That's what makes it so challenging.' Except, truthfully, it contained relatively few buts for him, especially where a woman was involved. He had never had to try, so he hadn't. His emotional life had never contained any areas of hesitations and certainly no *buts*.

Silence settled between them and then he said softly, 'Take off your clothes.'

'What?'

'Let me see you naked, in front of me.'

'I…I can't.'

'Why not?' Something suddenly struck him: her innocence. The way she blushed, the hint of unbearable youth lurking underneath the professional exterior. 'You're not a virgin, are you?'

'Would it make a difference if I was?'

'Yes.' He sat forward, alert. 'It would.'

'Why?' She edged towards him and dropped the shoes on the floor. It would have felt strange to have plonked herself next to him on the sofa so she sat on one of the chairs.

Talking was giving her time to doubt her decision. If she had fallen passionately into bed with him, she wouldn't have had time to think, but maybe this was a good thing. Maybe they both *needed* to talk, because this was not an ordinary situation, and a lot could change for the worse in its aftermath.

'Are you getting cold feet?' He shot her a crooked smile, reading her mind as though her thoughts had been written on her forehead, and that smile sealed her decision.

'No. Tell me why it would matter if I was a virgin.'

'You know me.' And she did, strangely. They worked so closely together and, although their working relationship was still new, he had the feeling that she *got* him. 'I'm not looking for…anything. It's what I tell every single woman I have ever dated and it's what I'm telling you now. Sex is a pleasurable pastime, but it's not love and it's not commitment, and it's not…going anywhere… If you're not experienced enough to take that on board…' He shrugged but his dark eyes were glued to her face. 'My…past experiences have not programmed me for any kind of commitment.'

'I'm not a virgin,' Alice told him abruptly. 'And talking about this makes it feel like an arrangement.'

'And that's a bad thing because...?'

'Because...' She faltered, thinking of the right way to say what she wanted to say, and he stepped into the breach without hesitation.

'Because you're looking for romance?'

'No! This is crazy. I'm going to go now. I should never have—'

Gabriel reached forward and circled her wrist with his hand and Alice shivered. Talking was a mood killer, whether it made sense or not. But that touch, the heat of his skin against hers, reminded her why she had stopped him in his tracks before he could enter his bedroom.

'Come closer and I'll show you why this might be crazy but why you shouldn't walk away.'

Mesmerised, Alice leaned towards him and half-closed her eyes. His cool lips against hers sent an explosion through her. She slid trembling fingers through his hair and caressed his neck. She could hardly believe what she was doing.

Was this really *her?* She wasn't a risk taker. Her life had been too unsteady for her to nurture the sort of devil-may-care attitude that encouraged spontaneous, careless behaviour. She was cautious, careful...

Yet she knew that she was about to take the biggest risk of her life in doing this and she didn't want to stop.

She kissed him slowly, drowning in the sensuality of his tongue melding with hers. As she kissed him, eyes closed, she blindly traced the contours of his beautiful face with her fingers. The wrap had slid off her shoulders and his hands were moving along her collarbone.

He drew back and she looked at him, still dazed from sensations she had never felt before.

'Undress for me, Alice...and don't tell me that you can't. Turn around. I'll unzip you.'

'I've never done a striptease before.'

'I'll show you how, in that case.' He stood up and began undressing. Very slowly, watching her as she watched him, her mouth half-open, fascination oozing from every pore.

Did it get better than this? Gabriel couldn't remember the last time he had been this turned on. She had the star-struck expression of a kid in a candy shop and it went to his head faster than a dose of adrenaline.

When his shirt was off, he began unzipping his trousers, and he grinned when she half-looked away, then looked back, then looked away again and finally returned her riveted gaze to his semi-clad body.

He was down to his boxers—dark-striped, silk boxers. Alice thought she might pass out. He had the highly toned body of an athlete: broad shoulders and a muscular torso that tapered down to a washboard-flat stomach and lean hips. Even in the most unforgiving of lights, he would still be beautiful.

Nerves gripped her.

What would he think of *her*? Was she opening herself up to humiliation? He might have waxed lyrical about finding her attractive, but it wouldn't do to forget that he went for small, voluptuous women with big breasts.

He didn't take off the boxers. Instead, he sat back down on the sofa and said with a wicked grin, 'Have I set an acceptable benchmark?'

Alice unzipped her dress herself. It was a long zip and it slid smoothly apart. She took a deep breath and then unlooped first one shoulder, then the other.

Another deep breath then it was off, sliding to the ground, the cool air hitting her bare breasts. He had looked at her with gleaming self-confidence when he had removed his clothes. She had her eyes shut until she heard him warmly, unsteadily tell her to open them.

The gentleness in his voice was like the waving of a magic wand and in that instant she shed her nerves as smoothly and as easily as she had shed her beautiful Cinderella dress.

She walked towards him wearing only her lacy pink panties and breathed in sharply as his hands settled on her hips and he sat up so that he could trail delicate kisses over her flat stomach.

She might not be a curvy Marilyn Monroe but she really turned him on. She could feel it in the way his hands shook ever so slightly and the way his breathing was just a little uncontrolled. Just for a brief window in time, her big, powerful boss was not the man who ruled the world but someone very human, someone driven by responses he couldn't tame, and she had done that. Her self-confidence soared.

'You're beautiful,' she heard him breathe.

She gripped his sinewy shoulders as he hooked his fingers into the waistband of her panties and tugged them down. She was completely naked and she didn't want to run for cover.

Two fumbling encounters with Alan before being ditched for a sexier model had left Alice with a punishing lack of self-confidence. If someone had told her that she would be able to do this—to stand in front of one of the sexiest men she could ever hope to meet and not feel embarrassed at her body—she would have laughed in disbelief. But that was exactly what she was doing now.

He parted her thighs with his hand and she curled her fingers into his hair and gasped as he traced the folds of her womanhood with his tongue. When he slipped it into her moistness, her legs almost gave way. The pleasure was unbearable.

This was refined torture as he teased her, bringing her

to dizzy heights before allowing her to subside. She was wet, throbbing, aching from wanting more.

He lifted her onto the bed and then laid her down and looked at her.

Her body was slim and graceful. Her breasts were just the right size. Her hair was like spun silk. He stepped out of his boxers. He was so hard for her that it was going to be a challenge to stop himself from doing the unthinkable; he knew that if she just touched him there he would release his seed like a teenager with no control.

Alice could scarcely breathe. She was overwhelmed with excitement. It coursed through her veins like a drug, washing away everything in its rampaging path. She had to squirm and resist touching herself to try to staunch the throbbing.

He settled on the bed and straddled her. She reached to touch him and he stayed her hand.

'No way.' Gabriel barely recognised the shakiness in his voice. 'If you do... I'm too turned on...'

'That's nice.'

'It's better than nice,' he growled in response. He lowered himself over her and she sighed and wriggled when he began teasing her breasts with his tongue.

'Hands above your head,' he commanded. Her nipples were big, pink discs and he tasted them delicately before taking one into his mouth and suckling on it, not letting up, enjoying her whimpers of delight and the way she moved, unable to keep still.

If she felt like a kid in a candy shop, then that was how he felt as well. The novelty of it was incredible, invigorating, exceptional.

When he could no longer bear the foreplay, he fumbled for his wallet, which he had dropped on the bedside table, and removed a condom.

Through the haze of her desire, Alice recognised a guy who took no chances. When he said that he did not involve himself in relationships for the long haul, he wasn't kidding.

She propped herself up on her elbows and watched as he put it on, fast and expertly. He was so big that she marvelled that he had not had any unfortunate accidents in the past from splitting one of them.

Their eyes met for the briefest of moments and he grinned.

'No risks, right?' she asked lightly and he nodded.

'Never.'

He nudged into her and then pushed harder so that she felt every bit of his girth rubbing inside her, sending waves of sensations shooting through her body. She clung. It was all she could do. Her short nails dug into his back as he moved harder and harder. Her legs wrapped round him and their bodies fused into one.

Her orgasm was deep, long and mind-blowing. Alice felt as if she was flying, soaring upwards, splintering into a thousand exquisite pieces. Her body arched as wave upon wave of unbearable pleasure coursed through her. One final thrust and he came as well, rearing up and groaning. Shudders of release ripped through his big body.

Unbelievable.

'Did the earth move for you?' he asked roughly, half-joking, half-serious, because it had damn well moved for *him*.

They had rolled onto their sides and were facing one another. It seemed perfectly natural. She had to lower her eyes because she felt so...*tender* towards him. That perfect moment of coming together was one of the few times when his guard was completely down, she suspected, and she supposed that it was the same for her. Now it was time for them to retreat to the people they were and tenderness didn't play any part in that.

'Shall I tell you how good you are?' she murmured teasingly and he clasped her fingers between his and kissed them one by one.

'That would be nice, and you can take your time. Feel free to be as descriptive as you like.'

'You're so egotistic, Gabriel.'

'Don't tell me you don't like it.' He kissed her and then settled his hand comfortably between her thighs. 'In fact, you have to tell me that you like it. I'm your boss.'

A timely reminder. She rolled onto her back and stared up at the ornate ceiling.

In the act of making love, she had lost the ability to think, but she was thinking now, remembering what he had said to her, how he had warned her off involvement: his little 'don't get attached to me' speech, the same little speech he would deliver to all his bed mates, of which she was now one.

Well, she might number among them, but she wasn't about to join their ranks in wanting more than he could give. She wasn't going to turn into another hysterical Georgia who had been silly enough to think that she could domesticate the jungle animal.

'You are,' she agreed lightly. 'Which is why this is only going to last for the duration of Paris.' Belatedly it occurred to her that she might have been a one-night stand. Had she jumped to the wrong conclusion?

'Is that a fact?' Gabriel murmured. He withdrew his hand to cup one breast instead and he gently stroked her until her nipple hardened.

'Being here is like playing truant…time off from normality.' Alice knew her body was reacting with wild abandon even though her voice was calm and controlled. She wanted him to flick his tongue over the tender nub of her nipple as he had done earlier; she wanted him to lick her between her legs until she couldn't breathe properly and then she wanted him inside her all over again, thrusting hard and sending her into glorious orbit.

Four days with him wasn't what she wanted but there was no way that she was going to lose control. She wasn't going to become his puppet.

And she wasn't going to let herself fall into the trap of thinking that, because maybe she had been harder to get than he was used to, he somehow was no longer the lazy guy who took what was on offer because he couldn't be bothered with the tedium of pursuit. She wasn't going to be another idiot who thought that he was capable of change.

'Normality being…?'

'Normality being London and the fact that I work for you. I'm being serious, Gabriel. I don't want to jeopardise my job. I can't think when you're doing…*that*…' He had slipped his fingers inside her and was absently teasing her tender, sensitive flesh.

'That suits me,' he drawled and Alice fought down the sudden flare of irrational disappointment. 'You're the best secretary I've ever had.'

'And besides,' she said drily, 'you like a quick turn-around when it comes to women, don't you?'

'Always.' Gabriel thought it best to remind her, although she was not like the other women he had been out with. She might be young, but she was cool, controlled, not in search of the inaccessible. Hadn't she told him that he wasn't her type? What, he wondered, was her type anyway?

It didn't matter. He wasn't risking anything. She wouldn't get emotionally involved with him any more than he would get emotionally involved with her. They understood one another.

'But while we're here playing truant,' he drawled huskily, 'I might see fit to limit the amount of client entertaining we do. You've never been to Paris and I know this city like the back of my hand. You're under orders to follow my lead...'

'Yes, sir!' Alice grinned. This was her big adventure and she was going to enjoy it while it lasted.

'Where did you learn to speak French?'

They sat in the sunshine outside one of the smart cafés close to the Louvre, where they had spent a couple of hours admiring the great works of art. He had been true to his word and work had been minimal for the past two days. They had entertained Francois and Marie after the deal had been officially signed, and had had lunch with another prospective client who had been charming and informative. But mostly they had made love.

She felt vibrantly, wonderfully alive. She had been living life in the slow lane and now she had been pulled into a Ferrari and was speeding up a highway, enjoying every second of the ride. It was thrilling, frightening and she was dreading the end, the brick wall at the end of the highway.

'Self-taught.' Gabriel sipped his strong coffee and looked at her, admiring the purity of her skin, the sharp fall of her hair, the fullness of her pink lips.

She was a revelation. They were lovers, but that did not impact on her ability to focus and work. They made love, but she didn't demand his constant attention. Neither did she give any hint that she intended what they had to last beyond Paris.

Which was good. In fact, it was great. They were having a no-strings-attached affair. She hadn't mentioned what exactly her type of guy was but he wasn't it. Admittedly, it irked him...

'Amazing.' Alice laughed. 'You must pick things up fast.'

'Necessity is the mother of invention,' Gabriel said drily. If only she knew...

Without the benefit of an expensive education, with his formative years spent either getting into trouble or else avoiding it, he had had to learn fast to compete once he'd got out into the big, bad world. His natural ability, talent and sheer untapped intellect had propelled him forward, but he had known from very early on he would need an edge, and that edge would be a second language. He had befriended a native Frenchman as soon as he'd hit the trading floor and had trained himself to speak only in French when they were in each other's company. He had learned to understand finance in another language, had learned the dialect of the stock exchange in French. He had earned his edge and it had come in very handy over the years.

'Meaning?'

'Meaning it's time for us to get back to the hotel. Looking at you is doing some very active things to my libido.' He drained his cup and stood up, and Alice followed suit.

This was what they were all about. She knew that just as she knew that she had done exactly what she had set out not to do: she had fallen under his spell. In London, she had seen the brilliant, inspired businessman, the man with formidable levels of energy who poured that energy into work.

But here she had seen the other man. The witty, charming, highly informative, sexy guy and she had fallen under his spell.

No, worse. With painful honesty, she knew that she had fallen in love with him. For her, this wasn't just a simple case of lust. No, this was the vast, unchartered territory of absolute love, the one-hundred percent absorption in another human being; the yearning and craving and not being able to envisage a life without them. In a perfect world, this was the sort of intense, soaring feeling that would be reciprocated. In her imperfect world, however, this was the nightmare that couldn't be contained and couldn't be ignored. Just thinking about her stupidity made her feel sick.

She had had searing sex with a guy who found her attractive but that was the end of it. She had launched herself down a one way street, had given her heart to a guy who certainly wouldn't be returning the favour, and it hurt. Gabriel Cabrera didn't do love. In fact, he didn't even do anything that remotely bordered on intimacy, or at least what *she* understood by intimacy. She hadn't failed to notice that when she asked questions he didn't want to answer, he abruptly, smilingly but very firmly, changed the subject.

The essence of the man remained hidden. That was the way he liked it, and that was something that was never going to change. How much more foolish could she have been? Against all the odds, against every scrap of common sense she possessed, she had handed over the most precious of emotions into the care of a man who would have run a mile had he but known. A wave of dizziness washed over her and she had to fight her way back to some semblance of normality.

They made it back to the hotel in record time. Dinner was going to be at one of Gabriel's favourite restaurants in Montmartre, somewhere chilled with an eclectic crowd.

It left them a couple of hours and she knew how those hours would be spent.

In his bedroom, in his bed…

She always made sure to return to her own bedroom, even in the early hours of the morning, but they always made love in his bedroom.

'I can't seem to keep my hands off you.' He pushed her

back against the closed door. 'Touch me,' he groaned. He unbuttoned his jeans and pulled down the zip to relieve the throbbing in his groin.

The touch of her cool hand as it wormed its way into his boxers was bliss, enough almost to send him over the edge.

'Let's make use of the bath…' He broke away to lead her into the bathroom, which was the last word in indulgence. A ridiculously large bath took centre stage with a walk-in shower to one side and twin sinks on the other side rested on black granite with a huge mirror behind.

He ran the bath, flinging in bath salts, and Alice watched him. He was poetry in motion and she couldn't get enough of him. He had stripped off her protective layer and the only one blessing was that he didn't realise that he had done so.

She had made sure to reveal as little about herself as he had revealed about himself, although he knew her thoughts on so many things. They had discussed literature, art, the paintings and sculptures they had seen, the food they had eaten and the wine they had drunk. They had talked about the people they watched, sitting outside and sipping coffee. They had compared notes on music. They had even talked about work and about the accountancy course she was due to embark upon.

'I can feel you watching me,' Gabriel said with a grin in his voice.

'That's because you're so egotistic. You think that every woman on the planet's watching you.'

'Ah…' He turned around, still smiling, and slowly got undressed. 'But you're the only one I care about.'

If only.

She had shed all her inhibitions in front of him. She had no idea how she was going to return to her role of perfect secretary—not when she was crazy about him, when he had seen her naked, when he had touched her in her most intimate places. But men were brilliant at detaching and she would be as well.

The water was beautifully warm and blissful. The bath was easily big enough for two and she slid between his legs, her back against his stomach, her head tucked against his neck.

He squirted some liquid soap into one hand and took his time massaging her breasts. She could feel him pressed against her, a shaft of steel, proof positive of how much she turned him on.

She sighed and slipped down lower into the water and, eyes closed, she lost herself in pure sensation as his hand moved from her breasts down over her stomach and between her thighs.

'Don't…' she protested as he found the sensitive bud and began rubbing it, eliciting broken, gasping groans.

'Don't what?'

'Stop or I'll…' Too late. Her body shuddered as she climaxed. Her breathing quickened and she cried out and turned in the water, thankfully not sending too much over the side of the bath, and she sat on him, but she knew as well as he did that without protection it was too risky.

So, instead, she did what he had done to her. Watching him climax was such a turn-on that she couldn't wait for them to get out of the bath and find the bed.

Was it her imagination or was there an urgency to their love-making that had not been there before? They would be leaving the following evening.

Gabriel could have just kept touching her, making love with her, and skipped dinner altogether but with just an hour to get ready and leave the hotel he turned to her and smiled.

'So…' he drawled, nestling her against him. They had

barely bothered to dry themselves. They had been too hungry for one another. 'We leave tomorrow.'

'We do.' Alice lowered her eyes and placed her hand flat against his hair-roughened chest.

'What do you think of Paris?'

'I think one day I'll be back. It's beautiful. I love the architecture, the art galleries, the museums… There's nothing about it I *don't* love.'

'And London? I don't think this thing we have has run its course…' He was as hot for her now as he had been on day one—as he had been even before then, if he was entirely truthful.

'Meaning?'

'Meaning, my dear secretary, that I'm not ready for our spate of truancy to come to an end.'

Alice raised clear eyes to his. *He wasn't ready for this to end.* She knew exactly what he meant—he meant that he hadn't yet grown bored with her. But he would, and when that happened she would be utterly destroyed.

More than that, having her around would begin to exasperate him. She would be just another woman to be discarded, except he would find that she was still there, still working for him, still *visible.* Would she end up buying a bouquet of goodbye flowers for herself?

'That's not how I see this panning out,' she told him and he drew apart and looked at her with a frown.

'What do you mean?' He smiled. 'We're still hot for one another. No point denying it, Alice. So you work for me and I've always had a policy of not mixing business with pleasure—but what's the saying about stable doors and a bolting horse…?'

'When we leave, Gabriel, it's over. That's what I said at the beginning and I haven't changed my mind.' Would she have responded differently if she hadn't done the unthinkable and fallen in love with him? Would she have been able to keep it as something fun and casual and then, when it was over, cheerfully return to life as she knew it?

Temptation to take that road dug into her and she fought it with the gritted determination of someone swimming upstream against a strong current.

'You don't mean that.'

She swung her legs over the side of the bed and began flinging clothes on, eyes firmly averted from his face. 'I mean every word of it, Gabriel,' she said. 'It's been amazing, but…'

Gabriel couldn't believe what he was hearing. He had never suffered rejection from any woman. He had always been the one to do the rejecting.

'But we can't keep our hands off one another!' he exploded, leaping out of the bed and snatching his boxers. He glared at her, challenging her to refute that, which she didn't. 'I don't see what the problem is!'

Fully dressed now, she at last felt strong enough to meet his glittering, bemused, demanding gaze but she still had to keep her distance.

'The problem is that we don't think alike, Gabriel. You take because you can and then, when you're bored, you move on to someone else. That's not me. I don't want to waste my time having an affair with someone unless I think it's going somewhere. Which is not the case here,' she added quickly, just in case he got it into his head that she was asking him to define what he felt for her.

'I'm just saying that we need to keep things black and white. This was a bubble. It's too late to say that it wasn't a good idea, but what's done is done, and now we can move forward and continue our working relationship and put this behind us as something enjoyable that won't be repeated.'

'I can't believe I'm hearing this,' he rasped, still incredulous. 'I've had my fair share of difficult women in my time, but you're not one of them! Or are you…?'

That cut to the quick. She was anything but, if only he knew. And thank goodness he didn't.

'I'm not,' she said shortly. 'But I'm realistic. Just like you. Except we have different realities. I want a man for life and I'm prepared to do my utmost to find him. You want a woman for two minutes and you'll never look further for anything longer.'

CHAPTER SEVEN

THEY HAD LEFT London with spring promising to be a fine one. They had returned to dank drizzle and the grey, cold weather had continued for the two weeks since they had been back.

Paris seemed like a dream. A wonderful dream to be locked away and only taken out at night, when she remembered everything—where they had gone, what they had talked about and, most of all, the heady excitement when they had made love.

She had been right to do what she had done. He had railed against her decision for five minutes, had tried to convince her that carrying on their affair was a good idea, but she hadn't failed to notice that in the end, when she had refused, he had ultimately let it go, already moving on.

And now...

She sighed and frowned at her computer, trying to focus. There wasn't a minute of the day when she wasn't aware of him. When he stood next to her to explain something, she could feel her weak, treacherous body begin to go into meltdown. Her head might try and box him up neatly but her body remembered the way it had felt under those roving hands and that exploring mouth.

He, on the other hand, seemed to have no problem with the way their working relationship had continued.

In her darker moments, she thought that he might be quietly relieved that she had made the decision that she had. It had certainly spared him the effort of having to engineer a break-up while maintaining the status quo.

The connecting door between their offices was pushed open and she tensed and looked up with a brittle, polite smile.

'I need you to book two tickets to the opera. Source me one that isn't too challenging. Best seats.'

Alice nodded. The rictus smile never left her face but something inside twisted painfully.

This was bound to happen. She had braced herself for it, for the moment when he found himself a replacement. A fortnight! What they had shared had barely been given a decent burial.

'When would you like me to book these tickets for?'

'Tonight.'

'That might be impossible, if it's one of the more popular operas.'

'Mention my name. I give generously to the Opera House. They'll find seats.' He strolled towards her and dropped a stack of files on her desk. 'And you'll have to get through these before you leave tonight.'

'But it's already five-thirty!'

'Tough.' He flicked back the cuff of his white shirt and strolled back into his office, shutting the door behind him.

Gabriel had never put himself out for any woman and he wasn't about to start now, but her cool detachment got on his nerves. It was as if Paris had never happened. She had even returned to her dreary grey garb, having tried to return the designer clothes he had ordered her to buy in Paris.

Naturally he had refused but he suspected that the whole lot had probably been given to charity. No reminders.

The worst of it was that he still wanted her. He couldn't

look at her without the memory of that slender, willowy body writhing underneath him. Another woman was what he needed, he had decided. He had had his change and it was time to return to what he knew.

He settled down to work and didn't look up until there was a knock on his door and he saw, with surprise, that it was nearly seven.

'Finished already?' he asked, swinging back in the chair and looking at her with brooding, unreadable eyes. 'Scanned and sent off everything?'

'Your date is here, Gabriel.' It was a challenge just getting the words out. So, he had reverted to type. Bethany Dawkins was small, curvaceous and dressed to impress in a figure-hugging black dress with a neckline that plunged almost to the waist, displaying bountiful breasts restrained behind a sliver of black netting. Alice had looked at the other woman and immediately felt dowdy, drab and unappealing, and she had known from the way the other woman's eyes had skimmed over her that she wasn't alone in that opinion.

She had already buzzed through to him that the tickets had been booked. She doubted sexy little Bethany with the flowing dark hair would be in the slightest bit interested in opera.

'Wonderful.' He stood up and began slinging on his jacket.

'Have a lovely evening,' she said through gritted teeth.

Gabriel paused, as though suddenly struck by an errant thought. 'With Bethany for company, I undoubtedly will. Opera interest you, Alice?'

'You know it does.' It was the first time she had alluded to one of the many conversations they had had over a bottle of wine before they'd had to return to the hotel, like adolescents unable to go long without touching one another.

'Of course. I'd forgotten. Care to join us? I'm sure it would be possible to have them arrange for a third seat to be made available.'

And witness first hand how easily he had moved on? Watch them holding hands and staring at each other in that 'can't wait to climb into bed after this' way? That was how he had looked at her in Paris. Over meals, in the back seat of the limo, he had looked at her with dark hunger, as though the time couldn't go by fast enough until he was in bed with her again.

'I'll give that a miss. Thank you. And, to answer your question about the files, yes, everything's been done so, if it's all the same with you, I'll leave now. I shall be going to visit my mother in Devon tomorrow and I thought I might stay over until Tuesday. I could look in on that customer we've been having problems with in Exeter. It's no trouble and it'll save you having to make the trip yourself.'

'How far does your mother live from Exeter?'

'Close enough.' Something else that he'd forgotten. She had told him the name of the little village where her mother lived, although she had kept all other surplus information to herself. Had he forgotten *everything* she had said to him? He had appeared so attentive, but had it been in one ear and out the other?

Well, he certainly had form when it came to that, she thought bitterly, but it hurt, because she had been one-hundred percent committed when she had talked to him.

'I think your hot date might be getting a bit impatient outside,' she reminded him coolly.

'And that's a problem because…?' He wondered why the sudden disappearing act for a long weekend. Since she had effectively walked out on him, he had been thinking about her non-stop, which alternately baffled and angered him— hence his decision to seek some replacement therapy. But not even the delectable woman waiting for him outside could kill the curiosity he felt when it came to Alice.

He knew that she visited her mother every weekend and, for the life of him, that seemed peculiar. It took filial devotion to whole new lengths.

And this weekend, she wanted to stay longer. He knew that the village was only forty-five minutes' drive from his client, so why the pressing urgency to stay the day?

Did she visit more than just her mother when she vanished on those mysterious trips to the back of beyond? The more he considered that option, the more likely it seemed, and of course there could be only one pressing reason for her to trek all the way down there every weekend without fail. A man.

She had slept with him and she had fancied the hell out of him, or so he had thought. Frankly, wasn't it a little suspect that she could move from fancying him to treating him like a complete stranger within a matter of hours? Women didn't operate like that. Detachment did not come as second nature to them. Why would Alice be the exception to the rule? It was as though the woman she had been in Paris had stayed there.

He had never been given to flights of imagination. He had always considered that the luxury of people who had too much spare time on their hands, but he was discovering that his imagination was playing all sorts of games now as he stood there, looking at her.

So, she had slept with him. Was it because the guy she really wanted was not available? Was the man married? Was that what those weekend visits were all about? Was it a so-called duty visit to dear mama, but really to hook up with some sleazy guy with a wife and kids who gave her sex now and again while promising to leave his albatross family one day?

Red mist settled over his eyes. 'I'll expect you back here first thing on Monday. Harrisons can wait. There's too much work here for you to take a day off.'

'I've already booked the day off,' Alice told him abruptly. 'I was being helpful when I suggested I visit Harrisons—it would actually have cut into my day. But they're only a hop and a skip away and I shall probably be in the area to do some…shopping anyway. I don't mind popping in and picking up the hard copy information we need.' *How dared he think that he could be heavy handed with her just because he had moved on and was involved with someone else?*

Just then Bethany appeared at the door, her face a picture of petulance. He had met Bethany several months ago at a company do. Her father—an Argentinian man in his late fifties whose company had surfaced on Gabriel's radar for acquisition—had brought her along in the absence of his wife, who'd been on a cruise with a gaggle of her friends, he had told Gabriel. Bethany had visibly blossomed the second she had set eyes on Gabriel and had followed him around for the evening, much to her father's delight. She was thirty, sexy as hell and, she'd confessed with a sultry little smile, bored out of her mind with all the dreary people talking about work.

Gabriel had taken her number, vaguely intimated that he might give her a call and promptly forgotten her existence, of which he had been reminded several times in the intervening months.

He had finally, two days previously, decided to take her up on her repeated offers. This was his comfort zone—being chased by women. His comfort zone was not one in which he pursued and was knocked back.

He looked between the women and the differences could not have been more startling.

Alice was nearly six inches taller in flats, slim, with her hair neatly tied back and her pale face intelligent and attractive rather than flamboyantly beautiful. She had a composure and a stillness that the much shorter, sexier woman lacked and Gabriel stifled his irritation at finding himself losing interest in his hot date for the evening.

'Have a really nice evening.' Alice couldn't bear to see them together, to see her replacement who was everything she was not. She hated the thought that she had been the temporary aberration, and she wondered whether Gabriel had been drawn to her because she was so unlike the women he went out with as a rule.

Bethany had lost interest in Alice altogether and was preening for Gabriel's benefit, smoothing her hands over her figure-hugging dress and then twirling round, demanding to know what he thought of her outfit.

Alice turned away, not wanting to see the rampant male appreciation in his eyes, appreciation that she had once seen directed at her.

'I'll leave you to it, shall I?' She interrupted the love birds and Gabriel turned to look at her.

'If you don't mind.' His voice was ultra-polite, his eyes flat and unreadable. 'And, Alice, have a good weekend... visiting your mother...'

Alice reddened. 'I happen to have other things planned,' she muttered, because he had made her sound sad and pathetic, and he had done it on purpose. Or maybe he hadn't. Maybe he had just pushed her back into the 'efficient secretary without a life' box whose weekend occupation was visiting her mother. Not that he knew the full story behind those visits.

'Oh? Anything exciting?' Gabriel's ears pricked up. Bethany's arm possessively linking his felt like a dead weight and it was all he could do not to shrug it off impatiently off impatiently.

'Oh, just seeing one or two people,' Alice told him vaguely. 'You know...'

Gabriel didn't know and the not knowing preyed on his mind for the remainder of the evening. He was irritated with his date, and then further irritated with himself, because before Paris Bethany would have been just the thing to relieve him of whatever stress he might have been having.

She had no interest in what was happening on the stage and several times asked him what the plot was. She spent quite a bit of time peering round her to see if she could recognise anyone, and was visibly relieved when the ordeal was at an end and they could get something to eat. Although, she said with a little moue, she really, *really,* would have loved to have something to eat at his place.

Sex was not going to happen.

In fact, nothing was going to happen.

Gabriel fed her, listened to her while his mind drifted in other, less welcome directions and then settled her into his chauffeur-driven car, made his excuses and headed back alone to his house.

So much for his attempts at distracting himself! The only thing on his mind was Alice's remark about having people to see at the weekend. The thought of her having a man down there had lodged in his head, utterly destroying the self-assurance he wore like a mantel on his shoulders.

There was no getting round it—if he had been used, if he had been some kind of sick substitute for a man who couldn't commit to her, then he had a right to know.

He knew where her mother lived. She had touched upon that topic in passing, had mentioned the house with a wistful smile on her face. She had talked about the little village and the picturesque country road which she was fond of walking down, breathing in the fragrance of the summer blossoms, the sharpness of the wintry air, dawdling in autumn on her way from house to village to appreciate the russet reds of the falling leaves.

Oh yes, he had a memory like a computer, and he hadn't forgotten a single thing she had told him in Paris when she had let her guard down and confided, told him snippets of her past which had seemed to slip out in between their conversations about art and culture, work and deals, the state of the world.

Alice, he thought with a frown as he retired for bed much later that night, would have appreciated the opera. She wouldn't have asked a bunch of idiotic questions, she wouldn't have stifled yawns and she wouldn't have kept looking around her like a bored kid at an adult gathering.

It all came back to Alice. He had never been this obsessed with a woman and he wondered whether it was because he still felt that they had unfinished business between them. If there was some mystery man in the background, then the business would be finished and she would be out on her ear looking for a new job. But if there wasn't… Maybe what they had started in Paris needed to reach a natural conclusion.

She might say that she didn't want that, but he did. Badly…and he was a man who always got what he wanted.

Alice finished preparing the supper and went to join her mother in the little sitting room that overlooked the tidy, pretty garden in which Pamela Morgan spent so much of her spare time, pottering and enjoying being outside where her phobia could not get a grip and drive her back to the safety of the four walls.

There was something that her mother was keeping from

her and that was worrying. True, she would be seeing her mother's therapist on Monday morning first thing, but she couldn't help wondering if there had been some sort of setback.

The sitting room was bright and airy and very different from the sitting room in the house in which she had grown up. Here, photos of her as a girl were proudly displayed on the mantelpiece and the sofa and chairs were deep and comfortable. It was a cluttered room, which was something her father had loathed, preferring to have as few reminders as possible around that he was a family man.

'You were telling me all about your trip to Paris,' Pamela Morgan encouraged as soon as her daughter was sitting down, legs tucked underneath her, cosy and comfortable in her faded jogging bottoms and bedroom slippers, with her hair in a stubby ponytail.

Actually, Alice thought that talking about her trip to Paris was pretty much all she had done since she had arrived. It had been the same last weekend and, whilst she had done her best to skirt round the topic of Gabriel, she had found herself talking about him, recounting some of the anecdotes he had told her. Her mother had made a very good listener, hardly interrupting, and Alice wondered if she had confided more than she should have.

But if her mother wanted to hear more about the Louvre and what they had seen, or the Jardin des Tuileries and how beautiful it was, then so be it.

Alice was accustomed to handling Pamela Morgan with kid gloves. She tiptoed around anything too intrusive, permanently aware that her mother was not one of life's more robust specimens.

Outside, the day had been surprisingly warm and sunny, and the sun was only now beginning to dip, throwing the garden into lovely, semi-sunlit relief.

In the kitchen, some meat sauce was simmering on the stove. Later they would eat together and, as always, it would be an early night.

As she chatted, her mind played with the thought of Gabriel and how he was enjoying his weekend with the pocket brunette. Had the opera been an aperitif, the taster course before the main meal? Of course it had, she chided herself scornfully. The main meal would have been the bedroom. Gabriel might be lazy when it came to every single form of emotional involvement, but he was just the opposite when it came to physical involvement. On that level, he was one-hundred percent active and engaged.

She wished she could eliminate him from her head, somehow press *delete* and get rid of all the inconvenient memories that were making her life a living hell.

She didn't want to quit her job but that was becoming a very real possibility with each passing day. Yesterday, seeing that woman in the office, had been the worst...

It was a reminder of how fleeting she had been for him. Her voice trailed off and she caught her mother looking at her speculatively; she grinned and tried to remember what she had been talking about. Paris? Work? Her flatmate Lucy's new boyfriend?

'You're a million miles away,' Pamela said softly. 'Have been since you returned from Paris. It's not your boss, is it? He seems to have made quite an impact on you.'

Appalled, Alice's mouth dropped open and she blushed. 'Of course not!' she denied vigorously. 'I wouldn't be so stupid! You know how I feel about the whole relationship thing, Mum, after...'

'I know, dear. After your father and that dreadful boyfriend you had. But...' There was a tentative silence and then Alice was startled when her mother said quietly, 'You can't let those experiences dictate your future.'

'I—I wouldn't *do* that,' Alice stuttered. 'It's just that you have to be careful when it comes to getting involved. It's all too easy to make the wrong choices!' She continued with heated earnestness, 'I will make very sure that, if and when I become *seriously* involved with a guy, he'll be someone who is right for me! Honestly, Mum, you want to meet my boss! He has a constantly revolving carousel of women who service his needs and, then, pouf! They're gone, straight through the exit, and ten seconds later another version is heading in his direction. He plucks them off the carousel the way someone plucks fruit from a tree! Has a little taste and then chucks what's left!'

'You're far too young to be so cynical about men...'

Alice bit her tongue but she and her mother knew each other well and she looked away because she could read what her mother was thinking.

If you're not careful you'll end up with no one because no one will fit the bill.

'I'd rather be on my own than make a mistake,' she said, her cheeks bright red, pre-empting the statement before it could be made.

Her mother sighed and lowered her eyes. She was not argumentative, and neither was Alice, but she had to be firm. She'd always had to look out for the two of them and it somehow felt treacherous for her mother to tell her that she was too cynical about men.

'What's the point of learning curves if you don't learn from them?' Fat lot of good that had done for her, she thought. She had been swept up in the same tidal wave of lust and desire that afflicted all the women who came into Gabriel's magical range. And she hadn't stopped at the lust and desire, which would have been bad enough. Oh no, she had taken it a step further and fallen in love with the man!

Her mother would have been distraught, had she only

known. Like her, Pamela Morgan had worked hard to cultivate a healthy scepticism when it came to the opposite sex. There was nothing wrong with that. It was called reality. How many times had they joked that men were more trouble than they were worth? For her mother, it would have been more than just a joke.

They usually ate in the kitchen, unless there was something on the telly they both wanted to watch, in which case trays were brought—although her mother never failed to complain that eating in front of the television was a sloppy habit.

But her mother watched a great deal of television and there had been times when some detective series or gardening show had been too tempting to miss.

Tonight, Alice set the table for them, leaving her mother in the sitting room, where she was happily flicking between her crossword book and the television.

She had almost had an argument with her mother and she felt awful about that.

Not only was the man intruding into all her thoughts, her waking moments, her dreams, but he was now managing to interrupt the easy flow of conversation with her mother.

She slammed place mats on the table and was reaching for wine glasses when there was a knock at the door.

Everyone used the kitchen door, but whoever it was had banged on the front door and, after just a brief hesitation, she dropped what she was doing and arrived at the front door at exactly the same time as her mother.

'You sit back down,' Alice said firmly. 'I'll get rid of whoever is out there.'

'No! I mean, dear, I'll get this. I don't like just telling people to go away. You know—it's a small village and I wouldn't want to get a reputation for being the sort of person who can't be polite to visitors...'

'Mum, if it's a visitor, of course I'm not going to send them on their merry way! But if it's someone trying to sell double glazing…'

'I'm not sure they do that any more, dear. Do they?'

As they stood there, vaguely quibbling, there was another loud knock on the door and, with a sigh of exasperation, Alice pulled open the front door and stared…

'What are *you* doing here?' Her mother was right behind her and she edged out of the door and half-shut it behind her, then she poked her head through and told her mother, who was avid with curiosity, that the caller was for her.

'Who is it?'

'No one! You…er…go inside and I'll be in, literally in a minute or two…' For a moment, Alice thought that her mother was about to ignore that suggestion but, after a brief staring match, Pamela Morgan tutted and headed towards the kitchen, not before casting another curious glance in the direction of the front door.

'What do you want? What are you doing here?'

Gabriel stared down at Alice. This was an Alice he had not seen before. Not the brisk, efficient secretary in the neat, uninspiring suit, or the glamorous, leggy woman in the designer clothes she had bought when she had been in Paris with him. A beautiful, fresh-faced girl who looked her age, with a ponytail and wearing stay-at-home, faded clothes and peculiar bedroom slippers with a cartoon motif.

Warmer weather had brought out a band of light freckles across the bridge of her nose. He had completely forgotten why he had come but he was damn glad that he had. Just seeing her did something to him and he fidgeted and looked away before resting his gaze once again on her upturned face.

'I couldn't get you out of my head.' Hell, had he just *said that*?

'What?' Alice was so shocked by that statement that her mouth fell open. Her eyes were glued to his face, which the early evening threw into shadow. He looked tired and dishevelled and drop-dead gorgeous. He had pushed up the arms of his long-sleeved cotton jumper and the sprinkling of dark hair brought back vivid memories of those strong arms around her. His low-slung jeans clung to him, delineating his long, muscular legs.

She felt her nipples pushing in anticipation against her bra, wanting to be touched and teased and licked.

'Shouldn't you be with…that woman who came to the office yesterday?' Alice asked huskily and Gabriel delivered a slow, amused smile that rocked her to the core.

Alice stared down at her feet. The pulse in her neck was beating fast and here, in these clothes, she had that weird, out-of-body feeling that she had had in Paris when she had thrown caution to the winds and jumped into bed with him.

He was making her aware of something better out there, something wild and free, and she *hated* him for that because she knew that it was all an illusion.

'It turns out that she didn't do it for me.' Gabriel had made a decision; it was one that had come to him when she had pulled open the front door and he had looked at her.

He was done telling himself that he was not built for pursuit. He was done pretending that he wasn't jealous whenever he thought of her with another man. If these reactions stemmed from the fact that what they had hadn't run its course, then it was up to him to ensure that it did run its course. How else was he going to get her out of his system?

'Are you going to invite me into the house?'

'No. You shouldn't be here, Gabriel.' But she was light with relief that the pocket-sized brunette hadn't become her replacement. It was stupid and it was cowardly but she couldn't help it.

'I know I shouldn't.' He raked his fingers through his hair, not too sure where he went from here.

Alice looked at him, perplexed.

'Is there a man in there?' he questioned suddenly, roughly, and Alice's mouth tightened with outrage.

'I'm not you, Gabriel. I don't hop from one bed to another without pausing for breath.'

'I didn't hop anywhere with Bethany. I put her in my car and my driver took her back to her house. End of story.'

'Just go, Gabriel.' She sighed and stared to the side of him, but his image was imprinted so forcibly in her head that every bit of him had been committed to memory. He was in her system like a virus which she couldn't budge.

'I'm not going anywhere.'

'Why? Why? I've told you…'

'Let me in.'

'You always think that you can get whatever you want.'

Gabriel stared at her and she squirmed under his unrelenting dark gaze. What would she do if he kissed her right now? Melt. She was melting now, liquid heat gathering between her legs, dampening her underwear. *He couldn't get her out of his head.* She told herself that those were just meaningless words, but they bounced around in her head until she was giddy.

'Let me in.'

He was as immovable as the rock of Gibraltar, standing there in all his brooding, intense glory, and with a little sigh of resignation Alice stood aside.

Her mother was hovering in the kitchen and introductions were made. Pamela Morgan launched into a series of questions, her curiosity on red alert, and Alice groaned silently to herself. If she had never said a word about Gabriel, she might have been able to channel him out of the house without too much difficulty—as just her boss who happened to be down to see a client and had popped in for…reasons best known to himself.

But she had spent far too much time telling her mother about him, describing him, inviting the curiosity that was now unstoppable.

How great to finally meet the man her daughter worked for! 'You never told me that he was so good-looking!'… 'My daughter loves her job; I can tell because she talks so much about it!'… 'And Paris…how wonderful that she had the opportunity to go there! She can't stop talking about it!'

'You *asked* me, Mum!' Alice avoided eye contact with Gabriel but she could feel him simmering with his own curiosity. 'I talked about Paris because *you asked me*!'

Her mother had chosen, however, to skirt round that technicality.

'I've intruded,' Gabriel murmured. Pamela Morgan was an attractive woman, with a frailty that her daughter lacked. Not even the loose-fitting dress or the long, cream cardigan could conceal her good looks. Was that why her daughter was so self-conscious about her appearance? Was there some sort of unspoken rivalry between mother and daughter? And, yet, no; there was clearly a strong bond there.

This was the first time he had ever met any relative of any woman he had slept with, aside from Bethany's father. Meeting the family had been something he had always heavily discouraged. Now, he was intensely curious, intensely curious to join the dots and make connections— intensely, inexplicably curious just to find out more.

'You're not intruding! Is he, Alice?'

'Well, now that you mention it…' She caught Gabriel's eye and noted the wicked gleam of amusement.

'That's very kind…may I call you Pamela? Yes? Well, you're very kind, but I won't be staying long.'

'Yes.' Alice stood up with a wide, false smile. 'Gabriel has to be on his way. Don't you, Gabriel? He's probably got all sorts of plans for the evening.'

'None,' Gabriel drawled. He settled down comfortably in the kitchen chair to which he had been ushered. 'But I will have, if you ladies would allow me to take you both out for a meal…?' His sharp eyes noted the quick look that was exchanged, and then Pamela Morgan was on her feet, clutching her cardigan tightly around her.

'You two go out. There's a lovely little restaurant in the village, just opened…'

'There is?' Alice gaped. 'And, no! We won't be going anywhere!' She glared at Gabriel who returned the glare with a comfortable smile of satisfaction.

'Yes, you will, Alice! I insist. We eat in every single weekend. It will do you good to get out and see the place for a change. Plus, there's food here for me, and what's left over I can pop in the freezer. And the weather is so nice at the moment. Such a lovely change from all that rain we've been having. Alice, darling, why don't you go and change, and you two young things can go out and have some fun.'

'Mum…'

'If you're sure, Pamela…' Gabriel stood up, exuding innate charm. 'Why don't you run along, Alice? Change into your glad rags? And, in the meantime, Pamela and I can get to know one another…'

CHAPTER EIGHT

ALICE FUMED. WHY had he shown up on her doorstep? It was utterly out of character for him, but then being dumped was out of character for him as well. Was that why he had said that he couldn't get her out of his head? Once you stripped that remark down to its bare bones, what you were left with was a man who wanted something of which he had been deprived, whatever the cost.

He was impossible!

She had practically nothing to wear. She didn't come down to Devon intent on having nights out. Her wardrobe consisted of comfortable clothes to hang around the house in. With a groan of despair, she rummaged through the bottom shelves where clothes from another era had been shoved and forgotten.

Gabriel here, in her mother's house, felt like an invasion of her privacy. He was seeing where she had lived for years; seeing the photos of her which were liberally scattered throughout the small house; the little drawings she had done which her mother had kept in a box during those long, miserable years when she'd been married, drawings which she'd had framed as soon as she had a house of her own.

He was a billionaire and she couldn't help wondering what he thought of her mother's house: too small, not smart enough, filled with mementoes and knickknacks that had cost practically nothing. Everything else, the more expensive stuff, had been sold off when her father had died and the family home sold. Her mother had not wanted to bring any bad memories with her to wherever she chose to put down roots.

Alice wasn't at all ashamed of where she had lived but it was only human to see your own particular circumstances through the eyes of someone else. In this case, her arrogant, super-rich boss.

She looked around her own bedroom with critical eyes. Nothing had been done to it since she had moved out. It was in good condition, but dated. The wallpaper was old-style floral and the bed and the dressing table harked back to a different era—the era of cheap reproduction furniture that was functional but lacking in style. It had served its purpose and, for the first time, Alice was slightly ashamed that she had not encouraged her mother to do some basic renovations to the house.

Yes, some of what she earned went on paying her mother's therapist, but there was always enough left over to spend a little on the house.

Her mother, whilst she probably would have been able to afford some of those renovations, would have swept aside the suggestion as being a waste of money. That, like so much else, was a legacy of her past, unhappy life, where money had never been thrown around and where the housekeeping had been frugal.

Eager to get downstairs and curtail whatever conversation Gabriel was having with her mother, Alice showered and changed as fast as she could. The black trousers, which had been folded on the bottom shelf, thankfully still fit; the red jumper might be baggy but its colour had not been diminished in the wash, and at least it looked jollier than the greys, blacks and dark blues that comprised most of the rest of the wardrobe of clothes.

As an afterthought, she applied a light covering of make-up—some mascara, a little blush, some lip gloss.

I couldn't get you out of my head...

She could feel his remark burning a hole through all her defences, worming its way past her conviction that it was just another example of his arrogance, and she groaned again.

She barged into the kitchen to find Gabriel enjoying a cup of tea and her mother giggling. Giggling! They both looked up as she entered, like a couple of kids found out in a conspiracy. Alice took a few deep breaths, gathering herself and resisting the urge to ask them what, exactly, what so funny.

She had been gone less than forty minutes and they had become best friends!

'This is all I could find to wear,' she said ungraciously, and was treated to a wolfish smile from Gabriel.

'You look lovely, dear. Doesn't she look lovely, Gabriel? You should wear red more often. It suits you.'

'It certainly does...' he murmured. 'We're going to an Italian restaurant. Your favourite type of food.'

Pamela looked between them with keen interest. 'How do you know that?' she asked with, Alice thought, a complete lack of tact.

'Oh, I know a great many things about your daughter, Pamela...'

'Because,' Alice snapped, 'when you're stuck in someone's company for days on end, you tend to find out superficial things about them. Like what their favourite cuisine is.'

'*Stuck in my company?* I got the impression that you rather—'

'Okay,' Alice interrupted hurriedly, before something was said that would have her mother's curiosity spiked even more than it already was. 'Shall we go? I don't want to be long, because...'

'Where will you be staying, Gabriel?'

Gabriel shrugged. 'Well, I hadn't thought ahead.'

'You'll save some money if you stay here. The spare bedroom is small but it's tidy. I use it as a sewing room, but I could just pop my bits and bobs in my sewing box.'

'Gabriel doesn't need to save money, Mum. And I'm sure he won't be staying overnight.'

'It's way too late for me to drive back to London,' Gabriel said thoughtfully. 'And don't we all need to save money?'

Alice controlled hysterical laughter. This was the man who travelled first class and only stayed in the finest five-star hotels. She doubted the concept of *saving money* had ever crossed his radar.

'It would be rude of me to turn down such a kind invitation.' He smiled at Pamela, the sort of smile that would have had any woman on the planet eating out of his hands.

'No,' Alice inserted firmly. 'If you really can't drive back tonight, then I'm sure we can fix you up with a pleasant local hotel. Closer to Exeter, of course, because I'm sure you'll want to visit Harrisons first thing Monday...'

'Of course you must stay here, Gabriel. I've never seen my daughter as happy and as fulfilled as she has been since she's started working for you. And if in return you want to buy me a new toaster, well, then it would be downright churlish of me to refuse...'

With which, she shooed them both out of the house.

Head held high, Alice snatched her jacket from the coat hook by the front door and stormed out into the cool darkness. She closed her ears to the friendly banter between

Gabriel and her mother and, when the front door had been quietly but firmly shut on them, she turned to him, hands on her hips.

'How dare you?'

'How dare I what?' He guided her towards his black SUV, which had made light work of the journey down.

'Become best friends with my mother!'

'You're being ridiculous.' He opened the passenger door and steered her into the car.

'I am *not* being ridiculous!' she hissed as soon as he was behind the wheel, starting the engine into throaty life. 'You shouldn't have come here.'

'Don't tell me you're not glad…no, *excited*…that I'm here. I can *feel* it.'

'I am *not*…'

Whatever she had been about to say was lost as his mouth hit hers in a crushing, hungry kiss, a kiss he had been waiting for ever since they had returned from Paris and taken up the charade of playing boss-secretary as though nothing had happened between them.

Hand behind the nape of her neck, he pulled her towards him and carried on kissing her, their tongues melding, their bodies yearning for one another.

Alice was giddy from the fierceness of her driven response. Her fingers curled into his hair and she moaned with a mixture of wanting and not wanting, unable to help herself, and hating herself for her weakness.

Finally, he drew back and looked at her.

'Don't spin me any yarns about not wanting me,' he growled. 'If I were to take you right here, right now, you wouldn't run screaming from this car. In fact, you'd get that sexy body of yours in all the right positions to have me in you!'

'That's not—'

'It damn well is! Stop running away from the obvious!'

'I never said you weren't an attractive man!' Her lips tingled from where they had been ravished. Her whole body tingled. He was right, he could have her in a heartbeat, and it was a shaming thought. She had spent the past two weeks fighting to maintain a controlled front and in a few seconds he had demolished it like a house of cards. She wanted to sob from frustration.

Gabriel smiled and turned his attention to the road. 'So…' He guided the car along the narrow road that led to the village. 'You've never been happier than you are now, working for me. Apparently, I'm an exciting boss.'

'Is that what my mother told you?'

'She's not what I had expected. Somehow I had it in my head that she was more like you.'

'Meaning what, Gabriel?'

'Meaning…strong, focused, opinionated. She's a beautiful woman, Alice, but she seems to live on her nerves.'

'I don't like you prying into my personal life.' But her voice was defeated. He had crossed the last frontier. In the space of a few weeks, she had gone from being the cool, together secretary he had taken on to replace his string of inept temps to a woman who had fallen under his spell, slept with him and now…the woman whose entire life would be laid bare.

'I'm expressing interest, Alice,' he said gently. 'Not prying.'

'I never asked for your interest.' She rested her head against the leather head-rest and stared through the window at the blurred, dark countryside racing past her. In a few minutes, they would be in the village. They could actually have walked. On a nice evening, it was a joy to stroll down the country lanes, breathing in the fragrance of the trees and flowers. It was a thirty-minute walk that she had always found therapeutic.

Sure enough, the village twinkled ahead of them, and he found his way easily to the village square, where he parked the car and then killed the engine.

He looked at her for a while. She had the most riveting face he had ever seen, even when that face was turned away from him. He wanted to drag her back into his arms, kiss her all over again, force her out of her coolness, which was unbearable now that he had seen another side to her.

He was baffled by the strength of his reactions to her. He wasn't just in hot, determined pursuit; he wanted more from her than just her body and her compliance. He had never been remotely interested in any of his past lovers' backgrounds or in trying to make sense of them.

He had taken what had been on offer and looked no further. Yes, so he had been lazy. He wasn't lazy now.

'Why is your mother hesitant about telling you that she has a boyfriend?'

Alice's head whipped round and she looked at him, shocked by what he had just said. 'Don't be ridiculous! You don't know what you're talking about. And I resent you poking your nose into my life, Gabriel!' She yanked open the car door and sprang out of the car, wildly looking round for whatever Italian restaurant they were going to. It wouldn't be hard to find. It wasn't as though the village was bursting at the seams with chichi eating places.

It took her two seconds to spot the red-and-white-checked awning where, from memory, a corner shop used to be, tucked away on the corner and easy to miss, if it hadn't been for the bright lights and the people inside.

'Don't run away from me!'

His hand snapped out, holding her firmly in place before she could flee to the safety of the crowded restaurant.

'I'm not running away!' No. She wasn't. She was staring up into those deep, dark eyes and bitterly resenting his presence here in her treasured, private territory. 'What did you mean when you said that...that mum had a boyfriend?'

Gabriel felt some of the tension leave him. She had kissed him. Hell, she had kissed him as hungrily as he had kissed her. And then, almost immediately, she had pushed him away. At least she wasn't pushing him away now. It was something.

'I'll tell you over dinner. I take it that's the restaurant over there?' He began walking, pointedly not tucking her arm into his, although he wanted to.

This, Alice thought, was what lust felt like. In Paris, when they had been playing truant, when she had fallen madly and stupidly in love with him, he had shown affection in all sorts of small ways: holding hands, turning to kiss her, reaching out to tuck her hair behind her ear when the breeze was whipping it across her face...

But they weren't playing truant now. They were back in England, and it was pretty clear that he might still want her, but those gestures of affection were no longer appropriate. His hands were very firmly in his jacket pockets and he was barely glancing in her direction as they walked briskly over to the restaurant.

'So, tell me,' Alice reluctantly demanded, once they were tucked away in the corner of the restaurant with two over-sized menus in front of them and a bottle of white wine on the way.

'I'm sorry if I said something you would rather not have heard,' Gabriel told her roughly. 'This wasn't a long, soul-searching conversation with your mother, Alice. She mentioned in passing that there was a man interested in her, someone she had started seeing recently, and then she laughed nervously and told me that she was working up the courage to tell you about him.'

Alice felt the sting of hurt prick the back of her eyes. She was lost for words. Her mother had given no indication of any boyfriend lurking backstage but then again, she thought with painful honesty, when was the last time she had encouraged confidences of that nature? No, she had held forth on men and the need to be careful with them; she had talked long and hard about them both learning from experience; she had bitterly and often harked back to her feckless father as a learning curve her mother should never forget...

That had never been fertile ground for her mother to tell her that she was involved with a man.

'I see.' Her face was stiff with the effort of trying not to cry. She wished he wouldn't be gentle with her. She wished he would just be the single-minded bastard who only wanted one thing, whatever the cost. She stiffened as he reached across the table and laid his hand over hers.

'I told her that I was sure you would be delighted to know that she had found someone, a companion...' Because, for all her assertiveness, her spikiness, her boundless ability to speak whatever was on her mind and suffer the consequences, she had a big heart.

How did he know that? He just did.

'Maybe I wouldn't have been *that* delighted.' She pulled her hand out from under his, instantly missing the warmth that had passed between them, and smiled at the waiter as he dribbled wine into Gabriel's glass and went through the performance of asking whether it was all right.

As soon as her glass had been poured, she drank it and looked to Gabriel for a refill.

'What do you mean?'

Alice threw the last of her privacy through the window.

He had made so many inroads into her life that there didn't seem much point hanging on to it. Fortified by the wine, she sighed and traced a little pattern on her empty white plate. Then she looked at him.

'I'm afraid my childhood wasn't a happy one,' she said heavily. 'My father was…a bully and a philanderer. I grew up having to deal with the effect that had on Mum. You're right—she's not like me. She's always been frail. You know…?' She darted a quick look at him, watching to see if he was repelled at what she was telling him, and then melting because his expression was so sympathetic. 'I can't believe I'm telling you this. I…I'm not usually the sort of person who confides.'

'You've grown up being strong for the sake of your mother.' Gabriel sipped his wine and impatiently brushed aside the waiter who was approaching them for their order.

So this was what it felt like, he thought, to involve yourself in someone else's life story. His lifetime had been spent as a solitary figure, forging his own destiny, never needing input from anyone else because experience had taught him that other people's input was always largely self-serving. He had grown up fighting his own battles single-handed and then, when the battles had been fought, reaping the reward without bothering to search any deeper. It was a formula that had always worked for him.

And still did, he reminded himself a little too vigorously, before he allowed pointless sentimentality to cloud the issue.

'When my father died, my mother was free to build a life of her own, but she had been damaged by years of having to put up with his selfishness. She became more and more anxious and now…' Alice shrugged her shoulders expressively. 'Over time she became fearful of leaving the house. It's been quite bad. In fact, I've had to hire a therapist to try and work some magic…and it's working. She's been out more in the last few months than ever before. Small steps. But I guess I've been guilty of laying it on thick about not getting involved with another man. I never said so out loud…' *But she had given that impression.* 'Who is this guy, anyway?'

'I don't know the details, Alice. Like I said, it was a fleeting conversation.'

'Whilst you were busy charming her, you mean.' Her retort was half-hearted. 'I wondered how she knew about this restaurant. I guess they must have come here, which is terrific, because it means she's getting out of the house, beginning to build a normal life for herself.'

And in the meantime, Alice wondered, how normal was *her* life? She had been so busy making sure they both learned valuable lessons about the nature of men that she had forgotten how young she still was. And her mother *had* tried to remind her of that, but she had unhelpfully brushed aside those conversations.

'So there you have it,' she said crisply. 'It would have been better if you hadn't known, but…'

'Why?'

'Why?' Alice laughed and there was an edge to her laughter. 'Because you're not interested in other people's lives, Gabriel. You're probably embarrassed that you've ended up here with me pouring all this out, but it's your fault for showing up unannounced.'

'Ah, we're back to the Alice Morgan who wants to pick a fight with me… It's not going to work.'

She was sorely tempted to ask him about *his* personal life but something held her back. Maybe she didn't want to hear that mantra about never committing to any woman. Maybe she wanted to believe that…that *what?*

That she could somehow change him because she was in love with him?

Hell would freeze over before that happened!

But, as they ordered food, she was keenly aware that she had let all her guard down with him, that the chance of returning to the fragile relationship she had worked hard to put back in place after Paris was changed for good.

And, for her part, she had seen yet another slice of this complex man—a genuinely thoughtful side that he kept well hidden under an armour of a ruthless, single-minded drive to succeed.

She ruefully thought that, while she had been busy never taking chances, while she had made a big deal of her non-relationship with Alan as yet further proof of how important it was to protect yourself from being hurt, her mother, for all her problems and her devastating marriage, had been courageous enough to take chances of her own.

The only chances Alice had taken were those snatched days and nights in Paris when she had thrown caution to the winds and had allowed her body to rule her head.

And she had made damn sure to scuttle back to the safety of what she knew the second they had returned to London.

From under lowered lashes, she watched as he worked his way through his food, the way he engaged her in conversation whether she wanted him to or not, the tactful way he desisted from prying further into her past. She took in those long, brown fingers curled around the stem of his wine glass as he sipped his wine and the brooding intensity of his dark eyes as they rested on her flushed face...

Sensitive to every nuance of her body language, Gabriel sensed the shift in atmosphere.

He had stopped being the enemy she had mistakenly

slept with, the enemy whose hot kisses she wanted to resist but couldn't…

He had her and satisfaction roared through him. He
had stopped thinking that he just needed to sleep with
her to get her out of his system. He now thought that he
just needed to sleep with her. He needed to have her body
under him, on him and alongside him. He needed to feel
the silky smoothness of her slender thighs between his
legs. He needed to touch her breasts and feel her melt
under his hands.

The meal couldn't end soon enough for him, although
he didn't think he could actually sleep with her in her
mother's house. Thinking about having to wait until they
were back in London brought a painful ache in his groin.
He could barely focus on the conversation she was having with him.

'If you'd rather I stay somewhere else overnight,' he
told her gruffly, 'then I'm happy to oblige.'

'What makes you say that?'

'The fact that you tried so hard to dissuade your mother
from her hospitality.'

'I've never known my mum to dig her heels in the way
she did,' Alice confessed, closing her knife and fork on
what had been a superb meal. 'But, no.' She shot him a
flushed, determined stare and her heart picked up speed
as he met her gaze and held it for longer than was necessary. 'She would be upset if you disappeared to stay in a
bed and breakfast. In fact, she would probably blame *me*.
She probably blames me for trying to over-protect her.'
The admission was forced out of her and she lowered her
eyes. 'If I hadn't been so…forceful, who knows? She might
have found Mr Right a bit sooner.'

'He may not be Mr Right,' Gabriel told her gently. 'But
he might just be the guy who takes her out of herself,

someone she's willing to have fun with even if it doesn't last the course…'

'What are you trying to say?'

'It's better to feel something, anything, rather than hide behind a wall in the hope that you don't end up getting hurt.' He was uncomfortably aware that this was advice he didn't actually follow to the letter himself, although his lack of emotional involvement had nothing to do with getting hurt or not getting hurt. He had no need to commit, so he didn't. There was no Mrs Right for him because that was a complication he didn't need. He was perfectly fine as he was, unlike Pamela Morgan, who wanted more. Unlike her daughter, who probably wanted more as well.

'And you think that's what I'm doing?' Alice bristled but there was a charge in the atmosphere that was thrilling. And she couldn't peel her eyes away from his lean, dark face.

'You want more of *me*…' He sat back and allowed his eyes to roam over her; lazy, indolent, darkly sexy eyes that made her body burn. 'Why don't you stop running scared,' he murmured, 'and just take what you want? Take what you can't tear your eyes away from.'

'You are the most conceited person I have ever met in my entire life!' She was breathing fast and, God, he *knew* exactly how she was reacting to him. Knew it and liked it.

'You want to touch…I can feel it. Do you know why? Because it's the same for me. I want to touch you too. Why do you think I spent hours driving down here on the spur of the moment?'

But you will never get hurt, Alice thought. *You can touch and then walk away unscathed…*

But was that enough of an excuse to run scared? If her mother could get involved with someone, as Gabriel had told her, then why couldn't she? How many times would she spend her life running scared when faced with the possibility of getting hurt?

And yet the thought of any other man having the same impact on her as Gabriel was far-fetched, almost beyond belief. He wasn't the gentle kind of guy who would gradually entice her back into the world of trust and love, the kind of guy she had vaguely pinned her hopes on finding at some point in her life. He was the dynamic, darker-than-sin, more-dangerous-than-the-devil kind of guy who would take her places she had never been and leave her broken-hearted when he walked away.

'Shall we go?' he asked huskily and Alice nodded mutely.

'This was never the plan,' she said shakily, once the bill had been paid and they were standing outside the restaurant.

'What was never the plan?'

'This. Me. You… It's not a good idea.'

'Life is about taking risks or else what's the point? I've spent my life taking risks. I wouldn't be here today if I hadn't taken risks.'

'What do you mean?'

Gabriel laughed but his dark eyes never left her face. 'Maybe one day I'll explain.' He threaded his fingers through her hair and tugged her towards him. 'Do you want me to kiss you? Because if you don't then this is your opportunity to say no and to walk away, and we can go back to playing our game of "it never happened".'

'Kiss me…'

Alice lost herself in that kiss. It was a crazy place to be doing this because she might get spotted. It was a small village and the fact that her mother had spent much of her time there confined to her house didn't mean that there weren't many locals who didn't pop in for chats, to see how she was doing, to have tea or the occasional supper. Any one of those locals would have hot-footed it right back to Pamela Morgan with tales of her daughter being seen outside that new Italian restaurant kissing a man.

But she couldn't resist. She breathed in his woody, clean aftershave, felt his firm, cool lips plundering her mouth and her body curved into his. She looped her arms around his neck and tiptoed to meet his searching mouth.

'I'm only thinking…' he broke apart to say in an unsteady voice that didn't sound at all like his '…about your reputation when I say that we need to take this somewhere else.'

'I don't want you to stop.'

'And I don't want to…' With his arm slung heavily over her shoulder, they half-ran to his car and picked up where they had left off the second the car door was slammed shut.

It was teenage, 'back row of the movies' stuff. That was what it felt like to Gabriel and he loved every second of it. He had never done that back-row kissing business; he was making up for lost time. If her teenage years had been spent caretaking her mother and being strong on her behalf, his had been spent digging himself out of the hole into which he had been born, forging a life for himself that would be strong enough to ensure that he would never have to look back or go near that hole again.

The fact that they had so much in common was a fleeting thought that was almost immediately buried under the urgency of his response.

He felt under the red jumper and found the obstruction of her bra, but made short work of that by plunging his hand under it, pulling free one breast that popped out, nipple already standing to attention, tightening to a rigid peak as he teased and pinched it into arousal.

The car was parked at a distance from the other random cars and the tinted windows meant that they were cocooned, protected from any curious eyes, not that there seemed to be many people around. Protected enough for him to feel comfortable raising her jumper so that he could cover that pulsing nipple with his mouth and suckle on it until she was whimpering and panting, spreading her legs in delicious invitation.

They were never going to make love in his car, he thought, wondering if his body would be able to tolerate the short drive back to her house without relief. But he could enjoy her for a bit longer, suck for a little longer on that circular disc.

With a groan of frustration at not being able to go the whole way, he flung himself back against the seat and groaned.

'I need a bigger car!'

Alice could still feel the warmth of his mouth on her breast. She pulled down the jumper, as regretful as he was and as desperate to get back to the house so that they could finish what they had started.

Making love with her mother a couple of doors down? True, her mother slept like a log, often with the aid of a sleeping tablet, but still… Never in a million years would Alice have seen herself as the kind of girl who would be driven to have sex with a guy in her bedroom because she just couldn't hold off. Since when had she ever been the kind of girl who lost complete control? *Since she had gone to Paris*, was the answer that came immediately to her. Since she had made love to him. Since she had discovered a carnal side to her that was insatiable…

Before he could fire up the engine, she reached across and fumbled with his zip.

More teenage stuff! Gabriel didn't bother to try to resist. He'd lost the ability to play it cool. Right now, what he needed more than anything else was release.

He unzipped the trousers and manoeuvred himself so that he could pull them down, along with his boxers. The cool night air was soothing, but not nearly as soothing as her mouth…

CHAPTER NINE

THE HOUSE WAS in darkness by the time they arrived back. Pamela Morgan was already in bed. It was nearly eleven and she was accustomed to retiring early.

Gabriel had no idea how he had managed to get back without going into one of the hedgerows by the side of the road. He couldn't concentrate. The woman next to him had taken his self-control and shredded it into a million pieces.

Yes, she had relieved some of that ache…

He caught his breath sharply, remembering the glorious feel of her mouth on him as she drove him to his climax. The release had been…indescribable.

Now he wanted more, much more.

He would have brought her to her own orgasm, would have put his hand and his fingers where his mouth would not have been able to go because of the confines of being in a car, but she had stopped him, breathlessly telling him that she wanted him in her bed.

Now, as she unlocked the front door with shaky fingers, he placed his hand over hers.

'We could wait,' he said gruffly. 'I don't want to. Hell, I would take you by the side of the house if you let me… But I don't want this to be seen as an abuse of your mother's hospitality.'

'I'm beginning to think that I haven't given Mum enough

credit for being a grown-up,' Alice said ruefully. 'She's probably been waiting for me to bring a guy home but not confident enough to come right out and say anything.' She pushed open the door and held her finger to her lips in a signal to keep quiet, then giggled softly, because she felt light-headed, young and very happy.

And he hadn't been able to get her out of his head! She gave herself full permission really to drown in that admission, really to luxuriate in it.

Paris had been an adventure but she had managed to convince herself that it had somehow been acceptable because she had been abroad…just a passing fever. But this was *really* an adventure because she was here, in her stamping ground, making a conscious decision to do something because it felt inevitable and somehow *right,* even if it was wrong.

She couldn't explain it, even to herself. She just knew that she had to sleep with him, had to follow this through to the bitter end, however and whenever that might arise, even if it meant saying goodbye to her job in the process.

They went up the stairs silently. Sure enough, when Alice looked to her right there was no light on in her mother's room. She turned left, thankful that her bedroom was at the end of the narrow corridor, and she pushed open the door, heart beating so fast she had to make herself take deep breaths just to steady her spiralling excitement.

She could still taste him in her mouth…it was a turn-on.

'Your bedroom?' Gabriel asked, looking around him. Moonlight streamed through the window, picking up bits and pieces of her belongings: a rocking chair in the corner, on which sat an oversized, battle-weary stuffed teddy bear; furniture that looked as though it had never been made to last; a dressing table with some framed pictures on it.

'Don't talk.' She pressed her body against his and her eyelids fluttered closed as he slipped his hands under her jumper. This time he undid the bra and she released him for a few seconds so that she could pull the bra and jumper over her head so that she was standing in front of him, half-naked.

'You're so damned beautiful…' Gabriel cupped her breasts with his hands and massaged them, rubbing the pad of his thumbs over her nipples as he did, and felt the breath catch in her throat. He leaned down and kissed her neck, then licked it, then nibbled his way up to her mouth so that she could lose herself again in another of those devastating kisses.

Alice pushed her hands under his jumper, seeking the warmth of his flesh. He had small, flat brown nipples and she teased them just as he was teasing hers and felt him respond.

Slowly they made their way to her bed, unable to break apart from one another, kissing and holding each other and stumbling a little in the dark until her knees made contact with the side of the bed and she fell, taking him with her and stifling another giggle.

This was nothing like the luxurious bedroom they had shared in Paris, with its fabulous, ridiculously lavish *en suite* bathroom. This was basic, but in fairness at no point had she detected anything condescending in his reaction to her mother's house.

He pushed himself up and removed his shirt and jumper, tossing them carelessly to the ground, then he stood so that he could rid himself of the rest of his clothing—trousers, boxers, socks. His shoes, he had already kicked off.

Then he was back on the bed and very, very slowly he unzipped and pulled down the black trousers, taking her lacy briefs with them at the same time.

He tossed them aside with one hand while using the other hand to part her legs.

Not that there was any need for him to do that. Her body knew just what to do when it came to making love with him. She settled back with her arm resting lightly over her eyes, her limbs wonderfully loose.

She knew what he would do. He knew how much she loved it, loved having him down there between her legs. And still, the moment his tongue flicked against her, she couldn't prevent the soft moan that escaped her lips.

She arched up, pressing herself against his questing mouth and exploding inside as he licked and teased the throbbing bud. She was so wet for him, so turned on, so ready to have him thrusting inside her—but he continued to torment her by remaining where he was, lavishing all his attention on her aching core and the soft, tender skin of her inner thighs.

Then he moved up to her breasts, leaving her on the very brink of coming. He drew one nipple into his mouth and played with the other, smiling against her body as he felt her desperate efforts to make as little noise as possible.

'Wrap your legs around me,' he commanded.

But first he had to get hold of protection, which was damned difficult, because it involved finding his wallet and then going through it in the darkness, while they both craved release.

He never took chances. Ever. It was one of the most significant things that indicated just how he felt about any woman being able to tie him down. Even at the very height of passion, he would rather walk away from making love than take a chance on an unwanted pregnancy.

Why was that? Didn't everyone, to a greater or lesser extent, have within them the urge to procreate, to see their bloodline continue? She had never asked him, had known that that was a boundary line she would cross only at her own peril.

Yet he knew everything there was to know about her now. He knew about her miserable childhood, the effect it had had on her, on her mother... He knew about the circumstances that had driven her mother to take refuge within the safety of her house, trapped by her own fears. He could make sense of her and the way she was from the background she had had.

But it was a one-way street because there were still so many questions that remained unanswered about *him*.

Alice knew that this was just one of the many reasons why it was so dangerous to get back into bed with him. She knew that somewhere in the very core of her, but she couldn't help herself, because fighting against that knowledge was the realisation that she would rather end up hurt than end up regretful for not having taken the chance.

With Gabriel, the probability of pain was always right there, huddled close to the promise of pleasure.

All her thoughts led somewhere, but she couldn't follow them, because the way he was touching and caressing her made her mind shut down.

She did as she had been told and wrapped her legs around him and felt him push inside her, big and hard.

Then he built up a rhythm and she stifled her moans against his neck. She was so highly charged that it took considerable effort to try and hold off so that they could dovetail their orgasms, but she did it, and they came together.

He reared up, stiffened, the muscles in his shoulders bunched as he gave himself over to wave after wave of pleasure, the same pleasure that was taking her into another dimension. But the questions that had been nibbling away slid out of the shadows and began nibbling again.

Was this all he was capable of—sex? Did he really have no interest in ever having a family, something and someone more permanent in his life? And, if sex was all he wanted, then why was that? She had seen so many facets of him and yet the way he was pieced together still eluded her and she would dearly love to find out more.

The pitfalls of being in love: it made you want to know everything about the person you loved. In Gabriel's case, that would be a suicide mission. That was something she felt in her bones, with gut instinct.

'That was…amazing,' he murmured, sliding off her, but immediately lying on his side and turning her to face him.

Alice murmured agreement. Making love had been a conscious decision on her part, but she could still feel tension seeping in, tension at knowing that, whilst she was fully committed to their relationship, he wasn't.

It was amazing for him because he had got what he wanted. What he felt was the satisfaction of the victor and it was a satisfaction that was not going to last for ever.

But she wanted for ever.

Her own innate honesty compelled her to recognise that she would take what she could for as long as it was on offer because any bit of him was better than nothing. Yet the prospect of the end would hang over her like the hangman's noose so that every time they made love, every time she laughed with him, felt his arms around her, it would be tarnished with a sense of sadness. She could feel the weight of the end on her shoulders even before what they had actually ended.

She wondered what difference it would make if she only knew what made him tick. Or at least *some* of what made him tick.

'Tomorrow's Sunday,' she said, languid and content after their love-making. 'What will you do? Head back up to London? My offer still stands to pop in to Harrisons in Exeter before I come back to work on Tuesday.'

So cool, Gabriel thought, so composed. No hint of any nagging or trying to wheedle him into staying on...

The perfect woman—but he couldn't help feeling a little piqued at her offhand attitude. A tiny amount of possessiveness might have been nice, he found himself thinking. After all, hadn't he made this trip down here just to see her? That in itself had been a break in tradition.

'What are *your* plans?' He turned the question back at her and Alice rolled onto her back and stared up at the ceiling.

Her plans were what they always were—except tomorrow, she conceded, would include an informative chat about the new man in her mother's life. Aside from that, as long a walk as Pamela Morgan could handle, maybe even making it into the village for tea, some light television and then she would make something for their supper.

What she would have really liked was to have Gabriel all to herself, but that was an admission she would never make...

'I shall relax.'

'In that case, I might relax here with you,' Gabriel drawled, propping himself up on one elbow and tracing the outline of her rosy pink nipple with his finger until the prominent bud stiffened in automatic response.

However cool she might be, her body was as hot as his.

'Really?' Alice injected a note of surprise into her voice. 'Surely you must have plans for the rest of the weekend?'

'As of this moment I consider them cancelled.'

'Because you'd rather spend time down here?'

'It's a beautiful part of the world.'

'Yes. Yes, it is.' She noticed that he couldn't actually admit to wanting to put whatever previous plans he had made for his weekend on hold because he preferred to spend the time *with her*. 'Although you might find it a bit boring,' she said truthfully. 'I don't suppose you have much experience of living out in the countryside…'

'I prefer the push and shove of the city. Suits my personality.'

'Aggressive?'

'You said it.' He idly inclined his head to suck her pouting nipple before settling back into his former position, looking at her, his face only inches away from hers. She had the clearest brown eyes fringed by sooty, thick, dark eyelashes; eyes that were open and wary at the same time. 'So, sell me this part of the world,' he invited lazily. 'Do your best pitch. Wax lyrical about walks in the open fields, tea and scones at somebody's little shop—maybe a barn dance later at the village hall.'

'Would you be interested in doing any of those things?'

'I think we can eliminate the barn dance.'

'Now, that just makes me wonder if there's one on at the village hall,' Alice teased. 'I can't see you enjoying walking in the open fields or having scones at the local tea shop, either,' she mused. 'Are you one of those city people through and through? Born and raised, would never leave it for longer than five minutes?'

'Not exactly.' He stiffened fractionally. This was where the caring, sharing had to stop.

'In the country, then? Don't tell me your parents used to drag you out for Sunday walks? My mum always made sure we went out on a Sunday afternoon for a really long walk, whatever the weather. She liked being out of the house, away from Dad. Although she always had to make sure to get back in time to prepare his tea if he happened to be at home. The closer we got back home, the more anxious and nervous she would become. Course, those walks stopped when I turned eleven, when I preferred to hide out in my bedroom studying or reading.'

'I didn't have country walks—or any walks, for that matter,' Gabriel heard himself say roughly. Restlessness surged through him, making him feel uncomfortable in his own skin, and he sat up and swung his legs over the side of the bed. Then he strolled towards the window, across which the curtains hadn't been drawn.

Stark naked, with his back to her, he gazed broodingly out to the dark shapes of fields, hedges, a copse of trees to the right in the distance.

That, Alice thought, was the sound of a door being firmly shut in her face. She sat up and pulled the duvet up to her chin.

Eventually he turned round but he didn't walk back to the bed.

'So...' A slashing smile lightened the passing shadow that had crossed his face. 'What exciting things shall we do tomorrow?'

'Aside from the barn dance? We can have a walk, perhaps with Mum, and then look around the village—go to that little shop for tea and scones...' *Enjoy pretending that this is a normal relationship...*

'But first thing in the morning,' she told him firmly, 'I will have a chat with Mum.'

Pamela Morgan was up bright and early the following morning but the coffee was still hot, ready to be drunk, when Alice made her way down.

Her thoughts were still all over the place. She had slept with him; she had lost the fight to put her feelings behind her and allow the common sense that had always ruled her life to take over, as she had told it to. As she had *needed* it to.

He didn't know the depth of her feelings—which was something, she supposed—but he knew how much she wanted him and, now, her life had been laid bare for his perusal. Not content with keeping what they had to London, he had invaded her life here in Devon…

And revealed things she herself hadn't even known about. Which showed just how much he had managed to ingratiate himself with her mother.

But then, he was the man who didn't have to try; the man who could move mountains with a smile, with a lazy turn of his head, with just a look…

'Alice, dear…! How was the meal last night?' Pamela Morgan was beaming. 'You never told me what a lovely man your boss was! Such a looker…'

'We need to talk, Mum.'

'Do we, dear?' But there was a tell-tale flush in her cheeks as she sat down opposite her daughter and fiddled guiltily with her coffee cup.

'A man…? A suitor…? You never said…' Alice had been hurt when Gabriel inadvertently had told her about a man in her mother's life but that hurt hadn't lasted. How could it, when her mother's eyes were glowing as she chatted happily and with relief about Robin, her friend's cousin who had moved to the village to start up his own small landscaping business. He was wonderful…they had so much in common. They had only seen each other a handful of times but thanks to him she had managed to venture more and more into the village; he had even taken her to see his company, which was still in the process of being set up.

Alice was dazed.

'But why didn't you say anything to me all this time?' she finally asked, but she knew why.

'Just a few weeks,' Pamela said uncomfortably. 'And

I knew you'd try to warn me off him, my darling, and I would quite, quite have understood, but…'

But she, Alice, her loving daughter, would have disapproved, would have issued stern warnings, would have dished out helpful advice by the bucket load, and in the end would have stifled anything that had a chance of surviving. Her mother had wanted to take a chance and she would have been afraid that her daughter would have killed that chance dead.

Alice wasn't hurt, she was mortified. Years of helping to prop her mother up had turned her into a hard-edged young woman who had allowed her own disillusionment to colour her behaviour.

Gabriel's entrance half an hour later helped to lighten the glum introspection into which she had been plunged and, with an unerring ability to cut to the chase, the first thing he said to her as they were walking out of the house was, 'You're upset. You spoke to you mother…and…?'

It was not yet nine-thirty but already the sun was warm and the open fields were bathed in the clear, unencumbered light so typical of the countryside where buildings and pollution didn't cloud the view and sully the air. He realised he didn't mind it. He quite liked it, as a matter of fact. A change from urban life.

'Do you really care?' Alice turned to him. The breeze ruffled her hair, blowing it across her face. She was slender and coltish in a pair of faded jeans, an old baggy jumper and a pair of walking boots.

'I'm interested; of course I am.' Gabriel refused to give in to qualifying what he felt. Naturally he cared if she was upset. He wasn't a monster. And, yet, when was the last time he'd actually *cared* whether some woman was upset or not? Had he been that bothered when Georgia had flounced into his office and thrown a hissy fit because she couldn't take no for an answer?

He had been irritated but he certainly hadn't been upset. Nor had he ever been curious about what happened or didn't happen in a woman's life. As long as they gave him what he wanted, he was absolutely fine and he always, but always, made sure that his conscience was clear by being upfront with them. Life was so much simpler when you made sure you didn't get wrapped up in complicated emotional situations that would always end up leading to dead ends anyway.

He had nothing to give and wasn't interested in trying to break that mould.

But he sensed that she had asked a leading question and he knew that he should repeat his honest, upfront, 'don't look to me for anything but sex and a good time' talk— just in case she had forgotten. And he *would*...but later...

He was *interested*. He didn't *care* but he was interested. Two completely different things, as far as Alice was concerned.

'And she's got a boyfriend.'

'Good for her.' Gabriel slung his arm over her shoulder and breathed in the fragrant, floral scent of her hair. God, what was it about this woman that drove him nuts? 'I want you so much right now that it hurts.'

Alice pulled apart and stared at him then she rolled her eyes and laughed. 'Is sex *all* you think about, Gabriel?'

'It's pretty deserted out here...'

'I was talking about my mother!'

'And I'm listening. I just want to touch you a little while you talk...' He slipped his hand under her jumper and circled her narrow waist. 'Tell me you don't like that.' Up ahead, the fields were broken with clumps of trees. It was an idyllic, picture-postcard scene. 'You're not wearing a bra. I like that…'

'I usually go bra-less when I'm down here. I don't have enough to warrant wearing one twenty-four-seven…'

'You have just the right amount.' He pushed up the jumper, ignored her half-hearted attempts to swat him away and gazed down at her small, pert breasts tipped with their rosy pink nipples.

Her breathing quickened as he rubbed the sensitive tips with his thumbs until they were stiff and aroused.

This was her wild adventure. She had fallen in love with the wrong man and had thrown caution to the winds because her heart was ruling her head. She *knew* that he was only in it for the sex, for the good time, but it was so hard to bury the part of her that wanted to find out where they were going, whether there was the slightest chance that he might want more than just sex.

He gently pulled down her jumper; his hand went to the button of her jeans, then the zip, and she gave a little shocked yelp as he began tugging down her trousers.

'We can't.'

'Why not? All right; we can find somewhere a little more private under the trees, although there's no one around. Is it always this deserted?'

'You need to get out of London a little more.' She was damp and hot as they walked hand in hand towards the nearest bank of trees. 'There're lots of places like this out here. It's quiet, peaceful. That's why Mum decided that she wanted to move here. It was restful after living in Birmingham. I also think she wanted to be as far as she could from any ugly reminders of her marriage.' She pulled him towards her and stretched up to kiss him, fingers clasped behind his neck, their bodies pressed so tightly together

that she could feel the hardness of his urgent, demanding arousal.

'Lying down might be a little uncomfortable,' Gabriel
said, but he had to have her. Nor did he want the substitute of her hand or her mouth. He wanted to be inside her,
needed to be inside her.

'Then let's forget about it and stroll back down to the
village,' Alice teased as she stroked his cheek and watched
the fire blaze in his dark eyes. 'We could have that scone
and that cup of tea. Tea can be very refreshing…might
cool us down…'

'You're a witch,' Gabriel said in an unsteady voice he
barely recognised. He tugged down the jeans, told her to
step out of them.

She kept the jumper on. Being half-naked like this, with
her bottom half-exposed, felt decadent.

'Now, legs apart,' he commanded.

Having him down there, standing perfectly still when
she wanted to collapse because her legs felt as wobbly as
jelly, was exquisite agony.

He explored her, taking his time. It surprised him that
he'd never made love outdoors and he thought that next
time he would make sure they brought a rug with them.

Next time? Yes, there would be a next time, because he
couldn't get enough of her…

Their love-making was basic, wild and hard. He hoisted
her up so that her legs were wrapped around him. She
could have been as light as a feather.

The sensation was intense. Her buttocks clenched as
he drove her down on him and she came over and over,
splintering into a thousand glorious pieces.

Afterwards, the walk into the village was languorous.
Sated, Alice had never felt happier. It was almost as though
they were a normal couple—ducking into shops, laugh-

ing at some of the souvenirs on sale, stopping to buy ice-creams. Mr and Mrs Average on a day out.

What a joke! She reminded herself that they certainly were not Mr and Mrs Average, or Mr and Mrs *Anything*.

He certainly wasn't average! In fact, he cut an impressive and madly exotic figure next to his paler counterparts as they dipped in and out of the shops. People stared. He didn't seem to notice, but *she* did. Women of all ages stole glances; wondered; maybe thought that he might be someone famous.

For the first time in her life, Alice felt as though she had stepped out of the shadows and become a person in her own right, someone who wasn't so surrounded by barriers, that she could be free to just...*be*.

They had a very long lunch in one of the three pubs in the village and it was only when they were emerging that she bumped into one of the ladies whom she knew visited her mother on a regular basis.

Alice had never socialised with Maggie Fray, but they had met on a couple of occasions, and now the older woman stopped and looked at Gabriel with twinkling, knowing eyes.

'So this is the young man your mother says you talk so much about.' She held out her hand with a smile while, mortified, Alice tried to shrink away from the grey, inquisitive eyes.

'My boss...' Alice said in a thin, high voice, but minutes before they had been holding hands and that begged the question of what exactly the relationship between boss and secretary was.

The older woman's smiling eyes seemed to be making all the right assumptions.

'Well,' she said comfortably, 'you two seem to make a very good match. And I know your mother would love to hear the sound of wedding bells in the not too distant future!'

On a scale of one to ten of hideous conversations, Alice rated this one at somewhere around twelve. She barely heard the rest of whatever Maggie was chattering about.

How much had she told her mother over the many weeks that she had been working for Gabriel?

A lot. They were accustomed to sharing. Even if she had made a big effort to play down the way she felt about Gabriel, she unknowingly would have given the game away because her mother could read her the way no one else could. Her mother would have been able to interpret her hitched silences, the expression on her face whenever she mentioned his name, the number of times she talked about him and the number of times she didn't…

Her arrogant, self-centred, infuriating, egotistic boss who was also brilliant, inspiring, unbelievably smart, charismatic and funny. And the fact that Gabriel had shown up at the house, uninvited, unannounced and apparently with no other purpose but to see her, would have given credence to whatever fairy stories her mother had been concocting in her head.

'People in a small village are inclined to gossip,' Alice said weakly as Maggie disappeared towards one of the shops, having given them a cheery wave goodbye. 'It's very annoying. Because…er…most of the time, what they say has no basis in truth *whatsoever*…' Alice couldn't bring herself actually to say out loud what the older woman had said. To mention that word 'wedding' would open a can of worms and she didn't know how she would be able to stuff them back in.

Gabriel was ominously silent.

He should have seen this coming. He had warned her

off but he should have clocked that there was something intensely vulnerable about her.

'Vulnerable' should have hit his radar and generated the automatic 'no trespassing' response, but somehow his guard had been down. It was what novelty and lust did when they came together—a lethal combination.

'What the hell was the woman talking about?' He beeped open the car and climbed into the driver's seat, but he didn't start the engine. Instead, he waited for her to follow suit, and then he turned to her with a cool, unreadable expression.

'I told you...' A hint of defiance had crept into her voice. 'In a village there's always gossip. Maggie is one of my mother's friends and somehow she's managed to get hold of the wrong end of the stick.'

'Because *out of nowhere* your mother somehow gleaned, erroneously, that we're...*what* Alice? About to tie the knot? Walk up the aisle? Start believing in fairy stories and building castles in the sky?'

'You're so bloody *cynical*!' she exploded. 'And *no*. I haven't been telling my mother *anything*. I'm not so stupid that I'd fall into the trap of thinking that you're there for anything but the short term, Gabriel!'

'I'm not going to get into a pointless argument with you over this.' He started the engine and began driving slowly away from the village.

Alice couldn't credit that they had been making love not so long ago. She couldn't believe that she had been so stupid to think that, if she blanked out the fact that she was hopelessly in love with him, everything could tick along nicely until such time as...what, exactly? He got bored? Became indifferent?

Was she so desperate that she would abandon all her principles just to steal a bit more time with him?

Was it any wonder that he had become so lazy over the years when women like *her* allowed him to get away with doing exactly as he wanted?

She had fallen under his spell and been mesmerised. She had slept with him in Paris; had kidded herself that she could walk away and carry on working for him without any repercussions. But there *had* been repercussions. She had been so aware of him, so acutely *sensitive* to his presence, that she had scarcely been able to function.

He had found his way to the very essence of her and he had taken up residence there.

She had never been an addict of anything in her life, but she had become addicted to him. Was that why she had fallen right back into bed with him— because he had happened to show up at her house and had told her, in that dark, dangerous, sexy voice of his, that *he hadn't been able to get her out of his head?*

Or maybe she had been injected with some sort of crazy, dare-devil urge because her mother—her always hesitant, always careful mother; her mother to whom she had preached the good sense of *not getting involved with a man* because *just look at what she had ended up marrying*—had had the courage to embark on a relationship?

Or was it just a combination of things that had galvanised her into the worst choice she had ever made in her entire life?

She could find a million reasons to justify why she had done what she had done, but in the end what it amounted to was that she had climbed onto a roller-coaster ride and now it was time to climb off.

Gabriel Cabrera was the equivalent of an extreme sport and she just didn't have the constitution for it.

She blanked her mind to the thought of the endless days and nights ahead of her which would not contain *him* in them. She would have to hand in her notice, find work somewhere else.

'It would only be a *pointless* argument,' Alice half-shouted, 'because you don't want to have it! And, just so you know, I'll be handing in my notice first thing on Tuesday morning.'

'You're being ridiculous!'

'And that being the case,' she continued as her anger, mostly with herself, spilled over, 'I might as well tell you that you may think you're being fair by warning women off you, just in case they get it into their silly little heads that you might actually have *a heart* buried there somewhere, but you're not. You're just taking care of your conscience. You don't want to have to try at anything that isn't work. You'll end up a lonely, sad man with stacks and stacks of money but no one to share it with!' She was staring at his profile which could have been hewn from rock.

There was no getting through to him. Why hadn't she been strong enough to wise up to that before? Dig deep below the charm, the looks, the charisma and the formidable intelligence and there was...*nothing*.

Those glimpses of gentleness, tenderness, vulnerability had all been an illusion. She shut the door on any other interpretation. She was shaking like a leaf and kept herself as rigid as a plank of wood to control emotions that threatened to burst their fragile containment.

'And on that note,' Gabriel drawled, 'I'll drop you back to your house. There will be no need for you to return to work. You can consider that little speech of yours a suitable letter of resignation.'

They were at the house. She hadn't even been aware that he was driving.

He reached across to click open her door and she drew

back, horrified at how her body reacted even now, when everything was falling apart.

'If there's anything personal that you need to take from your office,' he said coolly, 'then you can get in touch with Personnel. They can forward it to you.' Their eyes tangled and Alice was the first to look away.

She couldn't find room in her head to accommodate everything she was feeling: the horror of the end; an overwhelming sadness; self-recrimination.

'There's nothing I want to take with me.' Her voice betrayed nothing of what she was feeling. She stepped out of the car, walked towards the house and she didn't look back.

CHAPTER TEN

FROM WORKING IN one of London's landmark buildings, Alice's life returned to normality with a deafening thud.

One month after she had walked away from Gabriel, she was now back in employment, working as a legal secretary in a small solicitor's firm in the outskirts of London. She had gone from towering views of the city to the nondescript view of the back of a local supermarket car park. She had moved from the most exciting man on the planet to a middle-aged chap who handled small cases and apparently took himself off to play golf twice a week.

The highlights had grown out of her hair and Paris and everything else seemed like a dream.

She had not heard a word from Gabriel and, much as she had not expected to, the hope with which she awoke each morning turned into the sour disappointment that went to sleep with her each night.

Walking back to her house, her mobile phone rang and, when she picked up the call, it was from her mother.

Pamela Morgan's recovery was coming along in leaps and bounds. In fact, treatment with the therapist had been reduced to once a month. Now that her love affair was out in the open, it seemed to be all she could talk about, and Alice, having met the man in question, had to concede that her mother was in safe hands.

Time had moved on, her mother had told her; she was in a different place from the one she had been in when she had married.

The implication was that Alice should have reached a similar conclusion—that time had moved on and she was no longer the girl growing up in a scary, dysfunctional family or the girl who had had a brief fling with someone who'd turned out not to be Mr Right.

The implication was that there was a time and a place to be careful and Alice was young enough to take life by the scruff of the neck and take chances...

Alice had not become bogged down in discussing her situation. She could have told her mother that she had taken enough chances with Gabriel to last a lifetime, but she kept quiet.

Now, her mother was talking to her about a holiday she planned to go on and marvelling that her life had been turned around so dramatically.

Alice listened, contributing here and there as she stepped off the bus and headed back to the house.

It was an overcast, muggy day and although it wasn't dark, far from it, she was still surprised that the lights in the house were all off because she knew that Lucy would be in, getting herself ready for a hot weekend in Venice with the guy she had been seeing for the past few months.

It was a little after eight. Overtime was not expected but she had stayed on until just after six and had then gone out for a quick drink with two of the other girls from the office, who had a Friday-night routine in which she had been immediately included.

She was exhausted.

She let herself into the house, dropping her bag by the door, and heading for the kitchen whilst removing her lightweight summer jacket at the same time.

With the lights all switched off, the downstairs of the house was bathed in a grey twilight that Alice found rather soothing, so she didn't bother turning on any lights, instead carolling up the stairs to let her house mate know that she was home.

The last time she had arrived home unexpectedly without loudly announcing her arrival, she had discovered Lucy and her loved-up guy in the sitting room about to embark on a compromising position, and Alice had been horribly embarrassed. Since then, entries were always as noisy as possible.

The last person in the world she'd expected to see was in the kitchen chair and he'd been there for the past hour.

Gabriel had been driven to seek her out. The past month had been hellish, his worst possible nightmare. He had been unfocused, unable to concentrate and in a permanently foul mood. People had scuttled in the opposite direction the second they had heard him striding through the office, on the hunt for someone on whom he could vent.

He had even broken his own personal record by dating six women, none of whom had progressed beyond polite conversation over dinner. In their company, he had spent an inordinate amount of time checking his watch.

He had refused to give in.

Hell, the woman had burned him off not once, but *twice*!

It hadn't helped that he had not managed to find a suitable replacement for her. He was on secretary number three and the omens were not good.

He had cursed himself on more than one occasion that he had been lenient enough to let her leave without duly working out her notice. On reflection, he should have made her do the two weeks required.

His nights had been no better than his days. Work had

failed to do what it should have done, distracted him from thoughts he neither liked nor invited.

He missed her.

He missed everything about her. He missed the way she spoke her mind; the way she laughed; the way she looked at him. He even missed the way she smelled. And all that was why he was now where he was—sitting in her kitchen, having despatched her friend, who had allowed him entry only after a questioning the likes of which hadn't been seen since The Spanish Inquisition.

'I thought you'd never get back. Where the hell have you been anyway?' Casual voice to mask his far from casual emotions. Controlled but barely breathing.

About to reach for a bottle of water from the fridge, something to quench her thirst after three glasses of wine, Alice nearly fainted in shock at the sound of that voice which had haunted her for the past month.

She spun round and stared at the figure in the chair, speechless.

Her legs turned to jelly; she collapsed into one of the kitchen chairs facing him and just *stared,* unable to believe the evidence of her eyes.

'I've been waiting for over an hour.' Had she been out with a guy? No. If she had, she surely wouldn't have returned home so early. Maybe she'd been on a date which had been a disaster. He enjoyed the thought of that. He had been on enough disaster dates himself.

'Gabriel…' It was the only thing she could find to say. Her mouth was dry and her heart was pumping so hard that it felt as though it would burst.

'Your house mate let me in.'

'Lucy.' This was a surreal conversation. She couldn't peel her eyes away from him. He looked…haggard. He was still in his suit but he had disposed of his tie and the top two buttons of his white shirt were undone. For a man who always managed to look carelessly elegant, he was dishevelled.

'Right.'

'Why are you here?' Alice knew that she should sound firmer, angrier, more resolute. Her voice was thin and reedy and she cleared her throat and continued to look at him in the half-light: beautiful. Even drawn as he was, he was still the beautiful guy who had lodged like a burr under her skin and refused to budge.

And suddenly the anger that should have been there rose to the surface—because, she thought, she must not forget that this was the same emotionally lazy man who had walked away from her without a backward glance because he had got it into his head that she might, just might, be interested in more than just a romp in the sack!

This was the same guy who *had nothing to give.*

'No,' she said coldly. 'Let me guess why you're here. You can't get to grips with any of the secretaries you've had to replace me. Well, if you think that I'm going to come along and do a good deed by handing over, then you're wrong. I'm not going to be doing that. You've wasted your time, so you can leave. You know where the front door is.' She was trembling and she wrapped her arms around her to steady her nerves.

Gabriel had never lacked self-confidence. It was what had propelled him upwards, had given him the drive to leave his past behind and the confidence of knowing that he could do it. Right now his confidence had gone on holiday. He was shaken by the sensation of someone standing on the brink of a precipice with one foot hanging over the side and no safety net to catch him if he fell.

'I didn't come to try and get you to come back to work,' he said hoarsely. 'Although your replacements haven't been any good, as it happens.' That last offering failed to generate even a hint of a smile.

And why would she smile? She had given and he had taken and, in return, had stayed true to his lifelong motto of giving nothing back.

He had been a prize idiot.

'In that case, why are you here, Gabriel?'

'I'm here…because…because…'

He was stammering. Since when did the invincible Gabriel Cabrera *stammer*? But she wasn't going to let any sprigs of hope infiltrate the barriers she had been trying so hard to rebuild around herself.

'Forget it.' She clenched her jaw and forced herself to look at him, to meet his black stare without flinching. 'I'm not about to climb back into a relationship with you.' She laughed shortly at how lacking in veracity that was, because it had hardly been a 'relationship' by anybody's standards! '*Relationship*.' She spoke aloud, her voice thick with self-mockery. 'What a joke. As you've proudly told me, you don't *do relationships,* do you, Gabriel?'

'I said that. How was I to know that fate can sometimes have a nasty habit of laughing at all your good intentions?'

'Forget it, Gabriel. Forget all the fancy words.' Restlessness invaded her body like a sudden burning itch that needed to be scratched. 'Have you run through a few of your pocket-sized dates and decided that you weren't quite through with me just yet?'

'I've missed you. Have you missed me? Tell me that you haven't and I'll walk out of this house and you will never see me again.'

As ultimatums went, that one went beyond the barrier. She didn't *want* him here, did she, invading her life all over again? Smooth talking his way back into sex because of *unfinished business*…did she? But she hesitated because the finality of what he was offering terrified her. She might not really have expected to see him ever again, but now she could see that she had stupidly *hoped,* because her love was so strong that it seemed incredible that she could be left with nothing overnight.

Now she knew that if she turned away this time she really would never see him again. Fragile hope would be killed dead.

'Well?' Gabriel prompted shakily.

'So I missed you! Big deal. Does that change anything?'

'You're the first woman I've ever missed.'

'Am I supposed to be flattered by that?' But she was. And she didn't want to be any more than she wanted to feel the racing of her heart; any more than she wanted to be moved—stupidly, idiotically *moved*— by the way he was looking at her with eyes that were somehow naked.

She didn't want any of that because none of that changed the man that he was, a man who was incapable of giving.

'You can't give anything, Gabriel,' she said, reconfirming that simple fact to herself just by voicing it out loud; reminding herself that she had been sucked in not once but twice and that she was not going to be sucked in again. 'And you have *no right* to barge into my house, to sweet-talk my friend into letting you in so that you can sit there and start spinning stupid stories just because I didn't give you what you wanted!'

'I'm not here to spin stupid stories.'

But Alice was in full flow. Memories rained down on her, memories of how much she had given and how little had been returned. 'You're empty inside, Gabriel! One stupid three-second conversation with someone you met in the village and you took off in a hurry. The merest shadow of a hint that you might have been expected to provide more than just inventive sex and you couldn't escape fast enough! And now you have the nerve to come here and talk about *missing me...*'

'I get it, Alice. I should have got it sooner, but I get it now.'

'Don't you *dare* try and make nice with me for your own benefit!' *And stop looking at me like that...* 'Repeat: you can't commit! You can't even plan a month ahead with any woman because you might need to run away long before then! You don't just want to make sure that you don't put down roots, you want to make sure that you don't even leave *footprints!*' She was shaking like a leaf, all the hurt and anger bubbling up inside her.

'Oh God, Alice. Do you think that I don't know that every single word you're saying is true?' He sat forward, angling the chair so that he could lean his forearms on his thighs. Still hunched, he raised his eyes to look at her. 'You were right when you once accused me of being emotionally lazy. I am. Was. Always have been.'

Was...? Hope flared, as persistent as a weed and as tenacious as ivy. Drained by her outburst and by the desperate range of emotion surging wildly through her, she remained silent, her breathing heavy and laboured, as though she had run a marathon. She wanted to drag her eyes away from him but found that she couldn't, any more than she could stop her heart from opening up like a wound that had only been scabbed over, bleeding all over again. 'I want you to leave,' she whispered. 'You need to leave.'

'Please. Let me just… It's hard for me; just hear me out. There's something you probably don't know about me…. No, there's something you *definitely* don't know about me…' That standing-on-the-edge-of-a-precipice feeling was back, but he didn't care whether he fell or not, or whether there would be a safety net to catch him or not.

Nothing could have been worse than the past few weeks without her.

'I was dragged up in foster homes. You told me your story, and maybe I should have repaid the confidence, but confiding is something I've never done. I've never known how. It's something that's sucked out of you when you're a kid in care. You learn to get tough fast. So, I've never told anyone my story.' He smiled crookedly at her. 'Until now.'

'Foster homes?' She shook her head slowly.

'Correct. No privileged upbringing. No upbringing to speak of, in actual fact. Just driving ambition and, thankfully, sufficient brainpower to turn that driving ambition into career success. But someone consumed with driving ambition, someone who had to fight to clamber out of a crappy background. What can I say? There was no space left inside me for sharing—I wanted money and everything that comes with it because it made me invincible. And for a long time that was exactly what I was: invincible.' He looked at her, reading her thoughts, stalling them at the pass. 'No fancy words, Alice. Just me. Being open.'

'And then what happened? You were invincible...' She tried to imagine a youthful, defiant, angry Gabriel and her heart constricted. He had erected the same defences as she had, but his had been made of steel and he had never let them down, and she could understand why. 'You're not going to get me back into a non-relationship with you with a sob story,' she said half-heartedly because she knew that she should still be protecting herself.

'I don't want to get you back into a non-relationship.'

'Oh.' Disappointment seared through her like a blazing inferno. So he had come to explain himself. That was something—that he had thought enough of her to tell her about his past—but she wanted so much more...

'I need you to see that for me giving in a relationship

had always been a non-starter. I was dependent only on myself, the way I always had been for my entire life, and I had no intention of allowing anyone in to share that space. But you came along, Alice, and bit by bit you chipped away…'

'You never hinted that you wanted anything more from me than a sexual relationship.'

'I refused to believe that I did. I've been a fool, Alice.' He dared to reach out and was shaken with relief when she allowed him to twine his fingers through hers. 'I should have known that you were different, and not just because you were taller than the women I usually dated. Hell, I was *that* thick.' Another of those crooked smiles made her toes curl and did all those things to her body that she had become accustomed to whenever she was around him.

'I went from looking at you, to wondering, to fancying and then to wanting you more than I'd ever wanted any woman in my life before. And somehow, in the mix, came all that other stuff…'

'What other stuff?'

'The wanting…the craving…the needing and the loving…'

'You *love* me?'

'And I never even recognised it for what it was.' His voice was strangely shaky when he next spoke. 'So I haven't come here to restart a non-relationship, as you called it. I've come here to ask you to marry me so that we can start just the sort of committed, fairy-story, walk-up-the-aisle relationship I never thought I'd have. Because, Alice Morgan, I find that I can't live without you. And if you can't give me your answer now—and I'd understand, because I've been a hellishly poor excuse of a lover—then you can think about it.'

He stood up and he was already at the kitchen door

when her legs did what they had been programmed to do and sprinted after him.

'Don't you *dare* go anywhere,' she said breathlessly, her eyes shining. She flung her arms around him and held tight. 'Because I love you, Gabriel Cabrera. So, yes, yes and yes! I want to marry you. I want to be with you for the rest of my life.' She looked up and her eyes were glistening with unshed tears.

'No fancy words?'

She laughed and sniffed and laughed again. 'I had my own barriers,' she confessed, dragging him back to the kitchen table, but this time when he sat down, she sat on his lap because she just needed his arms around her. 'You know all about my dad, and I guess I always thought that it was safer never to let go, never to put myself in a position where I could be hurt. I was so determined that you wouldn't get under my skin. I'd categorised you in my head within days of working for you, and somehow I thought that made me *safe*.' She stroked his hair, kissed his dear face and submitted when he kissed her back, tenderly, lingeringly.

'You mean if I was a bastard then you could never fall for me…'

'But, bit by bit, that image started to melt and fall apart. And then there was Paris…'

'And then there was Paris…'

'I just…got lost in you, Gabriel. It was like you got hold of my heart, and I was terrified, because you'd laid down all those ground rules of yours; because I knew your views on commitment… I decided that the only way to deal with it was to back right off. I thought that, if I backed right off, there just wouldn't be the glue to keep you attached but it was too late.'

'Hell, Alice, it was too late for me as well. You were in

my head all the time and, idiot that I was, I never stopped to ask myself why I love you, Miss Morgan—and I can't wait for you to become Mrs Cabrera.'

'I can't wait either.' Her world had opened up the day he had entered it and she felt like she was soaring high when she thought about the whole bright future taking shape in front of her. 'I want you to hold me and never let me go, because I'll never let *you* go.'

* * * * *